SECOND
Shot

Pamela G. Hobbs

POOLBEG

ALSO BY PAMELA G. HOBBS

Previous books in *The Fitzgerald Family* series

Family Affairs

Roman Holiday

Just Desserts

Added Attraction

Published 2021
by Poolbeg Press Ltd.
123 Grange Hill, Baldoyle,
Dublin 13, Ireland
Email: poolbeg@poolbeg.com

A catalogue record for this book is available from the British Library.

ISBN 978178199-431-3

www.poolbeg.com

About the Author

A native of Dalkey, Co Dublin, Pamela's childhood dream was to write and illustrate her own books, and to that end she attended the National College of Art and Design, studying Visual Communications. Although she still uses her visual side, nowadays she definitely spends more time at the laptop than the easel.

As winner in the Novel Fair 2015, Pamela gained experience from being around other writers and was subsequently selected for 'Date with an Agent' (The International Literary Festival, Dublin) in 2016, 2017 and 2018. These events gave Pamela invaluable contacts and also the impetus to write her first short story, 'Time Heals', which was shortlisted for the Colm Tóibín International Short Story Award, May (2017), a part of the Wexford Literary Festival. She is a member of the online writing group, Indulgeinwriting.ie

A day job as an Adult Education teacher in Kilkenny is challenging and fulfilling but Pamela's evenings are spent in another world altogether – that of romance and intrigue – reading and writing. "Life can be tough," she says. "Find your happy ending wherever you can."

Pamela, her husband, and two sons lived in the United States, on both coasts, for 12 years and she includes many Americans in her writing, highlighting the numerous family connections the Irish have with the US.

She has written four previous books on the Fitzgerald family: *Family Affairs, Roman Holiday, Just Desserts* and *Added Attraction*.

Acknowledgements

Thanks, as always, to Johnny O', long-suffering cheerleader and chief supporter of all I do. A generous thank-you to the women and men who spoke to me of their own losses and shared their stories – your honesty is appreciated.

Heartfelt thanks must also go to 'the girls' – each and every one of you has encouraged me since the beginning and that means so much.

A shout-out to Suzi, who urged me to finish *Family Affairs* all those years ago and said she couldn't wait for Flynn's story – hope it satisfies.

To the Craig family in Moville – thank you for the warm welcome and for introducing us to the delights of Inishowen.

To my 'boys', their wonderful women, and especially our darling Lyra. And, finally, to my own siblings, all of us lucky to have been born into a loving, caring family – madcap though it was. Very lucky indeed.

Dedication

For all who never made it to loving arms –
we hold you in our hearts, always.

Prologue

One year earlier

It was a shock when he got the email. Momentarily speechless, and even though one doesn't usually respond to an email audibly, he let out a quiet *'unbelievable'* before digesting it and rereading the fateful words.

Heads-up, I'm pregnant. Yes, we took precautions. Yes, I was also on the pill, like I told you before our second round. But shit happens or, in this case, pregnancy. It must have been the dodgy stomach I had the few days before which rendered the pill ineffective – or you have super-athletic swimmers. I can imagine which scenario you want to believe. Either way, it's happening.

This is not to ask or expect anything of you. I don't want or expect anything from you. Ever. I'm financially stable and have a career. But I believe you have the right to know – considering our ties. I'm not telling anyone who fathered this kid. I expect you to also keep it secret. That may change down the line, for reasons, but for now all you need to know is your kid is due in late March. I'll let you know the gender when it arrives. I didn't plan this any more than you did but despite all the options available to me, I'm choosing to keep it.

G

Of course, there was no way Flynn Fitzgerald was not going to do the honourable thing. That child would have his name and its birthright. It would be a Fitzgerald, or at least partially. And he would know it and care for it in as much as he was able. As much as he was let. He didn't expect to move to another country or participate in an actual marriage, but married this child's parents would be.

That was non-negotiable.

The ceremony was performed in Brooklyn by a local Justice of the Peace on August 29th at 9am and he flew back to Dublin that evening. She had protested, loudly and at considerable length. But he was not known as determined, intractable and persistent for nothing. He always got his way. The underhand tactics he used, were, he felt, well thought out and convincing. She was no match for him. And if her morning sickness made her more vulnerable and open to suggestion, not *threats* as she had accused, well, he was not above using all the arsenal available to him.

Since there was no emotional attachment on either part it came as another, bigger and more earth-shattering shock when another email arrived in the middle of October.

I've lost the baby. Don't come over. I'll send you divorce papers when I can.

Flynn Fitzgerald, usually cool, calm, and collected, reeled. He had been a 'father' for but a blink of a moment, and felt the rug completely pulled out from beneath him. He didn't handle it well.

And that, in itself, was another shock.

Chapter one

Present Day
Brooklyn, NY

"Sully, get your ass upstairs, the Cap wants to see ya!"

Moretti was an idiot, Angelica Sullivan decided. Or more of an idiot than usual. Now that he'd yelled her business across the bull pen, she'd get all kinds of flack. Getting called to the Cap's office was rarely a positive. She tossed her head in acknowledgement and, reaching for her jacket, she shrugged it on as she headed to the stairwell. The Sarge had his office along a side wall of the pen, but the Cap had a more significant space one floor above. She rounded the stairwell and loped up, two steps at a time, but came to a stop before the door. It wouldn't do her any favours to appear unkempt, so she ran her fingers through her chin-length tousle and buttoned her jacket. Then she did what she'd seen her father and brothers do, usually right before church over the years, and rubbed the top of each boot over the back of her work trousers. It would have to do.

Captain Bellows pushed back from his desk and rose to meet her. She strode towards him, halted and saluted. It wasn't necessary or even protocol, but she preferred to err on the side of respect. Bellows' reputation was sterling and she was, in truth, in awe of him.

"At ease, detective. Take a seat." His voice matched his stature, big and booming in the auditory version, big and broad in the physical. He was always impeccably dressed and while his demeanour behind his desk was mellow to the onlooker, it hid a sharp intellect and a keen sense of judgement – the 'I know your worth' kind as opposed to the 'you are all dammed to hell' kind. Good judgement. Fair. Just.

As Gia took her seat, she realised her sergeant was already in the room, standing towards the back, next to a row of bookcases. He came forward now and took the chair next to hers. Okay, this was not normal. She'd been called to the Captain's office before, but usually with some knowledge of the reason. Quickly, she did a mental inventory of her latest escapades and case files. Nothing untoward, she hoped.

An hour later she was still reeling. God, your life could turn on a dime. She knew this better than anyone. And this was a turn she could do without yet wanted with every fibre of her being. How could that be? How could she simultaneously be dreading what was to come and, alternatively, longing for it to begin right *now*?

At not yet thirty and a newer member of her precinct, she was young to be a detective, but the circumstances had been extenuating. With three college degrees already behind her, she had the academic side totally wrapped up. And luck had played its part too. Both good and bad luck. Or good and spectacularly awful, depending on your viewpoint. Either way, she'd been promoted in advance of the pre-ordained route or timeline. Fortunately, her colleagues were on board, supportive even, but again that was luck. She worked with a great bunch, the proverbial 'family' that cops spoke about was alive and well here in Brooklyn. Gia wasn't afraid to get her hands dirty or use her intelligence to think laterally or outside the box to solve a mystery. But she wasn't usually a renegade – she liked the idea of teamwork. She thrived on it. Made sure she included others in her thought-processes and expected that same inclusion in return. It didn't always serve her well, but the fact that she'd been older by many years than the standard rookie when she started perhaps warranted her more rope or respect than was the norm, so she ran with it. And made a name for herself in her crew. You could depend, with your life, on Angelica 'Gia' Sullivan. 'Sully', it was generally acknowledged, was alright.

The first thing she did when she got back to her apartment was to see if her passport was in date. *Check*. She then hunted for a suitcase that would hold a variety of clothing suitable for possibly inclement weather – rain and wind, most likely followed a moment later by dazzling sunshine. *Check*. Those little bottles for toiletries so she could take her favourite brands? *Check*. Her supply of medications for pain, stress and allergies were all up to date. *Check*. Cancel her appointment with her counsellor for the following week, also *check*.

Completely ignore the massive elephant in the room that was her memory bank and worst nightmare?

Check, check, check.

Gia had a lot of time to think things over on the flight to Dublin. She'd visited with her parents, Rosa and Mikey, her brother Sal and his wife Louise and baby Valentine. They'd been concerned she was going so far, for a job, but she promised to be in touch on the regular and reminded them she was a grown-ass woman as well as a police detective. She could take care of herself. She was pretty sure they didn't believe her on that score. She doubted it herself sometimes, especially as dawn broke and she'd spent another restless night. It was always darkest before the dawn, right? She was allowed her doubts then, as long as they stayed well and truly vaulted the other twenty-three hours of the day. But dawn was hours away yet, so she put her doubts on hold. Time enough for that.

She pushed her pasta-bake version of food around the container with a plastic fork and sighed deeply. Her momma knew how to make pasta bake – this was not it. But needs must and all, so she swallowed a few more forkfuls, grateful she'd managed to eat a quick dinner a few hours earlier, unwrapped and ate the stodgy brownie and sipped her wine. By the time they were serving breakfast she'd have zero alcohol in her bloodstream and she'd make sure she gave her teeth a good brush before landing anyway. Plane breath was surely as gross as morning breath.

The flight attendant took away her meal paraphernalia and Gia opened her MacBook to peruse her notes. It wasn't really necessary, she could recite them verbatim, visualise every point, notation and summary. She knew this case. Or rather, she knew one of its predecessors extremely well. It was why she was somewhere over the Atlantic Ocean instead of eating New York pizza by the slice as she finished her shift. Like a cop. She wasn't just a cop anymore though, was she? She'd earned her detective shield the hard way. Not just by sitting the exam but by bravery and cunning in the field. And by getting injured on the job. Funny how that often got one up the ladder of the hierarchy, rather than down it. Surely getting shot while doing your specific task made you a liability, not a hero? In her case, she was offered the shield as a reward, rarely given without the usual climb, step by step, through the ranks. Of course, she'd refused the honour, at least until she'd proved her worth by insisting on sitting the exam.

Gia and exams had a spectacularly good relationship. There wasn't one she couldn't pass without a significantly high score. Luck? Perhaps. More likely just a trick of fate. Her brain liked facts and figures as much as it thrived on probabilities and chance scenarios. And she had an excellent memory. For most things. She shook that notion off as she closed the laptop and let her mind see the information unfold.

This new case was definitely connected to the particular one that had affected her precinct. That it was *directly* tied to the one she herself had worked, remained, officially, to be seen. Gia was pretty sure no proof was needed. Everything read the same as before. The modus operandi too familiar to be someone else. Hoyt Jansen was back, doing what he did, just in a different location. This time, though? This time *he* would pay, not the vulnerable girls he targeted so cleverly. Gia swallowed, did some slow breathing and mind-blocking techniques she'd learned in therapy, and let go.

She wasn't sure who to expect at the arrivals area, but tall dark handsome Gabe Mackenzie wasn't it. She recognised him, having met him briefly over a year ago at her brother's wedding, but had merely passed the barest of words with him. She did, however, know quite a bit about him. More than he would be comfortable with, that was for damn sure. She'd been staying with his partner, Ali Fitzgerald, sister of the bride, during the wedding preparations and had been privy to some of his handwritten notes sent to his lady love. When she'd finally seen him, it had been so incongruous, this big silent man with, apparently, a heart brimful of mush. She'd swooned a little herself, who wouldn't, but in truth her attention had already been snagged so she let his movie-star looks slide right over her.

Now he took her bag effortlessly, though she *did* protest. His calm gaze landed on her, still as stone, and she relented. She bet that worked on pretty much everyone. Except maybe Ali. She really hoped Ali gave him shit – she rather suspected that was the case. She smiled as she climbed into his jeep and they headed along the M1 into the city. There was no room, no time, for jet lag. That would come later. Right now, they needed to get to HQ and deal with some serious intel.

Gia was fine with that. Mostly.

The drive continued in relative silence. No point discussing the case when it would all have to be analysed again with the team. She could bide her time, keep her thoughts tidily in place and maybe get the measure of the man beside her as they drove. That, it turned out, was harder than it looked. He wasn't a man for idle chit-chat or small talk so the few contributions he offered were on point about directions and locations. Duly noted, Gia thought, and filed away the particulars. New cities were to be explored but time would be tight this time. At the wedding there had been way too much excitement going on – dress trying-on, champagne-drinking, tabletop-dancing, girl talk and catching up, though briefly, with her brother Nick.

Sightseeing it was not. Memorable? Absolutely. Surprising? Hell, yes.

They reached the station, Mackenzie parked with deliberate efficiency, removed her bag from his car and ushered her, with a hand to her back, into the bright if old-fashioned greeting area. It looked like every police front desk everywhere – just maybe a tad smaller than back home. It was bustling and loud. Same. Uniformed and plain clothes personnel hurrying about looking official and important. Also, same.

What was different was the complete lack of firearms on view. Gia would have thought that quaint, but she liked her firearm. It was part of her daily wardrobe and she was pretty sure she'd be feeling naked without her weapon. Advised not to bring her own she was promised they 'would consider' arming her on arrival. They'd better, she thought grimly, or people would know, pretty darn quick, just how stubborn she could be.

They climbed the stairs, Mackenzie having left her luggage behind the front desk, probably against regulations but he seemed like a man of importance. Twice in the stairwell people hurrying down gave deferential way to the two of them heading upwards. Nods and 'Sirs' were exchanged, but the silent man in front of her seemed oblivious. Gia focused on her breath. In and out, nice and simple, nice and easy. She was completely healed, physically, from her gunshot wounds, but every so often a nagging twinge would make itself felt and, since she'd been seated for the guts of seven hours and then some, she felt it now, as they neared the third floor. She shook it off, as she always did. It was muscle memory, that was all. The hallway they entered was standard, long yet wide enough to encompass passing traffic without standing aside. Mackenzie stopped outside a set of double doors and, knocking briefly, entered. He held one door wide for her to follow and she found herself in a boardroom. Despite the age of the building, this was slick and modern. Lots of chrome and blonde wood. A drinks station was along the back wall, offering tea, coffee, juice and water. There was a tray of muffins – look at that, she thought, they seemed homemade. Not a shop-bought donut in sight. Things were looking up.

Making herself at home amidst the bustle of bodies that swarmed the goodies section, Gia took a coffee and a muffin and sat at the table. She noticed that Mackenzie was sitting opposite her, a bottle of water at his place. Shit, she wondered, was there a seating arrangement? Glancing about, she noticed others taking various spots and decided, hey, if they wanted her to move, they'd say so. She bit into the ohmygodstillwarm piece of deliciousness and moaned.

"Yummy, aren't they?" The voice next to her was attached to a woman probably several years older than Gia but dressed in equally casual clothes. Jeans and a hoodie and, following a brief appraisal, hiking boots. The woman's hair was chin-length and arrow-straight, shiny as an obsidian stone but that was it for adornment.

Gia nodded her appreciation and, around a mouthful of muffin, said, "Yup, these are the shit." She wiped a hand on her trousers and held it towards the other woman. "Hi, I'm Sullivan. Just arrived. Good to meet you."

A firm handshake and introduction to Brigid Lennon helped Gia relax as others shuffled into seats, sipped beverages and wiped sticky hands with paper napkins.

"Who brought the goods?" Gia asked, scrunching the muffin's paper wrapper and tossing it into the purpose-left bowl in the centre of the long table.

"That would be Boyle," Brigid said, indicating the rotund gentleman opposite two chairs down. "He is a fecking fab baker. Gives Ali Fitzgerald, the TV baker, a run for her money, in my book. He could definitely be one of the contestants on her show, but he's too shy. We might get him to apply yet." She turned to Gia and studied her gravely. "Better not to mention what I said about Ali." She inclined her head to Mackenzie who was studying some reading material, "She's his other half."

Gia swallowed. Damn, it was happening already. She was well aware that Mackenzie and Ali were a thing – she'd been there, seen the romance, heard the love notes. But did she want to encounter a Fitzgerald in any shape or form, or even hear about them while she was here?

No. No, she did not.

A thin grey-haired woman moved with measured steps to the head of the table and flipped on the overhead projector. She pushed a few buttons, inserted a USB into the laptop and checked out the remote control to ensure it was all a go. She turned then and faced the gathering. She was not in uniform but may as well have been. Her navy trousers, blue shirt and navy jacket screamed 'person in charge' as loudly as the badge attached to her belt. She was strangely attractive, Gia thought as the woman's brown eyes swept the room. Her high cheekbones and subtly shadowed eyes were accented by a slash of red lipstick. Yes, very stylish, Gia thought, but with an air of undeniable authority. I want to be her when I grow up, she mused with a smile edging her mouth. It quickly left her face as the woman's gaze rested on her and Gia felt like she was back in school, caught by the teacher for being cheeky. It had, to be fair, been a regular occurrence so shouldn't have sent a shiver down Gia's back but, man, this woman could deliver the look. A slight nod of acknowledgement in Gia's direction had her sitting up straighter and brought her attention fully back to the issue at hand.

The woman at the front of the room cleared her throat,

more to gain attention from the collective than from necessity, Gia assumed. Everyone responded instantly. Interesting. This woman was definitely the boss.

"Good morning. For those new to the unit, I am Chief Superintendent Clare Healy. I am here at the behest of our friends across the pond with the FBI and those in Interpol, specifically the Netherlands. We have two imports to assist us with this ongoing investigation. On my left is Detective Kasper Menchen from Copenhagen." She indicated with an incline of her head to a man on her left, lanky, blond and tanned, presently sitting with his hands casually clasped in front of him.

Menchen nodded about the room, his eyes not resting on anyone in particular, but Gia filed the name away for future collaborative efforts. She'd check him out herself. She knew people who knew people in Interpol and she'd call on those connections now – favour for a favour. Healy then indicated in her direction and Gia realised all eyes would be on her, however fleeting. She needed her game face on. Straightening her spine, she looked directly at the Chief.

"To my right is Detective Angelica Sullivan out of Brooklyn PD who has worked a similar case and will bring her experience to the table. Now, let's get started."

Gia glanced about the room, catching the eye of each one, holding it for a beat and moving on. She had raised her brow at the 'similar' case idea – it wasn't similar – it was *the same* – but decided now wasn't the time to call out the boss on her error. Time, and the flow of information, would do that.

Healy went through a few slides, detailing images and explaining blocks of information to the unit. She spoke for about twenty minutes, clear and concise, laying out her expectations and concerns. Her deadline for closure. There were mumblings at that and she held up a hand for silence.

"Yes, it's tight. But not, if you lot are as good as I've been told, unrealistic. It's not hyperbole to say lives are being compromised here, you know this. For now, this case must continue to be completely confidential. If the media were to get a hold of it? A total shitstorm. None of us want that, least of all the vulnerable or their families. Now focus, use your intel wisely, do what you have to do. Within reason. Listen to our newcomers, especially about a person of interest named Hoyt Jansen – both have experience in this type of thing, albeit from different locations. Get to work."

Information and notetaking was shared and dissected. Gia eventually spoke about her knowledge of the ring she'd been investigating stateside, and its comparison to the modus operandi of the group presently under review. Her thoughts were organised as always and, mindful of the team spirit, she asked for input and reflection on her ideas and responded with acceptance and intelligence. She was good at this. Getting people on her side, working through the kinks of an operation. Listening to all the comments and sifting for the truth. This was her comfortable place. What she knew. She also knew so much more than was being put on the table but there was no way she was laying all her information out at once – a rookie move, for sure.

Menchen added a few titbits but Gia got the idea he was holding his cards close to his chest too. She wondered how much he knew of the Dutchman, aka Jansen, connection other than his being brought in via Interpol. Time would tell. She could feel herself flagging, fricking jet lag already, and she needed caffeine. In large doses. Healy had left the room some time earlier, leaving Mackenzie in charge. He had organised them into two work groups for the first hour, going through papers, taking notes and swapping ideas. The last hour was bringing the groups together to pool their resources and share their thoughts. Very little had changed. Gia still felt she held cards others had no access to. She would figure a way to bring them to the table and, though time was of the essence, today was not the day.

12

A natural break fell and Mackenzie told everyone to take five.

Grateful, Gia rose from her seat and said to Brigid, "I'm going for a coffee, can I get you one?"

Brigid smiled grimly. "I wish but I'm on a detox kind of thing this week, zero caffeine and zero sugar."

Gia stared at her. "And you call yourself a police officer? For shame, Lennon!"

Brigid grimaced. "Tell me about it. It was the stupidest idea I've had in a while but I refuse to give in, now I've started. And don't hold your breath on the coffee – it's police issue."

"I hear ya, sister. And kudos on the detox," Gia said, using her best Brooklyn twang and fist-bumping her. "But needs must and this is definitely a need."

Gia moved around the long table to the sideboard and pressed the lever on the silver flask. Empty. Shit. It must have been made in a kitchen somewhere. Perhaps this was an opportunity for a little exploring plus it would give her brownie points when she returned with a fresh brew.

She picked up the thermos and turned to leave the room. Boyle was just opening the door and spied her flask.

"Need help with that?" he asked, allowing her to pass in front of him.

"No, but thank you. Perhaps, though, you could point me in the direction of the kitchen?" She smiled as she spoke, aiming for friendly rather than desperate.

He stepped out into the hall behind her and pointed to the exit sign. "Those stairs lead to the kitchen, one floor below. You can't miss it, it's first on the right." She thanked him and he headed off in the opposite direction while she headed for the stairwell and pushed open the heavy door. Funny how all police houses smelled the same – that delectable touch of sweat with a hint of stale coffee and notes of pure sugar on the nose. She grinned as she rounded the turn, right into a wall of steel.

"*Holy shit!*" she gasped as her body felt the jar. Whoever

13

it was had been in a hurry. And no, she hadn't been paying attention but still …

She flipped her eyes upwards as the person, whose hands now braced her arms to prevent her toppling over, hadn't said a word.

She supposed, later, when she had time to think it through, that she should have expected it. Should have been geared up. She'd known it would happen. But, damn, she'd compartmentalised just a little too well and had put those blinkers on right and tight. Didn't help though. The person standing in front of her didn't morph into someone else, didn't disappear and wasn't a mirage. *Shit*.

"Fitzgerald," she said, crisp as a winter day.

"Sullivan." Flynn Fitzgerald inclined his head as he dropped his hands and stepped back to allow her to pass.

Pass she did. On down the stairs, knees like jelly, heart thundering in her ears. Her hands, clasping the empty thermos might have been shaking.

Okay then.

Chapter two

He didn't move right away. He couldn't. Her steps echoing lightly in the tunnel of the stairwell didn't falter but he didn't release his breath until the sound of the door thudding closed reached his ears. Silence. He rested a hand against the wall, unsteady and off kilter.

Unacceptable. He straightened, took a minute to regroup, to process what had just happened, and then continued upstairs to the boardroom. He was late, but justifiably. Healy couldn't castigate him, not that she would, in public anyway, because he'd been tying up a loose end on a case at her behest. He'd known Gia was on the way, had fought against it, been outvoted and, it seemed, left out of the loop on her arrival time.

He pushed open the double door of the boardroom and spotted Mackenzie, leaning negligently against the side wall, a half-empty water bottle hanging from one hand. He was, at first glance, staring into space but, as anyone who knew him could tell, that was a mask. Mackenzie's brain was on high speed at times like this, calculating and sifting nuggets of data into various compartments until they all slotted into place. Flynn made his way across the room, avoiding conversation when anyone attempted to engage him.

"A heads-up would have been in order," he said to Gabe, his voice cool.

"About?"

Flynn sighed. That's how he wanted to play it? "Ms Sullivan arriving today. My last notification was she would be here later this week."

"You've been busy so I was alerted to collect her this morning. There was no need to let you know. It was handled. Unless you're not telling me something?"

Mackenzie was a sly bastard. Not telling him something? Hell, how long had he got? But no. He was, in fact, telling him nothing.

"Not a damn thing," Flynn replied. "But I need to get the key from Molly for the flat in Dún Laoghaire. Healy, in her wisdom, has decided that Sullivan can stay there, as Menchen is to get one of the apartments in Ballsbridge and the other is being renovated. I offered the flat, with Molly's agreement, since it's empty right now, but I was not happy about it. We should switch her with the Dane, let him use the flat. It feels too personal this way. I don't like it."

"I don't believe anyone asked you to wine and dine her, Fitzgerald. Merely house her for the duration. Healy felt the two 'newbies' to the team should have separate living quarters. I gather that is based on past experience when two previous detectives ended up compromising an investigation because they were way too close and got caught in an entanglement of sorts."

"Entanglement? Jesus, Mackenzie, only you would call two cops having sex an entanglement. Anyway, I agreed to the living situation because Molly is looking for a tenant."

"Plus," Mackenzie added dryly but oh so truthfully, "if your mother found out Caro's sister-in-law was being shunted off to Garda-issue quarters, she'd have your head on a block."

"That is indeed true," Flynn agreed. Bloody family

relatives. Caro, Flynn's sister, was married to Nick Sullivan, Angelica's brother.

Complicated? Big time.

And Jo Fitzgerald, the matriarch of the family, would never see any relative, even one by marriage they had only met briefly during the wedding festivities, not being given the very best of a Fitzgerald welcome. In fact, Flynn realised he was probably expected to bring her to visit with his parents. Hopefully this new case would have them so busy it just wouldn't be possible.

He made a note to phone Molly later so she could leave the key under the granite block on the steps for Angelica 'Gia' Sullivan and then his part in this whole 'but she's a member of the family' fiasco would be over.

The woman in question sauntered back into the meeting room, thermos clasped in her arms. She looked cool and collected. Calm and capable. She eased the thermos onto the side table and filled a cup. She gestured to the others who were suddenly lining up now that task had been done, to fill their cups too.

A few minutes later, Mackenzie peeled himself from the wall and with the barest flicker of his hand motioned to the room to take their seats. Part two was starting. The part where an actual plan was formed.

Flynn took a seat at the back, his chair against the outer wall, away from the general groupings around the table. He liked to observe first and foremost. When asked, he would contribute, but he always liked to get a feel for what the detectives thought first. If he spoke too soon, they usually went with his suggestions. While that might be flattering, it was not what teamwork was about. Every person in the room had a part to play, had a skill that was needed for this case. They needed to understand that their input was valuable. Yes, by dint of being chosen one would assume they already knew, but hierarchal standings still had a play, and everyone, including Healy, deferred to Flynn. It wasn't that he was the smartest brain in the room, or building, or district, it was that he was experienced in a myriad of ways. He's been sequestered to so many different areas of crime-solving since he'd joined the ranks at age twenty, that his internal knowledge of how things got done, let alone his access to all the powerful people who had the budgets to get said things done, was legendary. And yes, he was smart. His head was a mine of information. Of puzzles. Of ciphers and of conundrums. Figuring things out, complicated things, came easy to him.

Or they used to.

Flynn let his gaze rest on Gia Sullivan. If ever there was a complication that was a complete anathema to him, it was she. He fervently wished she was not here. Not in this room, not on this case, not back in the lives of Fitzgeralds. He wished he never had to see her again. He wished he'd never met her in the first place.

He wished he wasn't, even now, lying, so blatantly, to himself.

Molly wasn't much help. Actually, she was the very worst kind of help.

"She's here?" his youngest sister had squealed. "That's fantastic! I'm at Mum's for the evening so swing by here first for dinner and I'll hand over the key and you can take her to the flat after and settle her in. Mum and Dad will be thrilled and I'm dying for Kit to meet her. He'll be by later. Oh, this is so exciting. I should tell Ali. Or, wait, has Gabe done that already?"

Fynn could feel his temples throb. "I neither know nor care what Ali has or hasn't been told. Not my concern. But if that's the only way to get the key, we will see you later, briefly. No need for food." It was a pathetic attempt on his part – he was on a losing streak.

"No need for food? Have you met our mother?" Molly chuckled. "See you about six. I'll suggest a casserole so no worries if late."

And it was decided. Gia Sullivan was going to spend a

period of time in Molly's flat – the same place where she had spent a few days last summer during Caro and Nick's wedding festivities. The same place where he and Gia had pretty much set the sheets on fire for one very enjoyable night of reckless passion. Unforgettable sex. And even more unforgivable consequences. Nothing about this arrangement was in any way positive.

But, before he took her there, they were going to dinner in his family home in Dalkey where the welcome would be as one would expect from a Fitzgerald family gathering.

The afternoon had continued what the morning sessions had started. Discussion, collaboration, brainstorming and at last the beginnings of a plan. He could see Gia was starting to fade and made their excuses to leave the ongoing meeting. She protested, of course, couldn't be seen to lose face on day one, but he used his wiles and ensured her new colleagues knew he was calling the shots. No surprise, she didn't like that either. And told him so. Roundly.

"You may be my boss, or one of them, but, Flynn Fitzgerald, you are *not* the boss of me." She'd slammed the car door as she'd taken her seat and, as he'd eyed her calmly, she'd muttered, "You know what I mean, so take that look and shove it."

The rest of the drive had been endured in almost complete silence. Until they neared his family home, Gia hadn't spoken.

Then, still without looking at him, staring out the window at passing views of apparent fascination, she said, "They don't know about us, do they?"

"Which part of us are you referring to?" His voice was calm. Steady. Not what was happening inside. But then there was no need for her to know how deeply she affected his inner workings.

"Any of it. All of it."

"No," he said. "They know nothing. And I have no intention of telling them. What went down with us is no

19

one's business. What happened after? No one's business."

"Good. Keep it that way," she said sharply.

"What about your family? Did they know?" He kicked himself for being curious. It shouldn't matter. It didn't matter.

"No."

"None of it?" He was incredulous. "They knew about the pregnancy though, surely?"

"Not a damn thing," she said as he parked his standard, nondescript sedan next to several other vehicles in the driveway.

She opened the door, hopped out, slammed it and strode to the open front door where his mother magically appeared, right on cue with her sixth sense for visitors.

Gia's own family hadn't known she'd been pregnant? Flynn was immobile. Couldn't get out of the car. Couldn't move. Reeling, he remembered the intensity of loss when he heard the news. How he had struggled with feelings he couldn't identify. How he had told no one even knowing he had *needed* to talk. And he had, talked to someone, eventually.

But *she* had gone through it alone? That wasn't right. No one, no woman, should face that loss solo. That was seriously fucked up. Why hadn't she told her family?

He needed answers.

Gia had forgotten. How had she forgotten the crazy family of Fitzgeralds? Stupid really, as it was quite like her own family's brand of craziness – different but familiar. She remembered Caro saying the same about the Sullivans, so it wasn't just her recognising the sameness. Jo, the matriarch, hugged her warmly and ushered her down the hall into the kitchen where several family members had assembled. Hugs and greetings were exchanged, and Ali screeched in delight as they immediately got caught up.

"MacHotness will be along shortly," Ali told her as she handed over a glass of clear liquid, ice and lime. "Best G&T ever, courtesy of Dad."

It took Gia a moment to realise Ali was referring to her partner, the one and only Gabe Mackenzie. "Okay, Ali, but seriously, I'll be working with him from now on – in fact, I was all day and he collected me from the airport. I *cannot* afford to have 'MacHotness' as my frame of reference for a colleague!" She laughed, sipping the rather excellent drink. "Cheers, Mr Fitzgerald!" she toasted Patrick, Ali's dad, as he winked in her direction.

"Now, darling, you know to call us Patrick and Jo – we *are* family after all," Jo chimed in.

And didn't that feel weird? Family. Yeah, she didn't need another one of those. Her own was fine and dandy and enough to deal with.

Molly dragged a man towards her, tall and dark with hair slicked back, the way Nick, Gia's brother, wore his. He had a sweet smile as he held out his hand to shake hers.

"Hi, I'm Kit Elliot, a fellow Yank – or at least partly. Boston. You?"

"Hey, I hail from Brooklyn – nice to meet you, Boston." She was going to like him, she thought, as they shook. And she really liked the way he looked at Molly. Like she was the icing on every cake he'd ever eaten. Good. Molly deserved the best. Did anyone ever say that about her? That she, Gia 'Sully' Sullivan, deserved the best? Well, they knew shit, if they did. She didn't deserve the best. Not even a little.

Flynn strolled into the kitchen, his casual demeanour at odds with the thunder in his light eyes and his slightly ruffled short chestnut hair, the same colour as all the siblings – bar Ali who wore hers dyed ice-blonde. He walked to the sink, poured a glass of water and leaned his long lean body against the counter, his eyes never leaving her face though he directed his comment to his mother.

"One Angelica Sullivan delivered, in person, Mum, as requested." His tone was cool, his eyes were not. They said, very clearly: *We will discuss this later*.

Gia smiled. *Not gonna happen, bud*. "Thanks so much for

having me, Jo, and Momma and Pop say hi. I hope you didn't go to any trouble?"

"Oh, not at all, darling, and how are your parents? Enjoying being grandparents? I bet your brother Sal is a great daddy. Have you heard our news?"

"News?" Gia looked about the kitchen at the collection of faces.

"Ah, here they are now," Jo said as the front door slammed. "That's Dev and Frankie. He always slams the door. You'd think he was raised in a barn."

Flynn pushed his hips away from the counter and moved towards her even as Jo opened the kitchen door with a big smile.

"I'm sorry. I didn't think. I should have warned you," he said quietly for her ears only.

"Warned me? About wh . . ." but the sentence was cut off as a glowing Frankie Jones entered the room in a rush. She and her very pregnant belly.

Oh. Gia took a breath. A gasp actually and was oddly comforted by a hand at her back, steady and calming.

Devlin Fitzgerald – Frankie's husband and Flynn's younger brother – sauntered in behind his wife. He wore 'expectant fatherhood' to the manner born. Even to Gia's suddenly numbed senses she could feel the tension emanating from Flynn standing directly behind her, that hand still in place. Damn him. He was trying to comfort her but she could see he was uneasy himself.

"Gia!" Frankie cooed. "So thrilled you're here. I know it's work-related, but still, we're so happy to see you again."

She surged forwards, belly at full sail, and before Gia could even think of backing away, she was enveloped in a warm embrace. Well, fuck it! Not what Gia wanted but it was very hard to avoid Francesca Jones when she was in full tilt. While not particularly tall or large, even heavily pregnant she was a presence. Always. As a famous model film star, retired, and now a travel writer, she was a force to reckon with. Beautiful, grey-eyed and dark-haired she radiated finesse and style. A member of the Fitzgerald family by default since she was ten, she and Dev had emerged as a couple a few years earlier, following a rather harrowing and disturbing adventure for Frankie. Now they were the most loved-up couple and disgustingly happy. Not fair, Gia chided her inner self. They did deserve it – they'd worked for their happiness and it hadn't come without loss. Just like that of her brother Nick and Caro Fitzgerald. Caro had endured a lot of trauma as she and her son Toby had travelled to Rome to look for his birth father. Nick had been an inadvertent part of that search and, after much drama, they had found a lot more than answers to long-held questions. They had found each other.

Even as Frankie disentangled herself and Dev hugged her, Gia tried to pretend the awful pain in her chest was just an illusion. An imaginary pain. Fleeting and unimportant.

She had turned out to be a very good actress, fooling, at times, even herself.

"Congratulations, you two," she gushed. "When is the big day?"

"October tenth. But we expect it to be late. They say most first babies are late. Did Sal and Louise's baby arrive on time?"

The tenth. October the fucking tenth. The day Gia's world had shrunk to pain and despair. To agony and heartbreak. To failure. At least Flynn didn't know the actual date she'd lost the baby so she could keep this shock to herself. Almost one year ago.

But Dev was talking now and Gia tuned back in.

"Yup, six weeks left to go before the bean arrives. I think we have everything we need but we're happy to pick up any advice from Auntie Gia. What did your brother and his wife need that they just hadn't planned for?"

Gia was momentarily stunned. He was asking her? But why wouldn't he? No one knew. And that was on her and on Flynn. By choice. She needed to remember that. She couldn't blame people for sharing their good fortune when they didn't know her total lack of it.

"*Um,*" she said, trying to remember Frankie's question, "I think baby Valentine was on time. I'm not great at things like that. Or, you know, kid stuff. Excuse me, would you? I need the restroom."

She escaped to the downstairs toilet, her skin clammy and cold. She closed the door and leaned over the sink, breathing heavily. When would it get easier? When would the day come when she could see a pregnant woman and not hurt, physically? There were days, weeks even, when she managed. When she was okay. Could do her job. Focus. This was not one of them.

She splashed water on her face, patted her skin dry with a soft hand towel and took a deep breath.

She unlocked the door and went out into the hall. Flynn stood there, silent and still. He glanced at her white face and handed her a glass of water. When she snatched it from him, guzzled and returned the empty glass to his outstretched hand, he offered her a glass from his other hand. Her G&T. Her eyes flew to his. That aqua gaze remained steady and to her mind, for once, it seemed, since they had met earlier that day, non-judgemental. She took that glass too and tossed the contents down her throat like a woman parched.

"Not a fucking word," she warned, as she turned to go back to the kitchen.

She paused on the threshold of the bustling room, donned her invisible cloak of armour and sallied forth to smile and beguile in a way she had almost perfected over the last year.

She may have been duping many, but she never lied to herself.

She was failing at this pathetic attempt at pretence.

Chapter three

It wasn't like him to feel rattled or unnerved. But, Christ, Gia's face when she emerged from the toilet was a blow he hadn't expected. None of this was what he'd expected. He hadn't taken the time to analyse what he *might* have thought awaited him with the arrival of Gia Sullivan to his part of the world, but it wasn't this. He had not expected to feel pity. Or worry. Or, fuck it, care.

She was supposed to be a thorn in his side. And she was. For many reasons. But her shock at Frankie and Dev's news was on him. He should have thought to warn her. He'd been too wrapped up in wondering why his body felt so tense all day, why his shoulders were tight and his stomach unsettled. And now he had to face an evening watching her deal with his brother and sister-in-law's happy forthcoming event. He'd had months to acclimatise. She'd been thrown in the deep end. So much for being the smart detective – he couldn't even head off an event that he'd known about. He'd not had his head in the game and that, too, was unacceptable. He had to do better.

Dinner was uneventful in the end. Mackenzie arrived late and he and Ali left straight after eating. Frankie and

Dev didn't stay for dessert either and Gia was almost asleep in the chair before eight. Jo packed a couple of portions of apple-and-blackberry crumble into a container and insisted she take it. Late August was perfect for blackberry-picking and she was great at making use of local bounty. Flynn refused to take any, not having a sweet tooth, though he had sampled the delicious fare for dessert.

They said their goodbyes. Molly handed him the flat key and a list of instructions for Gia about the electrics and kinks-of-the-house variety. Gia mumbled that she *had* stayed there before, but Molly wasn't listening. Fynn's youngest sister loved minding others and she regularly took people under her wing. It was how she'd met Kit. He'd been an undercover forensic accountant at the firm where she worked and, in mufti as a geeky nerd, dressed accordingly, so she'd been moved to take him under her wing. It had transpired that she'd had a few secrets of her own and before long the two were an item. Molly had not been pleased when she discovered that her eldest brother and her lover already knew each other, trusted each other, and had in fact collaborated working on some criminal cases together. The FBI were not shy about using their people in all sorts of ways and Flynn was very *very* good at acquiring the best people for the job. Any job.

This time however, he thought, as he drove a sleepy Gia to Dún Laoghaire, he had made a serious miscalculation and left the recruitment for his latest case to Mackenzie. That had been a mistake. He mentally kicked himself for not double-checking the names put forward. Mackenzie swore, when Flynn had tackled him on it, through a flurry of texts, that *she* had been put forward to them – they had not gone searching. The FBI and her captain thought Dublin could use her and her specific skills and knowledge on this case. Flynn decided the jury was out on that one. Time would tell.

He led Gia up the short flight of steps to the front door of the house. Caro actually owned the whole house but rented out the upstairs and basement and had used the main floor for herself and Toby. Now that she was living in Rome, Flynn's other sisters had shared tenancy. Ali had previously lived there for over a year and, earlier this year, Molly had taken a turn. She used it as her home office as well as her actual home as she studied and worked for a large accounting firm, BB&M. Now that she and Kit were putting the finishing touches to his home in Stoneybatter, this flat was usually empty. Molly hadn't officially moved out but was rarely there, so, yes, it was ideal for Gia, a sort of relative, to use.

Flynn inserted the key, swung the door open and showed Gia down the shared hall to Molly's flat door.

"I know where it is," she grumbled tiredly, the dark circles under her eyes deepening by the second.

Nevertheless, he carried her bag to the main bedroom and pulled the curtains before switching on the light. He did a quick turn about the flat, checking windows and the other bedroom, kitchen and bathroom, before returning to the inner hall door.

"Jesus, I'm neither a child nor inexperienced. I can check my own space, even if it's temporary. And why are you checking anyway? No one knows I'm here but your team. Stop smothering me."

She sounded disgruntled and cross. No, he realised. She sounded exhausted.

"Habit," he admitted. "No offence meant. I'll see you at the station in the morning. We aren't starting till ten so get some sleep. I assume you will either take a taxi or the train. Molly will have left directions to the DART and taxi numbers."

Gia let her head fall back against the doorjamb, holding the door open for him to leave. He took the hint. No one could accuse him of being slow on the uptake. Or not usually.

"Goodnight, Gia," he said and, before the door closed behind him, added, "At the risk of being insensitive ... I've just realised this is the anniversary of our marriage. I understand that you may not want to acknowledge it, or even remember it, but it will always be special to me."

Fucking hell.

August 29th. One year to the day when they had married in a small registrar office in Brooklyn. Just them and a witness that hung around waiting to be a stand-in, for a few dollars, to anyone who needed it. They had. Flynn had handed the witness fifty bucks and Gia hadn't even cared. She'd had no one there, had wanted no one. This marriage wasn't a thing. It was a 'kinda thing', she was calling it. A means to an end – the end being getting Flynn Fitzgerald, Baby Daddy, off her case. She had been specific, really specific that he was not wanted on voyage, so to speak, but he, stubborn man that she now knew he was, had not taken 'no thanks' for an answer.

Gia went through the motions of getting ready for bed, and by the time she flopped onto the sheet and hauled the duvet to her chin, her brain felt like it had just done a fast rewind to this day last year. One year. One decision. One mistake. No second chances. She closed her eyes, allowed the weariness of grief to flood her, for just a few precious minutes. Her baby would never be forgotten. Never. And then she forced herself to turn over and go to sleep. As awareness drifted away a stray thought struck her.

They needed a divorce.

She took the DART train to the city centre and walked to the main station. Taking the stairs two at a time she narrowly avoided colliding with a junior admin person hurrying down with an armload of folders. Gotta watch out for the unexpected, she reminded herself – it could always be deadly.

The conference room was full and the murmur of voices came from the several small task groups set up around the perimeter, huddled at tables. She glanced at her phone: no, not late. He'd said ten. And then it hit her. The bastard had given her a free pass because of jet lag. Well shit, that sucked majorly. Now she'd be accused of getting special attention from the head honcho. She and he would have words, no question.

She grabbed a coffee, not the worst police-issue she had tasted, and joined Brigid Lennon's group.

"Apologies, I was misinformed regarding start time," she said, pulling out a chair.

Brigid shoved a fresh muffin in her direction. "No problem. Here, I saved you one."

Gia gratefully accepted the fragrant offering and bit into chewy goodness. "Damn, he's good," she mumbled over a mouthful. She nodded appreciation towards the baker Boyle and took a drink from her mug. "Right, catch me up, guys, where are we?"

They were, it turned out, no further along. And they were frustrated. They all knew there was a baby-selling ring right in the heart of Dublin city. They had evidence but not enough. They needed inside information and, most importantly, they needed to know how the infants were being smuggled from the island of Ireland and, in fact even more urgently, where they were kept before that. And where were the mothers? The women who were duped into believing their children would be going to a good home, *chosen* for them, instead of being sold to the highest bidder.

This they knew because one young person had come forward when she was unable to track down her child to see how he had settled. "I was promised," Kylie wailed. "They swore that I could hear about him, get pictures and all. I'd never have given him to just anybody. But it was all lies! They said it to make me give him up, but they were never going to let me know. Never. They showed me the form I signed, but sure I hadn't read all the legal stuff, why would I? They'd said!" The tears had been real, and the anguish. Yes, she had received a chunk of change in exchange for her baby, but it was junkie money, a few thousand to feed her then habit. Not all the girls, as she'd

PAMELA G. HOBBS

said, were like her. Some were just against abortion, from strict homes or just needed the cash and not another human to feed.

Kylie had promised to take them to where she'd been introduced to a 'big fella with an accent' and then to where she and a dozen or so other young women had been housed in the inner city. Kylie was out of money and wanted (*needed*) more. She'd been made to see, by a *friend*, now that she was clear of drugs, that she'd been duped by smarter people who should have given her way more money. It was her right to get more, she'd said, and believed it wholeheartedly. She'd given them titbits of info, small hints of where the location was but, surprise, never turned up for the meet.

Kylie would only speak to a female garda and Brigid Lennon had been her contact. Brigid explained her frustration and sorrow when Kylie, no more than nineteen years old, had been fished from the river two days later. Overdose was the official verdict though she'd promised she was clean and Brigid, who had worked with many a junkie, had believed her.

Gia could see how that gnawed on Brigid, as it would on any detective who was following a solid lead. But now what? How could they find another woman to help lead them to the accented man?

"No guarantee it's our Dutch guy," Gia said to the others. "But scouting the last known location of Kylie seems like a good starting point. I have some ideas to run by you and then maybe we can take them to the group?"

Flynn couldn't believe his ears. *Lie* – he could totally believe it. "*Seriously, Sullivan? You think you should go undercover in the city of Dublin, slouching around ill-lit corners and pretend you are pregnant and looking for help?*" No, he didn't roar that across the room at her though, God, he wanted to. He was more professional than that. More measured.

"No," he said instead. "Not a runner. Any other ideas?"

Gia surged to her feet, unfazed by his dismissal. "Why not? No one knows me. It's not like I'll be spotted as a cop, or a local. They'll assume I'm from the country. At least let's take a vote, all democratic, and see what the others in the room think."

Flynn bit back a retort that there was no way anyone could take Angelica Sullivan as someone from 'the country'. And even this morning after a long flight, followed by a long day and probably, judging from the circles under her eyes, very little sleep, no one would mistake her for an innocent. She wasn't especially tall but her carriage was upright and forward-facing. Shoulders straight as she stared him down. Her figure was slight but, as his own body remembered all too well, soft in all the best places, and her long slender neck led to a fascinating face. It was what he'd noticed first. Or maybe it was the angle of that sharp jaw, or high cheekbones. Or the pert nose? No, it must have been her eyes, dark-lashed and a perfect hazel. Sometimes so green they were startling, other times topaz or amber. He could never figure it out – they were simply the colour of autumn trees. But no, he decided as he watched her tilt that chin up, daring him to listen to her plan, believe in her worth, it was her mouth. A plump upper lip that tilted up in a tiny curve at the side, placed so perfectly over a full bottom pad of lushness. Yes, he remembered that mouth and all it could do. All it *did* do. All he did to it. God, he needed to get a grip, and fast, or someone would notice him staring. Was that an uncomfortable silence while everyone waited to see what he'd say next? It was indeed.

She ran a hand through her chin-length, wavy, deep-brown hair, then slammed her hand on the table. Maybe she didn't mean to do it quite that hard but several people jumped at the slap.

Mackenzie stepped into the awkwardness with his usual aplomb.

"Thank you, Sullivan, for the offer. It should definitely be considered. Normally undercover work would go to the locals, those who know the area and the lay of the land. But Detective Lennon's face has been seen around the streets in question as has Sergeant Cullen's," he nodded in the direction of one of the other women in the room, "as she helped Lennon with the case. And no disrespect to the other female detectives here, but they do not fit the profile." There were a few snickers at this but fortunately they were led by detectives Jane Molloy and Helen Smith, both in their late forties.

Flynn caught Mackenzie's eye, a question in his own. Surely not? They had to talk this through. He couldn't be considering sending Gia undercover on her second day? That was . . . unthinkable. And pretending to be pregnant? Hell no. Granted, Mackenzie would have no idea how hard that ruse could be for Gia but, that aside, she was green. New to town and a bloody American. No one would buy her act.

"Let's take five," Flynn said to the room in general. "Sullivan, Mackenzie, a word." He stepped away from the table where he'd been doing paperwork while listening in to the small groups brainstorming around him. He moved to the window and peered out, unseeing. It wasn't a particularly charming view anyway. Grey plastered buildings side by side with those in faded ochre brick. A concrete yard, fenced in, a car park with all manner of nondescript vehicles. Nothing this view hadn't offered on any given day.

Stomach tight, he turned to the two approaching him but, before he could speak, Gia did. And stunned him.

"Don't fret about me, boy," she said in the most believable Cork accent he'd hear outside that city. "I'll be grand once I find my feet, like."

Well, now. That did change things.

Ha! Gotcha! *I'm not just a pretty face, Fitzgerald. I can do things. I have skills.* She smirked at him. Was it childish? Most likely, but the shock on his face was absolutely worth it.

"Yes, I did drama in one of my many incarnations over the years, plus I have a natural ear. And okay, my bestie and roommate from a summer I worked on Long Island in a motel was from Cork city with an accent so strong it took me weeks to understand. My personal challenge was to be able to answer the phone to her mom and pretend to be her. It took time. And practice. And a lot of whiskey. I succeeded. Deal with it and let me do the job. I'll wear a wig and I bet you have one of those prosthetic bellies I can wear – I wouldn't have to be hugely waddley, but enough to catch their attention."

"No, not a runner. If you must go undercover, we will find a pregnant garda to go with you – you can be the sister or friend. You are *not* faking a pregnancy." His tone was so stern yet flat that it startled her.

It appeared to surprise Mackenzie too as he glanced curiously at his cold-faced colleague.

Flynn's eyes stayed on hers, unflinching.

"But –" she began.

"I said no. Not open for negotiation. We'll find someone else but you can assist. Wear a wire. Take photos and notes. It can be brief and purely an information trawl." He turned to Mackenzie. "Set it up, Mac. Get Lennon to help select a garda. She knew Kylie so will know the type needed. We have to have a candidate somewhere local even if not in this house. Find her. Read her in. Get it done by tomorrow."

He turned then and walked briskly from the room.

Mackenzie raised an eyebrow at Gia. "Care to explain?"

"No," she sighed. "I really wouldn't." What could she say? That Flynn Fitzgerald was being honourable in an odd and old-fashioned way? That maybe he was concerned that she'd fall apart if she had to pretend to be carrying a child? In truth, she wasn't sure herself why she volunteered for the role. Instinct. To be in charge, on the frontline, included in all the ways. But on reflection, even within the last few moments, reality had struck her and, damn him, he was probably right. She'd be no use to the team if she fell apart. It probably wouldn't happen but she couldn't jeopardise the whole operation for her own ego. Sister or friend it would be.

She nodded to Mackenzie and went back to her group who were returning from break.

Mackenzie went to the top of the room and gave a swift outline of one side of the operation, the fact that she and an as-yet-unnamed garda would go to Kylie's haunts in the hopes of flushing out the 'big fella with the accent'. They discussed places and bars, cafés and, on Brigid's advice, the local women's hostel. Kylie hadn't stayed there but it seemed like an obvious choice. Gia agreed. Kylie could have been hedging her bets.

By mid-afternoon a loose plan was in place. As loose as these plans can be. Gia went to wardrobe and got fitted with a long blonde wig and some padding for a slight appearance change only. The fake hair felt itchy and the extra pounds neither flattering nor comfortable, but Gia didn't mind. She took the DART back to the flat, wearing her undercover outfit, planning her persona. She would meet her co-conspirator, if they found one, in the morning.

It was odd, travelling on public transport, and no one taking notice of her. Was this vanity, she wondered? The pale hair made her naturally tanned skin look like a dirty beige – nothing attractive about that. And the wads at her waist and hips were ungainly, to say the least. She had wiped the soft rose colour from her lips but was unable to hide the shape. There would be no mascara or eyeliner tomorrow but she felt naked already. She wasn't cocky but knew she normally had a certain appeal. Her hair had a natural bounce and she kept the cut sharp. Her eyes were usually touched with a slight sweep of blue eyeliner as it set off the tawny colour and, combined with a mostly unnecessary sweep of extra black lash and her favourite pink lippy, she turned heads. Maybe it was her attitude, her stance, her deportment. Or the fact that, for the most part, she basically didn't give a shit what others thought. Except . . . here she was, nearly bemoaning the lack of interest. What a crock! She was as vulnerable as the next girl to a bit of flattery and was never averse to a flirt. It was the

Brooklyn way. Mouth off at those jostling around you, holler across the street at a cab driver, greet the woman sweeping her stoop steps with a cheery 'How are ya?' and swagger on your way. She was a bit of a swaggerer, she realised as she now had to tone down that walk of hers in her new role. This woman wouldn't swagger. She wouldn't flirt or hurl an insult. She might curse though, probably would, but not the way Gia Sullivan did. This woman would be called Ciara, she decided, after quickly googling the most popular names for girls in Ireland from when she could have been born. She shaved a few years off her age knowing she could pass for mid-twenties, so hopefully she could play big sister, confidante to a younger, more needy woman. She could be the spokesperson for her shyer, nervy pal.

Yeah, she could do this. She walked to the flat from the DART, stopping at Molly's favourite Indian take-out restaurant. It had been underlined in red on the list of places to eat that Molly had left taped to the fridge. The fragrance of the warm food made her stomach rumble and she remembered she hadn't eaten since a coffee and a bowl of cereal – okay, and some of the crumble Jo had sent – and that muffin later. She needed to stop this. Her eating habits since . . . well, since, hadn't been healthy. She knew that, would happily point it out to another in her position, but was as yet unable to rectify the matter. These smells though? They were definitely working on her tastebuds. Shit, she was practically salivating.

She let herself into the flat, threw the keys on the inner hall table and kicked off her boots. She yanked the wig off her head and tossed it on a stool, running her fingers through her hair to loosen the awful tightness. She placed the food on the kitchen table, hunted down some silverware, a plate and a glass of milk, and opened the bags. Yes! Delicious. Her belly growled loudly and she laughed, or maybe snorted, as she opened the purchases. The food was a varied selection, enough to feed a small army, therefore leftovers for days. The best kind of food. And she had some of that dessert left in the fridge too. That she would take as a win.

She sat on the couch, her variety plate of food on her knees, and dug in. Her stomach thanked her, big-time, and she ate with enjoyment and relish. She was scooping the buttery tomato sauce up with some naan bread when she heard a perfunctory knock, followed by a key unlatching and the door to Molly's flat opened.

What the fuck?

Chapter four

The second he opened the door, he realised his mistake. This was not his sister. This was Gia Sullivan, and she would not appreciate his intrusion. With Molly he always gave a little warning knock and came right in. She expected that. Liked the familiarity. Knowing his error, he braced himself. He was right to.

"What the fuck, Fitzgerald? You can't come barging in here like you own the place! I could have been naked, for God's sake!" She had put her plate aside and surged to her feet as she spoke.

But she paused then as the word *naked* hung between them like a tightrope – taut and dangerous. They had been naked, gloriously, rapturously naked. And he, whatever about her, was likely never to forget it.

He paused, considering his approach. But there was nothing to consider, not really.

"I apologise, I shouldn't have come straight in. Force of habit," he said.

She gaped at him. "Ya think? And they give you the top job? Imbeciles."

Flynn bowed his head slightly. "Point taken. But I

meant with Molly. Since she moved in here in February, I had taken to swinging by every so often and checking on her. So, she gave me a key in case I got here before her. We would share a drink, talk about the day and then I'd leave – knowing she was okay."

"Why wouldn't she be okay? She's a grown-ass woman, big brother. Not your responsibility."

"True. And yet . . ." He broke off, not sure what to say. That he'd known she was floundering in her own way? A bit lost? A bit disconnected? As it turned out, he'd been right. "Did you know she is a fully qualified accountant?" he asked as he made his way cautiously across the floor.

"Molly? Isn't she the artist sister? The bohemian?"

Temporarily thrown off balance by his question, his intent of course, Gia gathered her plate and took it and her milk glass to the kitchen.

He sauntered after her, oh so casually.

"As we all thought. Turns out she was hiding a secret life from us all along."

"And you didn't suspect? You? The great detective?" She put her plate into the dishwasher and refilled her glass from a jug of milk on the table. She took a drink as she waited, her eyes on his now.

"No, I regret to say, and as she told me herself with great glee, I did not guess a thing. I knew she was troubled. We can tell that about each other, she and I, but I had no notion of her other talents. Her mathematical side. It was a revelation."

Gia put down her glass and folded her arms across her chest. "I can imagine," she said. "When Nick gave up architecture to run the hotel full time, we were all flabbergasted, Momma especially. But hey ho, he loves it."

Flynn reached for the kettle but, no slouch, looked to her for permission. A slight nod had him filling it and switching it on. He pulled two cups, again with a questioning look at Gia, from the cupboard over the counter and inserted a tea bag into each. He knew his way around this kitchen. Many an evening had been spent here with one or other of his sisters. It was comfortable. Homey. Warm. He liked his own apartment well enough and kept it exactly the way he preferred it, but this place? This flat held memories now, both good and, he supposed, challenging. But it was still, like his boyhood home in Dalkey, a welcoming space. He had a sudden hope that Gia would feel welcomed here. That she would feel at home. He had no notion where she lived in New York. Didn't think it was with her parents but he was lamentably clueless about her personal life.

Maybe that was for the best. Getting involved was not on the agenda. That hadn't exactly worked out the last time.

But somehow his brain wasn't paying attention. He poured boiling water into cups even as he asked, "Do you still share your parent's home? Or do you have your own apartment?" Once again, he owned his mistake the second the words were out. "Sorry, none of my business," he added quickly.

She narrowed her eyes at him and it was then he stopped short. She was different. God, he was an ass. And blind. She was wearing some awful get-up and had gained the poundage that only came with theatrical padding.

He couldn't help it, he really couldn't. "Nice get-up," and the grin that had been edging forth burst into reality.

It was fleeting, the grin, but fuck, it was effective. She remembered it from their night together, when he had flashed it at her having flipped her from being on top to beneath him and she'd shrieked. God, they'd had fun, that night. But not only fun. Passion and heat had seared her for months after, spoiling her for another. But that was another story. Now, all she could focus on, rather than pretending to tend to her own mug of tea which she didn't really want, was his comment.

"I'm getting into character," she told him as sternly as she could.

Her instinct was to match that grin. She used to be fun, happy, smart-assish and sharp-witted. Now, lately, she'd felt wrung out and so far away from sassy that it was a joke. When this was all over, when Jansen was dead or behind bars, she'd find that girl again. She'd trade grins with handsome guys and flirt her backside off. She'd do it, she promised herself. Her Angel would expect it of her.

"I see," Flynn said but she could tell he was doubtful.

So she gave him a taste. A flavour of who she could become.

"I'm Ciara, and this is my cousin Chloe. She's in a terrible state. Doesn't know what to do, like? Could you help us or what? She's scared and we were told ye could give us a hand." She knew her accent was spot on. And Flynn's face told her so even if she hadn't trusted herself.

But she was beginning to feel uncomfortable and, without thinking, pulled up her sweater to untie the padding.

A cough, low and coarse, stopped her. He was staring. For fuck's sake, it was just her stomach, he needed to get over himself.

"If you can't handle a little flash of flesh, go into the kitchen and take a stiff drink. This stuff is coming off whether you're here or not. Decide."

He turned on his heel and headed to the kitchen.

Fucking men. She undid her extra layers and tossed them down. God, the relief. But no whining. If Fitzgerald thought she wasn't strong enough to deal with a little discomfort, he'd pull the plug. "Hey, bigshot!" she called towards the kitchen. "Pour me one too!" She plopped back into her chair and unzipped her ankle boots. Back home, she would never wear outdoor shoes inside, but she'd forgotten her 'house shoes', as her family called slippers. Not fleece or fluff slippers – that was not her style – she wore a cool brand of boiled wool with a leather sole. And now she missed their comfort. Pack in haste, regret in leisure. Okay, that wasn't a saying, but it should be.

Flynn returned carrying two tumblers with a splash of amber liquid in each. He handed her one with the proviso, "Not sure of this brand of whiskey but it should do the job." He tilted his glass to hers in salute.

"Thanks." She was glad they weren't doing a 'cheers' ritual – that would have just been weird. She sipped, swallowed, gasped and sipped again. No, no clue what this was but it burned and hissed as it went down, so would do nicely.

She decided there and then that if she didn't learn to relax around this man, and pretty darn quick, then things were going to get very awkward indeed.

"So," she began exactly as he said, "We need to talk."

That brought a silence as they stared at each other. Flynn moved his hand in a 'you first' gesture that had her gritting her teeth. Okay then. Here goes.

"So," she began again, "how are we going to play this?"

"Play this?" His tone was frosty.

"Stop doing the Ice King routine. It doesn't suit you. Well, it does, but not now. You know what I mean. We have a history, brief though it was, and we can't let that get in the way again."

"Again?"

Jesus, with the tone, she thought, I'm going to murder him.

"Yes, asshole, *again*. You stopped me stone cold from going undercover as a pregnant target, and that kind of manipulation can't happen again. Our past is just that. Past."

"And yet, here you are, going undercover all the same."

"Yeah, but it's not the same, is it? Whatever!" She bristled. "Don't treat me with kid gloves. I'm not a delicate flower or about to collapse, so no more heroics or second-guessing me. Got it?"

"Loud and," he said. "Though in my defence, I never thought you couldn't do it, go undercover in that role. I simply felt it would be better for the team if you were less in the line of fire, so to speak."

"I hear you. And maybe you were a little bit right, but don't get big-headed about it."

Flynn pressed his hand to his heart, mocking but, she admitted, kind of cute.

41

"I wouldn't dream of it," he said.

And there was that hint of a smile. That rare, rare thing. Fuck, it really shouldn't be so tantalising. So precious. The only thing for it was to make him smile lots so she'd get used to it. Ha! That wasn't going to happen. Still, she certainly wasn't going to go goo-goo eyes over it every time either. She would become immune – she'd revisit that secretive upturned lip curve a thousand times in her dreams and then it would mean nothing. There, she had a plan. She loved a plan.

"I have a plan," Flynn said.

And she laughed. Maybe it was a bit of hysteria, delayed jet lag, deciding to go undercover, Flynn's smile, or just the synchronicity of it, but she found her laughter bubbling out of her and, yes, there were snorts.

"Sorry," she gasped eventually as he sat there, eyeing her with the Flynn special look, one eyebrow slightly quirked as if torn between bemusement and actual amusement. It was hard to tell with him. "I'd been just thinking of my own plan as you said that. Go figure."

"Care to share?" he asked dryly.

But she thought she detected a tiny hint of that lip curve.

"Nope, not even a little. But don't let me stop you. What's yours?"

She sat back in her chair, attentive and she realised, at ease. Maybe they just needed to spend time in each other's company, with zero sex stuff between them. Pretend like they hadn't been moaning and sweaty, gasping and eager all those months ago. Pretend it never happened. But no. A wave of guilt washed over her, then there would have been no Angel. Swallowing hard, she prepared to listen.

Flynn Fitzgerald had a plan – this ought to be good.

It was a simple plan, really, as the best ones often are. But he wasn't sure how she would receive it. It would involve them being together, working together, as partners and she might balk at that. But it was worth a shot.

"I suggest that we form a working partnership, you and I specifically, as opposed to the whole team. This plan will only come into effect after the undercover work is done and we will use that new information to take this case to the next level."

She looked at him steadily, unwaveringly. Narrowing her eyes, she said coolly, "First, you seem very sure we'll *get* information that can move us forward and, second, whatever it is might turn out to be useless. It could dead-end right there."

"Possible but unlikely. You, and the garda Mackenzie has found to work with you, Siobhán Barry, will discover whatever is out there. It's your job, it's what you both do. Whatever you find out can only move us forward – that is merely logic." Flynn hoped she wouldn't call him on the tenuous thread of his plan.

How could he explain that he needed to get her out of his head, and his brain told him the only way to do that was get an overdose of her. She'd irritate him soon enough. She'd bug him about everything, become a stone in his shoe. And then he'd be delighted to send her back to Brooklyn and distant family gatherings would hold no trepidation for him. Because, right now? He wanted to inhale her scent. Put his face to the curve of her shoulder where her neck looked both delicate and strong. After he inhaled her intoxicating fragrance, he'd nibble a little and then swirl his tongue to ease the slight sting of pain. He'd . . . well, he'd better get a grip because she was still looking at him and that look was now one of puzzlement.

"Logic?" she asked. "But of course. You're the updated version of Mr Spock, aren't you? So you of all people should know logic doesn't *always* play out the way we would like, or even expect. So why don't we wait and see, eh? If we get a decent lead from our undercover foray, we can talk. Otherwise, no dice. I'll take my chances with the team." She pushed herself up from her seated position and stood there, arms folded. "You should probably go. I'm still needing more than my usual hours of shut-eye."

Suddenly uncomfortable, Flynn returned his glass to the kitchen, placing it in the sink. He turned on the tap to rinse it out, but she spoke quietly behind him. "Leave it. I'll do them later. I just need to go to bed."

She was standing by the door, defiant and, yes, tired. Nothing could dim those eyes but the dark circles beneath looked more like bruises. He was an unthinking idiot, he told himself as he brushed past her.

"Apologies, I shouldn't have come over. I wasn't thinking. It won't happen again."

"I didn't say that," she said quickly. A hand reached out, touching his arm.

He froze, looking down at her slim fingers, her narrow wrist, the polish-free nails. She had practical hands but they were undeniably lovely. His stomach tightened and he felt such a strong urge to take that hand, bring it to his lips and place a kiss in the centre of her palm. To lay some claim, however minor, to her being. Stupid. He shook his head slightly and, perhaps misunderstanding his movement, she dropped her arm to her side. That was not what he intended but, Christ, he needed to go before he said or did something idiotic. Like hold her to him, tightly. Something, anything to take away the sadness he could see lurking in those autumn eyes. They were golden right now, the dark lashes creating sooty shadows on pale cheeks.

He walked through to the outer door, not pausing, knowing it would be a bad idea. Pausing led to poor decisions. He needed to be decisive, not dithering. But that didn't mean he had no manners.

"Goodnight, Sullivan, I hope you sleep well."

He pulled the door shut behind him, wondering did he imagine the soft "Goodnight, Fitz," as he did so. Wishful thinking, for sure.

He hated being off stride. The sooner this case was over the better. For both of them.

* * *

Gia's head fell forward and tapped once, twice and a third time against the doorjamb. She'd had to send him on his way. It was vital. Yes, her plan was to spend time with him, erase him from her system by the normality of it. The humdrum. But the problem was Flynn Fitzgerald was not now, nor probably ever had been, humdrum. He was, she knew, an extraordinary police detective. He was spoken about in hushed tones on both sides of the Atlantic. And beyond. His meteoric rise through the ranks was the stuff of legends. Yes, she knew all that. She also knew he cared, deeply, for his family. Not just his parents, but his siblings and, she suspected, their various partners. That would include her own brother Nick. Well, to be fair, hard not to care about that guy! Who wouldn't? Nick was stellar suff.

But Flynn was not just the outer cool customer. She wondered how many people saw beneath the surface? Saw *him*? She hadn't, not really. Not at first. But she'd experienced a side of him she doubted many had. The intensity of him. The heat and power of him, focused entirely on her. She doubted she'd ever forget that feeling of being the centre of his attention. It had been exhilarating and terrifying in equal measure. And so, *soooo* good. Flynn might be top of his career with regards to detection. To detail. To putting seemingly complicated issues into a simple form so others could understand. The Flynn she'd experienced, first-hand, had been a fucking *master* at the details.

And now she had to go to bed with those details all fresh in her mind once more.

Fucking Flynn Fitzgerald – in all the ways.

Chapter five

Siobhán Barry was an excellent choice for the job, Gia agreed, as she and the other undercover operative became acquainted. She was whippet-slim, with sandy-coloured hair that fell to her shoulders and a fullness of face that contrasted with her lithe body. She was also sharp as a tack, about seven months pregnant, thirty-two years old and, no word of a lie, looked eighteen.

"Are you sick of people asking you for ID?" Gia asked, handing Siobhán a cup of decaf tea.

"Heartily," Siobhán concurred, "but it has its uses. Like now. Before I got pregnant, I was constantly being sent to secondary schools and youth centres as a bait or spy, whichever they needed. That got old quickly." She laughed at how bizarre that sounded. "I mean, I had to pretend to fancy lads almost half my age, go crazy over some boy band or Goth group depending on the scenario. I could probably do a Mastermind specialist subject on teen tastes in all things angst." She reached over and, smiling, took one of the muffins Boyle had left for them as an early morning treat.

Gia tore hers apart, the scent of lemon and blueberry

filling her nostrils. Her stomach rumbled loudly and both women chuckled. "Yeah, my breakfast consisted of cold naan bread. God, these really are divine. They would definitely give Mackenzie's woman a run for her money."

"Oh, yes, I forgot you guys are related. What's she like – Ali? Anything like her big brother?"

See, this is what Gia hated about small towns. And yes, Dublin was a small town – relatively. Should she try to be all palsy with Siobhán and dish? Or be the cool New Yorker who kept others at a distance? Shit. Neither. She'd be herself, but circumspect – which was her natural demeanour anyway. Sometimes.

Deliberately misunderstanding, Gia said, "Like Devlin? No, they are all quite the individuals in that family. Ali is great, smart and so talented. She's very direct and outspoken so you always know where you stand with her." Except even that wasn't true, not strictly. Ali, it turned out, was a secret-holder and had unintentionally turned her family upside-down not a year previously. Gia made a mental note to ask Flynn how Ali was *really* doing. She'd seemed all blissed out, though still her sarky self, at the dinner the other day, so maybe she and Mackenzie had something real going on. Gia hoped so. She liked Ali – they'd clicked at the wedding of Nick and Caro and had shared some fun times.

Siobhán looked set to follow up on the Fitzgeralds but fortune in the form of Brigid Lennon's arrival forestalled her. Bullet dodged. The two other women knew each other slightly but their reputations of solid career work did the talking for them.

"Let's get down to it," Brigid said in her brisk manner and, avoiding the muffins, she whipped out a notebook and sat poised. "Well? What's the plan?"

Gia nodded towards the spiral-bound jotter. "Rather old school of you, Brigid. Haven't you heard of technology?"

"Yup, and I'm not a complete luddite. I just like my notes to be mine and not hackable or easy to access. I use my own form of shorthand so even if someone were daft enough to try to pry this notebook from my cold dead hands, they'd be none the wiser."

"I like your style," Gia acknowledged. She whipped her own small, battered book from her inside jacket pocket. "*Snap!*"

Siobhán laughed as she slid a finger across her iPhone and tapped open an app. "I'm techie all the way. Sorry, you two, but hanging with teens for so many jobs has shown me the myriad of ways this phone will never be parted from me. All the secrets, in so many different folders." She wagged her phone at them. "But all password-protected and no one knows the codes but me! Anyway, you start, Sullivan, since this was mostly your idea."

Gia moved her notebook off the folder on the table, opened the manilla cover and handed each of the women a sheet of paper. "This is the play. It's simple and underdeveloped for a reason. You two know the lay of the land, literally and metaphorically, and I have run several versions of this over the last year, so I know how it usually pans out. I accept," she held up a hand when Siobhán began to speak, "one hundred per cent that things may not pan out the same here. They didn't in New York or Boston either, hence the underdeveloped part."

"I get it," Siobhán said. "If it's too tight there's no wriggle-room, no manoeuvring. That would be a bigger problem."

Brigid tapped her own sheet with a finger. "Absolutely. Once we know our parts, we have to be able to work on the fly. Too scripted and we're screwed."

Gia relaxed slightly. Good. These women were as professional as she was herself. Knew the value of the street smarts that came with experience. Hopefully neither of these officers of the law would ever figure out just what a greenhorn Gia Sullivan actually was, on the force, whatever about life itself.

"I'm Ciara Sullivan, keeping my last name as it happens to be of Cork origin so fits, and you, Siobhán, are my younger, incredibly naïve cousin Chloe. Our mothers were sisters and since they were close, so are we. You, Lennon, have to stay in the background. The people we seek might know you and we can't risk the accented man, be he the Dutch guy or not, recognising you from before. We'll need you monitoring everything, yes, with technology I'm afraid, from a mobile location within running distance of us, at all times. By that I mean, so we can run to your spot easily, if we need to."

They spent the morning discussing, discarding and replaying the plan. Trying *not* to over-think it. Over-analyse. They all took notes, asked each other questions and brainstormed possible solutions to unplanned events should they arise. They were a team and it felt, to Gia at any rate, that they gelled. The trust was given, although not yet earned in reality. The badge did that for them. Didn't matter what station or house you wore it for, the shield was enough.

As it should be.

Chapter six

Ciara Sullivan linked arms with her young cousin Chloe and dragged her into the Well Women's Centre just over the River Liffey on the north side of Dublin. It was surprisingly clean and bright though no better or worse than any they had been in over the previous two days. They had also visited the Women's Refuges in several areas, but Brigid Lennon was sure the information they were seeking was through the intended support of pregnant women.

They had trawled a few for a reason. They wanted the word to get out, if anyone was watching, that a young woman was looking for ways to get her child adopted – but not necessarily through the official channels. At each place they had sat in the waiting room and had a version of the same conversation, ultimately leaving before being seen by anyone in charge. It wasn't to be assumed that the team running these places were in any way suspect – in fact, it was the opposite. Hence the scarpering before being admitted to an interview room.

Brigid had got the impression from Kylie that a woman would turn up at the centre – unfortunately she refused to say which one – and offer outside help to only specific girls. This was the last but one in the surrounding city limits but as the two women took their seats their 'script' took on a new level of intensity. They knew Brigid was close by, illegally parked, listening to everything on the wire that 'Ciara' wore. They didn't wire 'Chloe' in case things went in a different direction and she had to be examined for any reason.

"Would you not just keep it?" Ciara begged in a loud whisper.

"I can't. You know I can't. Me da would kill me. He hasn't seen me since me third month and I've lied about where I'll be for the next eight weeks. He thinks I'm off to London for work."

"Your da is a jerk-off. We both know that. But your mam? She'd mind it for you – she's a dote, like," Ciara said in continued hushed tones.

"No. I've told you, Ciara. They can't know. Maggie Lane from down the road had a baby on her own and my parents were disgusted. Said she should have been thrun out of the house. I have to get a home for it. I just wish I didn't have to fill in fucking paperwork. What if the child comes to find me in years down the road? Jaysus, this fucking sucks!" She flung her head back against the wall behind the hard plastic chairs where they were seated. Thumped it a few times for emphasis.

"Stop your whinging, Clo – you got yourself into this mess. You're old enough to know better."

"And you stop your nagging! I thought you were going to help me?" This time Chloe's voice rose, just a notch, just to allow that edging of anxiety.

Ciara sighed loudly. "I'm here, amn't I? But I don't know where to look for a place that takes your babby for you, do I? Not without red tape an' all. Maybe you should just ask them when it's your turn? Somebody has to be doing it, like. Shit, you should've gone to England like they used to. Look, I said I'll help, and I will. I just don't know how yet!" This was said with a weary sigh and a bit of a wail.

Neither of them looked at the older woman watching them discreetly from behind a newspaper. Neither of them even glanced in her direction. They didn't let on they noticed her attention riveted on them. Or that the page hadn't been turned. The woman's clothes were serviceable and nondescript. But she was not there to ask about an unwanted pregnancy. This woman was in her fifties, at a guess. She had been eyeing the few other young females in the room when the detectives had shuffled in. But as soon as they had started talking, her focus was all on them. It wasn't hard. The three other people were either flipping through phones or seated with eyes closed and earbuds in.

"I can't do it," Chloe said after a few minutes, a little more audibly. "There has to be someone who can take my baby and no one else will know. I mean, I don't even know if the hospital will have to record it? Fuck it. I can give a false name and then just leave without the child, right?" She turned to grab Ciara by the arm. "What d'ya think?"

"This place is creeping me out, that I do know. Maybe you *can* just leave the kid, but will you? Won't you want to know what happens to it? Give it to a good home?"

"Course I will, but what if the child comes for me later? What if I get married and a person shows up and says I'm their ma? What then? Oh, this is shite!" She allowed a few tears to track down her cheeks and sniffled inelegantly.

"Come on, let's go. This place won't help. They would want your blood on file here." With that, Ciara stood and hauled Chloe up with her.

Completely ignoring the still woman in the corner, they made their way out the door, closing it behind them. They went down the two steps and turned south to cross the bridge.

Wait for it, thought Gia, and three . . . two . . . one . . .

The door behind them banged closed again and a woman's voice called out, "Excuse me, girls, I wonder if I might have a word?"

Bingo!

***

52

"Report," Flynn said, his voice even, his gaze on her steady.

Gia pulled off the hot scratchy wig and plonked into a chair.

"Jeez, give me a minute, tiger," she said. "We just got here."

She exchanged a rueful glance with her 'cousin' who also sat, a hand resting on her belly. Siobhán looked as tired as Gia felt but must surely be even more uncomfortable due to her pregnancy. Gia unwound the padding from about her lower body and hips and tossed it to the floor. She noted Flynn's grimace. Hey, she was exhausted – if he wanted it picked up, he was welcome to play housemaid. He pushed himself away from his desk where he'd been perched and bent to gather up the offending wadded material and began folding it into a tidy parcel. God, he was a nitpicker. He paced back to his desk, placed the fabric there and turned back to her, his arms folded casually across his chest, for all the world like he was in no hurry. He propped himself there, on the edge of his work space, all nonchalant. It was a lie. His eyes, while still holding steady, couldn't stop the hum of impatience radiating from his person.

"Keep your shirt on, I need hydration and then will tell all." She reached for her water bottle and noted the rather surprised expression on Siobhán's face at her casual attitude to a superior. Well, he might be her temporary boss, but she owed him nothing and back where she came from this deferential crap was just that, crap. She wasn't going to treat the mighty Flynn Fitzgerald any differently to any other colleague. It wasn't her way and he could just deal with it.

"In your own time," he said with his jaw tight.

"Yeah, right." She took another gulp from her bottle, just because, and flipping back the cap settled in to relay their escapade.

It was pretty straightforward, at the beginning. She recounted, in a professional and practical manner, how they had visited the various Women's Refuges without result and then the Well Women's Centre.

53

"So, this woman, middle-aged, short greying hair, blue eyes, about five seven and 140 pounds, follows us from the building. We'd both pegged her instantly on arrival. She was out of place and too intent on her paper. Anyway, she said she couldn't help overhearing our little discussion and felt sorry for us. Did we have somewhere to stay? Had we eaten? Were we alone in the city? She came across as caring but there was a steely look to her. Someone less astute could well have bought her spiel, wouldn't you say, Siobhán?"

"Absolutely," Garda Barry agreed. "She placed her hand on my arm several times and asked if she could touch my belly. I hate when people do that so my recoil from her was real. Fortunately, Sully, in character, scoffed at me and I allowed it. It was the right thing to do. This woman was verifying I was really pregnant."

"And that's a checkmark in your favour, Fitz. She would never have bought a fake belly. She knew what she was doing. She also looked at Siobhán very thoroughly, including checking out her ankles."

"She got what she was looking for there," Siobhán bemoaned, glancing down at her feet.

Flynn turned and, locating a stool nearby, rolled it towards her and, with a brief "May I?", lifted Siobhán's feet to rest on the leather.

"I'm sorry you and your ankles were inconvenienced, but we appreciate the commitment." He rose and returned to his previous position of sitting on his desk.

Siobhán chuckled. "It was the walking, followed by the sitting and nowhere to elevate them, unlike now. Thanks, Detective Inspector."

He nodded to her and brought his attention back to Gia. "Continue."

"The woman's name is Jackie Carroll. We checked her in the system, or Lennon did, and she seems legit. By that I mean no criminal record. But she has her hand in some pies, that's for sure. She mentioned an address of a place

54

she said we could stay cheaply and that there might be people she could talk to for us, regarding a private adoption. She wanted our details but Siobhán complained that she needed a loo and we had to go. I asked for the address to be written down and told her we were fine for tonight but might look it up tomorrow."

Gia paused to have another drink and Siobhán took up the story.

"It's all on tape anyway, but Sully told the woman we couldn't afford a private adoption, deliberately misunderstanding that we would have to pay lawyers as opposed to being paid. I broke in with the fact that I wasn't giving my baby away for free, and Ms Carroll was suddenly very soothing, very motherly and all 'Of course not, dear, no one would expect that'. As we pulled away from her, not wanting to be too eager, she pressed us to come to the address she'd given us."

"So we'll turn up tomorrow and see where that leads." Gia sat forward, her eyes on Flynn's. "It's clever to use a slightly matronly, motherly figure. Young girls wouldn't feel threatened by her. Using a man would frighten young ones away, especially if their pregnancy was a forced one. And this woman, while not the height of fashion, was comfortably dressed – not flash – but not too drab either. Clever really. Well thought out."

"Was it similar to your New York case?" Flynn asked.

She thought about that. "*Hmm*, yes and no. Same modus operandi in that Women's Centres were the target to get the girls, but mostly it was a grandfatherly man who did the selecting. And as an inside job. He'd be hired as a male nurse or assistant and ferret out the vulnerable in the waiting room, ensure he got to them before the officials would and lure them that way."

"That was clever too," Siobhán said. "The girls would trust a member of staff, rather than a stranger."

"But not so easy here," Flynn said, moving to sit behind his desk. "Male nurses are still in the minority and an older woman would definitely be less suspect. And maybe not as easily hired as an assistant. And neither point is intended to be either sexist or ageist." He steepled his long fingers and tapped them against his chin.

It was a small insignificant movement but Gia suddenly remembered the feel of those fingers. The gentleness, the strength and, good lord, the *dexterity* of them. These were hands that were not only capable, but expert. She could feel herself flush at the memory and was furious. *No, no, no.* This man and his clever fingers would not derail her. Not now and not at all, ever again, if she had anything to say about it. Her memories? They could get the hell out of Dodge. Or in this instance, her wayward brain.

Unbidden, her eyes met those stupidly gorgeous aqua ones and she gritted her teeth. He couldn't know she was remembering the feel, the touch, the glory of his fingers. Could he? *Nah.* He was probably remembering a particularly nice bottle of brandy and that tiny smile that tugged his mouth was for an amber liquid, not a hot body. She needed to get real.

Clearing her throat, she said, "Tomorrow, then. We'll turn up at the address and see." She rose from her seat to end the interview and helped Siobhán up to a standing position.

"Check in here before you go," their boss said. "I may have some more news by then. Larkin is following up a few leads."

"Don't know who that is but okay, we can do that," Gia said and headed to the door, Siobhán following behind.

"Larkin is a local garda who does undercover work for various factions at the station," Siobhán said as they headed down the corridor. "He is usually very thorough so I assume he's been put to good use."

Gia paused, a hand on her partner's arm, outside the conference room.

"Wait," she said. "There is a possibility of Boyle the baker's leftovers. I, for one, am starved. Wait here."

Gia pushed open the door and headed into the empty room. It was dim and at first it appeared she was alone. She strolled to the side table where the goodies had been stacked previously and, yes, *score!* She collected up a couple of muffins and wrapped them in paper napkins – then yelped as a figure loomed behind her.

"Fuck, Mackenzie! Way to give a girl a heart attack! Announce yourself, pal. I could have decked you." She held her goodies to her chest, heart beating rapidly.

"Decked me?" The voice was full of sarcasm.

She hadn't thought he did sarcasm but you learn something new each day.

"I could have," she insisted but with a smile. She absolutely could. If she'd not been holding baked goods and lost in thought. She was slipping. "What the hell were you doing here in the dark anyway? That's just weird."

Mackenzie didn't even flinch at her directness. "Thinking."

Gia snorted. "Can't you do that like normal folk – you know, with lights on and stuff?"

"It's restful. And conducive to . . ." he hesitated and finished lamely, "thinking."

"I'd heard you had an odd way of progressing through a case but, thinking in the dark wasn't mentioned." She laughed, putting a finger to her lips. "Your secret's safe."

"Should I let Ali know you have gone to the dark side?" Mackenzie asked, with a nod at her clutched package. "She'll be most disappointed."

"And I suppose you didn't eat one of these yourself, being all saintly and loyal?" Her tone was scathing as surely no one could resist this yumminess.

Mackenzie merely looked at her, with a strong hint of incredulity.

"Oh alright, of course you didn't. I was jesting, jeez – take that scolding look off your handsome mug. And I'm not quite this greedy – Siobhán Barry awaits me outside and she is eating for two, so, see, I'm actually an angel of mercy!"

"Well, in that case," he said, "let me." And he took the

parcel from her, placed it on the table, pulled a piece of flattened cardboard from a shelf behind her, whipped it into its pre-made shape of a goody box and added several more muffins from the leftover stack. He then took two paper cups, put a decaf tea bag into one, topped it with boiling water, and poured coffee from the other carafe into the other. His movements were efficient and economical. He was used to being organised and capable, she could see. He fitted lids on the cups and picked them up. She happily took the closed box and preceded him from the room.

Siobhán was full of smiles but her grateful thanks at Mackenzie's thoughtfulness was simply brushed aside as nothing.

"It's my pleasure, Garda Barry."

"Tell Ali she's still the best, but if you let Boyle know I said that I won't be responsible for my actions," Gia said, as they turned to head down in the lift. She opened the muffin box and took one, insisting the rest were for Siobhán to take home. It was almost as delicious as it had been when fresh that morning, and the coffee though a tad bitter hit exactly the spot that needed assuaging. Mackenzie really was a thoughtful guy. Ali was lucky.

Gia wiped a crumb from her mouth as she said goodbye to Siobhán at the main door and sipped her coffee all the way to the train.

It had been an exhausting couple of days, with highs and lows and a lot of walking. Gia and Brigid had tried to get Siobhán to sit in the car and take a lift from one destination to the other, but the young garda wouldn't hear of it. Gia admired both women she was working with, for different reasons. Brigid was the eldest of the three of them, and obviously highly regarded as well as being thorough, organised and surprisingly tech-savvy. Her slightly brusque manner hid, Gia believed, a kind heart. Siobhán had great instincts which made her a natural for working the streets – officially, of course. She was funny and wore an air of innocence that wasn't strictly to be believed. From chatting during their walks to the various potential meeting places, Gia had discovered quite a bit about Siobhán's very tough upbringing. She deserved great credit for being on the force, with a dad in jail and a mother in rehab. She was, she said, determined to show her younger siblings how it should and *could* be done.

Gia had long become adept at evading the sharing part of any conversation. Even before – before everything, she hated explaining how she became a cop – at her age and via a very circuitous route. People, she'd discovered, either assumed she had an 'in' with the brass or she was playacting at the job. Neither could be further from the truth.

She let herself into the flat and threw herself down on the couch. It was a comfy one and, she gathered from the Fitzgerald sisters, had seen some action. Maybe it would bring her luck. Not in the sexy times way, God no, she was done with that, but in the general way. A happy new-part-of-life way. Not yet, obviously. She had some tough shit ahead of her, however long it took. Some demons would need to be faced, issues dealt with and people, certain individuals, handled. If he ended up in jail, that would do. If he ended up dead? So much the better. If she pulled the trigger? Ah, well, some things were too much to hope for.

Flynn stayed late at the office. He listened again to the recordings from the wire Gia had worn. He couldn't fault them. He'd heard the verbal report, seen the written one Brigid Lennon had forwarded, and heard the words as they had gone down. No, he couldn't disregard their findings or how they played it. It had been subtle and yet real. Gia hadn't dropped her accent once. He would have sworn she was Cork through and through. How did she do it? Waking his computer, he did a search on her. He'd done one before, sure, but this was more. Deeper. He bypassed several levels of security and found her application records for NYPD. Interesting read and a very chequered journey to the job. So many attempts at a career seemed reckless at best and unsure at worst. She'd graduated in English and Social Studies, Law, and Accountancy, all of those through accelerated programs and then an associate degree, more like a diploma he assumed, in Psychology and Drama, from a community college. Her studies totalled seven years but none, it seemed, was a perfect fit. So, he knew she was driven, and based on her subsequent speedy rise through the ranks, it spoke of a well-matched career path in the making. Finally. He glanced at reports from a few of her cases, all confidential and really not in his remit, but if he couldn't use his rank and sway for his own benefit once in a blue moon, why have it?

She was good. Not always orthodox but not a renegade either. By all accounts she thought on her feet, was proactive rather than reactive and a team player. He tried to access her medical records from last October but found they were sealed. He could, he knew, get them opened but he felt a twinge, a niggle of disappointment in himself at his subterfuge. They were sealed because she didn't want them known. Had anyone known she was pregnant? She'd been working on the Brooklyn Babies case at the time and maybe when she lost her baby, *their* baby, it had been too difficult to continue. So why was she here on this version of the same case? He agreed there were obvious similarities, patterns and links that were more than suspect but until they had concrete evidence that the supposed Dutchman was working out of Ireland – or at least Dublin – they should keep an open mind and look at all possibilities. That was their job. Their duty.

Damn. He shoved a hand through his short hair and pushed back from his desk. Something bothered him about Gia Sullivan. Not the something that had caught his attention over a year ago at his sister Caro's wedding. A different type of something. Last summer she'd been on fire – fun, sassy, flirty, and so goddamn sexy she'd left him breathless. And more satisfied than he'd ever felt in his life. And it had been only one night.

60

This other thing, the *off* thing was like a wave of sadness or weariness. Not that she came across as weary in the tired sense, just dejected weary. Of course, he completely understood a woman didn't just bounce back from a miscarriage. He wasn't a complete asshole. Shit, it had taken him months to process and he hadn't been carrying the babe. He fervently hoped she'd sought professional help and support. He still couldn't believe her family hadn't known and he couldn't fathom why. They seemed so close and Nick, the one he knew best, was a stand-up guy. He might not have been there to help personally, but Flynn bet Nick would have cared. It must have been so hard for her to face alone. He stood and paced, hands shoved in his pockets, and stopped by the window. This time last year he'd been holding two secrets, one bigger than the other and his family knew nothing about either. So, he was a bit of a hypocrite wondering about her choices when his had been exactly the same. But it wasn't the same, was it? She'd been the one needing someone, not him.

When he'd mentioned their anniversary the other evening, he'd heard her gasp. She'd forgotten. He hadn't. He'd never forget that day. What they'd done, for their child. Maybe he shouldn't have said it. Maybe her gasp was one of hurt, but to him their marriage was a good thing, came from a good place as it had been a promise for their baby's future. He wouldn't regret that. Couldn't. He hoped, in hindsight, she didn't either. Gia hadn't wanted to get married, had protested but it had still happened. He may have railroaded her, laid the family connections/ collective disappointment /traditional values on a little thick. He doubted his parents would have cared whether they were married or not. They had welcomed Caro's baby, Toby, into the fold with open arms and she'd only been eighteen. *They* would never have expected marriage, but it was important. To him. Flynn shook his head, looking out at the twinkling lights appearing over the city skyline as the early September evening turned to night.

He walked back to his desk, saved all the data he'd collected on Gia and switched everything off. It was an easy walk to his city-centre apartment but he always felt the car should be with him, in case. In case he got called out on an emergency, or his family needed him or, well, or. He parked in the garage below his building and took the stairs to his fourth-floor home. There was a lift but he felt the least he could do for his body on a day when he was deskbound was to use his legs. Some evenings it was more of a strain than others. The strain he felt now wasn't physical. Or at least not from tiredness.

He closed his apartment door and tossed his keys on the hall stand, then tugged his tie down and divested himself of his suit jacket. He was a suit man, owning at least two dozen, as he felt a certain respectability was never a step too far in the wardrobe department. By the time he hit the shower and let the hot pulsing water hit his back he was already pulsing elsewhere.

One hand to the shower wall, the other wrapped around his cock, his thoughts centred on the one woman he could not erase from his mind.

His wife.

Chapter seven

Being on the job was a thrill. Each and every day Gia walked the beat, did some sneaky detective work, wrote up never-ending reports or had the luck to go undercover, it didn't matter. It was all the job and she did not take that privilege, to work for the citizens of NYC and its environs, for granted. Here in Dublin, it was the same. Come to work, be grateful for the job and *do* the job, whatever the day brought. It just so happened that this particular job was of the upmost importance. To Gia. No matter what, she would see it through, this time. And she wouldn't let doubts and anxieties sneak their bastardly way through her protective shell. No siree, not her.

Her wig on, padding tied tight, her oversized 'shirt over leggings' style look in place, Gia took the train into the city. Now they were doing this, actually playing the role, she didn't dare go without her disguise– always better to be safe rather than sorry. She and Siobhán had met with the boss earlier in the day and gone over strategy. A part of her, a teeny tiny part, wished their very brief fling had not resulted in pregnancy and she could simply enjoy the memory, take it out and polish it when needed, without the inevitable pain that came too. Would she ever be able to separate them? Would she ever be able to look at Flynn and not notice his hands, his leanness that hid strength and ripcord muscle, a flat toned and defined stomach, narrow hips, and sculpted thighs and arms. His chest alone was a thing of sexy dreams. That smattering of dark chest hair, those dark flat nipples that peaked as she touched and tasted them. Good lord, she needed to take a breath. A flush was stealing over her cheeks and that was a look that did not go with dirty blonde hair, saggy hips and baggy clothes.

What to do? She would have to teach herself to ignore that damn flutter that teased her belly when she was close to the man. When she interacted with him. It wasn't so bad when it was totally work-related. But any conversation that involved just the two of them? Flutter, flutter, *flutter*. She did her best to slag him off, treat him with a large dose of irreverence, just like she had last summer during those glorious wedding-party days. She refused to let his status here daunt her. After all, the first time they laid eyes on each other, neither had a clue who the other was. They both knew *of* each other, through Nick obviously, and the shooting involving his stepson, Flynn's nephew, Toby. But when he walked into the flat, the very place she was now staying, and she, Ali, Caro, Frankie and Molly had all been swigging cocktails two nights before the wedding, well, that had been a meeting of eyes that had held as the air crackled around them and time had, she believed, actually stood still. Those eyes, that stare, that intense focus and then as she'd tilted her chin at him, her own eyes unwavering, the tiny smile that tilted the left side of his mouth. And she'd been lost. A goner, as Molly would say. She wasn't a goner anymore, of course she wasn't. She was mature and well able to compartmentalise her silly belly flutters with the best of them. If only she could in fact train said belly to behave, all would be well.

She and Siobhán had arranged to meet on the DART so

they could emerge together at the city-centre train station –
in case anyone was watching. Overkill, maybe, but nothing
wrong with being cautious. Siobhán plonked herself down
on the space next to her at Monkstown station and the two
fell into desultory conversation about nothing specific.
Both took turns scrolling their phones and insisting that
each other look at the memes or Tik-Tok videos. Nothing-
to-see-here vibe, just two young women on their way to
town. One largely pregnant, the other fussing and irritated
at times.

It was late, after seven, and they carried backpacks and
jackets. Siobhán aka Chloe also carried a blanket as she
might be encouraged to stay at the address and as
someone who had been supposedly staying on and off
with friends till her cousin arrived from Cork, it was
conceivable she would have a small amount of bedding
with her.

The station was busy as they bustled through the
evening crowd and made their way, at a measured pace,
pausing frequently to give the mum-to-be a rest, to the
address Gia held in her hand. It was north of the river, but
only a short walk from the main thoroughfare. It was
down a series of long narrow side streets and when they
arrived at it, they noticed a couple of young women standing
outside, smoking.

"Jesus," Siobhán said, softly, "wouldn't you think they'd
know better?"

"Same with us, in the US," Gia replied. "Young women
still smoke despite all the public awareness. I have a pack
with me, as a prop, but I'll make sure they know it makes
you ill."

"Good thinking – one of us should be smoking. I have a
couple of cans of Coke in my bag, some bars of Cadburys
and some packets of Tayto, the Irish-girl staple in times of
stress." Siobhán nudged Gia in the arm.

"Even I know Tayto," she said, grinning. "I had my first
taste last summer and found them delicious."

"I'll keep them as bartering food, if necessary, but I'm hoping they'll let you stay too and we can work on distribution of all things calorific together. Feeding people who doubt you or are potentially suspicious is always a good gambit. Did you bring sandwiches as Larkin suggested?"

Dave Larkin had figured they would both be 'required' to stay at the house, and he, having checked it out on the sly, interacting with one of the girls loitering outside, realised that the kitchen facilities were limited. The young woman had offered the information that there was only breakfast and dinner offered but they were good, and that the kitchen closed at six thirty for the night. She said most of the girls swapped food and treats well into the night. The no smoking or drinking policy was strict, in house, but the people in charge knew they couldn't restrict the girls outside their doors.

Gia and Siobhán approached the entrance, nodded briefly to a few stragglers and entered the building into a bright though narrow hallway. A neon-lit sign directed them to the office and they presented themselves as 'guests' of a Ms Carroll. The attendant, a young gum-chewing, pale-skinned woman, was so uninterested as to be laughable. Their customer service needs work, Gia surmised. She noticed the rounded belly of the woman and wondered was her baby up for adoption too? Was she getting paid? It would be fascinating to see how all this played out. How much did the young women actually receive in payment for their infants? And was there a sliding scale? Time would tell.

Three flights of stairs later and Siobhán was huffing and puffing. "Jesus," she moaned, loud enough to ensure she was heard, "could they not set us up in a fecking bungalow?"

"Stop whining, Chloe, you're lucky to be here. These people could be the answer to your prayers – you'll be minded, have your baby, and get a wad of cash for it. What more could you want? It *is* what you want, right?"

There was a snort from the woman attendant showing

them the way. Her steps had slowed too, the higher they climbed.

Gia was interested in the response to their exchange. "Hey," she said, catching the woman's arm, "what was that for? Are we missing something?"

"I didn't say nothing," she grunted. "Here's your room." She shoved open a door and directed them inside.

There were twin beds, a table between them, a chest of drawers and a single wardrobe. Not exactly the high life, but then, if you were a lost soul in need of shelter, you would not be complaining. It looked clean though spartan. There was a laminated list tacked to the door of the closet and Gia sauntered over for a read.

"What's all this? Seems a bit like boarding school to me." She made her voice dismissive, angling for a bond with this person who might have access to more information – crucial documents or files that might hold keys to the chain of command.

"It's not like any school *I* went to," was the response. "This is way better."

Okay. No help there, then.

"If you say so," Gia mumbled grudgingly.

They dumped their bags on the beds and sat, wondering what happened next.

"Ms Carroll will come and talk to yiz soon, so better not unpack yet. She might change her mind."

Siobhán glanced nervously at Gia. "Fuck it, what'll we do if she tosses us out? I've nowhere to go." She looked pleadingly at the woman who shrugged thin shoulders.

Gia crossed and sat beside Siobhán. "You'll be grand. The woman said she could help and she will. I wish you could stay in my gaff but then my mam would tell your mam. I really wish I had a flat or something, but I can't afford it. Prices in Cork are wicked high, like."

"S'not your fault, Ciara. Stop feeling bad. It's enough that you're here with me. I'd be terrible lonely otherwise."

Their chat was interrupted when the attendant was

pushed aside and the woman from the day before, Jackie Carroll, entered the room.

"Ah, you came. I thought you might." She brandished a clipboard at Siobhán and spoke in a very matter-of-fact tone. "Right, you need to fill this in, truthfully. I assure you it is all confidential, but you must be accurate as to dates and doctor's visits so far. If you are to stay here, if we are to help you, I must insist on honesty. I must also insist that you speak to no one about our little home away from home here. It is only for those in need and others do not understand the extremely valuable service we offer to you unfortunate young women. As for you," she turned her glacial stare, all traces of matronly warmth vanished, on Gia, "you may go now. I will take care of everything from now on. I'm sure you've been very helpful but you are no longer necessary to your friend's requirements."

"No!" cried Siobhán. *"Don't go, Ciara!* You can't make her leave – I need her! She's me cousin. Her mam and mine are sisters. I need her!" Tears trailed pathetically down flushed cheeks and she clutched at Gia, her head swinging from the Carroll woman to her supposed relative.

"I'm not leaving her, not until I know what ye are up to. Till I know she'll be well cared for and that her babby will go to a good home. I'm staying or we both go," Gia declared, aiming for terrified bravado, if there was such a thing. She thought there might be. She could see how one could be scared shitless yet still stand up for oneself. Hadn't she done it many a time?

Ms Carroll ignored the outburst and sent Gia a glare that would stop traffic. "We'll see," she harrumphed. "Now, Chloe, fill this in and I'll send Marcella here back to collect it shortly. Sign everywhere there is a highlighted X."

And with that, she exited the room and trundled down the stairs.

Marcella followed in her wake, leaving the door open.

"Born in a barn, were ya?" Gia called after her and got up to close it firmly after her. She noted the key, on the outside

of the door, and no way to lock it from within. Interesting. Were the women kept under lock and key? But why? Why, if they chose this place would they be tempted to leave? So much to learn. So much to unearth.

She sat down with Siobhán, whipped out her phone and quickly took pictures of each of the pages on the clipboard and emailed them straight to Brigid Lennon. She then deleted the photos, just in case she was searched.

They waded through the form – it was pretty straightforward, until you read the small print. It was complicated and full of legalese and would no more stand up in a court of law – in any country – than the writing on the back of a cereal box. But a young, worried and alone woman wouldn't know that – the terminology was meant to intimidate. Siobhán happily signed – she knew it wouldn't fly – but beside that, the station had given her a fake PPS or identity number and had created a backstory for 'Chloe'. They weren't so worried about Ciara as she wasn't the one ready to hand over her body's offering. The form stated pretty clearly that no contact of any kind would be allowed between mother and baby in the future and to that end, the mother was not to know the identity, nationality, ethnicity or religion of the new parents.

The exact amount of payment was not mentioned. A significant amount, a substantial sum, a generous gift – the phrases were all scattered throughout the printed material. There *was* a sliding scale – a blond boy, of good weight and length, would garner the highest price. The scale went down from there, offering considerably less for a female child of colour. Again, no specific figure was mentioned.

Yet, obviously, Gia and Siobhán surmised, many women took this nebulous offer. With abortion now legal in Ireland and easily available up to twelve weeks, Gia wondered why this service, such as it was, was even necessary.

"Why do they wait until it's too late?"

Siobhán shrugged. "I genuinely don't know. But it's certainly worth finding out. I assume they're hoping it's just not true. Maybe some think the father will step up or family will help out. There are still some staunch conservatives in this country and a small village in rural Ireland can be a lonely and desperate place. In fact," she continued, warming to her theme, "don't know why I picked the rural part of Ireland. Many cities, especially parts of Dublin are so image-conscious in certain neighbourhoods, they wouldn't want an unwed mother walking their streets either. People can be shits, basically."

"Truth." Gia raised her arm and they bumped fists.

They studied the papers and thought through a plan. Gia would stay the night, leave in the morning with as many names of contacts as possible and return for Siobhán/Chloe the following evening. She would have found them a bedsit, she'd tell Jackie Carroll, but they'd still avail of her services to take the baby. Neither woman wanted to stay a second longer than necessary in this weird and uncomfortable place.

Gia sauntered down the stairs, along the corridor and out to the street to join a couple of the young women gathered around a waste bin, smoking.

"Got a light?" She held up a cigarette and hunched her shoulders against the slight evening chill. "I'll share my sandwiches later if ye like," she offered.

"Go on," said one, a skinny redhead, handing her a lighter.

Her protruding belly, unseen from behind, was the perfect TV belly – a round ball sitting on her middle. It looked so fake Gia almost asked to touch it.

"Cheers!" she said, lighting up. The once familiar taste of tobacco and pungent smoke wafted through her lungs as she inhaled. How had she ever done this for fun? It took control, but she managed not to cough, returned the lighter and took another drag. Might as well get deep into character. "Are ye all selling yeer babies, like? Would ye not just have gone to the clinic months ago?" She figured she should brazen out the whole 'I may be Chloe's cousin but I think she's mad' persona and see where that led.

"That'd be murder, me ma says," Redhead offered by way of explanation. "This way I get a few quid to go back to school and not have to worry."

"But isn't it hard? Like, won't you be upset?"

The redhead's companion, a heavyset equally pregnant girl who could surely be no more than sixteen, glared at Gia. "Won't matter in the end, we'll get the few bob and start over." She paused and rubbed her stomach. "I didn't know I was preggers till too late. Me periods were never regular and the fucker who done it to me is well gone, so I've no choice. I'm still in school. Me mam is in the bed most of the time so I can't bring a kid home. The social welfare doesn't stretch that far, even for single mothers."

Oh, good lord, thought Gia, really wishing she hadn't asked. But she'd known the stories wouldn't be pretty, wouldn't be whitewashed for her benefit, so she needed to suck it up. "What about the father of your baby? Can't he help?" she asked the thin girl.

"Me uncle is the da, and he wouldn't let me keep it. He's got six of his own already."

Charming. Quite the shitstorm in that family. Gia took another pull on her dwindling cigarette and eyed them both with apparent coolness. "Well, I'd want to know more about who is running this racket if it was me," she declared, tossing the butt into the bin and crossing her arms over her chest. "It doesn't seem right, selling babies."

"Well, it's not you," Redhead snapped. "It's your pal is doing it."

"Sorry, no offense meant," Gia mumbled. "I want what's best for her. She's my cousin and I want to help. I'd just be happier if I knew more about it. If I knew this Carroll woman could be trusted."

"Course she can. This is Marcella's third baby going to Ms Carroll so it must be okay," the younger girl said. "She wouldn't keep doing it if it was dodgy, now would she?"

Indeed. But if Jackie Carroll was paying a so-called

PAMELA G. HOBBS

decent sum to Marcella for her offspring, why was the girl still working for her? Why not leave? Get a different job, one that would give her a career path or at least some modicum of credibility for a future? And why have the appearance and attitude of an indentured servant? Gia knew that if she could get Marcella to talk, they would be onto a good lead.

Shrugging against the evening air, she turned to go back inside.

"We've tons of food, so if ye want to come to our room, and bring Marcella or any of the others, we'll share it with ye." The comment was delivered in an offhand, doesn't-matter-to-me tone, and she went inside hoping the bait was taken.

Chapter eight

With an air of both misgiving and distraction, Flynn watched Gia enter his office. This woman brought so many complicated feelings into his well-ordered life and he didn't like or appreciate or want any part of it. He knew she could do the job but was aware her methods weren't always by the book – they weren't unsanctioned, per se, according to his research – merely unusual. He wasn't sure that was a word he wanted applied to any detective working one of his cases. Yet here he was. And here she was, bedraggled blonde wig in hand.

The distraction was easier to identify. Everything about her was a distraction, from her head to her toes. And all points in between. He had never, not once, been as rattled by another person as he was by her. Her short dark, not quite curly, not quite straight hair angled into her chin at exactly the right spot, showing her slender neck to perfection, the way it blended into strong, yet narrow shoulders. He remembered those shoulders. Bare, soft to the touch, scented in some mysterious perfume that had his senses reeling. Her winged eyebrows, dark as her hair and so expressive, her pert nose, determined chin and that stunning mouth – that delicious upper lip, the most kissable mouth he had ever seen. But it was her eyes, those incredible amber eyes that twisted his gut as she sauntered into his office.

"So, here's the skinny," she said as she threw herself into the vacant chair in front of his desk, adjusting the padding about her lower body.

He took a breath, steadied himself and sat upright, his usual posture at the ready – as normal, like this was his usual type of visitor. It was not.

"There's a whole heap of shit going on in that house and I didn't feel real happy about leaving Siobhán there this morning. In fact," she leaned forward, her elbows resting on the desk, "I'm heading back as soon as I give my report. The sooner she is out from under the purview of Jackie Carroll the better, but we can't just swan back out – it needs to look like Siobhán's staying and we need to give her the opportunity to get more intel. It's a balancing act, for sure."

Flynn, aware that they were still awaiting further information on Ms Carroll, noted Gia's concern. He picked up his desk phone and asked for Detective Lennon to be brought in.

"She may have more insight," he said as Gia raised her brow.

"Sure," she said. "Whatever works, but it better be soon. You need to hear this."

And succinctly, with little inflection and only a minor pause when Brigid arrived, Gia gave her verbal report.

"I'll write it up by this evening so don't even think of stopping me going to get her. I didn't like the way that Jackie was watching her this morning at the breakfast table. She was way too focused on her."

"Any particular reason?" Brigid Lennon asked. "Had Siobhán mentioned the father of her baby?"

Gia switched her gaze from Flynn to the other detective and he felt its absence keenly. That was patently ridiculous.

He had lived without her gaze on him for a year.

"She did. We decided, when reading the forms, that a blond, blue-eyed man of good education was going to be of most interest so she said the baby's father was a solicitor from Rathgar, wherever that is. That's what she wrote and handed in last night and there was definitely more of an interest in her this morning."

Brigid nodded. "Yeah, that's what Kylie said too. That the girls who had 'strong' parentage on the father's side would get extra of everything." She had made air quotes using the word strong but both Flynn and Gia understood her point. These girls were favoured. Their babies would fetch more money. Bigger pay day.

"And now that they are winding down the business here in Dublin, as we know from Marcella," said Flynn, "that must put pressure on them to get the best possible stats."

"Wait, what?" said Brigid. "Who is Marcella and how do we know?"

Flynn stood, rounded his desk to a small fridge, opened it and handed Gia a bottle of water. "Take a break. I'll fill Detective Lennon in."

Since his co-worker had arrived with her own water, he didn't offer any, but got straight into the retelling of Gia's report. It wasn't complicated. Not really. Just a different version of 'we've done what we can, here, time to move on'.

"According to Marcella Jennings, a pregnant employee of Jackie Carroll, the business, or at least the branch located in Dublin, is coming to an end. There are fewer women available to offer infants, most likely due to the new legal situation regarding termination. There are only four women presently at the Dublin premises and, according to Ms Jennings, no more on the books. It appears that of the four there, one young woman's baby is fathered by a relative and therefore not a viable purchase. Another woman's is fathered by a Brazilian immigrant, so down the list and Marcella is, apparently, unable to recall the father of her child. This leaves Siobhán as the only person with a potential winner and Detective Sullivan fears that this may put Siobhán at risk. Am I missing anything?" He looked from his notes to Gia to verify his understanding of the situation.

"Spot on, chief," she said, her voice as sassy as always. "However, I don't just want to get Siobhán out – those other three need rescuing whether they know it or not. And Marcella also let slip, after her fourth shot of vodka, that Jackie Carroll was complaining about the loss of specific buyers. I gather they are looking for some new people to buy babies here in Ireland. They have the last few births about to happen and they need buyers now. Babies up for official adoptions are way down for all manner of reasons, hence their hitherto lucrative business, getting them on the sly."

"Irish people have tended to go abroad for adoptions in recent years," Brigid interjected. "And it can be a long and costly wait. I can see why some people would be happy to buy on the black market." She raised her hands in a 'don't shoot the messenger' pose. "Hey, I'm not saying it's right or that I agree. Of course I don't, but I can see why the market is there. That said, we need to stop it."

Gia nodded. "It's a criminal offence and those babies are being bought and sold for profit. There is nothing okay about that. Let's go." She hauled herself from the seat and turned to the door.

"Not so fast," Flynn said, not raising his voice but stalling her in her tracks nonetheless. "Detective Lennon and I will accompany you." He got no further.

"*Absolutely not!*" she barked. "This has to go down easy and quick. In and out. There is nothing about you, Fitzgerald, that's either of those things."

He stopped, actually unsure what to say. He was *never* unsure. But those words, *easy and quick*, held a resonance that she was well aware of. Their first time had been quick. Too quick. And they had laughed about it as they fell into the easy. *Damn and blast.* He needed to rethink everything when she was around him. Everything she said had all kinds of double meaning and inuendo or maybe it was just him. But now was not the time. He caught her eye.

He could see the snark in her eyes. Now definitely wasn't the time, but it would come and he and she would hash this out. All of it. It might not be pretty, in fact it could get downright ugly, but it needed to be aired – every damn bit of dirty linen and hidden fabric, if that was a thing, had to be taken out and discussed. Then it would be over. Finally. But not till then.

Now though? Now they needed to get to Garda Barry's aid, if Gia was in the right of it. He was fairly certain he could rely on her gut in this respect.

"We *are* coming with you and you will be wired again. Not up for debate," he continued at the instant refusal that didn't quite make it past her lips. "But we will stay out of the way unless you give us the signal. Let's go get you rewired."

He stood, herded them from his office and downstairs to meet with the tech guys. If time was of the essence, they would be done and dusted by mid-afternoon, and then, well, then things between himself and Detective Gia Sullivan could be thrashed out, once and for all. The where did they stand part, the how did they behave around their families in future, part. All of it. They needed a plan, a map of their status, so to speak. Flynn liked a good, well-thought-out plan. And he definitely needed one for their murky waters.

Chapter nine

Wig back in place, Gia entered the building as if she owned it and darted straight up the stairs. She heard Marcella calling out but ignored the shout and headed to the bedroom she and Siobhán had shared the previous evening. When she left this morning after breakfast it had still looked like the remnants of party central after they had hosted an 'impromptu' get-together the night before with Marcella, the redhead whose name was Buffy, genuinely, and the younger girl, Emma. They had swigged vodka as if none of them knew what alcohol could do to an unborn child and sneaked cigarettes which were smoked out the window. They ate sandwiches, chewed toffees and scoffed donuts. They made crisp sandwiches, courtesy of Buffy's hoard of white bread and butter, and how Gia had kept her surprise at that culinary delight to herself she would never know. Siobhán had kept her 'vodka' in her own container, refusing to share because she was susceptible to cold sores, and she and Gia had marvelled later, when the others had left, how Jackie Carroll allowed any booze on the premises at all. It was covert for sure, but they had assumed regular sweeps would be made.

They had also marvelled at the tales told by the increasingly loquacious Marcella as she let slip names of those involved, women who had given up their children, and locations around the city that had been used in the past. "All gone now," she had lamented. "Bloody abortion laws have changed everything. I nearly had one meself, but Jackie found out I was up the duff and said she could get me five grand for this baby. So sure, fuck it, why not? But looks like this will be the last. They're moving up north, and some lads from out foreign have already taken over, Jackie is pissed cause she wants to go too, but the fella with the accent says no, and the foreign lads want nothing to do with Dublin, so it's curtains for her and me. And you lot." She had swept her hand majestically about to encompass Siobhán, Buffy and Emma. Then she'd burped loudly, laughed hysterically and fallen into a dead sleep. Neither of the other two had anything of major value to offer, both attending Jackie's 'hot house' as it was known locally. Siobhán had almost choked on her sandwich on hearing that sobriquet, imagining, she said, them all tucked up in a glasshouse till they were ripe. They'd had a good chuckle at that and then, when all the food supplies were depleted, the younger women had left, dragging a grumpy-to-be-woken Marcella with them.

Gia and Siobhán had talked in low voices for a while, writing notes in their phones and emailing them to their work accounts, then deleting. Neither had slept well and Gia had hated leaving her partner behind, but they needed to stick to the plan. It would be suspicious if 'Chloe' left with nowhere to go, but equally unusual if 'Ciara' had stayed in a place for pregnant women, and she not in the family way.

Breakfast was porridge and toast, scrambled eggs and bacon and endless strong tea. It was the diet of champions and all the women from the midnight feast partook heartily. Gia had only nibbled on the toast and avoided the tea – she was a coffee gal all the way. She was not eating for two, had never even got to the part of her pregnancy where that had been a thing. Her abiding memory was the constant nausea, the never-ending urge to empty her stomach of all that rested there – but it never happened. She'd eaten saltines, a type of cracker, every morning before attempting to get out of the bed, and it had helped. She'd kept a supply in her car and handbag and both were called upon on way too regular a basis. As she watched the other women tuck in, a wave of regret washed her. Would she ever know that delight of eating for two?

Shaking off the melancholy, she'd risen, said a public goodbye to her cousin, nipped upstairs for her bag and left the clean-up to Siobhán as pre-planned. Siobhán wanted an excuse to stay in her room and even if it meant being reprimanded for having 'guests' there, it would hopefully buy her time till Gia returned to get her out.

Stepping into the bedroom now she stopped in her tracks. It was bare of any sign of occupancy. Nothing but two beds, minus the bedding, the table and wardrobe. Nothing. No sign that anyone had ever been there. No sign of Siobhán Barry.

Shit.

Gia whirled on Marcella who had come clomping up the stairs after her. "Where's Chloe? Where's my cousin?"

Marcella looked at her, dumfounded. "What d'ya mean? She left straight after you this morning. Jackie said Chloe got a message to go meet you. *Let me go!*"

Gia released the grip she hadn't been aware she had on the other woman's arm. She stepped back.

"I didn't send any message. I went looking for somewhere for us to stay and I'm back to bring her with me. Where'd she go?" As soon as she asked, she knew it was useless. Marcella believed what she was told. She did what she was told. She was a follower, not a leader. "Where's Jackie?" Gia demanded, brushing past Marcella, heading for the stairs and the office below.

"How do I know? I only work here. No one tells me

nothin'," Marcella grumbled as she followed in Gia's wake.

The office was on the ground floor, towards the back of the house. Probably a parlour, back in the day. Now, as Gia flung open the door and walked boldly in, it was neat, clean and very much a modern office set-up. A main desk in front of the window and two smaller ones against a side wall, all sported desktop computers and one of the smaller desks also held a printer. Gia quickly catalogued the supplies and furniture, making a mental note to ensure the hard drives were searched for any and all information.

Jackie Carroll looked up from her work and, having glared at Marcella in the doorway, snapped, "I thought you'd left, Ms Sullivan. Your cousin said she heard from you and went to meet you. I suggest you go find her. I'm busy."

She lowered her head to some papers and began shuffling them. This woman was up to her armpits in nefarious doings.

"We both know that's a crock of shit, don't we, Jackie? She didn't message me and she didn't leave here, unless she was forced! Which was it? I want to know where my cousin is and I want to know now!"

Jackie Carroll glared again, and a moment passed where Gia stood her ground, unbending. The older woman broke the stare and twisted in her seat to reach for some paperwork. She shoved a bundle in Gia's direction. "Here! They took her to one of those locations. No, don't ask me which one, I didn't ask. I don't want to know. That way I can have plausible deniability." She shoved her chair back and stood. "Go, Ms Sullivan, and don't come back. I tried to help your cousin, but perhaps she doesn't want this enough. She certainly resisted going and needed a little persuasion."

Gia snatched the papers from Jackie's hands and snarled, "If you've harmed a hair on her head, it's your head that will roll, you conniving cow!" She turned on her heel and marched for the door. "And don't think I won't be reporting you to the guards, making girls sell their babies."

As she strode to the front door, she could hear the woman shout after her, "*I never make anyone do anything! It's their choice! I'm helping them!*"

"Yeah, yeah, sure you are," Gia muttered under her breath.

She walked briskly to where the car was waiting, double-parked on the quay a minute or so away.

"Hop in," Brigid said, as the back door swung open.

Gia slid into the seat and shoved the papers at the detective. "Siobhán's not there. They've taken her to one of these locations but I haven't a clue where they are. Jesus, if they harm her or her baby, I'll –"

"Stop." Flynn's steady voice came from the driver seat. "They need her. They won't hurt her or her child. They can't afford the loss." His attention once again on the traffic, he asked Brigid to read off the list of potential places. There were four. He and the detective discussed possible routes and options as Gia seethed in the seat. She had fucked up. She should never have left Siobhán alone. Stupid and, as it turned out, dangerous. Christ, she hoped Siobhán was keeping her cool. She must know her colleagues would not leave her high and dry, but still. When Gia had been on the case, the previous year, there had been scary moments but she'd trusted her house to keep her safe. To get her out. To save her. It had been a close call, but here she was, so there was that.

The loss was not on them. That was on her.

As Flynn and Brigid discussed the best bet on where Siobhán might be, all Gia could do was listen. She yanked off the scratchy wig, and undid the padding, figuring wherever they went next, it wouldn't matter what she looked like – her role as Ciara was over. Flynn spoke to the dispatcher and organised three of the places to be searched immediately. He and Brigid had a hunch about the fourth, a warehouse along the quays on the southside but close to water transport or the East Link bridge if they wanted to head to the airport.

Gia wondered aloud why Carroll's people might want to take Siobhán out of the country and Flynn's take was that they wouldn't or at least not right away. His reasoning was sound – they would obviously have obstetricians available here in Dublin – ones they trusted, or at least used – and that would ultimately be easier. And with heavily pregnant women, time was of the essence.

"Do you think they will try to induce her?" Gia asked, trying not to let the worry come through in her tone.

Brigid shook her head. "Kylie said Jackie Carroll took very good care of her. So hopefully whoever Siobhán is with now will be of similar vein."

"Yeah, they took care of Kylie until she wasn't useful anymore," Gia said.

"That was me. I dropped the ball on her. Shit, I'll never forgive myself for letting Kylie out of my sight. She'd be alive today if I'd stayed the course."

"You don't know that," Flynn said. "All we know is she was telling you things that she was told to hold secret. That was her decision. For her own reasons. If she hadn't told you, she would have told someone else who may not have followed through. This way you get justice for her."

Gia listened as Flynn spoke quietly and with such authority. He had a point. As police detectives, all they could do was hope a person would trust them with their story and allow them to help. You can't make a person do things. Not really.

"Flynn's right," she said, laying a hand on Brigid's arm. She ignored the lifted eyebrow in the mirror as she continued. "From what I read in the reports, you were there for her, offered her all the help you could, gave her assistance and promises that you could in fact keep and still she led you on a merry dance. She made mistakes and didn't deserve to die, but that's on those who tossed her in the river, not on you. You were her beacon when she needed it. Remember that."

The irony of what she was telling Brigid when only minutes earlier she'd been beating herself up over her own performance in similar circumstances, was not lost on her. But Gia believed both truths, hers and Brigid's. There had been times when things had gone south on the job and they hadn't been her fault. So she knew the difference. She knew when and where to assign blame. None was due to Brigid. Herself? All the blame. She may not have pulled the trigger, so to speak, but she was solely responsible for the outcome.

She drew a deep breath as Flynn pulled the car to a stop. They got out, devised a quick plan, and while Flynn called for back-up and Brigid took up a lookout position, Gia sauntered up the alley towards the river to knock on a big wooden door that looked like the old-fashioned entranceway to a warehouse that it was. She glanced back, and around. No one to be seen. Her partners were out of sight but still in audio contact. That was some relief. There was a van parked at the side of the road and she surreptitiously took a photo of the registration plate. Cover the bases, basic training 101.

She rapped hard on the wood, the flaking paint drifting to the pavement with the sudden movement. Silence. She tried again, hollering when she paused. *"Hey, open up! I haven't all fucking day!"*

There. A distant thump, then another. She waited, adrenalin starting to pump through her. Reminding her she knew how to do this. Was good at it. Loss and pain had taken up too much space in her brain, made her doubt her abilities at times. *Focus,* She knew when to put things aside. Had become, by necessity, quite the compartmentaliser.

The sound of a bolt sliding. The door opened a crack.

She went on the attack. *"For fuck's sake, yiz took all fucking day! I'm here to see yer wan, Chloe something. Hurry up, I'm not gettin' any younger."* Her accent was pure inner-city Dublin. She had the briefest of moments to wonder if Flynn was impressed as he listened in via the wire.

Pushing open the door against a tall skinny man with dreadlocks, Gia barrelled in. "Where is she? I'm to check her." She figured the more insistent and impatient, the more assured she was, the more likely whoever was here was likely to believe her.

"You can't just barge in here," Skinny Guy said as another man walked over to join the fray.

"Jackie sent me," Gia lied. Except it wasn't a lie, not really. The woman had given her the list, maybe because her conscience pricked at her, but equally maybe to catch her out too. Had she phoned ahead? Too late to worry about that now.

In her ear, Gia heard Flynn's quiet words, *"The other places are clear, she must be there. Give the signal if you need us."*

When, thought Gia, because she knew she would.

The second man was huge. Not just in height but in stature. Bulky and brawny, a sleeveless vest showed massive arms covered in tattoos and a vast chest. His shaved head was shiny, whether from exertion or heat, she didn't care, but it made him just a tad more intimidating.

"She never told us," Bulk and Brawn said, his voice cold and hard. "What ya want to see yer wan for anyway? She's not due for weeks. Unless you're here to hurry her along, get lost, bitch!"

Charming. What a delightful addition to the world. "Not that it's any of yours, but I'm trained to see what's what in that department. I'll tell *you* how many weeks she has, sonny, not the other way around." She strode forward into the large space. It was dim, with windows high up close to the roof. About halfway across the space a flight of stairs rose to another floor, like a mezzanine, and Gia quickly realised there was probably only one way up and down. That could pose a problem. She needed to readdress their plan.

Skinny Guy whipped out a phone and began tapping. "I'm calling her cos she never said you was coming."

"Sure, phone her, but she wants this done quick like, so don't be wasting my time or hers when I can be in and out in a few. Your funeral when you interrupt her meeting, but hey, fire away, just don't say I didn't warn ya!" She shrugged all casual, all 'who gives a shit if you're fucked over' and headed for the stairs. "Up here, I suppose?" she threw back over her shoulder, unbelievably relieved they didn't try to stop her. Confidence in one's movements, manner and patter usually did the trick. But she wouldn't bet on for how long.

As she took stairs two at a time, she heard the men arguing behind her and tried to ignore the words. Siobhán, her health and her baby, was her goal. Their squabbling over contacting Jackie or not had to be, for now, low on the list of priorities. She hurried along the wide floorboards of the partial upper floor – only one door, down to the left, was closed. She made straight for it. The handle wouldn't turn but there was a key.

Quickly unlocking the door, she entered on a breeze, speaking loudly so the men, now following fast on her heels, could hear. "Okay, up you get, let's check you out, see if what Jackie said about you feeling unwell is true!" She spoke directly to Siobhán who was lying listlessly on a narrow bed.

She raised her eyebrows in silent inquiry as to Siobhán's emotional and physical status. The pregnant woman sat, swung her legs to the floor and gaped at Gia.

Nodding briefly in understanding just as the men arrived and crowded into the doorway, Siobhán gripped her belly and winced.

"Who are you? I want to go home. I want my mam!" Siobhán whimpered. "Do you know where my cousin is?"

"*Shut up, you!*" Skinny man growled. "This one is here to check you out. You can stop your whining and let her at it. Me and him will be right outside the door."

Gia whirled on him. "What? Aren't you staying to gawk at a woman's privates? Stomach a bit too weak for that, eh?" She put a sneer into her voice.

Shedding her jacket, she briskly walked to the small

sink and washed her hands. She moved swiftly to Siobhán, pushed her back with a hand to the shoulder and spoke brusquely. "Shut up and lie still, I'm going to do an internal exam and check your cervix. Jackie says you were complaining of pain earlier and she thought you might be in premature labour. We can't have that. We'll have to stitch you, give you meds. She said this baby can't be a premie."

With that announcement she began pulling down Siobhán's maternity pants and shoving her knees apart as she mouthed a silent 'I'm sorry'. She bent down and sat in front of her spread legs, doing her best to obscure the view.

It wasn't necessary. The two men backed out and slammed the door. *"We're right here so don't try any funny business!"* Brawny called out. *"There's no way out!"*

"Shut up, I'm busy!" Gia shouted back.

Siobhán continued to moan and groan loudly as Gia, whispering in her ear, told her the plan.

"No, you can't do that," Siobhán mouthed. *"That's crazy."*

"It's the only way, it will be fine. I've done it before."

"No way."

Gia reached into her sock beneath her jeans, whipped out a small blade. She was always prepared. Depending on the outfit or situation, Gia wore a concealed blade in her sock or her belt. Both had stood her in good stead over her admittedly brief but definitely adventurous career. With an indrawn breath, she quickly made an incision on her scalp, above her left ear, underneath a swathe of hair. Blood appeared and just as quickly she swiped at it and transferred a smear to the upper inside of Siobhán's thighs. She did that a few more times and, as Siobhán theatrically moaned and cried out, Gia placed a pad of tissues to her cut head, pressing firmly. Shit, it hurt like a mother and it had better fucking work.

With one hand holding the rapidly soaking tissue, Gia used her other to help Siobhán up. They decided to leave her pants off, it looked more staggeringly real this way, and hurried to the door.

"This has got to be quick and dramatic," Gia warned.

"Just imagine you're in labour and the baby is massive. Be explicit. Be loud. Be real. Ready?"

Siobhán nodded and Gia crumpled the bloody tissues in her hand, flipped her hair over the wound and yanked open the door.

"Fuck it, lads, she's bleeding! Race down and open the door, I have to get her to Jackie's on-call doctor. Now!" she roared as she and Siobhán staggered through the door and aimed for the stairs.

The two men were taken off guard and scrambled to catch up.

Siobhán was Oscar-worthy.

"Me baby," she moaned. "I can't lose me baby! Stop it, why don't you? I thought you were supposed to fix the pain. Help me, Jaysus, help me! *Get me drugs!*"

She shouted and moaned so loud that they could hardly hear the ruckus of the two men thundering down after them.

"Hey, yousz two, ye're not going nowhere." Skinny reached out and grabbed Gia's arm which she freed with a quick elbow-jab to his chin.

"You tosser, can't you see she's bleeding?" She spun on the larger man and, waving the bloodied tissue in his face begged "Call Jackie – tell her I'm on me way with the Chloe woman. Tell her to have supplies ready and call Dr Hayes. *Do it!*" She barked the last two words as if she was the one in command. Most likely unused to the sight of female blood – or not the 'running down the legs from possible imminent childbirth' kind, the big man flinched and did as he was told.

The two women charged for the door, flung it wide and raced to the car pulling up alongside the kerb.

"Get in!" shouted Brigid as the back door opened wide.

They didn't need to be told twice.

Chapter ten

"Hold still," Flynn grunted as he held Gia's jaw in one of his hands, holding her steady while dabbing with an antiseptic wipe. "This might need stitches."

"*Ouch!* No. No hospital. No stitches. Don't you have those Steri-Strip things in your box?" She tried to angle around to see into his first-aid kit.

Flynn changed the angle of his hold and gripped her chin tighter. "*Hold. Still.* And I'm trying to apply those if you would be so good as to remain immobile." He looked into amber eyes and could feel his stomach clench all over again. He was hurting her, he knew it, but this had to be done.

He wasn't sure he'd ever forget the moment he saw the blood trickling down the side of her face.

They'd hightailed it back to the station, Flynn driving with unaccustomed speed. He had already sent out alerts to have the two goons arrested for holding a person against their will and Jackie Carroll and Marcella had been delivered to the interview room some time earlier.

They'd pulled up to the Garda parking area where Dave Larkin was pacing the lot waiting for their arrival. As Siobhán tumbled from the vehicle into his arms, Flynn had heaved an inward sigh of relief. It was an unofficial secret those two were an item and Dave was the father of Siobhán's baby, and Flynn was grateful he was returning an unharmed partner to the other man's arms. He could see the slight shudder in Siobhán's frame as she tried to hold it together and decided he and Sullivan were de trop. He inclined his head for Gia to walk in front of him and they entered the station house.

The Carroll woman was in one of the interview rooms and Marcella was in another. The other two younger pregnant women had been long gone. He'd suggested Gia take Marcella and he would focus on the older woman as Gia had already built some kind of rapport with the younger one.

When they'd met up to discuss notes a half hour later, he'd thought Gia was looking rather pale. Had he missed something? Before he could ask if she was okay, he spotted it. A streak of vibrant red snaking its way down the side of her cheek and below her collar. *What the hell*?

He'd taken her arm, dragged her to his office and turned on her.

"*Explain*," he barked, sliding his finger through the blood and shoving it in front of her face. "Just what the hell happened in there? And why the fuck did you not say something?" He saw her blink of disbelief at his use of language. "*Sit*," he ordered as he went to the shelving unit behind his desk and returned with a first-aid kit.

Working efficiently, he unearthed the disinfectant wipes and traced the line of blood up the side of her face to a gash about two inches long on the side of her head. "I'm waiting."

Gia sighed and then winced as he cleaned the cut. He should say sorry, apologise for causing pain, but *shit*, this was beyond ridiculous. How had this happened?

"*Well?*" he prompted.

Another sigh, this one with a definite grumpy yet defiant edge. "I had to get blood somehow. You must have heard that on the wire. I obviously couldn't cut Siobhán so

I did what was necessary. It's no big deal."

"This has been bleeding since the warehouse? And you are only getting it seen to now? If I hadn't noticed, would you have told me? Got it checked out at a medical centre?" He could hear the fury in his voice as no doubt she did too, but he didn't care. He *was* furious. And strangely terrified that she was more hurt than she let on. This woman had cut her own head to save another woman from who knew what. She did it for her partner, for the case. But he didn't know many who would. He reached for the pretend stitches and applied them as best he could. He'd parted her hair, clipped some back and razored off the barest amount possible, just enough to allow the strip to cover the wound. When he took the clip out it should be covered and not look too obvious. If his hands weren't quite steady, it was the sight of the blood, not the knot in his stomach at what she'd done, was the culprit.

"*Ouch.*"

"*Hold still. Please.*" No, he wouldn't take her to the hospital. He imagined she'd had enough of those. But he could take care of her. If he could just stop his mind from going all the places his body had been clamouring for since he saw her in the stairwell several days ago. He'd been dealing pretty well with all the Gia Sullivan issues he had bottled within. He had processed, gone to see a therapist, for Christ's sake. How much more mature could he have been? Well, maturity had sneakily taken flight because even the feel of her head beneath his hands was affecting him in a most inappropriate way, knowing she was in his care, however temporarily. Her skin under his fingers, when he brushed his knuckles down her cheek before using the razor had felt as soft and dewy as he remembered. His hands, when they had held her shoulders, could feel the strength he knew she possessed. Her glossy short hair, while presently sporting a proportion of dried blood, brought instant images of his face buried in her scent as she had moaned beneath him.

The kisses he had bestowed along that slender neck now tainted with her own blood, had thrilled him as much as they had affected her.

He took a breath, applied one more strip as discreetly as possible, unclipped her hair and let it fall softly back into place. He discarded the soiled wipes and took a fresh one to clean away the remnants along her cheek and along her neck and heard her gasp.

"I'm sorry, I'm trying not to hurt you."

"No, it's not that, it's fine, I just . . . nothing."

She turned her head, angled away from him, eyelids swept down, casting a shadow with her thick lashes. A light pink stained her cheeks and he hoped like hell she wasn't running a fever. There was no way she was spending the evening on her own, that was for damn sure.

"Come on, let's get you out of here," he said briskly, doing his best to appear normal. In control. Behaving like the Flynn Fitzgerald everyone expected to see. If anyone could see how jittery he felt below the surface right now, his credibility would be shot.

Gia slipped slowly from the tall stool he'd dragged over to give better height for his ministrations. She wavered and his arm was about her before she could right herself.

"Easy now, you've had quite a day," he said, shoving the fear aside. "Slow and steady."

Typical Gia, she brushed him aside. "I'm fine," she snapped. "Just want to catch Siobhán and Brigid before I go back to the flat."

"About that," he began, but she'd already strode from the room, back ramrod straight. "That went well," he grumbled as he followed her to the boardroom where the others had congregated.

Siobhán was seated next to Dave though they had put up their professional wall. They were fooling no one, but it was their business how they handled their personal life. It rarely came into play and even today Dave had been working away in the background, digging for further information on Jackie Carroll and her as yet unknown associates. Maybe Siobhán would have heard info worth delving into. Flynn and Brigid had not asked about her ordeal, in the car – it had seemed unnecessary at the time and they knew they'd get to it, eventually. Siobhán safe back at the station had been the priority.

As Gia entered the room, Siobhán rose and, crossing to her, wrapped her arms about her. They hugged tightly and as they moved apart Siobhán let her tears fall.

"You were amazing. How can I thank you? You were brave and fast and clever and ingenious and, well, everything. Seriously, I can never thank you enough." She swiped at her eyes and groped for a tissue.

"Don't be silly. It's the job. You knew I'd come." Gia tried dismissing what everyone in the room knew. She was a stand-up cop, Brooklyn based or not.

"Yeah, I knew you'd come. I hardly know you but I knew that. Partner." She held out a hand to shake Gia's as if she hadn't just held her in an embrace. Women were funny about these things but Flynn knew that making light of a serious situation was second nature to some officers of the law – it appeared Angelica Sullivan was one of them.

Dave stood, moved forwards and offered his hand, murmured a few words that made Gia's cheeks pinken even as she shook her head and then it was Brigid's turn.

It was she who noticed the wound on Gia's head and, in her blunt way, said "What the fuck, Sullivan? Did you swing at someone?"

It seemed no one was the wiser as to how the gash in her head had come to be. Siobhán had said nothing, probably hoping to prevent Gia getting into any trouble. It wasn't exactly by the book to cause yourself harm in order to dupe the enemy.

"Didn't you guys pay attention on the wiretap?" Gia asked, throwing herself into a seat at the table. "Follow along, boys, it's not rocket science."

"In fairness to the outside listeners, you never actually said aloud what you were doing and I didn't either in case the gobshites outside the door heard," Siobhán said. "It was all pretty fucking covert, Sullivan. And to be honest I was stunned into silence anyway."

She sat down next to Dave and Flynn wasn't surprised when she leant a head on his shoulder. She must be exhausted. On that point Flynn flexed his muscles. His official ones anyway. It was late in the day and his crew had put in an extra amount of work. He made some executive decisions. Because he could.

"Siobhán, go home. Dave, go with her. Brigid, finish the report and be out of here in half an hour, even if it is not complete. Jackie Carroll and Marcella will remain in house overnight, courtesy of our government. If our two warehouse chaps are brought in, they too can cool their heels in a cell overnight. We will reconvene at eight in the morning when Siobhán can tell us exactly what she learned from our duo. Until then, thank you, and good night. Detective Sullivan, I'm taking you home."

The trouble began when he realised he hadn't clarified *whose* home.

"Wait, where the hell are you taking me? I want to go to the flat. I want some food and some sleep. Lots of both, in fact, so I've no time for a mystery tour."

Gia glanced out the window in the early-evening sun, taking in the soft hues of colour in the sky. Flynn drove down various streets unknown to her but she was clued in enough to know it wasn't in the direction of Dún Laoghaire. She turned her head to glare at him, trying really hard to hate him right now. That was proving so damn hard. He'd been so gentle with her, tender, caring even. And it confused the hell out of her. It was a flesh wound for God's sake, not a broken limb. When he'd touched her earlier, held her head in his strong hands, those fingers moving fleetingly across her skin, she'd almost lost it and begged to be held. It wouldn't do, of course. She was well capable of getting over a shock-and-chase, as she used to call a quick getaway.

But his touch? Damn, if it didn't send tingles racing through her body. It had been clinical. Almost. And shouldn't have affected her in that particular way. Shit, the memories though. Those hours of him, focused on her, *intent* on her, had fucking ruined her for every other man. And all he had to do was run his fingers along her cheek and down her neck, with a fucking antiseptic wipe, and she was putty. Melting. Heat flooding every orifice. And the memories? With everything that had happened to her since that precious summer, she'd done her best to block it out. Block him out. Ignore the wistfulness and longing that crept in every now and then. The yearning for what, it seemed, only he could give.

She was not going down that road again.

Flynn spoke into the silence. "I'm taking you to my place. I'll give you food and a place to sleep, but there is no way you are being left alone tonight. And if I take you to Mum's, trust me, you'll be overwhelmed by kindness and I'm not sure an abundance of that is what you need right now."

"So, what, you're going to be nasty to me all evening? Yeah, I can see it now. The great and mighty Fitzgerald losing the cool and issuing curses and dissing my work ethic. Somehow, bud, I'm not buying it. Take me to my place and end this farce."

"I'm not sure to which farce you are referring, detective. The one where you go rogue and behave in a manner unsuited? Or the one where you pretend you are all fine and able to make yourself food and take a bath and get yourself to bed without analysing your actions and what might have gone wrong. That farce?"

The battle was lost and she knew it. Too exhausted to argue, she turned her face to the window. "Fuck it, take me to your place and feed me. That's as much as I'll allow for now."

She couldn't see the twitch at the corner of his mouth,

PAMELA G. HOBBS

but she could *feel* it. Down to her toes. The sexy bastard and his cute little rare and unusual smiles. She'd woken to that smile once. The tender sweet one. It had been fleeting, but Christ, it was embedded in her memory bank. She'd also encountered, in their mad fling, the wolfish smile and the *holding back an actual laugh* smile. She'd give good money to see that one again. Just as well she wasn't floating in the moola because she was pretty sure hell would be freezing over before he laughed at anything she had to say.

The car pulled into a ground-level space whose door opened at the press of a button and Gia sat up to take interest. This was the mighty man's domain and she better take notes as they could be worth money or at least some decent blackmail material. She had a hunch not many people got invited here. He wasn't exactly a party guy, despite being very close to a brimming family. He reversed smoothly into an empty space in the garage – except it wasn't really a garage – it held about half a dozen spaces, four of which were filled with vehicles. Three were nondescript cars, like the one they were in, the fourth was an SUV.

He got out and rounded the front to reach for her door.

"I can open my own door," she snapped as she swung her legs out. Why did men think that was a thing? A form of gallantry perhaps? An old-fashioned throwback to assisting fine ladies from carriages? She really wished it didn't make her feel cared for. Minded.

He took her arm as she stood and, damn, she was glad. Lightheaded for a second, she closed her eyes and when she opened them, he was right there, just standing, holding her, not saying I told you so. Not smirking.

"Ready?"

"Yeah, ready. Thanks." She knew she sounded grudging but, hey, she felt it in equal measure with the gratefulness. Call her fickle, she didn't care right now. Hunger was making her stomach ache and a bone weariness was seeping in. If she felt like this, she only hoped Dave Larkin was pampering the lovely Siobhán big time. Her fears and

96

anxiety as she lay waiting in that locked room must have reached some level. Sure, it hadn't been long, a few hours, but Siobhán hadn't known that. And the not knowing was often the worst in any hostage/kidnap scenario, no matter how well trained you were.

He put a hand to her back, easing her forward and, like a lamb to slaughter, she went. They entered an elevator and he pressed five as the doors swooshed closed. He didn't remove his arm and she couldn't decide how that made her feel. His hand, strong and firm, but not too close was a presence at her waist, but was she batty to think she could feel the warmth?

He ushered her out into a small hallway with only one door opposite. When he beeped in a code and opened the door, she moved forwards, curious now and brightening a bit to finally see the lair. She wasn't sure what she expected but it wasn't what she found.

The interior was softly lit, showing a long hallway with several doors on either side and what looked like an open space at the end. She walked forwards along a wide pale-oak-planked floor. The walls on either side were a warm sage. The trim was the colour of putty, the doors, painted wood panels, the same shade.

The open space was a revelation. Opposite were four Georgian sash windows and as she turned in a circle, she could see she was in a corner apartment. More windows lined the right-angled wall and, to her right and slightly behind her, was a partial wall and an island separating the living space from a kitchen. Taking in the wooden rectangular table right in front of her and the large couch and chairs to her direct right she made for the windows. There were blinds but, wow, she was glad they were up. It was almost dark and the light from the old-fashioned streetlamps along the quay, dancing reflections on the river below, was mesmerising.

There was no chance of being spied upon – the buildings across the river were a floor lower and one would need binoculars even if they'd been on a par. She moved from window to window, taking in the panorama of the city before her. This was a find, for sure. The side windows faced a street with an opposite building of slightly smaller height, below his window level. Clever that. He lived in a place where he could see all about him, but no one could see Flynn Fitzgerald. Or at least not without contortions. Farther to the right, the famous O'Connell Bridge hosted bustling traffic both vehicular and pedestrian. The apartment was so central yet had an air of quiet and solitude to it; it was calming, serene. The walls in here were dark grey and this time the trim was white. The Roman blinds appeared to be navy and the big leather couch was also navy. An area rug, with an oriental design, echoed the colours with plenty of deep red and warm sand added to the mix.

She turned to face him – surprise, she knew, apparent on her face.

"I'm impressed," she said and watched as he peeled himself from the wall where he'd been waiting for comment.

He took his hands from his pockets and gestured to one of the armchairs across from the couch. "These are actually quite comfortable unless you want to stretch out while I organise some food." The armchairs were the kind found in a stuffy library, old brown leather but faded and with scatter cushions on each that could be used or tossed.

"Go make yourself useful and feed me, I'll explore my options."

"Should that worry me?"

"Probably. Definitely." She tossed him a side grin because she knew that would piss him off. There was something so delightful about getting under Flynn's skin.

"Right. I'll change and be right back to make dinner. Make yourself relatively at home." He turned and headed down the hall as she snorted at his use of the word *relatively*. She heard a door open and close and prepared to snoop.

The wall behind the dining table held a bookcase which, while it certainly held a mixture of hardbacks and paperbacks, also held a selection of photographs. This open living area was surprisingly spacious and felt welcoming and comfortable as well as very manly and stylish. How did a man like Flynn Fitzgerald pull that off? An interior designer? His siblings? A wide square coffee table sat on the rug between the chairs and the couch and it had several stacks of books neatly placed. The main dining table had a laptop at one end with more books and a stack of papers. In the centre was a wide low pottery container holding fat church candles of different heights and she bet his youngest sister Molly had given him those. Interestingly, they were melted down quite a bit so either he liked his ambience or he'd had company. Most likely female company. Now why did that make her take a deep breath?

Not her business.

Shaking her head, she dismissed the image of him with a woman, dining, chatting, flirting. When she first met him, she'd have sworn he'd never flirt. But, to her detriment, she discovered he had his very own brand of the art. Saving the perusal of photographs for later so she could embarrass him while studying them, she made her way to the island to investigate the kitchen.

The countertop on the island was marble and spotless. She wondered did he mean he'd take a pizza from the freezer because it looked like no one ever cooked here, or maybe he was a nitpicker when it came to cleanliness? She'd ask, she decided, rather than guess. She loved calling him on shit. Even though they'd shared but a moment in time, she knew stuff about him. She was good at discerning and she liked nothing better than the puzzle of a person to solve. She turned from the island and studied the U-shaped counters with stove top and oven, stainless-steel massive fridge, what looked like a dishwasher and above the polished wood, slick cabinets with glass doors. One held only glasses, another plates, another cups. It was strangely satisfying, the way everything was laid out. The countertops held a toaster, kettle, a knife block, a small Lazy Susan with spices, a three-tier wine rack, almost full, and a wicker basket holding a pile of folded fabric napkins.

Gia pulled out drawers and opened cupboards. The cutlery was neat, the saucepans and skillets stacked on a wire contraption so nothing was pushed into anything else. There was a trio of composting bins and two tall larders – one a pull-out that had all the cans and pastas, the flour and the nuts. The other held a broom and mop, and other cleaning supplies on one set of side shelves. Everything, so painfully neat, had an air of usefulness and of being used. He really did live here – actually *live* here. Interesting.

But now for the litmus test. She opened the fridge.

Chapter eleven

"Verdict?"

Gia, still crouched with her head in a cold drawer, spun at the sound of his voice.

"Shit, Flynn, cough or, you know, make noise, unless you want to give a girl a heart attack! I could have been holding a bottle of this expensive wine and dropped it. Then where would you be?" She pulled a bottle of Chablis from the door and tilted it tantalisingly at him. It had been previously opened and the cork stuck back in, so she stood, helped herself to two glasses from the designated cabinet and poured them each a measure.

He watched her movements but didn't interfere. Wise man. She needed a shot of alcohol, and this very nice white would do the job. She tipped the glass in his direction as a salute, shy suddenly at the thought of doing a cheers routine with him. That seemed so intimate. So date-like. This, them being together in his kitchen, was nothing like that. It was functional. Necessary, she assumed he believed, to ensure her health and well-being and nothing more. She'd do well to remember that. And then she noticed his clothing change.

Aw, fuck it.

He wore jeans. Denim *jeans*. Like he wasn't a stuffed shirt who lived in a suit. And to add insult to injury, okay, to add more sexy to the situation, he wore a faded grey T-shirt that skimmed his body in a shamefully delicious way. He was barefoot and it wasn't even ugly. *I mean, come on,* Gia thought, there was no need for that kind of trickery.

"This," she waved her hand, the one not holding her wine, up and down in front of his body. "You did this on purpose, right? To throw me off my game. It won't work. I'm made of sterner stuff." God, she hoped she'd find some stern in there soon because the heat that was filling her looking at his body, shoulders, arms, well, that needed ice, and stat. It wasn't like she hadn't seen him naked. That was an image forever, indelibly, printed in her brain, but other than his sculpted body laid out before her, and above her and under her, she'd only ever seen him in a suit. And while that was a fine sight indeed, this casual ensemble made him so, *so* much more. What a bastard he was, to do this to her while she was at a low ebb!

But there was hope. He might turn out to be a shit cook, so she could at least gloat on that.

He didn't (wasn't).

Dinner was delicious and she *knew* delicious. Her momma was Italian and the food that had graced their table since she was old enough to sit at it, was legendary in Brooklyn. Everyone knew Rosa Sullivan was the queen of Italian feasts. Her tomato sauce had poems written to it. When she told this titbit to Flynn as she whirled spaghetti and his homemade sauce around her fork and bit into the yumminess of it all, he'd raised his eyebrow and she could see his disbelief.

"Okay, not actual poems, but many have praised her food in fulsome terms. But this, Fitzgerald, this sauce is damn good. I applaud you. Or I would if I had the desire to put down my utensils. I don't." She winked at him and, to her astonishment, she could have sworn he blushed.

"Thanks," he said, not quite meeting her eyes. "I like food. My family is a bunch of foodies – or rather we all like to eat what our mother cooks. And, of course, there is Ali and all her talent. I learned basics from Mum when I was in my early teens, mostly because she was overrun with my younger siblings, and someone had to boil water for pasta, or potatoes or rice and shove a chicken or roast in the oven. The more adventurous meals I learned from books and cooking shows. I don't like the idea of eating processed food, or relying on take-aways, and I equally don't like the notion of a person, like a housekeeper, being in my space. So, this is the result."

He offered her more grated parmesan and she accepted, swirling it into the nutty sweet sauce.

He'd put on a pan to boil water, taken out a container of sauce from the fridge, tossed spaghetti into the boiled water, glanced at his watch, and emptied the sauce into a smaller pan to heat through. It was all effortless, easy. Capable and competent.

Fucking manly.

She was fairly sure she was doomed.

He'd opened a solid spicy Portuguese red to go with the meal and, as she sipped her wine, she figured it was bull-by-the-horns time. She needed to get her big-girl panties on and deal with the elephant in the room. Maybe she was the only one aware of that grey pachyderm but deal with it she would.

"So, about last summer," she said, swirling the deep red liquid. She knew the psychology behind the activity and didn't care.

"What about it?" His glass was poised halfway to his mouth.

"Oh, come on. You know. Are we going to discuss what happened? I don't mean the consequences, obviously, not going there, but the reasons for it."

"The reasons?"

"Are you going to repeat everything I say?" It was

103

almost funny but he was dodging her question and now she was curious about that also.

"No. Nor are we going to repeat last summer's activity."

Why did that make her feel just a little crushed?

"Get off your high horse, smarty pants. I wasn't offering a repeat, I just wondered if we should process it. Because of working together. So there's no awkwardness."

He rose abruptly from the table. "There is nothing to process. We had sex. We won't be doing it again. There's no need for awkwardness."

She stood up too, gathering cleared plates to take to the kitchen area. Her cheeks were warmed with the wine or it could have been a tinge of embarrassment.

"That's it then. I won't bring it up again."

"Good."

"Fine." God, they sounded like squabbling schoolchildren. Gia set the plates next to the dishwasher. "I'm sure you're as pernickety about stacking as you are about everything else, so I'll leave you to it."

"Everything else?"

See, he shouldn't do that, she thought. Finish a conversation and then make a flirty comment that brought heat right back between them. It wasn't fair. In the sex department, pernickety was not a word to be ascribed to Flynn Fitzgerald. Other words maybe. Words like raw, hungry, rough, strong, *knowledgeable*, insatiable. Intense. Those words.

"Okay, you win that one," she said. "But I thought we weren't discussing it."

"My apologies. I stand corrected. My ego got in the way."

She laughed. How could she not? She found him funny in his odd almost endearingly truthful way. He didn't hide things.

"I'm using your restroom," she said and headed down the hall.

She'd lied to herself just then. He did hide things. She

knew nothing about how he felt about their fling, how he felt about the baby. Well, she knew a bit about that. She knew he was so damn old-fashioned that he'd pretty much badgered her into marrying him. But how he felt, inside? Not a damn thing. They hadn't discussed the baby in those few short hours before and after the registry office. There had been no time, which seemed odd now, with all that happened after. He hadn't said if he was happy to be a dad or wished it had never happened. Just that no child of his would be without an official father. When she lost the baby, she'd seen he'd sent emails, texts. She'd deleted them unread. She hadn't needed his reprimand for being so careless with their child. So unable to do that one thing. So, in reality, *she* had let him hide in that instance. And now, when she tried to begin a conversation long overdue, he cut her off.

Fine. Good. All as it should be. *Jerk.*

She appraised his bathroom with a critical eye. This had definitely been done by a designer. All cool greys and French blue. The odd deep red accent added quite the Nantucket flair. The floor was Italian tile, non-slip, at a guess. All these furnishings were 'at a guess' as far as Gia was concerned. What did she know? Her own apartment in Brooklyn was a mishmash of hand-me-downs, garage sales and roadside finds. She loved it. But she had to admit Flynn's apartment was not just stylish but decidedly welcoming and comfortable.

Deciding on further snooping, she walked back along the corridor towards the front door. She'd found the bathroom because the door had been ajar, but now several door handles beckoned. The first on the left opened to a fully stocked gym. Holy hell. In fact, holy *fucking* hell! It was a large room and, as she flicked on the light, she saw it had a treadmill, stationary bike, a weight bench and a staggering amount of weights sets. It also had a huge screen on the wall opposite the treadmill. That, she did not expect. She didn't see Flynn as a TV watcher but maybe he

PAMELA G. HOBBS

had secrets? Sport? News? Nature? Surely *not* thrillers. She needed to investigate that thread.

Chuckling to herself she backed out, flipping off the light. She was about to open the door opposite, figuring for some reason it was probably Flynn's bedroom, and she absolutely wanted a peek in there, but something drew her to the next door down. It was closed like the others but there appeared to be a strip of light escaping from under it. Curious, she took the few steps, dismissing the tingle down her spine as nonsense.

She opened the door.

Listening to the tingles should be a thing.

Because Flynn Fitzgerald definitely had things to hide.

Flynn closed the dishwasher and tucked the tea towel that had been hanging from his back pocket onto the rack. He reached for the cloth and swiped over the already clean counter. It was habit, okay, maybe veering towards an obsession, but he hated crumbs and an untidy workspace. A kitchen was a workspace as much as his desk at the station so he treated it with the same respect. Strangely, he hadn't minded Gia's ribbing over dinner. She had a smart mouth to go with that smart brain and it never occurred to him till this evening that she was the only woman who gave it back the way his sisters sometimes did. Gia let him get away with nothing. Christ, when she mentioned last summer, he actually thought his brain would burst and he would babble like a lovestruck teen and tell her all the things he *did* think about their fling at his sister Caro's wedding. And her brother's. Therein lay some of the problem. Nick had become, if not exactly a friend, then certainly someone whose company he enjoyed and whose intelligence he admired. Do you sleep with that man's sister? Your new sister-in-law by marriage? Or whatever complicated relatives they were now? No. You did not.

And yet they did. There hadn't been much shut-eye that night. It had been all energy and very much awake

106

and active goings-on. As he stood in his kitchen, palms pressed to the island counter, he let his mind wander.

The first time he saw her. The first time they spoke, when he couldn't take his eyes from her incredible mouth. Unless it was to snag those amber eyes with his. He knew he didn't imagine the electric current that flowed when they touched. They had both stilled, eyes locked to the joining of hands and then raised to stare at each other in blatant surprise. She had pulled away first, stepped back, turned to the other women in the room, but he could still feel her skin on his. The sound of her voice, that slightly raspy tone and Brooklyn accent went straight to his gut. And lower.

He hadn't slept that night. Or at least not easily. The sheet twisted about his long legs as he went over every second of their short encounter. He had brought some food from his mum to her eldest daughter so she wouldn't be cooking the couple of nights before her wedding. And as she had 'the girls' over, Jo had not wanted their time together spent worrying about recipes. So, he had come bearing a casserole and bread. He knew they had wine aplenty, but he'd brought another bottle anyway, Caro's favourite. Frankie, his sister-in-law, let him in and took his food and beverage offerings to the kitchen while he sauntered, unsuspecting, into the living room to greet the party.

Angelica Sullivan had been standing, no, dancing, on the coffee table. Hips, in low-slung jeans, swinging to the thumping beat coming from the loudspeakers. Ali, Molly and Caro were also dancing but their feet remained on the floor. She held a large cocktail glass in one hand as she raised it over her head in a swaying motion. Thankfully, he noticed, his gaze determinedly avoiding her flat tanned belly visible beneath the short T-shirt, the glass was almost empty. They'd obviously already begun their celebrations. He was no grinch. He hoped they were going to have a blast. He was to meet his brother Dev and Nick later in the local for a celebratory pint, so was in no position to point fingers.

"Flynn! You're here!" Caro had shrieked as he approached.

Her shrill cry had caught Gia off her guard and, as she toppled from her stage, he caught her easily in his arms. The smell and feel of her was a shock. Light yet solid, breathy and laughing, her eyes had met his and time had stopped. He'd put her down immediately, because the heat racing through his body had thrown him off balance. Flynn Fitzgerald didn't do off balance.

They were introduced formally, of course, and he couldn't resist sneaking a look at her upper arm where she'd received a gunshot wound while saving his nephew Toby from a nasty piece of work in New York the previous New Year's Eve. It was there, not too obvious, but there. A reminder of her bravery. Her courage in putting Toby's life ahead of hers. A kid she barely knew. Yes, it was the job, but not everyone took it to that extreme. He knew he was going to find a way to thank her personally. If that involved a meeting of mouths, and tongues and lips, well, he had best just man up. Even then Flynn knew he was diving into danger but for once in his rather staid life, the social side of it anyway, he wanted to throw caution to the wind.

And throw it they did.

He had stayed for a while, shared a small glass of wine, refused the food options including his mum's, and stayed mostly silent as he watched the women engage with each other. Gia was the blow-in, new to this tightknit band, yet she laughed with them as easily as if she'd known them for years, that husky sound searing through him in a way that made his breath catch.

When he could bear it no more, he stood to leave, saying his goodbyes with a special hug for the bride-to-be. "Don't worry, I'll look out for Nick this evening," he said, smiling as he kissed her forehead.

"He can look out for himself, Sir Knight," Gia had said, laughing. "He's all grown up."

"Indeed," he said dryly, knowing grown up and good behaviour didn't always go hand in hand. "Walk me to my car." Then he added, "I'd like to discuss something with you, related to the New Year's Eve case." In case any of his sisters were surprised by his demand. Because it wasn't a request.

"Sure." No hesitation. No questioning. Did she know what he really wanted? Did she want it too?

He angled a hand to her back, that sliver of skin so tempting, and eased her way out to Caro's door in the communal hall and over to the outer door. He backed her up against it so her back was flattened to the wood. Her hands were splayed behind her for traction and he leaned in, his face mere inches from hers.

"If I'm reading this wrong, say so now. Otherwise, hang on."

He gave her the beat of time. A moment of decision. Her eyes didn't leave his, but that slightly overlarge upper lip curled up at the corners and with a growl he took her mouth.

One hand slid behind her head, holding her at the angle he needed, the other slid to her neck and circled it, keeping her still. Not tight, not to scare her, but to show her he had this. He was in charge. As he devoured her mouth his thumb and forefinger caressed her jaw, but his hand never left the skin of that slender, glorious column of her throat. Her lips parted beneath his and tongues crashed and parried in a fever of mad desire, and he was definitely not reading it wrong. The kiss felt like it was the most on-point thing in his entire life.

Getting his breath under control, he'd drawn back, hands still in place. He didn't smile. This wasn't about fun and games. This suddenly felt very serious. But he knew he had to lighten it or one or both of them would melt to the floor.

"Welcome to the family, Sullivan."

Flynn let his head fall forward as the memories swamped him. Damn. He could feel every second of that first kiss. It had been spectacular.

She'd been spectacular. For a slight, lean woman, she had packed a mighty punch. And thinking of that, where was she? Not still in the bathroom, surely. He glanced about the room. Her bag was flung on the couch where she'd chucked it when she came in. So she hadn't left.

The silence in the apartment struck him as incredibly present. A cool chill invaded his skin as he pushed away from the island and rounded the corner wall into the hall.

The door. He should have locked *that* door.

No. *Fuck no.*

Chapter twelve

Fury flooded him. How dare she prowl and snoop? No one was allowed in that room. He rarely went there anymore and it was private – strictly off limits to everyone. He could feel a thunderous anger rage through his mind, numbing everything but fear. She couldn't be in there. He'd feel like the biggest fool. She'd see him as pathetic and lost. He hated that those were the feelings he'd projected on himself and that she might see him like that too was unconscionable.

He strode down the hall, managing to be silent due to bare feet on the woven runner. He wanted to storm into the room, drag her out, berate her, send her packing. Not just for tonight, but for the foreseeable. Taking a deep breath, the sensible side of his brain kicked in. He couldn't send her away. The case needed her insight, her knowledge. And she'd been stellar today, damn her brave hide.

But he could still read her the riot act.

He pushed open the door and entered the moonlit space. He'd bought a blackout blind for this room, as it not only was in direct line of the rising moon but two streetlamps seemed to invade the space as well. But the blind remained in its box. No point now. It could be as bright as day for all he cared. He didn't see her right away and ducked around the furniture only to pull to a halt.

There. She was there, sitting on the floor, her back to the wall, knees pulled up, her head resting on them, head to the window. Before he could lash out, he moved quietly towards her on the carpeted floor, and a cool beam caught the slash of tears across her cheek.

Aw, shit. Shit, shit. It was then he noticed the slight shaking in her body. Either she was still crying or very cold. Neither was acceptable to Flynn, regardless of his instinctive anger at finding her here. He crossed to her, hunkered down and took her face in his hands. She barely resisted. Her drenched eyes slowly lifted to meet his and he felt the kick to his chest. *Damn.* Her pain was palpable. Releasing her for a moment, he swung to sit next to her, stretched out his legs and hauled her slender shaking body on to his lap. He was still angry, he reminded himself as she curled into him, clutched his T-shirt in her hands and simply held on. He couldn't help himself. Cursing inwardly, he wrapped his arms about her and let her weep. His head fell back and rested against the wall as he waited her out. His throat tight, he didn't speak, didn't know what to say. No matter what happened next, whether he let her know how mad her invasion of his privacy made him or not, she deserved to be allowed to grieve in whatever way she wanted.

He knew this grief. Maybe not to her level. Maybe not as intensely. How could he? But he recognised despair when he heard it. Felt it. Breathed it in.

They sat there, in almost silence. The only sound her soft keening, but even that faded to gulps and sniffs. He shifted, reached into his pocket and pulled out a handkerchief. "Blow," he said, trying to remain calm. While she'd been crying, he'd allowed himself to hear her. Really hear how distraught she was. How desperately sad she must have been. No one at the station or on the job would have known this volcano was just below the surface. He hadn't known. Hadn't imagined *this* was right there, only millimetres from her natural, casual yet professional demeanour. Why hadn't *he* known? Considered it a possibility? Just because his own emotions were locked down, it was pretty arrogant of him to expect she was moving on with apparent ease. Was this what he'd felt was different about her?

She blew her nose, hard and long and the sigh that emanated from her was world-weary beyond measure.

"Want to tell me what that was all about?" He knew, with sisters as his reference point, that it was always better to ask, not assume.

She straightened on his lap, crawled off and returned to her previous position, but this time she mirrored his stretched-out legs.

"Seriously? With all this, you can ask? You don't look dumb, you don't usually act it. But, man, right now that's the dumbest of questions." She waved her arm about, gesturing to the furniture, the paint, the bedding, the chair. The blasted rocking chair.

He should never have bought it.

Flynn grunted in acknowledgement. She was right, he was being obtuse. On purpose. Anything to forestall the conversation he knew was coming. Gritting his teeth, he figured it was time.

"I, well, I felt the baby, our baby, should have an Irish home too. So, I, well, I just got a few things. To be ready. Of course, I realise that was stupid. *I* was stupid." He stopped, hearing his own bumbling explanations of something he couldn't seem to explain.

"Oh Flynn." Her voice was soft. Understanding.

God, he didn't need softness right now.

She levered herself to her feet and ran her hand over the end of the wooden crib. "It's beautiful. It's all beautiful. I had no idea." She turned then and picked up a baby blanket in palest green from a pile set on the rocking chair seat. She held it to her face and inhaled.

He'd washed it as soon as he'd bought it. Another stupid idea as it turned out. He'd washed all the bedlinen he'd bought in person and the few baby clothes he'd got online. He'd heard that was what you did. Now of course, nothing was returnable, but since he hadn't been in this room for months, he'd packed that discomfort of his child's special things being just a few feet away, into a far, far recess in his mind.

Gia put the blanket back down and reached into the crib. She lifted the stuffed animal up and hugged it to her body. "An elephant? Any significance?" Her voice remained gentle, unobtrusive, and he found himself rising to stand next to her.

"I had one as an infant. Kept it for years. I thought the baby might like it too." He sounded maudlin, and childish, if indeed both feelings could exist together.

"And elephants never forget, right? That they are loved. Your son would have loved this so much. He would have been lucky to have you as a dad."

"Son? We had a boy?" His voice cracked. He hauled in a breath. He didn't mind at all what sex the baby was, but hearing it claimed as a boy made it so real. Too fucking real. They'd made a baby boy. Their son.

Rasping a hand across his mouth he walked to the window and propped one hand against the frame. Why was it suddenly so hard to breathe? To swallow? This was so messed up.

"I'd like you to leave, now," he growled, his voice low and unsteady. "Call a taxi. I'll see you tomorrow at the station." When there was only silence, he closed his eyes against the sudden sting. "Just *go*."

When the door closed quietly behind her, he sank to the floor, completely and utterly undone.

She didn't leave. Of course she didn't. Gia took a long drink of water, and another, crying so deeply and intensely left one very dehydrated and she needed to replenish her

114

reservoir. She rummaged in his kitchen, found the booze and coffee pot, both of which she knew from experience he would need shortly. For now, he needed alone time, but she'd be there for him when he emerged, despite his earlier command.

She made a cafetière of not surprisingly decent coffee, considering his family's love of all things epicurean, and poured two fingers of Scotch into each of two glasses. They would both need that too. She rummaged and found a tea cosy, it would have to do, and angled it about the coffee pot. Taking the beverages and two mugs, with sugar and cream in small handmade pottery vessels, she laid them out on the coffee table.

Tucking her feet under her she settled onto the couch and prepared to wait. He wasn't a wallower, she believed, so would not spend the rest of the evening in his son's room. Even though he expected her to be gone, she believed he'd come back to this room when he had allowed himself to let go, just for a bit. To give himself permission to unleash his pain, his loss. It wasn't easy and it would continue to hit him at the oddest of times. Especially now he had an image – a little boy, who might have had his eyes or his hair colour. Or his smarts. Never to be. It was the loss of potential that broke her so many times, so she got that. What he might have been like. A laughing cherub? A mischievous rascal?

She limited those wandering images now; they only made her feel like shit. Every so often she opened the door to his lost childhood, teen years, young adulthood, but it got her nowhere except right back to pain. So, though it took serious mind games on her part, she stopped that journey short when she felt herself drifting. She needed to heal. Move on. And with the help of her therapist, she was doing okay.

She'd do even better when she had this case wrapped. When she had Hoyt Jansen well and truly trapped and in prison for the rest of his miserable life. That thought, and that thought alone kept her sane. Some might say *in*sane but she knew what she needed. Gia Sullivan was not giving up, not on this.

Nursing her Scotch, she rested her slightly throbbing head back against a soft cushion and, closing her eyes, began some slow steady breathing exercises.

"Why are you still here?" His voice was weary, resigned. Not angry or shocked. Not quite sad, but close.

"Come on, Fitzgerald, you honestly believed I'd do as you ordered? Hah, you know me not at all. Here." She swung her feet from beneath her and reached for the second glass of golden liquid. "Drink this. I needed it and I'm damn sure you do too."

He took the Scotch and swallowed it in one. Glaring at her, he immediately lifted the cosy and began pouring the still warm coffee and, without adding a thing, sat in the chair opposite and studied her.

"I'm impressed," she said, trying for a touch of lightness. "You didn't even flinch, tossing that drink back. Are you that practised? Now that's a smidgin worrying. Do your colleagues know the great and sober Flynn is not as he seems? *Hmm?*"

"Stop talking. I have so much to say to you but I don't think I can find words right now. Hearing you talk isn't helping."

"Sure it is. I'm always a delight to hear talking. I remember you liked listening to me very much at one stage. You liked my bossy tone, my acquiescent tone, my begging –"

"*Christ, Gia. Enough.*" He swallowed some coffee, replaced the mug on the table and leaned forwards, elbows rested on his knees, hands clasped together in front of him. "I'm still catching up. I'm sorry you had to see the ba– the room. It's private. No one has seen it. I meant to take it down, donate it. I intended to."

"It's okay, Flynn. You weren't ready. There's no right time. I feel . . . I feel privileged to have seen it." Gia drank some coffee, irritated that her hands were a little unsteady.

"That room reduced you to tears," he snapped. "That's on me."

"For fuck's sake, Fitz, don't be an idiot. Crying about something so beautiful, so special and thoughtful and, fuck it, *kind*, would reduce anyone to tears. I just wasn't expecting that level of commitment from you. That's all." She topped up her brew even though it was cooling fast.

"Commitment? Is marriage not enough of a show of commitment?"

"That's not what I meant. And you know it. I never asked for marriage. I never asked for anything from you. I was happy to take care of my baby myself. You did your bossy boots routine and railroaded me when I was at a low ebb. Morning sickness sucks, I'll have you know –" Gia stopped on a gasp, her hand flying to her mouth to stop the words. "I didn't mind, I swear. I'd welcome it back if only . . ."

"Christ, Gia, I'm sorry. I didn't mean for us to be arguing over this. I was embarrassed you saw my attempts at baby-decorating. I don't know how to pack it up. How to dispose of it. Twice I tried but . . ."

Gia watched this intelligent highly revered man misplace his words and felt humbled. He had been so much more affected by their baby's loss than she had given him credit for. In truth she hadn't thought about his reaction at all except to assume he'd be partly relieved and partly pissed off at her. Both of those beliefs were wrong on so many levels. And she needed to own that.

"It looks like we have both learned some things about each other tonight," she said. "And that's not a bad thing. I, for example, learned that you are a Peter Rabbit fan. That I had not expected. And the soft yellow on the walls is perfect. Quite the decorator, Mr Fitz. Very stylish. I had assumed, looking at this apartment, that you had people in to create it for you but, seeing our son's room, I'm betting not."

Gia heaved an inner sigh when a smile, just a little one, stretched Flynn's lips for a moment.

"You like the frieze around the wall? I felt our baby

shouldn't be exposed to Disney characters too early and that Beatrix Potter might be a more gentle introduction to the world of literature. And since I was unaware of the sex I went for neutral colours." He sat back in the chair, easier now.

The tension that had vibrated from him when he had emerged from the room had lessened. He still looked raw. Broken, but not into pieces. Not unfixable. She could help with that. She owed him that.

"Did you really do it yourself?" She began to gather the cups and coffee pot, more to give him space to answer than any housekeeping urgency.

He rose too, his body limber and fluid. He collected the glasses and followed her to the kitchen. "I did. I even enjoyed it. I was going to order the bedding and blankets online but felt I should actually feel the fabric in person so I got those in a fancy baby shop in Dundrum. I got the cot there too. Or crib as you call it."

"That is one swanky crib, very chic, very on trend with its cool oval shape. Is it the one that can be a toddler bed too?"

He looked obviously surprised she knew of the make. It wasn't like she hadn't done some dream-shopping herself. Except she hadn't purchased anything.

"Yes. It made sense. And before you berate me for buying things so early, in my defence I thought it best to plan ahead as I can get cases that take up inordinate amounts of time and I didn't want to scramble at the end. Turns out planning in advance can be a fairly fucking terrible idea."

"Don't be so hard on yourself. Your intentions were above and beyond. Of course, I wouldn't have let the baby out of my sight so I hope you had a room available for me to stay in too?"

"Hardly. I'm afraid your comforts were way down my list."

She snorted at that. I mean, this was Flynn. Sex God.

Even if he'd managed to put that night of passion out of his mind, she certainly hadn't. "Liar," she said cheerfully, opening the dishwasher to place the cups and glasses inside. "There's no way we could spend a night under the same roof and not scorch up the sheets. We both know that's true."

She flipped him a grin and her heart tripped as she noticed him watching her move about his space. He was definitely lighter now. They had, while not exactly fixed things between them, opened doors, physical as well as emotionally, it seemed. She noted the tightness about his mouth, that sexy tic in his jaw. Yeah, he was no more oblivious to the string of heat tightening between them than she was.

Interesting. Very interesting. She could use that to ease his tension that little bit more. And if she got something from it too? What was the harm?

"Hey, could you do me one more solid?" she asked, a hint of coy slipping through.

"I haven't exactly been your Sir Knight, now have I? But ask away."

"You held me while I wept, without, I may add, telling me to stop or indeed running a mile. That's pretty fucking knightly in my book." She stepped closer to him, mere breaths from his solid chest, that grey T-shirt looking more manly by the second. She needed fistfuls of that, now. So, she moved. One hand grabbed the fabric, the other reached up behind his neck and pulled him towards her. It only took a beat. He wasn't a stupid man. Or slow. She hadn't, in fact, asked, she'd taken.

His mouth landed on hers like the heat-seeking missile it was. His lips didn't take the time to tease and taste, they didn't linger to relearn her shape. He knew her mouth, and from the way he was devouring it, he remembered it extremely well. *Thank you, Jesus.*

Gia had acted on instinct, needing to have this man touch her again. Hold her like she meant something. Their

PAMELA G. HOBBS

madness last summer had been hot, intense and tender all in one. She didn't know what Flynn she was getting when she pulled his mouth to hers, but it was both different and the same. How could that be? How could she recognise the essence of him right down to her bones, but still have this kiss feel so new? In reality, they barely knew each other. Not intimately or at least not emotionally. Wait, intimacy? Yeah, they knew that part. Had the prize for that.

He'd been standing, all casual, hands in jeans pockets when she'd grabbed him. Now? His arms banded her, hands splayed across her back, holding her so close it should have been uncomfortable with her own hand squished between them, but this kiss was so far from uncomfortable. The taste of Flynn Fitzgerald was uncanny. Unique. He unleashed a hunger on her she'd almost forgotten but as the kiss deepened, as his tongue reminded her of just how talented he was, she remembered it all. Those nights since Flynn, when she had pleasured herself, alone in her apartment, trying to recapture the magic had been so paltry she realised now as her knees gave way and her stomach dipped. As heat pooled in her belly, and below. As her heart thudded and bells rang out. Bells. Lots of ringing.

"*Shit.*" It was a hoarse sound as Flynn pulled away from her and reached for the phone on his counter.

She braced herself against the marble. She had to, or she might just have collapsed in a melted ball of wax on the floor. He barked his name into the phone, his eyes never leaving her face. She knew, intellectually, he was speaking, but although she watched that sexy mouth move, the only sound she heard, as she tried to catch her breath, was the screeching of brakes.

What the fuck had she been thinking? This was a disaster. An unmitigated disaster. What a fool she was! What a blithering idiot of all idiots. One didn't kiss Flynn Fitzgerald and move on. Obviously.

Well, in a way it was a good thing. He'd never want her

back. This was merely a reaction to the closeness and sorrow they'd shared earlier. A physical release to the tension and pain he'd suffered. She was glad she could do that for him – *liar, you want so much more* – and once he remembered they were colleagues now, he'd never let it happen again anyway.

Best to come out swinging.

Flynn ended the call and briefly typed into his screen. He ran a hand through his short chestnut hair that had the tiniest amount of grey edging the temples.

Sexy as fuck. The bastard. *Focus, Sully, focus.* He is saying words: pay attention.

"And I've ordered a car to take you home. She's agreed to see us first thing in the morning. I'll help you get your things. Your ride will be here in five."

All business. All hotness gone. *Liar.* "Wait. What? Who's agreed to see us?" She felt like a fool asking but better a fool now with questions, than a total fool tomorrow morning arriving unprepared.

Flynn frowned down at her. But he didn't look angry, he looked amused. "Jackie Carroll," he explained patiently. "She's ready to talk. To give up her boss. I had laid out a tentative deal for her earlier when we talked, but she gave me nothing."

Gia was stunned. This was excellent news. Could be the break they needed to find the instigators of this awful baby-market ring. Could be the way forward for her to finally put her issues to rest. Or at least aside. She crossed the living-room space, grabbed her bag and shoved her feet into the shoes she kicked off earlier. Seemed like hours now. Days. So much had happened in this apartment tonight.

"Wait, how is your head wound?" Flynn took her arm to stop her hasty exit.

She really needed to leave before another discussion about where they were, and where they were definitely *not* going took place. Definitely best to forget all that kissing stuff. All that closeness, the sharing.

"What?"

His hand cupped the side of her head where the Steri-Strips lay, almost hidden by her hair. Well, shit on a stick. She'd forgotten the reason for coming here in the first place.

"Stick with me, kid, and you'll see I'm tough as old boots," she said. "It's fine. Not a bother. Can't even feel it." As she spoke his phone buzzed.

"Okay then. Get some sleep. Your car is here. It's a station ride, so on the house. See you in the morning." He walked her down the hall, hands back in his pockets. It was a good look on him. She turned to say good night but he slipped his feet into boat shoes by the door and ushered her out.

"I'll see you down," he said in a no-nonsense and don't-even-think-of-resisting voice. Since Gia was, at this stage, all out of resistance, she was fine with that.

She was too damn aware that if he gave even the slightest encouragement for her to stay the night, her feeble body would cave. Big time. If his phone hadn't rung with case news, who knows where the kiss would have led? She was grateful for that phone, she told herself as Flynn closed the door on the car and knocked the roof in salute. Grateful, she convinced the aching between her thighs, that things had gone no further. Because they couldn't. Their past was the past. Their sorrow, though she now understood it was a shared, if different, experience, was no basis for a new relationship. Or any attempt at one.

Plus, she needed to be realistic. One day Flynn Fitzgerald would discover what had happened. What she'd done.

And he would never forgive her.

Chapter thirteen

Flynn was a mess. Or as much a mess as he ever allowed himself to be. It was ironic, he supposed, as he folded baby clothes into a box, that it took this evening's drama to give himself permission to let go. To say goodbye. He thought he'd been okay. The therapy sessions had been helpful and he'd believed he was in a good place. He had been incorrect.

The softness of the fabric against his cheek – he hadn't even realised he'd held it up – brought a new tightness to his chest. It could have been wrapped around his little boy, he could be snuggling a wee one right now, pacing the floor as his son dropped into a safe and secure slumber. He added the tiny shirt to the box.

Dragging a hand across his eyes, trying to erase the sting, he counted breaths. Focused on the removal of all things baby-related. He'd take the cot apart next and put it in storage. It would never see the light of day, he knew, but he simply couldn't pass it, or the selection of other infant items he'd purchased, on to Dev and Frankie. He wasn't strong enough to see their beloved child in his baby's things. If it had played out differently and his son was outgrowing the new-born things, he'd have been proud to

123

pass them on. To share. It was a shock to find the loss of a baby could make him selfish. Maybe he was being hard on himself. This could be normal behaviour. He'd drawn the line at a support group so wasn't sure of what normal baby grieving looked like. He'd bet the moon there *was* no normal.

Flynn took a break to drink a Scotch, the burn of it in his throat an urgent reminder of what had happened earlier with Gia. How to unpack that scenario? Christ, another mess to deal with. Probably better that he dealt with the right now. The baby room to be dismantled and stored. He'd never seen himself become a father before Gia's pregnancy, and he was certain he'd never have the chance again. But he had Toby, Caro's son, and the new arrival shortly to make its appearance. That would be enough. It would have to be.

By two thirty the room was clear. Empty of memories bar the Peter Rabbit frieze along the wall. He'd repaint the room the next free day he had. He needed it all gone. Or not quite all. If the stuffed elephant had been unearthed from the taped boxes at the last minute and placed on the top shelf in his wardrobe, well, who would know?

He fell onto his bed, exhausted and weary in every bone and sinew. More tired than he remembered being in years, he recognised it for the emotional barrage it was. It would be better tomorrow. Day by day it would be better.

When he woke before dawn, his hand wrapped around his cock and the image of Gia Sullivan tasting him where his hand stroked, still fresh from his dreams, he felt a wave of betrayal. How could he be thinking about her hot body, her smart and clever mouth, her small perfect breasts as they had pressed against him earlier. How could he think like this, dream of this, when his baby was gone? Would the two emotions of heat and loss be always intrinsically linked? If he got the chance to have Gia beneath him again, could he do it and not think of the pain?

Stop fooling yourself, you idiot. Hadn't he done just that earlier? Hadn't they kissed with only thoughts of skin, and touch, and more, more, *more*, with only pleasure and relief on their minds? Yes, they had. It had been so fucking good. And, he acknowledged realistically, so necessary. His brain knew that the body needed the healing as much as the heart, and if that came through sex, wasn't that the most natural thing in the world? Flynn relaxed in his bed, let his mind wander and regroup. While he might desire Angelica Sullivan with every fibre in his being, and he accepted that that was unlikely to change any time soon, he knew they were done.

He was her boss now, so even if they had the slightest chance, and that was slim at best, given, well everything, any relationship between them was verboten. Was he a coward to feel a certain amount of relief in that? He was indeed. He looked at his watch and with a groan knew further sleep was beyond him. He got up, pulled on some sweats and, grabbing a water bottle and keys, headed out into the cool grey light and hit the streets for a punishing run.

He was glad for the early light misty rain, glad when it masked the taste of salt, already damp on his face when he ran past Holles Street Maternity Hospital and avoided a man handing a heavily pregnant woman from a taxi into a waiting wheelchair. Glad he could keep running, glad the early morning bakers and delivery staff didn't know who the hell he was or the sharp jabbing pain behind his ribs that had nothing at all to do with exercise.

And mostly he was glad to know.

He'd had a son.

Gia arrived on time, barely. Sleep had evaded her and that had not been a shock. It had been a night, that was for sure. She tried to blame the relief of having Siobhán safe for her poor judgements but, even as she swung up the stairs to the interview room, she knew she was kidding herself. Emotion, pure and simple was the root cause of

125

her issues. Grief, shock at the baby room – then the sheer tenderness of it – and passion. Thrown in there for good measure was forgiveness. For herself for not believing in the man who helped create their baby. The man who had set her panties on fire, for one night only, last summer and had then stepped up to do the honourable, if old-fashioned, thing. She hadn't really given him much thought once the pregnancy was over. She was too busy reeling from her own horrors.

But now she knew differently. Now she knew there was a depth of kindness to him, a well of thoughtfulness and caring that would have made him a great dad. And of course, in the small hours of the morning, when things were at their shittiest, her guilt gnawed and bit, its sting direct. A very hot shower and strong coffee had helped, but she knew another night like that would rear its head again. And then there was the kiss. Bad judgement it may have been but so damn worth it. That, she was not regretting.

She peeped in the glass square on Interview Room 3's door and noted an agitated Jackie Carroll sitting alone at a table. A garda stood sentry close to the wall, but from his stance it didn't appear that Ms Carroll was in any way a threat.

"How is she?"

Flynn had approached unheard and Gia jerked with surprise. How did he do that? Had he had stealth-approach training? She'd find the time to ask; it was a skill she'd dearly like to acquire.

"Seems a bit off her game, which should suit us. How do you want to play it? The classic good-cop bad-cop?"

"Actually, I don't think you should be in the room. She knows you. Or at least a version of you. Can't imagine how that would help."

"I disagree. I have to be in there. I want her to know I was undercover. She needn't know Siobhán is on the payroll but, knowing we have that much intel now, that we already had the goods up to a point, will scare her into giving up more. She'll know I've seen the others, the girls, that I know the set-up. She can't lie about it. Trust me, Fitz, it will be better this way. To our advantage."

He studied her closely, considering. Nodding, he rapped briefly on the door, opened it and gestured her inside.

The room was not unlike an interview room anywhere – no window, bare walls, a table bracketed to the floor. Three chairs in this one – Jackie Carroll claiming the one behind the table. It was moveable but also chained to the floor. One never knew when a suspect or person of interest would choose the fine old art of furniture-tossing for a bit of diversion.

Gia loved this part of her job.

She loved the story that would emerge and watching how the person of interest would try to play the room. That was always fun – and noting the clever way the various interrogators plied their trade. They all had unique techniques. And yes, sometimes when it was a team, it fell to good cop/bad cop or a version of same. She liked the straight talk – the 'Look, you be straight with me, I'll be straight with you'. She also threw in some empathy and humour as the situation warranted, but she never lied to the perp. There was no future to that. And ultimately, she simply liked finding the truth. The way and how of the truth, and the fascinating way one person's truth was not another's. How cool was that?

Growing up in an Italian/Irish household, there had been only one truth. The Catholic one. By high school, Gia knew that, in fact, it wasn't her truth. The truth she believed in was nothing to do with religion, organised or otherwise. It was a moral code. An inner belief in innate kindness and a whole heap of justice. How the justice was meted out varied, though, and that was where Gia had her own issues. She believed in law and order. She believed in appropriate punishment, sentences or reprimands. And she also believed that way too often the courts got it wrong. So wrong.

So here they were, about to hear one person's notion of their truth. Gia was really looking forward to it – for so many reasons.

Flynn introduced himself and Gia and offered a seat. Jackie Carroll stared hard at Gia and frowned. "Do I know you? You seem familiar."

"You do, Ms Carroll. You spoke with me yesterday morning as you denied any wrongdoing in the case of Chloe and her unborn child. Fortunately for her, I did not believe you and you reluctantly gave me the address where she might have been located. We found her, but not as you suggested we might. She was in fact detained, against her will, in a locked room in an upstairs floor of a warehouse. Two gentlemen, and I use the term loosely, were standing guard. They are not doing so any longer."

Jackie shifted in her seat, her hair unkempt and her blouse and skirt wrinkled. She tilted her head to one side, curious now as well as slightly unnerved. "But who *are* you?"

Sliding seamlessly into the persona of Ciara from Cork, Gia placed her elbows on the table and leaned towards the bewildered woman. "You mess with me cousin, like, ye mess with me and all the Sullivans!"

Startled, Jackie reared back. "But . . . you're with the *gardaí*? What about your hair? And you sound like a Yank!"

The last part was definitely accusatory and Gia realised that was, in Jackie's narrow-minded opinion, the worst of her sins.

Flynn crossed one long leg easily over the other and folded his arms across his chest. "Detective Sullivan is a United States Police Officer, detective rank. To you, that may seem far-fetched and even unrelated, but we are using her intel and experience with a similar case to help us here. And help us she has. She has unearthed a goodly amount of information regarding your little scam, Ms Carroll, and is almost ready to throw the book at you. She has connected you to several crimes both here in Dublin and elsewhere. You have one chance, one, to get her attention in the best possible of ways, before she does her sworn duty. One chance to save your skin before a locked cage is in your immediate future."

It was hard for Gia to hide her almighty glee listening to Flynn speak. He was giving her the reins and she loved it. He was also playing fast and loose with the facts. But, whatever.

"You better believe it, Jackie, I'm not in the mood for games after the stunt you pulled with Chloe," she said. "She could have been seriously harmed. I need details of the person pulling the strings. Obviously, I and my learned colleague here know exactly who that is, but if you want to stay away from a very long stint in jail, you will give us full disclosure. I will, I assure you, take your co-operation into account when I hand the judge the case. My advice? Start talking."

With that, Gia got up, strode to a side table and, after unsealing a new tape, inserted it into the recorder, pressed start, announced details of who was in the room, date and time and some obligatory restrictions.

"Jackie Carroll, please state, for the record, that you are giving this information of your own free will, in a voluntary capacity and that you are aiding us in our attempts to bring down the notorious baby-selling operation, of which you are a significant part."

She smiled at the older woman. Encouraging and sympathetic to the difficulties she found herself in. A supportive, *trust me* smile.

Jackie sighed deeply and began to speak.

He was impressed. But then, why wouldn't he be? She knew exactly what she was doing. By the time Jackie Carroll had told her story on the tape recorder, she was also willing to write the whole lot down on paper and sign it. Gia was relentless. But never mean or vindictive. Having been labelled by himself as a tough nut, she belied his words by asking open, non-directed questions. Jackie gave it all up. Not only was she willing, by the time Gia was finished with the interview, Jackie was thanking her for letting her tell her side. Unbelievable. If Flynn hadn't been there, he *wouldn't* have believed it.

It was a clever and insightful technique. It wouldn't work for everyone, but Gia was skilled in the art of the devious and he'd be wise not to forget it. She'd lulled their suspect into a total sense of security and trust. Jackie had told them more than Flynn had expected. They had a name now, not the one they'd hoped for, but a real connection to the system in place. The man who was running the show locally and, once they had him, they had the boss. He knew it was only a matter of time, but based on this new information they needed to have a meeting right away and come up with a new and more long-game plan.

To that end, Flynn took out his phone, sent a group text and when Gia came out of the bathroom, her face still lightly flushed with success, he was reminded, viscerally, how this woman, this smart, capable and beautiful woman made him *feel*.

Her intelligence shone through in the interview room. She never made the suspect feel less or on the back foot, yet, equally, she never let up. Didn't shy from the tough questions. And still managed to have Jackie eat out of her hand. They now knew Jackie's own back story and why she was involved. Knowing the why, in any case, was crucial. Without it, without the motive for any crime or any involvement even in the peripherals, the case could go dead in the water.

Bouncing on her toes, Gia grinned impishly at him. "That went better than I hoped," she confided. Rubbing her hands together in glee, she added, "I love a good suspect interview, don't you?"

Flynn pondered the question seriously. "I hadn't really thought about it as something to enjoy or indeed look forward to. You seem quite delighted with yourself."

"I am," she agreed. "So much information for the taking if you just know how to ask for it. Come on, let's go meet the others and make plans."

He had the feeling she would tug him along like a child with her favourite uncle, and that didn't sit well with him. He liked being an uncle just fine, but he never wanted to appear avuncular to her. She'd obviously put last night's kiss out of her thoughts and he really should do the same, but Christ, when he looked at her, when that upper lip, with its little side quirk, was right in front of him, smiling up at him, it was hard to remain unmoved.

"You are assuming a lot, Sullivan," he said coolly, getting his wayward wants back in check.

"*Nah*, you've definitely contacted them by now to get them to gather asap."

"Sure of yourself? Or of me?"

"Both." She walked backwards, in front of him, running a hand through her hair, showing off her cheekbones. "It's what I'd have done."

If only that didn't make him feel a surge of satisfaction.

They met, Siobhán, Brigid, Menchen, Larkin and Mackenzie, and Gia gave a verbal report of the interview even as she handed around photocopies of the statement. It was succinct and professional, with a balance of Jackie's own story and the present situation.

The gig was basically up, as far as selling babies was concerned. Jackie's involvement came from her own hidden past. She'd been left in a home, one of those awful Mother and Baby institutions that had only recently come to public light. People had known about them for years – certainly the parents who sent their daughters there, the girls themselves obviously, sometimes the fathers of the babies, and all the religious community that served them. It was a disgraceful cover-up, reaching dark nasty depths that most citizens wanted to ignore. But not any longer. Jackie's experience was sombre and painful. How she survived at all was beyond anyone's comprehension.

However, survive she did with a zealous mission to save any baby she could from being thrust into a home of any kind, even an orphanage for regular adoption.

Jackie's belief was that if perspective parents were to pay a lot of money, they must *really* want the baby and would therefore be unlikely to mistreat or discard it – both occurrences that had happened to her. As a teen she'd ended up in a foster home and encountered who they now believed was the 'fella with the accent'. Not the Dutchman Gia was hoping for, not Jansen, but plain old Gary Miller from Belfast. As a lad from that inner city, Gary had been involved in many scrapes which escalated when his parents deserted him. His Protestant father had been shot by the IRA, seemingly for simply walking near the Falls Road area. To make Gary's family background even more complicated, his Catholic mother, according to Jackie, now a widow, took off with a deserted British Army soldier. The boy had been handed to relatives who abandoned him due to his many escalating misdemeanours. Finally, an aunt in Dublin took him in and he was subsequently dumped, his words, she said, in the same foster home as she was.

From what Flynn gathered while Gia slowly pried this information from Jackie, Gary was not only a piece of work, he was an equal-opportunity shyster, doing anything for anybody if the price was right. His boss, Jackie swore she didn't know this name, lured him into this latest scheme by offering a huge financial reward for saving babies. The word *saving* was used with discretion here as Jackie swore Gary's heart had finally been softened by the notion that he could do some good. Reading between the lines, two things were obvious to Flynn. One, Jackie was smitten with said Gary and two, he was using her and her demeanour of respectability to be his dupe. Jackie had taken a secretarial course and worked as a mid-level typist for years in an unexciting, going-nowhere job. Gary offered her a dream, a calling, a reason for her very existence. Gary said, Jackie announced with no small degree of pride, that she, Jackie Carroll, was the best recruiter of pregnant lost souls of women they'd ever had.

It was equally clear that Jackie hung on Gary's every word and believed that they had a future together. That they were a team. It was unbearably sad, in one way, that this lonely unhappy woman had come to this. She'd had no real childhood and all she wanted now was to ensure that small unwanted babies, like she had been, would benefit at her hands. She was doing God's work. And Gary's.

She was delusional.

The intel that was most critical came towards the end of the interview, when Gia had Jackie eating out of her hand. She'd had tea and biscuits brought in, and a shawl of some kind as Jackie had complained of the cold. The baby caper was nearing its end. Society in Ireland had changed with recent laws and women had more options available to them. No longer the lonely boat trip or cheap Ryan Aer flight. Now, a woman who was, for whatever reason, unwilling or unable to keep her child, had a choice. Flynn was in no position to judge and was just grateful backstreet operations were far less likely to be the only way out.

Gary Miller was winding things down. He was moving out of Dublin and returning north to where all the 'shipments' originated. 'There are no more babies coming,' he'd told her only weeks ago, which was why she'd gone looking for more, hoping to keep his business interests local to her. Kylie had been her latest near miss before 'Chloe'. The girls from the inner-city house were no good, Jackie confided, they hadn't the pedigree the buyers wanted. Chloe had seemed more likely, more the thing. Jackie was disconsolate, afraid now that Gary was moving on and she was being left behind. She was just trying to help, she'd pleaded to Gia, to save those poor mites from her own fate. To be a conduit for good.

And she believed her own press, Flynn thought, as he listened to Gia wind down her report. She would stand charges, but leniency had been promised and he would see legal aid was contacted and informed of the whole scenario.

"The trouble is," Gia said to the small group of people, "that there appears to be three or four infants due within the next week or two but the mothers-to-be have already been relocated."

"Where?" Brigid asked. "Belfast? Miller's turf?"

Gia looked at Flynn. "You'd better take over – I don't know the lay of the land up there."

Flynn eased away from the wall where he'd been leaning and took a seat at the oval table. "They have been moved to East Donegal, according to Ms Carroll. To Greencastle specifically where there is, apparently, a ferry that takes the new-borns to, we think, Derry. We are not sure what happens then, as yet, since they are then geographically in the United Kingdom, and out of our jurisdiction. Clever really, as the babies are born in Ireland and thus have an Irish birth certificate, which according to Miller, via Carroll, is what most of the buyers want. Not sure why but apparently, being Irish is just European enough, while still having a certain amount of individuality. The buyers like the Caucasian look, the fair skin, the usually light eyes – go figure." He linked his fingers in front of him on the table and looked about at his team. "I do not want these infants to leave the country. What we need to do is figure out a way to stop that."

Gia stood. and paced, her hands shoved into her jeans' pockets. "Jackie said that this time Miller's boss would prefer if they didn't have to go to the expense of bringing the babies from Donegal and further on to God knows where, so we need to focus on that. It looks like they want these infants processed here on the island. She also said at least one of the sets of buyers had backed out, so we need to ensure nothing happens to the women or the infants if they are now on the unwanted list."

She walked around the room to the coffee layout table

and offered them all a drink. Flynn declined, sticking with water, Mackenzie went for some herbal tea but the others all took theirs appreciatively. When she placed a plate of muffins in the centre of the table, Flynn wasn't sure who groaned the loudest in hungry anticipation. He didn't mind. They all needed sustenance. Nothing wrong with a burst of buttery sweetness, loaded with tangy blueberries. He took one himself, wrapped it in a napkin, and while the others tucked in he joined them.

"I have an idea," Gabe's quiet voice interrupted the mini-break while they ate.

He, of course, wasn't eating sugar or butter, God forbid. Just sipping some concoction that probably had all manner of healthy vile-tasting properties in it. But this man's ideas were always worth listening to, always had a reason, and often an edge. Yet a tiny shiver of, call it apprehension, crawled up Flynn's spine as he caught Gabe's eye. However, the case came first, so the idea must be aired.

"Let's hear it," Flynn said.

Chapter fourteen

"No." It was a firm negative, no question about it.

Gia rolled her eyes on principle, even as her skin prickled at Gabe's plan, because Flynn's immediate response was to knock it down. She wasn't surprised, considering their past, but it still pissed her off.

"I think it bears considering," she said, glaring at her boss.

"I said no." His return glare, for her eyes only, made her even madder. Who the fuck did he think he was? She wasn't made of tissue paper, she could handle Mackenzie's plan, even if it meant swallowing a whole lot of pain. She could do it.

"I can do it," she insisted. "Brigid and Siobhán are out for various reasons and I've been in disguise till now, on the off-chance someone other than Jackie and the two assholes has seen me. Dave or Mackenzie could partner me. We could do it. Stop being so bossy and so up yourself and look at the big picture."

She could feel the tenseness in the air as she uttered the words. It seemed no one spoke to the almighty Fitz like that. Too bad. He was being a dick.

"I can't let you do it, regardless."

"It's not your decision – well, okay, maybe it is, *boss*, but think it through. Be reasonable. I've been undercover, you know I can do accents and, in fact, using my own would probably work better. But I can sustain character. You know that too. And I bet you've looked at my record. You know my home station boss would trust me with this. Pick me a partner and let's get on with it."

"It's not that simple," he began.

She was having none of that. "It's exactly that simple. Tell him, Mac." She turned to the other senior detective, hoping she sounded decisive not pleading.

"She *is* who I had in mind when I thought of the plan, Fitzgerald. She is the right age, we can give her a back story and we already know she's steady under duress."

Jesus, Gia thought, he had no idea.

"I think the best man for the job is debatable," he went on. "We need someone who can act, someone who can blend, someone who can fake rapport. Someone who is not averse to pretence. And who can match this woman in wit and charm. Anyone spring to mind? Bearing in mind she and our mystery man will be in close quarters for an undefined amount of time."

As Flynn proceeded to knock back the candidates' names offered, Gia grew irritated. "Why not Menchen, he's as invested as I am for his own reasons. He'd be –"

"*Absolutely not!*"

There was a moment's silence as Flynn's barked negative had everyone turn to him in shock. He rose and paced the width of the room before, with a hand dragged along the back of his neck, he explained. "No. We need someone who knows the lay of the land in Donegal. He wouldn't understand the locals. Could misinterpret colloquial signals." He paused as if trying to come up with other reasons. He jerked a head at Mackenzie. "You do it."

"I have never been to Donegal. I would serve no better than the Dane. You," he looked at Flynn steadily, "on the other hand, know the county well, I understand."

She could see Flynn's shoulders tense. She could feel his resistance as if it was an actual steel wall. Well, fuck him. He didn't have to hate her that much.

"Great idea, Mac!" she declared, all cheery and bright and positive. "Flynn and I could definitely pretend to be a couple in need of a baby." The second the words were out of her mouth she knew she was in trouble.

Flynn blanched even as she felt her stomach heave.

"Excuse me," she mumbled and darted for the door. The bathroom was very, very far away. The corridor walls got narrower and narrower. She couldn't breathe, couldn't . . .

"I've got you." Gabe Mackenzie caught her as her body crumbled and her knees gave out. He gathered her to him, and simply held her. He took long soothing breaths and then pressed one of his large hands to the top of her head, using increasing but gentle pressure.

She felt the most incredible warmth move through her entire body and her stomach unknotted. She stared up at the intense serious face above her. His eyes were closed and a frown crevassed between his brows.

"Who are you?" she whispered because it felt unreal, this moment. As if she was having an out-of-body experience. "What are you doing to me?"

"I'd like to know the same thing," Flynn's voice snapped. "Let her go. I'll handle it from here."

Mackenzie opened his eyes and with a smile that could indeed have been a grimace, he released Gia. He was pale and the breathing that had been steady and strong moments ago had become choppy.

"Ah shit, sorry, Mac. I forgot for a moment what you do. Go. Take a break. I've got this."

Gia thought the two men were speaking a foreign tongue for all she made sense of it.

"Somebody want to clue me in here?" she asked, feeling so much better.

"Fitzgerald will explain," Gabe said. "I'll go drink water, it helps. And I'm so sorry, you two. I had no idea."

138

And on that cryptic note he walked slowly down the corridor, one hand occasionally bracing the wall for balance.

"What the fuck just happened and what does he know? What did you say to him? You promised!"

"Slow down, Sullivan, you have it wrong. Nobody told Mac anything. Come with me and we'll get a tea. I'll explain then."

He took her arm and for once she didn't think to protest. Perhaps she was glad of the assist as her knees weren't quite what they should be. *That* fact she'd be keeping to herself. They entered a small canteen and Flynn directed her to a table and chairs in a quiet corner and he headed to the serving area.

When he returned, he was carrying a tray with a pot of tea and two almond and raspberry slices. "I have it on good authority that Boyle actually donated these cake things to the canteen this morning, thus they're worthy of being eaten. The tea – I asked for extra bags to make it strong. You may kick back, but you've had a shock – your body knows it even if you are being stubborn and disagreeing." He poured the tea and, yeah, it was a strong, almost rusty colour, and he added a drop of milk. He added a packet of sugar though she shook her head. He put the mug in front of her with a look that forbade comment.

Fine. She'd go along. She wanted the dirt on Mackenzie anyway and it would be a good distraction, from, well, from whatever her body was yelling at her.

"Why did he go all weird on us? I swear to God I could feel my body go cold, then hot and just as suddenly I felt like I was relaxing in a warm bath. What the fuck, Flynn? I'd heard he was odd but hadn't experienced it personally. Spill."

She took a deep drink from the tea, enjoying its depth and aroma. And the kick of sugar. She was surprised when Flynn added a spoon to his own before cutting his almond cake into three precise sections. Was he shook by her words, or as freaked as she was by Mac's behaviour? The former, she decided. He'd have seen the Scot in action before. Strangely, or maybe not, this thought, both thoughts, comforted her.

"Mackenzie is reluctant to reveal anything about his abilities but I have seen him do a version of what just happened with you. Several times. It drains him."

"*Huh*. It was like he was indeed draining me of all my energy, or at least the ugly stuff. I thought I was going to collapse and then suddenly it was like I was floating. Free. Clean. But Jesus, he looked wrecked, didn't he? I feel shit, now, knowing I've done that."

"Stop." Flynn reached across the table and took her hand. Squeezed it. "It's what he does. You feeling shit counteracts everything he's just done."

"How does he do it? Is he a healer? A modern-day witch doctor?"

Flynn raised a brow. "He would really not like that term. Now isn't the time to go into it, and his story, his back story rather, is not mine to tell. Let me just say his parentage, both Osage Nation and Scottish, have people with interesting seeing, feeling and yes, healing abilities. He inherited boatloads of them all. And then some. He uses them only when absolutely necessary." He paused for a moment, considering. "Now, let it go." As if realising he still held her hand, he relaxed his fingers and slid them away.

She felt that. The loss of their warmth. How right they felt around hers. How steady, normal and comforting. They also, to be fair, gave her a tingle. She'd think about that later.

"You're right. My feeling crap about him feeling exhausted does neither of us any good. I see that. But fuck, it must be hard for Ali to live with that. With him knowing things about her, feeling her feels."

Flynn sat back in his chair, a cup of tea in his hand. "I believe he rarely, if ever, does that for Ali. She won't allow it. She's tough, my sister. Tougher than any of us knew." He dragged a hand across his jaw at that, a weariness invading him.

140

"I don't know the whole deal, nor do I have to, but I *do* know she puts full responsibility for keeping everything from you and your family on the shoulders of the bastard who hurt her, not anyone else. That's healthy, right? So, you can let that one go."

He gave her a wry smile. "Easier said, Sullivan. Easier said."

She smiled back. They could do this. They could have a normal conversation. They could share. "Sorry about earlier," she said quietly. "I didn't expect to feel so exposed. Maybe because we'd spoken about it last night. I don't know. But I've handled missing kids etcetera since last October, and was not affected, so it could be the *you* quotient."

"Excuse me? The what?"

"It's you. You're the added element to my stress. Oh, not intentionally. Stop puffing up like a fricking angry bear, *yeesh*. Get a grip. It's that I didn't have the Baby Daddy anywhere near me when I dealt with things before. And nor did I know said Baby Daddy was as soft as mush under that hard exterior." She stopped, suddenly aware that Flynn's eyes were boring into her. And now she was visualising the aforementioned hard exterior. It was not, in any way, an unpleasant task. But she needed to get focused on the task Mackenzie had brought up. Not daydream about Flynn Fitzgerald's six-pack.

She blinked. Took a piece of almond cake from his plate, bit in, swallowed and drank some tea. She knew his eyes hadn't left her face but she was steadfastly ignoring his gaze. If she looked, if their eyes connected, if she saw the flare of passion she remembered, oh so clearly, she might well beg him to whip off his blasted starched shirt and let her lick him all over. Yup. That was a distinct possibility.

"Come on, let's face the gang. We're doing this, Fitz. We're going undercover. Together. As a team. As a married couple. Oh wait, we *are* a married couple!" And on that note, she pushed back from the table, stood, stacked the tray, remembering to wrap the extra slice of yummy goodness in a paper napkin for later, and strode back to the conference room, considerably lighter. Thank you, Gabe Mackenzie.

Married. They were still married. As if he could forget it. Had she applied for divorce papers? No matter. Right now, that was one less thing to worry about if they were to go on this mad undercover operation together. He supposed it made sense. There was planning to do, documents to collate, backstories to compile. He had a good team to get these things done in a hurry but it would still take a few days. They needed those for a bit more research. A bit more digging and information gathering from Jackie Carroll. He carried the tray back to the kitchen counter and took a deep breath before joining the others. He'd been struck so intensely by so many emotions in the last hour it was hard to process. Shock, when Gia had fled from the room, white as a ghost. Sheer raging jealousy when he found her wrapped in Mackenzie's arms and relief when he understood the truth of it. He was a fool. As if Mac would ever betray Ali. Or himself. Gabe Mackenzie held himself to similar high standards as Flynn. They both respected the badge. And those in their care. For Mac it was even more obvious since he had found Ali. But Flynn knew, gut deep, that Gabe would only ever use his abilities to help others, so even the betraying thought that he'd had nefarious intentions deserved an apology.

And then there was the assailing memory. Baby Daddy. What a silly term! Who came up with these names? But, Christ, whatever the way she'd said it, it alluded to the night of conception and his brain had zeroed in on the heat of that night. The rawness of it. The fucking *rightness* of it. He shook his head as he neared the conference room. If he and Gia were to survive pretending to be a couple, he needed to keep his thoughts under lock and key. In fact, he needed to throw away the key.

His phone buzzed in his pocket and as he pulled it out,

the message he saw had him sigh in part frustration and part pleasure. His mum: **Dinner here tonight. 7pm Caro Toby and Nick home unexpectedly. And a proper welcome for Gia.**

Well, hell.

He pushed open the door and caught the woman in question shoving her phone into her pocket. She'd most likely got a similar message. But now was not the time to think about those ramifications. They had a plan to make. And decisions to formulate. God, this was going to be an adventure he felt sure he'd regret for a long time to come. But needs must. Or at least the case came first.

Whatever. He took his seat, avoided looking at Gia and when a pale but reasonably put-together Mackenzie rejoined them, he leant over and said quietly, "I owe you an apology. Thanks, Mac. Appreciate it."

Gabe looked at him, in that unblinking way of his, and just nodded. But Flynn felt it. Felt the understanding and the forgiveness. And when Gabe added, "I am here to listen when the moment is right for you," he knew that his colleague and friend understood so much more than he was revealing. Somehow Mackenzie knew about the baby. Flynn sighed and returned his attention to the plan. They had to get this right – the timing, the backstory, the play. Otherwise, young women could lose their babies forever. For the proverbial thirty pieces of silver. There was nothing right or just about that.

Flynn, Mackenzie and Gia drove to Dalkey together. Or rather, Flynn went in his subdued sedan and Mac took Gia in his jeep. The house was lit up even though it was early September and the evenings were still bright at seven. There were fairy lights still strung about the garden and it certainly added festive cheer, though which festival was on offer was up for debate. Flynn greeted Caro with a hug and studied her face carefully. Marriage to Nick Sullivan had her blooming. She was as beautiful as ever, just softer maybe? Was that a thing?

143

His nephew Toby arrived at the door, all gangly fifteen-year-old arms and legs. But he was never too old to be hugged by his eldest uncle and Flynn held him close, this precious boy, who had entered their lives amidst secrecy and hurt. Not anymore though. His sister Caro was a woman of strength and integrity and had gone about finding Toby's birth father when she'd felt the time was right. The plan had failed spectacularly but they had all gained so much in a roundabout way.

Toby pulled back from Flynn, spied Gia and rushed over to hug her and deal with exclamations of how tall he'd become.

"Does everyone comment on how you've grown?" Flynn asked Toby as the boy returned to his side.

The kid laughed out a "*Yeah*" and, with one arm slung around his shoulders, Flynn headed inside, leaving Mackenzie and Gia to follow.

He was hanging his jacket in the hall closet when he heard a squeal of delight along with a "Hey, brat!" and knew that Nick and his sister had just met up. They were close, he knew, but wasn't sure if Gia might end up confiding in him about the past year. Time would tell. If he had to take one to the chin from Nick, so be it. Back in the day, when Caro had first announced her pregnancy, he and Devlin had begged for the father's name. They'd seen red, on her behalf, and wanted justice. Or at least child support. So he got the protective brother routine. Couldn't fault it, in fact.

Sighing, wondering what the evening reunion would bring, Flynn straightened his shoulders, hating the feeling of uneasy anticipation that was creeping in. Hoping his gut was wrong, he turned to walk down the hall and enter the fray.

It was wonderful, simply wonderful to have her brother in the same room as her. To see him with this extended family of theirs. The serendipitous quality of it all, the magic of warmth and laughter and teasing. It was a bit like her own family back in Brooklyn, though hers was smaller of course. Sipping a glass of crisp white wine, she studied the players, the couples and the various interactions. She was especially interested to see how her brother engaged with his stepson. What must that be like? To be a new parent of a teenager? Scary as shit, was her thought. But then, what she knew of Toby kind of defeated that notion. He was one of those kids that should be odd and uncomfortable to be around – he wasn't. Not even a little. He was funny and easy, not to mention smart and curious. Raised by a single mom with the help of her family, Toby Fitzgerald was the product of good parenting and good genes. Sure, her side of the family too on her Italian cousin's side. She'd never known their Toni, Toby's birth father, the way Nick had, but she remembered him as light-hearted, fun and yet a clever kind young man. She could only imagine how his parents must feel, at such a loss. Noticing Toby roll his eyes at a comment from Nick who just laughed and gave his shoulder a playful cuff, she felt her eyes mist. That young lad was the spit of his dad, and how much joy must that give to his paternal grandparents?

Dinner was the usual Fitzgerald performance, she was beginning to realise. So much food, so much nimble manoeuvring around the kitchen, baskets of warm bread, buckets of chilled wine and carafes of room-temp red. It was a roast this time, pork with crackling, apple sauce, roast potatoes – the kind that were forgotten in the oven and all the better for it. A kale salad for health reasons, joked Ali, as she placed it on the table and added: "To counteract the individual fruit and cream pavlovas for dessert!"

Gia patted her stomach in anticipation, knowing that the woman could bake for presidents, she was that talented. When Frankie came over to chat, Gia was able to breathe normally, ask questions about the upcoming event and was relieved to discover she was able to be happy for them. Genuinely happy. When they sat about the table,

Dev made jokes about the size of his wife's belly and when they all shushed and groaned at him, Gia noted that Flynn joined in. Maybe he was healing too. She hoped so.

As she ate, tasted and enjoyed the delicious fare, she listened to the family about her. The several conflicting and intertwined conversations all being held at once, the tone of seriousness in conjunction with bursts of laughter. It was easy, she thought, and normal. If she ever did have a family, sometime in the future, she'd like it to be a mix of this and her own Brooklyn Irish-Italian kind of crazy. Then she blinked in realisation – that's what she *would* have had, in a small way, if she hadn't screwed everything up so badly. If she hadn't failed at her one job of being a parent: protecting her unborn child.

She could feel the tightness in her chest, feel her breathing begin to ratchet up but before she actually made a fool of herself, Nick stood and with a fork pinging against his glass to gain everyone's attention, began to speak. "We have an announcement to make . . ."

This was what Flynn must have felt last spring, she thought, as she cheered and smiled along with the others. This visceral pain lancing through your body as you heaped congratulations and delight on the happy couple. The knowledge that someone else was living a version of your happiness, your future, your family, and they were entirely oblivious.

"I know," a quiet voice said in her ear. "It's a lot. Here." Flynn handed her a glass of brandy as everyone milled around back-slapping and hugging and, in several cases, wiping happy tears. "It hurts."

She took a bracing gulp and agreed. "It fucking does. I'm so sorry you had to face this twice, Flynn. How can we be truly happy for someone and at the same time viciously jealous? How? How can our bodies and our hearts process those two violent emotions at the same time?"

The hand at her lower back rubbed gently and, God forgive her, she leaned into it. She needed it. His touch. His

146

care. He was the only person in the room who understood. What a sorry pair they were. Tossing back the rest of the amber liquid, she set the glass down.

"I guess we'll find out how good we are at acting, right? I mean we're going to have to pretend a whole heap of emotions over the next however long we're undercover so we'd better start practising on this happy lot."

"Agreed," he said.

His hand had somehow travelled up her back and now rested at her neck, his long fingers caressing and massaging at the same time. Now was not the time, she told her traitorous body, to get all the shivery and spicy feels. His touch felt both hot and comforting at the same time. *Not. Fair.* But at least she could focus on *not* getting turned on instead of feeling miserable for herself. She was genuinely happy for Nick and Caro. They were obviously over the moon and Toby was doing a crap job at pretending to feel put out. He would finally be a big brother and, wow, that brought such delight to his young face.

They moved through the throng and greeted and hugged the two parents-to-be. It was astonishingly easy to do, after all. Maybe the fact that this bittersweet moment was understood and shared by another made it more bearable, but easy it turned out to be.

"Are you two managing?" Gabe asked as Flynn handed Gia a cup of coffee in the drawing room sometime later.

She took the cup and glared accusingly at Flynn.

"Don't blame Flynn," he said. "He has been the very soul of discretion. I mean no disrespect by referring to your loss, merely letting you know I am aware and can hold my own counsel."

Gia rolled her eyes. "You're an odd chap, you know that, right? But thanks. Ever since you caught me when I almost fainted, and you did your voodoo shit on me, I feel strangely lighter. Or I did till now. But even this, this is easier with support." Without thinking, her hand rested on Flynn's arm and when she felt him go utterly still, she snatched it away. Heat suffusing her cheeks she took a sip of coffee, mortified at her lack of judgement. God, what was the right thing to do? She was usually so able, so confident in her actions and always, *always* owned her behaviour. But Flynn Fitzgerald and his manly cool and sexy presence threw her for several loops. Fuck him and this crappy situation. She pasted a smile on her face and was about to haul herself from the armchair when she felt a hand on her shoulder. Flynn's hand as he sat on the arm of her chair.

Alrighty then. Maybe she wasn't as bonkers out-of-her-normal zone as she thought. Maybe them casually touching was going to be a thing. A normal. A new version of them.

Gabe was speaking and she tuned back into the conversation when she heard her name being mentioned.

"Do it," he was saying. "You need to let your family know you will both be away for a while. On the job. They don't need to know details, but you know from past experience that it is better to alert your loved ones to your absence rather than have them worry and try to track you down. That can become . . . complicated."

"I never tell them anything I don't have to," Flynn said.

"The strong silent type?" Gia quipped. "Does that not get exhausting? Being the Lone Ranger type can pall after a while surely?"

She patted Flynn on the thigh, a hard muscle unbending beneath her touch, and could feel his body tense again. Interesting. This time she wasn't sure it was because her touch was unwelcome. Very interesting and definitely to be thought about when she was next alone.

"Tell them what you like," she said, meaning it. "Just don't tell them we're already married." And slapped a hand to her mouth in horror at what she'd blurted out.

It was one of those moments, Flynn reflected several hours later, when time stood still. One sees them in a movie: the loud chatter, the bustle and hustle of noise and then someone says something of note into a second of silence and suddenly the whole room is agog.

That. That happened.

"*What* did you just say?" Typically, it was Ali, the sharp-tongued sister, who spoke first.

"It's for a case we're working," Flynn said, trying to laugh. "We're not actually married! Gia was just joking."

Christ, he could feel a wave of heat sweep his body, followed by a chill of sweat down his back. Why? It wasn't anyone's business if they *were* married. What was his issue? But he knew. Of course he knew. He was embarrassed about the whole bloody thing. Getting her pregnant, though some would argue it did take two, marrying her in such an underhanded and covert manner. And being so lost at the thought of his little boy, his son, never to be known. The whole fucking situation sucked and Flynn *hated* that a lot of it was on him.

"Right!" Gia agreed. "It's a pretend scenario coming up for us in which, yeah, we are the devoted lovebirds! Isn't that a hoot?"

The chatter broke out then as they all laughed and made jokes at the thought of Flynn as a marrying man. He found it rankled. It shouldn't have but, Jesus, was he that ineligible? He had never given his marital status or previous lack thereof any thought. He was, in old parlance, married to the job. He had to be, to do it properly. To give it his best. *Hypocrite*, his inner voice chided, you'd already planned a new lifestyle around your baby, starting to rewrite the workload and work type. Having never assumed it would be for him, that he would be a dad, let alone a husband, it was shocking how easily he had allowed himself to wear the role, however briefly.

"You are all being unfair," his mum interjected. "My Flynn will make a wonderful husband one day, when the exact right woman knocks him for six. Mark my words!"

"Good one, Mum," Dev laughed. "What kind of woman would take on this long drink of misery?"

149

"A strong-willed, equally stubborn, good-humoured, sassy and intelligent woman, that's who!"

"Don't want much, do you?" Ali laughed. "Just a paragon, really, right?"

Jo smiled at her collective offspring. "Oh, I don't think the woman I have in mind is a paragon. Just perfect for my first-born."

And damn if she didn't walk through the group, pat Gia on the shoulder, and swan out to the kitchen.

Chapter fifteen

"That was close," Gia said as she snapped her seatbelt closed. Flynn was giving her a ride back to the flat, against her better judgement. But bickering over a train or a lift seemed so childish considering, well, everything.

"What were you thinking? Christ! You announced to the room we were married, having put yourself at pains warning me not to. I can't believe you did that!"

"Jeze, keep your hairshirt on, buster. And it was an accident – I didn't intend to say it. No harm done. You handled it. Take a bow and get off my back!" She hated that he was right. She'd let the cat out of the bag, however unintentionally, and was kicking herself hard enough without his boot in the ass too. She shoved a shoulder against the window and turned to glare at him across the width of the car. It was a shit car and it pissed her off even more. "This is a shit car, Fitzgerald – surely you can swing for something more upmarket?"

"Really? That's your comeback? You slag my *car*? Come on, Sullivan, you can do better than that!"

Was that an almost-smile? Nah, must be the dim light playing havoc with shadows. But wouldn't it be nice if they could argue and slag and laugh all in one conversation?

"Well, I'm not going to slag your parents, your siblings or my own brother so other than pissing you off the alternative is to feel crap about myself and I'm done doing that." She was *trying* to be done doing that, but he didn't have to know how low her success rate was, now did he?

"Insulting my vehicle choices won't piss me off. I know what they look like, and more importantly *you* know why I chose them so pick another option upon which to vent your anger."

"*Upon which to vent my anger?* I know you don't normally speak this formally, like you are straight from the casting couch of a nineteen-forties movie, so drop the act, Fitz. It won't work with me."

"There's nothing untoward about my speech patterns," he said so articulately she had to laugh.

He was making fun. *Of himself.* It must surely be a first.

"Look at you, all self-deprecating. See, I know words too. Big words. Fancy-schmancy words. But to get back to the point, I do know why you drive this hunk of boredom when on the job, obviously, but visiting your family? A frigging bike would be better."

"You saw my garage. You know I have options. But we did come straight from the station so, as time was of the essence, I chose not to go back and retrieve the jeep."

"Your garage? Were those other cars not belonging to the other tenants?"

"No. I own the building. I own the garage. I only let out some commercial space on the ground floor and one flat on the first floor. The elderly couple there don't own a car but can use a few of mine if they're stuck. They have spare keys for all of them and Jack, one of the couple, used to be a mechanic so he keeps them in decent running order. He never drives my jeep, just the selection of sedans."

She digested this information and pondered on its practicality. "Huh. That's a lot to take in." She shifted so one knee was pulled up on the seat and one leg kept on the ground. "Some of the detectives in our home house do the same. Keep a variety of cars and drive them in a random selection but having someone else drive them too? That's extra smart. And you own the whole building? In downtown Dublin? Shit, man, you must be on the take!"

Flynn tossed her a raised eyebrow. "I'm not sure where to begin to respond to all that. Obviously, I'm not on the take, as you so politely phrase it."

"Of course you'd zero in on the insult first! You're too easy, Fitz, Too easy."

"If I may continue?"

That eyebrow quirked again. Damn, he was cute when he was being semi-playful. She gave a 'please go ahead' sweep of her arm.

"I invested in the building several years ago on a bursary, if you will, from my grandmother. We all inherited a considerable amount and chose to use it in different ways. Ali bought her restaurant, Dev his studio, Caro the flat where you now reside, Molly funded her secret education. Because I lease the ground floor, I earn an income too. Plus, as I hold a senior position within several forces, although on a contract basis, I do get a healthy pay packet. And I also invested wisely at the time of the inheritance. As to the car driving, I like that Jack and Diego can head off for a weekend in one of my vehicles. They also take care of the building. Their rent is relatively paltry due to the tasks they do for me, as opposed to the commercial rent. But it works. For all of us. And seeing others in a car, supposedly attached to a police official, throws doubt in the mind of anyone watching me so, yes, that works too."

Gia folded her arms and smirked. "Jack and *Diego*? Look at you all politically correct and 'woke'! I have to say you continue to surprise me. Ah, you're blushing – aren't you adorable!"

Flynn's head snapped around. "I'm not blushing. I never blush! And I thoroughly dislike the term '*woke*'. I was never asleep when it comes to people's own personal business. Jack and Diego have been together for over thirty years. They are decent humans, regardless of what their sexual life might involve. It makes zero difference to me. Speaking of swinging a different way, do you remember Mariana, your cousin Toni's widow who has moved away from Rome?"

"I met her once years ago on an Italian trip while Toni was still alive – she was a quiet, almost insignificant individual but her daughter Mia was real cute and lively. What about her? Have you some *gossip*?"

"It's not gossip," he insisted. "But much to everyone's surprise, Mariana has a new partner. Bernadine, a local farmer in their hometown in the Po valley, has turned out to be a very positive and delightful influence in their lives."

"How do you know about Bernadine? Oh wait!" She slapped a hand against her chest. "You had her checked *out*? Shit, Flynn, it's not your business. You can't play God like that."

It was his turn to shift in his seat. "It's not playing God if you're looking out for family. Mia is important to Nick and Caro. And Toby. It was only right I check that Bernadine is right for them. She is. She appears to be fiscally responsible, a pillar in the community and most importantly, loves Mia. And, of course, a contented Marianna is good for Mia too. Everyone wins."

"You mean, you win. Because you decide who is or isn't right for someone. Jesus, next you'll tell me you had Nick checked out before he and Caro married!"

The silence was such a giveaway.

"For fuck's sake, Fitz. She's a grown woman!"

"A grown woman who'd been badly hurt by a member of his family in the past. Of course I ran him." He paused a moment and with a sigh admitted, "I ran you, too, if you must know. After you were shot protecting Toby."

Her mouth dropped. Literally dropped open. Snapping her teeth shut, she sat straight in her seat and banged her head repeatedly against the headrest.

"Don't. You'll hurt yourself. You already have a wound

there." He reached over and rested a hand on her arm. "You would have done the same. I know you'll say you were only doing your job, but it helped me, knowing that you were already building a stellar rep and that saving Toby wasn't an aberration. It was what you'd do for anyone. That helped me. You were a stand-up cop. You still are. Don't tell me you've never run anyone – even if not you personally, then you definitely got a contact to do it."

She stayed silent because, yes, she had. Drat that man and his high moral tone and his fucking high morals in general. Why couldn't he be a complete schmuck? A regular Joe asshole she could dismiss easily. She closed her eyes as reality seeped in. She never would have felt that pull, the shimmer of desire that fanned to fierce flames and burned so brightly. She wouldn't have reached those heady delights of release if he was an asshole. She was never attracted to men who treated her like shit. That wasn't her jam. She had friends who walked that path, she wasn't one of them. She and the sexy man beside her had both known, the second they saw each other that something would happen. They had also both known it would be fleeting and very *very* hot. No promises were made because she was leaving and he was staying. It was lust and sex and passion all the way. Two bodies recognising each other as exactly the right one for right then.

Sure, things changed when she realised she was pregnant but there was still no commitment on her part. It was the caveman currently driving her home that went all traditional and conservative on her. Even then, it was an 'in name only' deal. Which reminded her, she needed to get divorce papers drawn up. She'd sworn to do it months ago but, somehow, she'd forgotten. She didn't feel married. She wasn't married in real terms so the paperwork should be merely routine. She'd definitely get on that. She would. She'd email her attorney tonight.

Flynn pulled the car to a stop outside her flat and switched off the engine. That did not bode well.

"You're not coming in," Gia stated flatly. "I don't trust you."

Flynn ignored her, got out of the car, walked around and opened her door just as she was struggling with the handle and her bags.

"You're right not to trust me. I don't trust me when I'm around you. Too many memories of one single night. I've tried shaking them off but, so far, I'm playing a losing game." He walked her to the doorstep and taking her bags from her arms placed them on the ground. "So, here's the deal. I'm going to kiss you senseless right now, Since the apartment kiss was rudely interrupted. And then I'm going home."

"What makes you think you'll be *able* to go home after I kiss you back?" Fuck, where had that sass come from? But, let's be real – it could happen. She'd experienced his kisses. She knew of what she spoke.

"I'm going to trust that you'll make me leave. That we will both see the wisdom of getting this next kiss out of the way. We need to go into this fake marriage with neither baggage nor yearnings. No unspoken, unacted-on desires. One more kiss, we're done. Agreed?"

Well, when he put it like that . . . She hadn't time to finish the thought before he read the consent in her eyes and moved.

She tasted like . . . everything he never knew he wanted. Her lips were soft, yielding. Opening to his, but he wanted to slow it down. His instinct was to devour but his brain wanted slow, steady, and *more*. He pressed his mouth to hers, softly, gently, but with intent. She groaned, shifting her position so her arms wrapped about his waist and she nuzzled into him. He wished she didn't feel so damn perfect against his body. That she didn't fit him so bloody well. He tasted her, once, twice, again and again. Light touches that pressed lips to lips. Together apart, together apart. He was teasing them both. Tantalising them with a slow, deliberate introduction to what was to come.

156

"Flynn . . ."

Her voice was a husky plea and he couldn't deny her. He cupped her face in his hands, angling it slightly as he paused, a breath away from her mouth and said, "Hold on, Sullivan. Just hold on."

It was glorious. Better than he remembered, if that was possible. Maybe it was because he knew more about her now. Admired her. *Liked* her. Found her cheek and sass a frustrating turn-on. Last summer it had been pheromones of lust, pure and simple. The other night had been a spontaneous but grief-driven delight. This? This was stand-up sexy as fucking hell. His tongue invaded, twisted and danced with hers. Skid along the side, swirled slowly and started all over again. *More groans. Gasps. Grunts.* He was pretty sure he was the one grunting. *Fuck*, he wanted to take her right here, on her front doorstep. He moved his hands, one to hold the back of her neck, the other slid down her back, down in a long slow sweep to grasp her ass and haul her right against his straining body. This was torture. Gorgeous, dangerous torture.

Her hands slid up his back, moulding into his muscles, sending frissons of pleasure deep into his bones. He widened his stance as she wiggled her body to settle right there, her heat to his. He backed her against the door, *he had to*, he needed his other hand to touch her everywhere he could. He grazed his knuckles along her neck, feeling the throb of her pulse, as his fingers edged down. He needed to feel her breast, her hardened nipples already like peaks pressed to his chest. He needed to tweak, squeeze. Jesus, he needed to taste. It was a long time since he'd been this hard, this quickly. It was like his cock knew her, recognised his happy place and was begging for more. He tore his mouth from her luscious softness and kissed her gently on her jaw before stroking his tongue along the column of her throat, drawing more sexy rough gasping sounds from her. It was music to his ears. She was as affected by this as he was. It was more than a kiss now. It was an assault and would continue till he had his fill of her. Reaching down he yanked up her T-shirt and in a fluid movement had her practical white bra pulled from her breast, and that beautiful puckered tip beneath his lips. He wasn't a plodder. He was an experienced, deftly moving man on a heatseeking mission. *Oh, the feel of her!* Her taste, so perfect. So *her*. He let his tongue explore the tip and its raised surrounds, before grazing his teeth across, back and forth and finally taking the whole nipple suckled deeply into his mouth.

"*Fuck, Flynn.* I feel you *everywhere*." She gasped, her head falling back, a soft thud on the wooden door, her arms removing from his body and her hands now grasping his head, holding him to her breast, urging him on.

He gave the other breast the same attention, one hand kneading its twin and both sensations flooding his body with want. Raising his head, he stared into drugged amber eyes, lids half closed, the crescent of dipped dark lashes almost hiding her expression. "One more," he rasped and took her mouth again.

It seemed Flynn Fitzgerald was indeed able to go home. Damn him. But also, thank goodness, because when she came up for air the danger was real. This man was her addiction. Knowing he was as turned on as she was, helped. She didn't feel so needy, so desperate. His grunts and groans had matched hers, one for one. When she closed and locked her door she barely made it to the bed before yanking down her jeans and using her fingers. The relief when her body let fly was unreal. She'd almost come when he'd inserted his thigh between hers and used it against her. Sweet frigging hot cakes, that man was sin on legs. She'd felt him too, long, hard and hot, but he'd backed away at her touch, groaning about it being *too much*.

Too much was fine with her, but the oracle had spoken. He rested his forehead to hers for mere seconds before pushing back, his face impassive. She was pretty sure her heaving breath gave off anything but impassive, but she knew. Seconds earlier he'd barely reined it in. He was being the adult, and she hated that she was glad of it. They really couldn't have sex right before an assignment where they had to pretend to have sex. That would just be weird, right? As she lay panting, allowing her breath to return to a pattern, she did her best to convince herself of that.

Gia rolled to her stomach, her head comfortable on the pillow and let herself remember. The kisses and touches she'd experienced moments ago had stirred up so many images, so many feelings. Her first sight of Flynn Fitzgerald, the zing she felt when their eyes met and she toppled into his arms. The next zing, even stronger as his arms wrapped, briefly, around her. Their first kiss. She closed her eyes, visuals of Flynn Fitzgerald, dashing in a navy suit, white shirt and pale-blue tie, taking his seat in the church in Dalkey where Caro and Nick married. The look in his eyes as she sashayed down the aisle after Communion, irreverently sneaking a glance from beneath her lashes as she passed him.

The reception back at the house was a blur, at least at first. She felt ignored as he brushed past her, several times, not making eye contact, not stopping to chat, except once briefly acknowledging her in an official and officious manner. And then that changed. She was leaning against a door jamb, a G&T hanging from her fingers, ice clinking gently in its Waterford crystal container. The music had started and the happy, strike that, stupid-in-love, couple had taken to the floor. They looked deliriously delighted with themselves. Nick glowed. Yeah, it was supposed to be the bride doing the glowing, but he really did. She'd never seen him like that and swallowed over the sudden lump as she watched him rub a thumb back and forth over Caro's lower lip. While they fucking danced. *I mean, who did that?* Gia had wondered. That was for Hallmark movies, not real life. He looked like he wanted to devour her. And Caro looked like she wanted to be dessert.

"Fuck," she'd said, unaware that it was audible.

"It has crossed my mind." Flynn's voice was low and right behind her.

She should have felt the sizzle except her eyes had been on the sizzle in front of her.

"Dance with me."

It had been a statement, not a request. An order, if you will. He took her wrist, lifted it, glass and all, took the drink from her hand, placed it on a side table next to the door and pulled her, willingly it must be said, behind him.

When he turned to hold her, one arm about her back, his hand resting low, just above her ass, the other holding one of hers in the old-fashioned way, like a waltz but closer to their bodies, she couldn't help but slide her arm up, her hand resting on the back of his collar. They moved, him leading, her following. She didn't usually dance like this, so it took a moment but he, the Fred Astaire of south County Dublin, swung and stepped, dipped and glided.

"Aren't you the dapper surprise of the night?" Damn her voice for sounding too breathy, too husky, too wanting. "I was not expecting this level of expertise."

"I aim to please." It had been low, rough. So laden.

"I bet you succeed, too," she said. She could smell him, a subtle but heady mix of spice and lemon, and her core tightened in response.

He angled her closer, that hand low on her back urging her flush to his lean body. *Oh, sweet Jesus.* Her eyes flew to his and she would have stumbled except for his quick reactions.

"I've had no complaints," he said, his gaze steady on hers. Those eyes and their odd colouring made her skin prickle and take notice.

"*Hah!* That's cos most people are terrified of you and your strong silent persona. You're probably not nearly as expert as you think."

"Care for a wager?"

"We both know we're not talking about dancing, right?"

"We are not," he agreed, his voice steady and calm and, if she hadn't seen the flare of heat in those eyes, she might have been fooled into thinking he was not remotely bothered by the exchange.

"What's the bet? I'm not afraid of you." Such brave words from a woman on the edge of combusting from need.

He leaned in, his mouth against her ear, his breath causing tendrils of hair tucked tidily away, to lift as he spoke. "I wager I can make you come so hard, so fast, your head will spin and you won't be able to stand."

She swallowed. Hard. "But if I'm lying down, the bet doesn't count. It won't matter if I can stand up from a bed or not."

"Who said anything about a bed?" He did some more fancy dance moves and she realised the music had changed tempo. He was performing for the other guests and family members. She would have been rooted to the spot if it was up to her. Fortunately, it was not.

"Are you trying to scare me?"

"I'm trying to tempt you."

"Can it be a little of both?" Gia's heart was racing so fast she feared it would crash-land.

"No. I don't believe you're afraid of anything. And I only work with a willing partner, certainly not a scared one."

"Then consider my speeding pulse a willing sign."

"Excellent." The word was clipped, sharp even. His look was anything but. Without releasing her he moved them across the small dance floor, and onto the paved pathway that led down the garden and split into several different directions. He chose one that led to the boathouse, a small structure built on the rocky shoreline.

He tugged her behind the shed, away from possible prying eyes and before she could catch her balance, let alone her breath, he had her backed against the slatted wood, his hands flattened on either side of her head, his mouth on hers. She would never know how she could simultaneously melt and heat at the same time. It was certainly a scientific conundrum but not one she was willing to consider right then. Seconds later, his hand slid the fabric of her dress up her thigh, his beautiful fingers skimming seductively along her skin, closer and closer to where she ached for his touch.

"You look particularly stunning in this dress but it is definitely cramping my style and will be coming off before this evening is out." He kissed his way down her neck, along her exposed collar bone and back up, taking her earlobe in his teeth. He tugged, gently, even as his fingers traced her, front to back along her lace thong.

She wasn't normally a thong wearer, but this dress was unforgiving and she wouldn't have contemplated leaving her ass cheeks bare if not for the fitness regime being a cop called for. She was never so grateful for the dozens of squats, the kettle swings and the running. She gasped as his fingers slid under the lace and she felt his touch on her body. Her hitched breath coupled with his hoarse *"You're so wet!"* had her angling into his hand in a wanton and needy manner. If she'd had brain cells available to use, she'd have been mortified at her actions but, no brain cells were forthcoming. So, she did what any righteous, turned-on, consenting woman would do; she held on for the ride.

When the orgasm barrelled through her moments later, she had to wonder at his magic fingers. He'd slid two inside her, angled them, twisted something, pressed against something else all the while his thumb had circled her with increasing pressure in exactly the right spot. The man had form, that was for damn sure. Expertise? Hell, yes. Would her lace undies ever be the same again? Hell, no. She'd happily let them take the hit. And there was something very sexy about ripping lace, not that she'd admit *that* to the sisterhood.

"You won that bet, hands down. Or wherever you had them," she said, when she could.

"I assure you it was my pleasure." He peeled his body

from hers, allowing air to circulate between them. It was chilly and she missed his heat an inordinate amount. Stupid really.

She reached for his belt. "My turn. It's only fair. And I want to."

His hand grasped hers, holding it still. "No. Not here."

"Why not? You didn't seem to mind exposing my nethers to the world!" she said indignantly. The sound of the waves lapping at the shore was interrupted by a burst of rowdy laughter and Gia recalled just how unprotected they were.

"It's not that. I'd like nothing more than to have your hand wrapped about my cock. But I heard a group of Toby's pals approaching so I think we should make ourselves scarce. Come with me. I, for one, want that dress on the floor, and you naked beneath me." He straightened the fabric, inching it down and smoothing the creases. "Is that acceptable to you?"

Always the gentleman, she was beginning to understand. Was it? Acceptable?

"Yes."

It was a ridiculous notion, thinking he'd actually sleep. He knew better. Flynn threw off the duvet and reaching for shorts, stood, slipped them on and shoved his feet into sneakers. He headed for his home gym, switched on the treadmill and started his run. It wasn't his usual habit. He preferred street, or even woodland running but he knew he had to wear out his body now, and try and get a night's sleep before the early meeting scheduled for the whole team the following morning, or, he amended looking at his watch, even several hours.

The old 'it seemed like a good idea at the time' scenario was jeering at him now. It *had* seemed like a good idea. Kiss her senseless and walk away. What a fool he'd been. A blind, idiotic thoughtless fool. The kiss itself wasn't the problem – far from it. That kiss had been as close to damn

PAMELA G. HOBBS

near perfect as a kiss could get. The only thing marring its complete perfection was that he knew it would dead end. It had to, that's why he'd instigated it. They had to move forward with no past issues lurking and rearing their heads when least expected.

Had it worked? He pounded a few more steps as he changed the incline setting on the treadmill. No, it bloody hadn't. If it had, he'd be asleep in bed, dreamless and rested. Instead, he chased up an imaginary hill, remembering things that were all too real. All too intense. Instead of finalising things, the kiss had opened up his tightly shut memory bank and damn if he couldn't recall every moment of their night together at Caro and Nick's wedding. Every bloody moment.

After the assault on her body with his fingers, up against the boathouse back wall, he'd ushered her upstairs, discreetly of course. They'd barely made it inside his old bedroom, and locked the door before he'd taken her mouth with an urgency he'd never before felt. It had all been so new. Not the having sex part, or even fingering a woman to orgasm. It was the unbelievable need that had surged through his body, the desire for her, above all else. The desire to please her, to make her beg for him and him alone. Those notions belonged on cable TV or within the pages of a romance novel. He'd wanted women before, enjoyed bouts of sex and fun play with them, but this? This was next level. This was frankly terrifying. He barely knew the woman and she was practically family. It was off the charts wrong on so many levels, and he didn't give a damn. He wanted to taste every inch of her skin. He wanted to touch every crevice and curve. He wanted her begging and moaning his name. He wanted her legs wrapped around his hips as he surged into her. Christ, he felt like a wild animal and that was also terrifying. He wanted his mouth on all the secret places her body had to offer.

He wanted all of her.

It wasn't working. He slowed the machine down,

stopped it. Got off and towelled his sweating skin. Not enough. He needed a shower and at this rate, the way his memory was rehashing things, a cold one was in order. He started with the hottest water he could handle and let the steam fill his bathroom. Not working. He propped one arm against the shower wall and grabbed his hard cock with his free hand. He wasn't a jerk-off-in-the-shower-on-a-daily-basis kind of guy, but here he was, doing that. Again. Needing that, while a film reel of his taking of Gia Sullivan ran like a chart topper in his mind. They'd eventually made it to the bed. But first he'd unzipped her, eased the dress from her shoulders allowing it to fall to the floor. One of many fantasies of the night fulfilled in an instant. He let his mouth travel down, all the way down until he ended on his knees before her, drinking her in as she gripped his hair in her hands, holding him where she wanted him most. Her eagerness, her desires, fuelled his own and he gripped her ass, kneading that flesh in his fingers as his mouth and tongue went to work. When she shattered beneath his touch, the pride he'd felt in giving her pleasure was new to him. He was always, he hoped, a generous and thoughtful lover, but seeing Gia bite her lip, head tilted back as she let the flow of feeling move through her body, brought on a possessiveness he didn't know he owned.

His mother always had his bed made with fresh linens. It was the small things that made a difference and he was never so grateful for that simple gesture. Jo liked each of her grown offspring to feel their family home was always there for them, even long after the coop had been flown. A tousle-haired, sexy, naked Gia sprawled on his bed was an image indelible in his brain forevermore. He lowered himself over her, still fully dressed and the contrast of her skin against the fabric of his shirt and trousers was both frustrating and erotic.

"Off," she'd said, tugging on the buttons of his dress shirt and he'd taken a moment to oblige. He let her undo the buckle then, watching her every move, her tongue peeping out from pearly teeth, her concentration was so intense. *Fuck,* that was hot. She unzipped him, slowly, watching him from under her lashes, her sexy lower lip begging for kisses. All he could think of was those lips wrapped around what she was now uncovering. He never asked for it. It was a gift given freely by some women but not every woman wanted or enjoyed it. Gia, thank all the gods, was very much on board with discovering just how much torture she could inflict on him before he hauled her away, slid on a condom and entered her in one fluid movement before he made a fool of himself. God, she was snug. He could feel her clench and unclench her inner muscles and between them they set a pace and a rhythm that had them sweaty and groaning before he felt her shudder and gasp his name as she came again. Finally, he let go, joining her in a complete collapse of blissful exhaustion. They slept.

Until they woke and did it all again.

Chapter sixteen

The planning and paperwork took three more days. Everything had to be in place. Gia chose not to wear a wig or disguise herself in any way – if anyone who might turn up in Donegal had seen her, it was in a wig so she felt safe. How to disguise Flynn Fitzgerald though? A clothing change for one. Gone were the classic conservative suits. She chose a wardrobe of jeans, button-downs and cotton sweaters for him. Chelsea boots and a navy sports jacket were added, a sharp haircut, styled more au currant, and a pair of slick black-rimmed glasses. She brought everything to the station and had him try them on. He definitely looked *not himself* when he walked into the conference room. He looked, besides being as confident as usual, like a man straight from the pages of *GQ* magazine. How did he swagger suddenly when normally he walked with a simple assurance? This walk had attitude. He could wear a character as well as she could. Wasn't he the dark horse! Two garda walked past him without acknowledging his presence, did a double take and grovelled accordingly. Smoke and mirrors were a thing, a ruse learned early in the Academy. Show people what you want them to see, and they'll believe it.

Her own clothes she selected from a boutique in Sandycove, a small village in the south suburbs of Dublin, with the help of Frankie, style guru extraordinaire. Gia wanted a simple sophisticated look, one that exuded lots and lots of money. She was going with a 'my family came over with the Mayflower' vibe of a New Englander and to that end kept her palette in creams and navy. Old money colours, old money fabrics of linen, wool and silk. She even tied a marine-patterned Hermès scarf around her neck – courtesy of Frankie's own wardrobe. The local police were *not* going to dole out for that level of role play. The clothes fit well, felt well and made her look the part. She hated the part. She hated the lifestyle her character was projecting. Bored socialite in want of a baby but unwilling to ruin her figure to get one. Flynn had to project a wealthy IT consultant, hence the happily spending time in Ireland part of their act. Everyone knew Ireland was a hotbed for IT and all things internet and web-based communications.

They went over their back stories, again and again. They grilled each other on details, made some up on the fly, ones that made sense for the people they were fake-creating, noted the changes or additions in a notebook, and questioned each other repeatedly. It was all work and they both sank into it eagerly. Gia knew, from her viewpoint, she needed the normalcy of working with Flynn to take the mystique out of him. He was much too interesting to her in so many different ways. She enjoyed the way his mind worked, how savvy he was in picking up on others' trains of thought, how he could develop an idea in quicksilver time and have it mapped out in a sensible and clear way while those around him were still grasping the concept. His IQ must be off the charts, she thought, as she listened to him explain some intricate point to a junior garda. He wasn't mansplaining to her, the way many did, just outlining specifics and encouraging the young garda to speak her mind. Gia liked that. Approved of his methods and wished more in the hierarchy, especially the males, would do just that: take a minute to talk someone through something, not simply override them by doing it themselves or talking down to them.

Flynn never talked down to people, Gia was learning. He could be an ass, and frequently was in her opinion, but he wasn't mean and he wasn't unkind. And all he had to do was turn those ice-blue eyes of his in her direction and she frigging melted. That was her problem though and she was working on it. If she could delve deep into her new role, she'd be so bitchy she'd automatically hate her supposed husband. That would help, surely? God, it had better. Trouble was she was also *supposed* to hang on his every word, believe he'd give her everything she wanted. Trouble was also that he was panty-melting hot in his new glasses and hairstyle. The way those denims hugged his ass should be made illegal.

"So you're booked into the Airb&b situated between Moville and Greencastle on the Inishowen Peninsula," Brigid informed her. "The belief amongst the team is there isn't a hotel swanky enough for your back story in the area, but this house is on the waterfront overlooking the lough and is an architect-designed gem. According to our intel, the boat taking the babies leaves from Greencastle so this way you are close, but not obvious." She showed her a map, opening it out, old school, on the centre table.

She pointed to the two places and Gia could see the port of Greencastle had easy access to Northern Ireland. Was that where the babies went? Or did the gang bypass the obvious and go further afield? But where? They needed to get talking to Gary Miller himself, infiltrate on one level by Menchen, going to ask for work as a deckhand, and she and Flynn would be out in the open as a couple needing a baby pronto. Thanks to Jackie Carroll giving up the goods, they knew of a couple from Boston and another from New York who had each received a baby via Miller. As a pretend couple from Greenwich, Connecticut, they could easily move in the same social circles, know the same people. Mingle with the families – in the case of the Boston couple, they could have met the baby. The background team in Dublin had contacted the adoptive parents and were following up on legalities both from the Irish side and the US. How that would pan out, for the birth mother and the new parents, was up for debate. At least they had the details so could wing it, if asked.

The night before she and Flynn were set to head to Donegal, Gia asked Ali, Molly, Frankie, and Caro, who was due to fly back to Rome the next day, to come over to the flat in Dún Laoghaire. It, of course, still officially belonged to Caro, but since they all seemed to be getting a turn, they had dubbed it 'the girls' flat' and whoever was temporarily in residence got to be in charge.

They ordered in from the local Indian take-away and Molly regaled Gia with the story of the Korma Incident. It was one of those stories that was hilarious in the retelling but not so much when it had happened. When she got to the part about swinging a bag of hot food at the head of one of the intruders, Gia laughed along with the others but when Molly went on to say they were so hungry, she and Kit had salvaged some to eat, she collapsed in mirth, visualising the whole incident.

"The cavalry, or should I say, Flynn, arrived, and took over and when he uttered those immortal words, 'Ain't korma a bitch?' I would have wet myself laughing except Kit fainted then and I was kind of distracted." Molly held up her fork full of lamb korma and they all chuckled again even as they filled their glasses.

"Your family seems to get into a lot of scrapes," Gia observed, adding more pilau rice to her plate. "And your brother seems to spend a considerable amount of time involved in those scrapes."

"Oh no," Frankie said. "He's not involved, he just puppeteers everything from the side-lines!"

"I was pretty happy for him to truck up here that night, I tell you," Molly agreed. "But yeah, he can be a total jerk too, like, you know, keeping people in the dark and holding secrets."

"Is that directed at me?" Caro asked, sipping sparkling water. "Because as it turned out I wasn't the only one keeping pretty large things from my family, now was I?"

"No, it's totally on him. And I shouldn't have said anything, anyway. Flynn has his own issues and it's none of our business."

Ali took a swig of beer, her preferred beverage with Indian food she had announced earlier, arriving with a six-pack. "Are you referring to his weird behaviour last October and then again at Easter? He sure was a pain in the ass. Grumpy and distracted. But he seemed better during the summer and almost human again this last week. What gives?"

Gia swallowed her wine, lowering her eyes. *Shit*. That was a lot to hear. She knew, cerebrally, that Flynn had been affected by her situation, or what he knew of it. She knew. But hearing that his family had been aware of something too? That was, for some reason, deeply saddening to her. It made him and his feelings real. Too real. She was responsible for all of it.

"Excuse me." She stood and headed to the bathroom to take a much-needed minute. She splashed water on her face. The cool water was a balm to her heated cheeks and helped her focus. *They didn't know. Not really. They didn't know why, or who, they didn't know the ins and outs. The facts.* Flynn didn't either, but that was something else entirely.

"Top up, anyone?" Gia waggled the wine bottle when she re-entered the fray. Nope? She filled her own, pissed at herself that she wanted Dutch courage from a green bottle.

"We were just laughing at the idea of Flynn being undercover!" Ali said. "I've never seen him out of suits, well, except at the lodge on holidays. What's he going to wear?"

171

This was naturally directed at Gia and she hesitated. How much did they know about the job ahead? Probably very little, as was only right. So, she spilled the beans without, of course, spilling the actual beans.

"He looks very different. To me anyway. The suits hide his physique on any given day. The shirts and sweaters we selected to emphasise his shoulders and are a closer cut to his body. He looks fit."

"Wait," Frankie interjected. "Fit as in 'he exercises' or fit as in *hell, yes!*?" She used air-quotes for the exercising part and fanned herself for the rest.

Frankie was funny, she came across as quite demure for a world-class actress and model but there was a core of kindness and humour that only those close to her saw. Gia appreciated that she was allowed into that circle.

"Both, actually," she admitted. "I mean he has abs for days and arms that could put any gym rat to shame, plus those runner legs? Man, they're hot."

She stopped because, fuck, they were all staring at her. What? What had she said? *Nooooo.* She'd let the wine do the talking. She was giving away far too much. Not about the op ahead but her knowledge of their brother. *Intimate* body knowledge. She looked at her glass – *fucking traitor, you're supposed to help, not dob me in it!*

Caro spoke first. "As his eldest female sibling, may I enquire how you know this?" Her voice was high-pitched and formal.

"Get off your high horse, Caro. We all want to know. Spill, Gia!" Ali pleaded laughingly.

Molly sat back, nursing her glass, a frown between the lovely Fitzgerald eyebrows all the girls were blessed with. Gia guiltily avoided her stare but it was too late. Molly knew something, or at least suspected it. Wasn't she the one who had a touch of ESP? Well, it was going to be a shitstorm unless she held her ground and lied through her teeth. She took a deep breath right as Molly spoke.

"Did you sleep with him?"

When they eventually left, Gia cleared away plates, giving herself a virtual pat on the back for her quick thinking. Did they believe her? It didn't really matter. Flynn could deny it if challenged, just like she had. Vigorously.

It was the gym, she'd insisted. She'd had to go to his home for work, she improvised, and he'd been working out. She couldn't not see.

"He has a home gym?" Ali had been incredulous.

"Was he not wearing a shirt?" Caro, ever the clothes police.

Gia had laughed them off, successfully she thought, and threw it back on them. "I can't believe you haven't seen his workout room. It's really well stocked. He uses it daily, I'm told."

Molly had harrumphed. She wasn't buying it but for some reason she didn't pursue the whole 'you had sex with our brother' part. Gia was grateful for small mercies.

She tidied the rest of the living room, disposed of the recycling and got ready for bed. Her bag was packed for the early start and although she'd demurred, Flynn was collecting her at seven. He was intractable when it came to a schedule. Maybe that was a good thing for his line of work, but Gia liked a little flexibility in her life. And her work.

She'd told the Fitzgerald women they could come and go to the flat while she was away, to have a presence there, as no one had any idea how long their sting operation would last. Short and sweet was the aim but they were all professionals and knew to be open to any number of possibilities. Besides Kasper Menchen hopefully getting work in the dock, they had two local garda from the Moville area on alert. It was both polite and protocol to include the station concerned with any job being conducted by an outside team, and their Dublin team was on it.

Gia was impressed with the way things ran here. There was a chain of command, of course, there had to be, but it was, she felt, a looser version of what she was used to in New York. There was respect for the command but, also, the word they used here – *craic*. Having a joke about macabre things was vital when on the job. Every cop knew that. There had to be a relief valve, a way to decompress. The Irish took it to another level and it was taking some adjustment for Gia to understand when it was fun and when it was serious. Some of the 'lads', as everyone was collectively called, slagged with such sombre expressions it was hard to tell. She'd been caught out a few times already, the butt of everyone's humour, but Gia was good at laughing at herself and didn't mind in the slightest. It made her feel like she belonged. Or at least was starting to. She must remember that she didn't in fact belong here. Other than the comradery in arms that all who served felt, she belonged in New York. Getting too vested in what happened in Dublin would only lead to misery.

She set her watch for an early wake-up and, stopping herself from over-analysing the evening's events, she turned out the light and fell into a dreamless sleep.

Chapter seventeen

Donegal might be a particularly lovely and scenic county but it was a pain in the ass to get to. As they bypassed Monaghan town, south of the border, Gia nodded off, her head resting against the window. Flynn didn't mind. She was a distraction just being next to him. With over two hours at least left to go, if they didn't stop, he hoped she'd stay asleep. It was easier than listening to the chatter. They'd done homework too, the professionals they were, but one could only second-guess backstory questions for so long without losing focus. They knew who they were portraying and were smart enough to wing it as needed. She wore navy linen cut-offs, pressed and neat, paired with a crisp white shirt and navy linen jacket. Her shoes were red – ballet pumps, he was informed – and the leather belt about her slim waist was the same red. As were her nails. He wished, fervently, that her nails were a normal clear nothing kind of colour. Her everyday nails. She'd worn red polish the night of the wedding, to match her siren's dress, and he could still see them wrapped around his body in all manner of ways. Shaking his head, he took the road from Aughnacloy, the border village, to

Omagh the county town of Tyrone and they were at last, officially, in the North of Ireland, short-lived though it would be. If she woke, they would stop in that town for a late breakfast and then head on to Derry and across to Moville in Donegal, back in the Republic.

There had been one of those iconic moments earlier when Gia had opened the map on her lap and followed the route with a highlighter.

"Will we stop in Londonderry?" she'd asked and he had almost stalled the car.

"It's called Derry when you're with me. And for future reference, be careful what you call it, especially when we are going through the North. It's way too easy to say the wrong thing to the wrong person. I've heard those who live close to the border, unless they know for sure a person's political leaning, refer to it as 'the city', purposefully omitting the name. It's clever. And a useful tool. Remember it."

"Why can't you guys figure this North-South stuff, out? It can't be that big of a deal surely? You're such a small country."

He had laughed at that, but not in humour. "I could tell you, but there are not enough hours in a week, let alone a day."

"Ah, give it a shot, why don't you? We have nothing else to do over the next few days as we settle into our new home away from home. I'll listen without comment."

That of course had made him laugh out loud, in genuine amusement. "From what I know of you, Sullivan, no commentary is an impossibility."

"Try me," she'd said. "You might be surprised. I'm pretty smart. I took history. I only said the Londonderry thing to get a rise out of you."

He'd turned to look at her then, raising his infamous eyebrow. "Not a successful ploy, you may find out to your detriment. You might well receive a long, involved history lesson before this case is over."

"Bring it on, bud. I'm so ready."

He'd rolled his eyes and continued driving. He, Flynn Fitzgerald, was at the eye-rolling stage of this *relationship*. He was not, never had been an eye-roller. He behaved differently around her and he wasn't sure he liked it. It didn't feel odd with her, but he was sure as he was of anything that it was only she who brought about these changes. Despite their charged history, their shared pain, she made him feel . . . lighter. He found her funny. And charming. Intelligent and a quick thinker was a given but her sexiness? That was creeping in all over again. Stirring him up when he had no right to it. She was so beyond off limits it was almost funny. Ironic then, that here they were, driving for hours, starting their new roles as a married couple in search of what they'd already lost.

Ironic and perhaps unfair. Time would tell.

In the end, she slept through Omagh and Derry so he didn't stop, but he nudged her awake as they drove along the west side of the Foyle. It was such a pretty view and she deserved some pretty. It was the least he could do. It wasn't because he'd missed her chatter and her jibes and her quirks and her divine and kissable upper lip. It was time she woke and got her bearings, that was all.

"Here." Flynn handed her a bottle of water from the centre console, studiously ignoring the stretching of fabric over her bra as she yawned awake. "You might need this."

She took the bottle, her fingers grazing his and he could feel a jolt all the way up his arm. Ridiculous. Was the carpet in the car giving him static?

She held his eyes as she twisted off the cap. "Damn," her murmur was low, but he heard it. "You felt it too. Shit, that doesn't bode well."

Gia gulped the water as he kept his eyes peeled for, well, for anything other than her and her sleep-flushed cheeks. They slowed down through Moville, the long narrow street with all manner of shops and cafés lining the sides. She sat up straighter and looked about expectantly.

"This is a cute village and they have a supermarket.

177

Should we get supplies for later?"

"No, Brigid said our host, who will thankfully be absent, has left a full fridge and larder, on her instructions. Beds are made up and towels and spare linens are on hand. I don't think it's much farther."

"They'd better have left a shitload of alcohol and snacks too," she said, opening up her phone GPS. "It's another two miles, a turn on the right. Oh, that must mean we'll be on the water!"

"Did you not see the property when it was chosen? I hope you like it." He cursed inwardly. Now why had he said that? He wasn't some eager bridegroom out to impress his bride. *This. Was. Work.* He'd do well to remember that.

"There, turn there," Gia said a few moments later.

He indicated, turned the vehicle and they drove slowly down a narrow winding road. More like a lane, really, discreet and well hidden. He pulled the SUV to a stop at the only house nestled at the dead end. Somebody had upped the ante. Usually, undercover agents got very middle-of-the-road accommodation. But then they weren't usually playing upper-end folks with a lot of cash to flash.

This house was low, split-level by the look from the outside and wrapped, on three sides, in glass. The view was spectacular and he turned to Gia to realise she was already out of the car and scampering to the low stone wall overlooking the inlet.

She spread her arms wide and tilted her head back to the noonday sun. *"It's glorious!"* she shouted, turning slowly in a full circle, arms still outstretched. She looked impossibly young, impossibly joyful and he couldn't contain the grin that split his face.

He unbuckled his seatbelt and got out. Shoving his hands in the pockets of his new jeans to avoid doing something stupid like grab her and twirl her about, he sauntered over to investigate the vista. He'd been to the Inishowen peninsula before but it was years ago and he'd forgotten this side, and the charm of it. He paused behind her, taking it in. The inlet was sparkling, a beautiful deep blue and the odd puffy cloud drifted by overhead. Even as they watched, in companionable silence, the wind changed and the previously gentle waves turned choppy.

"Man, that was fast," she laughed. "*Yikes*, it's chilly!" and she jumped down off the wall without giving him a chance to move out of the way. He wrapped his arms about her, an instinctive move, he told himself later. Pure instinct to catch her. To hold her. To wrap her in. Her shriek of fright and fun faded within seconds. Flynn wasn't finding the situation in the least funny. He was finding it deadly serious. If this, her accidentally falling into his arms, made him hard, he was in way deeper than he'd thought. But so be it. He stilled. Holding her steady, his eyes on hers, drinking in the gorgeous ever-changing rainbow of rusty hues. Now, they were slightly dazed as she looked right back at him. Was it his heart that thudded so loudly it was heard over the stiffening breeze, or was it hers? He glanced to the hollow of her neck where a pulse jumped and jived. Not just him, then. Good. Or maybe very bad.

Aw, fuck it. He lowered his head, heard her intake of breath, that sexy intoxicating gasp, and touched his lips to hers. He pressed them gently, lifted, pressed again. Changed the angle of the kiss and did it again. He could feel his chest tighten, his groin tighten, his belly tighten, all from lips to lips. But they were *her* lips and that was everything.

He pulled back and waited. Would she berate him? Chide him? Kiss him?

"What was that for?" she asked, her voice small and husky.

What could he say? *Because I saw your joy and needed it too? That I needed your lips like I need the air I breathe? Because I'm finding it increasingly harder to resist to smell of you, the feel of you, the essence of you?* No. He couldn't say any of that.

"Just getting in character," he lied, and released her to get the bags from the car.

***

Liar, she thought as she followed him into the cooler than cool house. The floors were a pale, wide maple plank, the walls, or rather *the* wall in the main room was a soft blue-grey tone bringing the sea right through visually. The sectional couch had a modern retro look in deep grey velvet and the armchair a splash of cherry. A stainless-steel coffee table was centred on what she could only assume, based on the surroundings, a Persian rug. Damn, but this place had style. Was a juxtaposition of old and new that really gelled. She loved it, or at least what she'd seen of it so far.

She walked back across the vestibule area, a pale stone floor with colourful abstract design rugs, high ceilings and a couple of matching occasional tables against the wall. Huge mirrors above the tables reflected all the light from the glass beyond and whole area spilled with bright light. Gia explored the long hall as she went to discover the kitchen, down two steps and into another bright airy room. The appliances, all super-modern in stainless steel. And fuck, each one a Smeg. This owner had serious money. It was a perfect fit for their pretend coupledom scenario. She wandered the room, skimming her hand across the surface of a concrete island tinted pale blue. All the extra touches were in tones of blue and grey, keeping the sea theme. It really was spectacular. Even the high stools for eating at the island were padded with pale-blue leather. No expense spared here, then.

She opened and closed cupboards, checking out the crockery and silverware, yup, all top of the range. The fridge, with its fancy double doors and icemaker, was stacked with all manner of goodies as was the walk-in larder. There was a note propped against the fancy espresso maker, welcoming them to the home and detailing a few things re keys etc. It also stated there was fresh bread in the wooden bin and a selection of cheeses under a glass cloche in the larder. She realised she was peckish, having slept through their intended brunch stop so set about brewing the coffee.

"Hey, Fitz!" she called. "Come help with food. I may be your real pretend wife but I'm not your housekeeper." Start as you mean to go on, she reminded herself.

"I'll be right with you. Just putting the bags in the main bedroom for now. I'll let you have that one, I'll take the other," he said.

She heard the opening and closing of doors and went back to her task.

Flynn strolled in a moment later and for a second she stopped, frozen. He was a handsome man in his suits and ties, but in this smart casual gear he was devastating. And he was completely unaware, which was just as well. She could only imagine the ego on someone else. The assholery that could ensue. Not Flynn Fitzgerald. He embodied the classic silver screen hero. Cool, calm and collected. An odd mix of James Dean and Cary Grant. Gia knew her old movies – her momma was a sucker for them and many a late afternoon on a rainy day she'd curled up on the couch in Brooklyn next to her and binge-watched. Grant, Cooper, Astaire, Sinatra, Howard, Stewart, Brando. The genre didn't matter – from western to musical, buccaneers to mobsters, her momma loved them all. As a child Gia had ignored them, too boring. As a teenager she had initially sneered at the old movies channel but, following a bout of flu, home off school with nothing to do, she'd agreed to watch. And got hooked. Her mother worked hard as a seamstress from their home, so making her take a much-needed break to relax eventually became a shared pleasure.

"Cheese is in the larder, cold cuts in the refrigerator and bread in the wooden bin. I'm on coffee duty and will get the plates. Oh, and don't forget the butter." Irish butter had ensnared her once again. When she'd been over for Nick's wedding, she'd discovered its creamy salty flavour and become a big fan; now it went on everything, even, sacrilege to some, her roast potatoes.

"On it," he said and went about gathering the food.

They set up on the island and when she drank her Americano, hot and dark and full of smokiness, Gia groaned aloud. "Man, this is good brew," she declared. Opening her eyes, she noted Flynn studying her intently. "What? Have I got a coffee moustache?" She wiped at her mouth and checked her hand for coffee stain.

He continued to stare, this time right at her mouth. "You have a very kissable mouth, you know that, right? And when your tongue peeps out, and strokes that upper lip of yours? Well, it's quite the sight. That's all."

He bent his head to his crusty bread topped with salami, Parma and creamy blue cheese and bit in as if he hadn't just said those words.

"You can't just say those words and then eat!"

"I can. I just did. Do you have a problem with my husbandly remarks?"

Oh. He was playacting. Irritated with her stupid sense of deflation, Gia glared at him. "I hope you don't expect me to make those kinds of comments back to you. My repertoire is a bit scarce when it comes to complimenting men."

"Men in general or just me?"

"Both. Either. You already know you have a great body, a handsome face and an irresistible charm, so don't go begging for more. Your ego won't handle it. And I'm lacking in the vocabulary."

"Irresistible, huh?"

He grinned, the bastard, and took another bite.

"See? I should have known you'd pick up on that one. Seriously, don't hold your breath. I'm not that person." She lathered more butter onto a torn-off piece of baguette before adding a slice of gouda and some brie. Might as well go for full fat all the way.

"I don't need the words, darling – just throw me some melting glances and we'll be all square."

182

She snorted a laugh. He was funny when he relaxed. "That's going to be even harder than the words, husband. I'm particularly low on smoulder."

"Well, then. I see I have my work cut out for me. I need your smouldering as you put it, when we are with Miller and his cohort. They need to believe *you* believe I'll get you whatever you want. Even if it's someone else's child."

Gia sighed. Back to business. It was all very well to tease each other, but they were here to stop a baby-buying ring and she'd do well to remember it. She had to remember it. *As if she'd ever forget.*

"You're right. I'll try to look longingly at you at all times when in public. But don't expect miracles. I'm good but not that good."

They ate the rest of their lunch, discussing an afternoon plan. Kasper Menchen had arrived in Greencastle the day before and had secured dock work. Not with Miller, but at least he'd be there, eyes and ears open. If Jackie Carroll stuck to her end of the bargain, Miller would know to expect a glamorous couple from America on the lookout for an instant baby. Carroll was to tell him they'd be in the area over the next few days and would eat each evening in the local fish restaurant. He could find them there. It wasn't an ironclad plan, sure, but it was something.

Since Jackie Carroll had also said they were getting out of the baby business imminently, this could be their only chance. Diamonds, it seemed, were back in fashion. She'd sworn she didn't know why they used Greencastle as a way off the island, but said she'd heard mumblings about Scotland and the Netherlands. That, and how it might work, as opposed to straight across to the UK was being investigated by a selection of detectives on the force in those countries. Gia and Flynn went over the possible outcomes. They had brought a bag of baby clothes, a travel cot and a baby seat, in case they actually ended up with a real live baby. They were pretty sure they wouldn't, but preparation was key. And Miller had to believe their story.

Flynn stacked the dishwasher as Gia went to the bathroom to wash her hands.

Another showstopper fashion plate. All tile and open shower with a massive stand-alone tub in the centre. Heated towel rails covered most of one wall and a huge frosted window let more light filter in. There was a slightly different colour theme here, sage green and pale grey, and with the muted tone it felt warm. She noted the sumptuously soft hand towels, Egyptian of course, she discovered, checking the labels. Seriously, didn't these people do anything on the cheap? No, they did not: even the soap was Dior. A pump soap called Lucky? Lucky her, as she washed her hands in the admittedly divine-smelling contents. If this was the main bathroom, God knows what the en-suites would be like. She was pretty certain both bedrooms would have an en-suite. It was that type of house. She'd enjoy that part of the tour later. Work came first. Always.

For now, they needed to get into the small village, one that hid big secrets.

Greencastle was small, true, but had all the necessary makings of a fishing port. The nets, the crowds, the piled-up piers with boats on dry dock, as well as timber pallets and empty lobster pots. And the smell of fish. Lots of fish in barrels and in basins, for sale both for private vendors and commercially. Several vans, again, both trade and personal, were parked in a typical haphazard fashion along the main pier itself. The water hosted a dozen or more trawlers and as Flynn parked his own vehicle and rolled down the window, the smell and the noise intensified.

"Christ, I'd forgotten what a small port can feel like. Smell like. Hope you don't have a delicate stomach, it can get . . . pungent."

Gia threw him a sarky glance. "I've got this," she said. "I spent a lot of time around the docks as a kid. My dad was a regular at the fish market, for the restaurant. I went with him as a kid. Earned a few bucks swabbing open market stalls when the trading was done. Not so much as a teen. It wasn't cool to turn up to class with *eau de poisson* the scent of the day."

Flynn laughed. How could he not? Imagining Angelica Sullivan giving stick to the fishmongers as a kid! Pure delight. Imagining her swanning into her classroom giving her mates the finger? Totally credible. He had to watch himself, he thought as he climbed out of the car, all suave and sophisticated, easy money, easy life. He walked around and opened his 'wife's' door, handing her onto the uneven stone ground. She dropped her sunglasses to her nose and slid her blazer over her shoulders. She took his arm, like royalty, her hand resting on his proffered forearm and he had to chuckle. To the fucking manor born.

They began sauntering along the small pier, he letting his gaze slowly, unobtrusively, take in the names of the shipping vessels. Gia, in character, peering over her sunglasses with an element of disdain was the perfect foil for his pretended interest.

"Fitzgerald, you can't possibly think these people will have anything for us?" Her voice was pure Mayflower mixed with Nantucket and a dash of Kennedy.

"Honey, appearances can be deceptive, let's give these folks a chance." They'd decided he'd keep the Fitzgerald, but as a first name and he'd have a mid-Atlantic twang. Someone who'd lived in the US for years but was originally Irish. It would account for his knowledge of the area, his understanding, for the most part, of the Donegal accent, and his reason for choosing an Irish person to find him a baby. He was playing an asshole though and Flynn hoped it would come easily. They'd also decided that they'd keep Gia's name and use the last name of Kennedy as their identity. He doubted anyone they'd be dealing with would get the joke but if they commented, he would tell them his parents had a wry sense of humour. They both knew, when undercover, to keep everything as close to real as possible.

185

He wanted to be in character, all the time, so he wouldn't let his guard slip when it came to *real* Gia and how he felt around her. Every moment in her company was a challenge. A challenge not to hold her, kiss her, taste her. Every word he'd said to her, in character, was as true in real life and that scared the shit out of him. But also exonerated him for all his feelings, which kind of felt like a pass. He could touch her in public, kiss her, say all the romantic or sexy things, and she would believe it was pretend. With any luck it would rid him of these dastardly thoughts, once they were spoken out loud. Maybe they'd vanish. Simply melt away *because* they had been said.

It was worth a try.

He was an idiot, believing that but that couldn't be helped.

Flynn edged them around the perimeter, knowing she was taking as many mental notes as he was and having her clued in, alert, helped keep him sane. Somewhere in the milieu of fisherfolk, Gary Miller could be hiding in plain sight. They had a description from Jackie Carroll and a rather faded ID photo from his driving license on file for a misdemeanour years earlier, but that was it. He would have to approach them, sure in the knowledge that they were awaiting his contact.

"The guy leaning against the bollard at two o'clock, pretending not to notice us, is a definite possibility," Gia said, sotto voce.

"Check," Flynn agreed. "Let's not give him too much. We're not supposed to know he's here, just that he will appear in the restaurant. Menchen is at ten to two, talking with an older, looks like a local, guy."

"Yeah, spotted him. The other man is definitely local. I got a whisper of the accent as we turned and honest to God, between Menchen's accent, excellent though his English is, and that guy's, not sure how they will converse at all."

"Grunting and swearing, I would imagine. It works for

186

most men."

She poked him in the shoulder. "Look at you, all aware and clued in. Go, Flynn."

He looked down into her laughing face and bent his lips to hers, a light but definite kiss. "That's my girl," he drawled loud enough to be heard by those nearby. "Always keeping me on my toes."

Gia looked momentarily startled but, taking her cue, snuggled into him more pointedly. "That's my job, honey, but you have to keep your promise." She reached up and kissed his cheek, followed that with a gentle pat and then shuddered pretty obviously.

"Are you cold, baby? You know how I like to keep you warmed up."

She pouted. "Honey, you like to keep me running hot as Hades. Let's go back to our house and you can do just that."

He did his best leer. "Anything for you, sugar. Anything at all."

Flynn angled her back towards the car but not before the guy they suspected was Miller rolled his eyes and spat.

"Delightful," Flynn muttered. "Our work here is done. He thinks we are moronic Yanks with all balls and no brains." He opened her car door, ever the perfect gentleman.

"Speak for yourself, Fitz. I've plenty of balls."

And on that cheeky rejoinder she hopped up into her seat and he shut the door firmly, a smile sneaking out when it really shouldn't.

The short drive back was accomplished in silence but they began discussing their impressions as they entered the hall. Gia headed straight for the kettle and switched it on. She reached for china cups and tilting one at him, asked if he'd like.

He nodded and went to hunt for biscuits. A large tin held the goodies and he fetched a plate and slid several oatmeal cookies out. Tea was a given in the Fitzgerald household and he supposed Gia, being of part Irish descent, might have the tea ritual too. But no, she made a small pot of coffee for herself yet still brewed his tea perfectly. It struck him as inordinately thoughtful. They drank and chatted, discussed and debated. It was like any case except it wasn't. Nothing against any of his female colleagues, but no one stirred him like Angelica.

When he saw her again, this time, not in New York for their expedient wedding, but on the stairwell at the station he'd felt the wind knocked out of him. Not for the loss or the sadness, but because she affected him as much as she'd ever done. If not more.

He wasn't blind. Or stupid. He knew she felt something too. You don't kiss like that if you're not into it. If you don't want it. Trouble was, he was starting to suspect he wanted so much more than kisses. Than sex. Than a fling. He wanted *more*. He wanted her.

He took notes; she abstractedly ate cookies and paced about the open space. She asked questions about the area, about specific geographical aspects of their location. What he didn't know, he googled.

"There has to be a specific reason they use Greencastle," she said. "It's not the hub of the universe, which in itself could be a good reason, but why else? Derry is part of the UK, right? So why not just have a location there? Why go through another country? What's the angle, surely it's more than Irish passports, dammit?"

Flynn didn't disagree. He googled some more, and searched for accessible ports, not in Northern Ireland. Ports that were close enough to not be a huge crossing for either a pregnant woman or an infant straight from its mother's arms. They didn't know the ins and outs, but Jackie Carroll had said they didn't normally deliver the babies to the new parents in Ireland, just have them born there and then get shipped elsewhere. But where? The obvious place was the Netherlands because they knew from intel from New York as well as the Hague that it was the buying region, but, again, how?

"We will have to play it cool this evening, suss Miller

out without letting him wonder why we'd care."

He looked at his watch. An hour before they had to head back into the small port for food. They were supposed to be American, so they'd booked for an early dinner.

"Go ahead and get ready," he told Gia. "I'll use the shower in the main bathroom, so you can use the master bedroom ensuite."

"OK."

"Right."

They cleared their things from the counter to the dishwasher and he then strode out to get his washbag from his case.

The master bedroom was as well styled as the rest of the chic abode. A massive bed, all white linens, a textured wallpaper in tones of gold and bronze, what looked like four thousand cushions and throw pillows on the bed. He shook his head, baffled. Why? They were only going to get tossed.

"*Oooh*, look how they dressed this room!" Gia exclaimed, coming in behind him. She ran her hand along the surface of the bedspread, groaning at what she felt.

His groin tightened at the sound, wishing her hand was smoothing over his body. Christ, now he was jealous of fabric? Gritting his teeth, he turned to leave but she darted in front of him and dragged him with her into the ensuite

"Don't you want to see it? See if it's as cool as the main bathroom? Oh, Holy Mother. It is. Look!" she said excitedly. "It's all marble and glass. And the colours! That ochre with the navy is divine."

Was it? Flynn neither knew nor cared. He needed a shower and, at this rate, watching her lean over the tub stroking dulled gold taps and fixtures, her rounded ass *right there*, it was going to be a cold one.

He waited. He was good at that.

She pulled out every drawer, lifted towels, smelled them, fingered soap, flipped open the glass of the vanity cabinet. "Oh," she made a disappointed sound. "I thought we'd discover all manner of things about the owner. Medicine cabinets are great for that. Maybe in the other bedroom? I'll check it out." She headed out into the hall and made a left towards the second bedroom.

He waited some more because he knew what was coming. He'd discovered it before they left for their first scout of Greencastle but thought it was prudent to stay quiet. Perhaps, he admitted, as she stormed back down the hall, that had been an error of judgement.

"The door is locked. Have you the key? Why is your room locked?" She looked flushed as, he suspected, the reality of their situation was beginning to dawn on her.

"It's locked because, like a lot of Airb&b patrons, the owners choose to keep one room separate, off limits. Ergo, I don't have a key."

"Find it!" she snapped.

"That would defeat the purpose, would it not? The reason it's locked is because they don't want us using it."

"Oh, shut up, smarty pants. I get that. But what are we going to do?" She started to laugh but a tad on the hysterical side. "I feel like I'm living the trope of a romance novel."

Flynn peeled his body from the doorframe where he'd lounged. "How so? What the hell is a trope?"

"There's only one bed!"

Gia took her shower in the master bath. She'd spun on her feet, grabbed her bag from the stand at the bottom of the ginormous bed where Flynn had left it, and shoved him out the door to his own ablutions. What the actual fuck? She soaped her body and washed her hair, her mind whirring too speedily for her to thoroughly enjoy the very expensive fragrances wafting amongst the steam. Why hadn't somebody on the team requested two bedrooms? Too late now anyway. It was certainly large enough to host an entire family, let alone two adults.

She dried off, taking a moment to enjoy the softness

enveloping her. She wasn't avaricious. She didn't need designer things, or lust after certain makes. Her parents believed in saving and buying once because you bought well. It had been drummed into them as kids. She'd seen her parents make sacrifices and treat credit cards as the very devil. Gia wasn't that much of a purist; she happily used her credit card when the need arose but didn't like the guilt of not paying it off monthly. But it was a good lesson, she mused, taking her underwear from the heated rail. Yes, it was early September and no heat was needed, but hey, when in Rome and all.

The dress Gia had chosen was one of those clever little numbers. All discreet and slightly prudish until it went on. A deep rose, the length was just above the knee, not in any way risqué or daring, but the skirt of it was cut on the bias, and swirled around her legs as she walked. It kicked up a bit, in a flirty way. As the top part was snug to her torso, short sleeves but with a boat neck, she decided to forgo the bra. Ha! Let that be a lesson to you, Mr '*I wasn't aware there was only one bed*' Fitzgerald. See how you like these beauties hanging free. Slight exaggeration – there was no hanging in the breast department for her. They were small and perky and she was happy enough with what her Maker had given her.

She slipped into a pair of nude heels – the shop assistant had assured her they would make her legs look longer – and grabbed a wrap in a swirl of colours that included the pink of the dress. A dusting of rose lip-gloss and a toss of her hair and she was set.

Flynn stood in the main room, his back to her, hands shoved in pockets, looking out at the sea.

The view would have been enough for the enthusiastic reviews this host would no doubt receive from guests; even with the classy and stylish furnishings, nature still won the prize. The shift of blue on blue, the direction changes of the wind, the sails of some leisure boats whipping by, all created a painting by one of the French Impressionists.

Flynn turned at the clip of her heels and she stared, hoping her mouth wouldn't drop open. Still in jeans but with a fresh white shirt, open at the neck, and a navy linen jacket he looked so handsome her breath actually caught. She'd thought him fanciable before, obviously, since she'd spent hours drooling over his body, but with the new hairstyle, the new non-Flynn clothing, well, he was a sight. He pulled a hand from his pocket and glanced at his wristwatch.

"We better get moving, it's almost six."

She was peeved he didn't comment on her outfit. She was dressing for a part and needed the reassurance. Odd, that. She never needed reassurance when on the beat, or running into a building, weapon drawn, or chasing a suspect down a street. Those actions were second nature to her, dressing up wasn't. She didn't have an ounce of the famous Frankie Jones panache, but he could have at least said something.

Instead, he walked towards her, a crease between his eyebrows. "Isn't that a little . . . short?" He waved a hand towards the skirt of her dress.

Shit. She'd wanted a remark, just not this one. "Don't be any more of an asshole than you have to be, Fitz. It's just legs. Have you seen them before? Oh, wait. You have! Wrapped around your hips, I believe. Or had you forgotten?" There, that should work.

It didn't.

"I find I can remember both the look and the feel of your legs more perfectly than is comfortable. I also find myself irritated that other men may notice them this evening. If that makes me an asshole, so be it. Let's go."

He angled his hand to her lower back and ushered her from the room.

Outside, he locked the house and opened her car door. As she slid in, she knew she owed him a truth, even a little one, after that rather backhanded but rather panty-melting compliment.

"You look very handsome, and I remember exactly how you felt too."

He didn't look at her on the drive to the restaurant but, when she stole a glance at him, she wondered if he would grind his teeth to nothing his jaw was clenched so tightly.

She'd take it.

Chapter eighteen

The restaurant wasn't what Gia had expected. At least not the outside nor even the slightly rustic interior. It had a good reputation – the freshest fish and seafood – *obviously* – but she thought it would be more upmarket, chic and trendy. She said as much to Flynn as they took their seats.

"It's been a family-run establishment for over thirty years, I believe," he said, "and I have never heard a negative thing. Why don't you hold your review till after we eat?"

"The menu looks great but I'm trying to stay in character and not overeat. I'm supposed to be obsessive about my figure which is so far from my real life it's laughable. I could inhale the crab cakes for a starter but, if I do that, if anyone was watching they'd expect that would be it for my food intake. They have John Dory on the list here – I love that fish. My dad used to get it from the Citarella Market in the West Village. This is so not fair!" Gia couldn't help the edge of whine in her voice. Of all the blasted undercover work to get, she got the 'eat nothing at a famous seafood bar', kind. *Grrr*.

"I'll get the crab cakes, and you can sneak some. Get the John Dory, enjoy it. I'll have the turbot and we can share a dessert, if there is anything you fancy." He placed the folded menu back on the table and opened the wine list.

She watched him from beneath lowered lashes. Everything he did was so in control. So steady. So professional. She really wanted to rattle him, throw him off guard, make him falter. Was that mean? But she knew it would have to wait. A successful outcome for this job was way too necessary and important for her to screw it up on petty notions of flooring Flynn Fitzgerald. What would it take, to make him bend? She didn't want to break him, just test him.

She wanted him to feel as shaky in his feelings for her as she was for him. What it boiled down to was simple. She wanted him badly and it was a sore point that she might just be a sexy memory for him.

Aiming for sophisticated nonchalance, she let her gaze wander over the other diners and then out the window to the view of the Port. *There*. It looked like Miller *was* the man leaning on a bollard, again, this time talking to Kasper Menchen. Interesting. She waited till the waiter went back to the kitchen with their choices, Flynn, in character, having ordered for her as well as selecting the wine without including her. He was supposed to be a pushover when it came to his wife's demands, but a total micro-manager in everything else. Those traits would help them be excused for being extra particular in the details of the contract and, hopefully, if the bait had been set correctly, Miller and his crew would buy it.

"Menchen is chatting to our man," Gia said quietly as she sipped some water. "I imagine he'll let us eat, and drink, before he comes looking. Plus, he'd probably want a few more patrons here to camouflage the conversation. Do Irish people really not eat this early? There is hardly anyone here."

"When people go out to eat it's usually later, maybe from eight. Unless it is a theatre crowd looking for an early bird before curtain-up. I have no set time for dinner anymore. Like you, back in the States, I eat when the job allows."

Gia nodded. "Yeah, so true. When I was on the beat, we had a shift to cover and, unless something went down, a day could be planned and that included dinner or even breakfast. But since earning my detective shield, all food-planning bets are off the table."

"Does that mean you only date cops, as they get the strangeness of your life?" Flynn sat back, looking like it was a casual, nothing to see here, kind of question.

She wished her heart didn't pick up at the thought he might care.

She turned it back on him. "Do you only date co-workers? Is that even allowed?"

"I don't date on a regular basis. And you didn't answer my question."

"Why not? No one good enough for you? Or is it because of seniority? You might fancy a subordinate but can do nothing because of rules? That must suck." Before he could react and she could *so* tell he was ready with a response, she added, "It's easier for me. I can date whomever I choose." She didn't add that she hadn't dated, not really, since him. Since the wedding. Since she'd been pregnant. It was too scary.

But she'd had sex with one guy, a complete stranger, because she'd had to. She'd been terrified that she'd never trust her body again. She'd wondered what would happen if she fell for some guy and then froze at the exact wrong moment because, well, her body had failed her baby. *She* had failed her baby. So, she'd gone to a bar in a different town, on a weekend away by herself. She'd selected the most handsome of guys, an inked pool player with an amazing body. Chad or Brad or Tad, she didn't remember, it didn't matter. They'd had sex upstairs in her rented room and it had helped. She hadn't come, she didn't need that. But he had, and it proved she could allow a man enter her body without freezing, without her mind numbing to a place of loss and pain. He'd left, a kind guy who would, nevertheless, never be for her, and she took care of her own pleasure. Tad/Chad probably thought her bonkers because even though she was back on protection, she'd asked him to wear two condoms – to be extra sure.

No one else, at work or in her admittedly limited social life, appealed. Her mother, the ever-lovely Rosa, tried setting her up with 'nice Catholic boys' but to no avail. And everyone knew being brought up in a religion was no guarantee of niceness. Of decency. Look at her, for fuck's sake. A walking, talking bloody disaster of a Catholic.

"And do you? Date? Whomever you choose?" he asked, his clenched fists resting on the table, knuckles showing white.

"All the time," she lied airily. Was that a slight shoulder-slump on the mighty Flynn? Surely not. "Why? Does it bother you?"

"It's none of my business," he replied, removing those fists from view.

"Then why ask?" See? Look at her, continually improving her interrogation skills. Go, her! *Yay!*

Flynn was saved by the bell, or in this case the waiter, returning with a plate of crab cakes. Her stomach growled and she groaned. They smelled divine.

"Go on, try one," Flynn pushed the plate in her direction. "No one is paying any attention. Miller remains outside."

"But what if he has a minion in here, watching?" she almost moaned, her taste buds chomping at the bit.

He raised his eyebrow.

"Okay, that would be overkill. I'm convinced." She cut open one of the crisp cakes, took a forkful and swallowed. "Holy Mother, these are the bomb!"

Flynn's eyebrow went up again. "I assume that means they are palatable?"

"Oh, get over yourself with your fancy words. They are damn delicious. Here, try one." Unthinking, she forked up some more, held it up to his mouth, waiting for him to take a bite. Both eyebrows rose this time, and she rolled her eyes. "We're supposed to be married. Married couples feed each other all the time. Open!"

He opened. Chewed, swallowed. "They are indeed *the bomb*," he agreed laconically.

She grinned, delighted. "*Ha!* Bet you wanted to air-quote that!"

"I don't air-quote. You should know that about me."

"Oh, I do. I was messing with you. What else should I know? In case we are quizzed separately, like on *Mr and Mrs*?"

They shared the rest of the starter and then their mains, both beyond compare. He told her other things she should know: he liked hill walking, his favourite ice cream was praline, he had his suits made bespoke as he didn't have time to shop and always went to the same tailor – they merely differed in fabric weight and colour variant.

She'd laughed at this. "You mean several versions of grey and several versions of dark blue?"

"It's easier that way," he'd agreed and he wasn't wrong.

She almost missed her blues now that she was out of uniform. You never had to ponder wardrobe choices, or worry about what would match. Now, in mufti, she always also chose a sombre palette. Like he said, easier. But at least she added the odd dash of colour with a T-shirt in summer, a sweater in winter.

She found out that he loved his parents, Toby and his siblings, in that order. He didn't say as much but she read it, not so hidden between the lines, when the subject turned to all the comings and goings of his crazy family over the previous few years.

Gia listened, took mental notes, observed how his face changed, softened when he spoke. He loved Frankie, too. He cared for so many and had so many in his care. He liked to appear all nonchalant and unaffected but she could see so clearly it wasn't true. And from the snippets the women of his household had let slip, she gleaned that he, not their father Patrick, was the decision maker, the 'go to' person. The fixer. A bit like Nick, in her own family.

Maybe that's why they got on; they understood each other on a very base level. Protect and serve, though not just for the law.

He read a lot, including the classics and old mysteries. No romance though, but that wasn't unusual for most men. He didn't read true crime unless it was work-related, and he hated baths. Such odd little nuggets of information, such unusual glimpses into his life. She felt warmed by his openness, cherishing his confidences. They decided against dessert but thought to give the coffee a try when the man they assumed to be Miller approached the table. The restaurant had filled up while they'd been talking, so Miller's approach went largely unnoticed.

"Sit," Flynn said in an imperious tone. "Are we to assume you are Mr Gary Miller, baby finder to the rich and needy?"

The man flinched. "Keep yer fuckin' voice down, Yank. Do ye want all about to hear?" He pulled out a chair, the wood scraping on the stone floor. A waiter arrived and placed a pint of Guinness in front of the new guest. "It's on yeer bill," Miller said diffidently and took a deep drink.

Flynn looked down his nose at Miller, a fairly impressive feat, Gia decided. She did her best to look both mildly revolted by the man and grudgingly fascinated.

She propped her head in her hand, elbow on the table. "Well, sir, can you get us a baby or not?"

Miller rubbed a grubby hand across his mouth. "What's the hurry? Got some problem in the lady department, have yeh? Or is it his nibs, here? Shooting blanks, are yeh?" His head swivelled from one to the other.

Flynn's eyebrow was at its autocratic best. "There is absolutely nothing wrong with my sperm, thank you very much. However, my lady wife would prefer not to go through the process of childbirth herself and we heard from some close friends in Boston that you might be the gentleman to help. Are you? Or are we wasting our time?" He tossed his napkin down impatiently and reached for his wallet, as if ready to give up on the potential deal.

Miller waved him back. "Keep yer shirt on, fella. You're talking to the right man. I'm only a runner, so to speak, so I'll have to get details from ye and pass it up to me boss. If he says okay, then we can see if a deal can be made."

"Darling, don't let him fob you off with an excuse," Gia said. "Insist you meet the boss! You, sir, are being insulting. My husband and I will only speak with the person who can arrange for us to have a baby within the next few days. Time is money as you dealers regularly say, so get us what we want, in a timely fashion, and your boss will get the money." She sat back and waved her hand in Flynn's direction. "Give him our details, darling, and get this business moving. I find I am tiring and would like to get back to our house."

A document of sorts was produced from Miller's pocket, smoothed out and handed to Flynn to fill in. A biro was also produced, but Flynn, a man of considerable means, glared at the offending article and reached into his trouser pocket to provide a fountain pen. *Oh, nice touch*, Gia thought as her 'husband' perused the paper with the perfect amount of sneer.

"No," he said, tossing it back without signing. "This is ridiculous. It allows us no say in the infant. What if we don't like the look of it? I must insist we see the gestational mother before making any promises to purchase. If your boss doesn't like our terms, fine. We can go elsewhere. Here is my cell number . . ." He wrote briefly on the crumpled sheet. "Call when you and your boss have the information we want."

He stood and held out a hand to Gia. "Sweetheart," he said, "we shall depart." He helped her to her feet and ushered her forwards.

Without a backward glance to see how Miller was taking the turn of events, they approached the bar counter, paid the bill and left. Neither spoke, but Flynn made a point of wrapping his arm around her as if supporting a person in a state of upset.

She wished she didn't like it so much. She wished it wasn't pretend. She wished a lot of things and, trying to get her thoughts straight and back to the case, she desperately wished, *hoped,* they would get to meet whatever young woman was about to sell them her baby.

There is only one bed, he thought. He was accounted to be all kinds of smart, had an extremely enviable IQ, was a member of all sorts of smart-people clubs, was sought after for his insight and intelligence on a range of topics, many of which involved figuring things out, thinking latterly, *using his fucking brain.* One bed. One bedroom. How in the ever-living hell had he assumed two rooms would be available? The team knew they were pretend. Who had booked this? He was pretty sure he could make heads roll for this. And a house this size, suitable, it would appear, for entertaining should definitely have two bedrooms to offer. Why the hell hadn't the owner locked the small study down the hall if they'd wanted valuables under wraps? And then it struck him.

Mackenzie. Surely not. There was no way that taciturn bastard would have played matchmaker. Was there? He couldn't, of course, have asked for only one bedroom to be available, but most bloody likely knew it to be the case. Well, screw it, there was always the couch.

Flynn unlocked the door and Gia shot past him into the bedroom. It wasn't late, they had a couple of hours before they needed to face the *one bed* scenario and he eyed the grey couch with renewed interest as he sauntered to the drinks cabinet to select a nightcap.

"Here, we've some more work to do." Gia hurried into the room, her laptop tucked under her arm, her sexy dress a thing of the past. She wore sweats and a large grey Brooklyn PD T-shirt that pretty much enveloped her. She sat on the couch, cross-legged, her computer on her lap.

Alert to her vibe of enthusiasm, Flynn poured a second shot of the excellent whisky and brought her a glass, placing it next to her on a side table. Shrugging off his blazer, he folded it, placed it over the back of one of the armchairs and sat down next to her. She eye-rolled him and he smothered a grin.

"Get this," she said, flipping her gaze back to the screen. "Did you notice the tattoo on Miller's arm?"

Flynn closed his eyes briefly, thinking back. "Yes, some kind of animal, and a sword maybe? You were closer to that arm – what did you notice?"

She hummed a little to herself, her excitement catching. "Can you get your own laptop and look as well? I'll tell you what it's about when you get back."

He did as he was asked and returned, sitting down next to her. He unbuttoned his shirt sleeves and rolled them neatly to his elbows. He flipped open his screen and could swear he heard Gia mutter "Bloody typical" as she glanced at him and then back to her own screen. Women never ceased to baffle him, but he would soldier on.

"What am I looking for?" he asked, opening a search engine.

"Okay, so I know I've seen this tattoo before and I'm looking through my work records to see if it is where I think it is. Can you google Dutch tattoos of lions with swords on the sail of a ship? Yeah, I know it's odd, but if I'm right it ties Miller directly to the gang I dealt with out of Staten Island last fall. The lion is an ancient symbol of the Dutch, twelfth century maybe, and the sword was added by the time of Charles the Fifth. It was originally a symbol of bravery and courage but was annexed by a criminal gang about eight years ago. They used that symbol but set it into a ship's sail. One of the other classic tattoos from the Netherlands is of the typical Dutch sailing vessel. Both have been bastardised by this gang, supposedly showing their idea of bravery while they conquer the world. Yeah, crazy, I know," she said, giving him a look, "but go with me on this, please."

She went back to the screen, her fingers flying across

the keyboard as she opened file after file, cursed, typed some more, opened another one. She muttered along with her work, processing verbally, asking and answering her own questions.

He left her alone and began his own hunt. He closed the search engine and used special websites from Interpol and the FBI to dig deeper. There was silence, or rather her low mumblings, as they worked, side by side. She had the red nail polish on her toes and he shifted, uncomfortable in his jeans, as unbidden and unwelcome visions sprang to mind. *Out of the gutter,* he scolded himself and averted his eyes. Every so often he noticed she stole a look at him, or rather his forearms, as he worked the keyboard. Was she as fascinated by simple body parts as he was? They were in a shitload of trouble if that was the case because there was nothing simple about her body. It was a package of perfection to his mind. Small breasts that responded to his touch so majestically, nipples that stood to attention the instant they were touched. Her waist was narrow, her ribcage uneven. He remembered the left was larger than the right and she said she was born that way. He'd kissed every line of it that night, peppering her skin with licks and touches as eagerly as she'd explored him, telling her it was the most beautiful ribcage he'd ever had the luck to see. She'd pushed him away, laughing, but that soon died as he'd demonstrated his devotion to her body, again and again.

With a heavy sigh she glared at him. "Could you move? Take the chair or go put a blanket about your shoulders or something?

He studied her quizzically. "I'm fine here," he said.

"That's the trouble. You *are* fine. You're a complete frigging distraction. You and your long lean legs and broad shoulders and those fucking forearms. I can't concentrate worth a damn. *Move! Scram!*"

Chuckling, he rose and sat down in the armchair, one ankle crossed over his knee, balancing his laptop. He focused on his keyboard but spoke to her. "You are rather a distraction yourself. I wasn't sure how much longer I could resist the red toes, the smell of your perfume, see the gentle curve of where your neck meets your shoulder, and not take action."

"Wait, did you say my toes? Shit, Fitz, do you have a foot fetish? Cos I didn't sign up for that!"

He laughed. "No fetish, not that I'm averse to anyone else's joy, but they remind me of that night. The red dress you wore. It's hard not to go there, in my mind."

She grinned at him. "Look at us, all grown-up-adulting, discussing our desires and needs and working away at the same time. My guess is, if we are honest that there is still some lingering hotness factor between us, we can navigate those murky waters more easily."

"Lingering hotness? Your turn of phrase is rather apt. If we are being honest, I have to admit the lingering is a little untrue – it denotes small or unimportant or less. I find you as hot as ever, sitting there cross-legged in your sweats and T. How is that for honesty?"

She fanned herself theatrically. "*Ooooh!* You're good at that. Now, stop looking at me and work. We can face this little dilemma of ours when all this is over." She waved her hand expansively to include their work, and the room.

"Oh, we can, can we? Good to know." And damn if it wasn't. Would they explore this thing between them when the case was over? And other than enjoying some great sex, what would it achieve? When she left, because she would, he'd have to face that feeling of emptiness that had been gnawing at him since she'd flown back to NYC after Caro and Nick's wedding. He didn't like that reality one bit and, besides that, how could they sleep together with the pain of a lost baby between them. He had so many thoughts about it, so many concerns. So many what-ifs.

But now was not the time. Maybe it would never be the time.

"*Gotcha!*" Gia exclaimed and did a wiggly bum-dance on the couch. "Here," she angled her laptop towards him.

"This guy and his several accomplices were all at a building where I was on a stakeout for the baby-selling ring in the Bronx. This *is* Hoyt Jansen and take a look at his upper arm? *Bingo*. The same tattoo. All the guys had it."

Flynn leaned forward and studied the screen. "What happened to Jansen? My understanding is that although you got a couple of his crew, he escaped. Your boss wasn't sure the case was linked to ours, but this pretty much proves it. It also gives us new leads."

Gia frowned as she turned the screen back to face her. She looked paler and her skin had taken on a waxy sheen. Before he could speak, she said, "Yeah, Jansen got away. Word was he was giving up the baby-selling and moving on to diamonds, like Jackie Carroll said her big boss was. The Dutch connection and all. The research I was able to do on him shows he has lineage back to when the Dutch originally landed in what was then New Amsterdam. His family is wealthy, he has no need of the money."

"Maybe he has need of the thrill. Many a crime has been committed for less. I'll get in touch with some other colleagues I have in Amsterdam and have them look into Jansen's family there. See if there is a gem link. Are you okay? You look a little off."

"Aren't you the charmer? I'm fine. I probably ate too much. Could you please go to bed now so I can too? And before you go all knight errant on me, I *am* taking this couch."

Flynn rose to his feet, his laptop closed and put aside. "Absolutely not. I'll be perfectly fine here."

"No, you won't. I'm almost a foot smaller than you, and I won't take kindly to you playing the hero. You'll just be in shit humour tomorrow when you won't have slept and that will go worse for me. I'm doing myself a favour. Now, make yourself useful and bring out the spare blanket and pillow I left at the foot of the bed. Don't," she held up a hand, "just don't. If I was a guy, of the same stature, this conversation wouldn't even have taken place."

"I wouldn't have been pretending to be married to him, though, would I?"

"That won't wash. You might have – gay couples do find ways to get babies too, you know." She paused. "Though this gang, particularly the dealings that Jackie Carroll was involved with seemed a touch on the 'Holy Joe' side, so they probably wouldn't have taken a gay couple as clients. Moot point. When I come out of the bathroom, I expect bedding to be awaiting me out here."

On that, she marched out of the large living area, into the master bathroom and he heard the snick of a door lock.

His gut was torn. That famous instinct that propelled him down right path after right path was warring inside him. He waited a moment then followed her to the main bedroom, heard the sound of running water, ignored it as best he could, gathered up the pile of bedding as requested and returned to the couch. He knew he would be extremely uncomfortable on this couch and she would fit it perfectly. If she was male, he would definitely pull rank and take the bed as his due – he'd spent many an uncomfortable night on many an uncomfortable couch as he worked his way up. But he wanted her to be comfortable. He wanted to care for her, to tend to her.

And she'd hate it. They'd switch tomorrow, make it a fairer field. He shook out a flat sheet, tucked it under the seat and laid several blankets on top of it. They must have been in the chest at the end of the bed as he hadn't seen them earlier. His family had a chest just like that in their holiday home in Clifden. His mother called it a Hope Chest, originally for the trappings of a bridal trousseau. Did women have those anymore? He'd google that. He tossed two pillows against the couch arm and picked up his folded jacket and laptop.

When Gia returned to the room, wearing sleep shorts and a tank top, his mouth went dry. *Fuck.* Irrationally pissed at her, and at his instant reaction to her, he snarled, "You couldn't wait till I'd left the room, I suppose, before sauntering in wearing next to nothing?"

She tossed her short swing of glossy hair at him. "Oh, for fuck sake! These are my PJs. Get over yourself. If you think this is hot, you are more sex-starved than I am. *Out!*"

She pointed dramatically towards the bedroom door and, in spite of his hardening body, he couldn't help but grin at her reaction. This was the problem in a nutshell. He'd been snarling at her a moment earlier and now, as he headed obediently to the bedroom, he was grinning. She had him completely upended.

"Goodnight, wife!" he called over his shoulder. "I hope you don't fall off the couch. And if you do, remember it's your choice, not mine."

"Oh, fuck right off, Flynn Fitzgerald!"

But he could hear the smile.

Chapter nineteen

No one to blame but herself, wasn't the most comforting of thoughts. But she thought them anyway. Gia finally got up from the couch, the blankets falling to a tangled mess on the floor. It wasn't an uncomfortable place to sleep. Quite the opposite. The lack of mattress was not what was stopping her falling into a dreamless slumber. *Those frigging tattoos.* All she could see, every time she closed her eyes, was Hoyt Jansen, his big arm flexed as he pointed his gun at her, the lion-and-ship tattoo, undulating beneath his muscles. He was a big man, like a lot of the Dutch, blond, and, it had to be said, handsome. A smooth talker, a winning charm, he cajoled innocent and vulnerable women to offer him their babies in exchange for a chunk of cash.

Like the Dublin girls, they were mostly abandoned and living in hostels. Kicked out of home and either too late to have a termination, or unwilling, they were lured by the idea that their infants would be going to rich, well-educated parents. The offspring would have a great life, better than any they could provide. Sure, they could have gone the official adoption route, but Jansen promised his parents were handpicked, willing to pay large for the privilege of their little babes. The payoff from the Bronx gang was certainly more than the Irish gang paid out, but it was all relative.

As Gia paced the floor, the dark expanse of window capturing her image in a shadowy, eerie way, she tried to think clearly why Jansen would use Ireland instead of merely going to a different state when things got too close for him in NY. From discussions with the team before they headed to Donegal, she'd inferred that although abortion was now legal in Ireland it would take time for women to feel confident or secure enough to avail of it, what with everyone knowing everyone else's business. But it was happening. Not so many boat or plane rides to the UK. And yes, that was why the baby business was closing here, but why had it started?

Brigid had said there was a horrible history in Ireland of sending young pregnant girls to homes run by nuns where they worked till the baby was born and then, more often than not, they would never see the baby again. Like the home where Jackie Carrol had been born. Some were adopted out in Ireland and even more sent to rich families in the US. The desire for a white, Christian, healthy baby was gold dust then, as now, it seemed. Whatever the reasons, it was so wrong, so damaging to all concerned.

Gia rested her head against the cool glass, peering into total darkness and hoped they could meet the young woman lined up for them and maybe persuade her to . . . what? Keep it? If the girl was hoping for money, keeping her child wouldn't scratch that itch for her. And Gia, thankfully, hadn't ever known that desperation. She'd known a different kind of desperate, but not ever that, so what right had she to tell the mother-to-be what to do? A mile in my shoes was all very well but the law would still be broken and it was her job, hers and Flynn's to thwart the endeavour, no matter the outcome for the mother and child.

That sucked. Because maybe that mom had no other option? Gia hated playing Devil's Advocate, hated that two sides to every story was a real thing.

She closed her eyes against the night and the sadness and the pain of memories those blasted tattoos had brought back. A lion waving a sword, inserted into a sail. Not an awful vision in daylight, not even at night, but in her sleep it became a nightmare she dreaded. Until seeing Miller's, she'd blanked it out. Almost forgotten it was that image that used to wake her from her worst everything. The therapy had helped her replace it with a different image and it was now she realised she should give her head doc a bonus.

Maybe she should face it again, awake, not alone in the house, but alone right now. Safe. Secure, with no demons to launch a sneak attack. And Flynn there, in the background, should she need him. She sank to the floor, twisted so her back was to the glass on one wall but facing the sea from the other glass expanse.

She let the night in, she let the memories return. Her head back, her eyes closed, hands resting loosely over pulled-up knees, she remembered. Oh God, why did she think this was a good idea. The stillness of that gloomy October night, the chill in the air. She'd sat with her partner in an unmarked car, not unlike the crap-heap Flynn drove, and waited. They'd had a tip-off that things were on the move, that this night would involve the moving of several young pregnant women to a different location in order for them to deliver their babies. They'd heard a truck would come, the women would be transferred, and the old hanger where they'd been staying, in an abandoned airfield in Flushing, would be defunct. Their inside intel was solid. One of the girls was an undercover agent, pregnant herself, but totally up for the job. No one knew Gia's own condition. No one knew she was also carrying a baby. She barely had a bump, but cradled it tenderly every time she was alone. She'd already begun speaking to her infant, explaining her day-to-day tasks. She'd heard a baby liked the sound of your voice and she wanted her son or daughter to recognise its momma when it arrived.

The car was parked off the road in some scrub bushes but near enough to get a view of the old road leading to the hanger. Several jeeps and SUVs were parked outside and Gia and her partner, Kai, knew that the women inside had been there for over a week, were supposedly cared for by a medic and pre-natal nurse, were well fed and had cleaning and bathroom facilities. That, however, did not excuse Hoyt Jansen from organising this band of misfits and scared young women and coaxing and enticing them with a cash pay-out for the bounty from their bodies.

The dreary night wore on. Kai took out his sealed container of noodles and shrimp and began eating. Gia excused herself, opened the car door, raced into the bushes and returned her earlier lunch to the earth. Wiping her mouth on a wad of Kleenex she kept with her for these episodes, she straightened and returned to the vehicle. She didn't get in, though, simply leaned against the driver's door and watched the night. Kai eventually finished his food, tossed the closed (blessedly) container into the back and eased open his own door. They chatted, in a desultory fashion, taking the edge off the waiting. Kai's daughter's upcoming Fall Fest ball, his son's football game. It was easy. They were used to each other now. Trusted each other. But not with everything, obviously. In hindsight, she should have told him about her pregnancy. But hindsight is twenty-twenty for a reason. It has all the facts.

The bus came for the women a little after midnight. Gia and Kai crouched low behind their car, and Gia called for the back-up they knew was supposed to be on alert. They had made the decision that not all would be hiding their cars in the long grass, but would be cruising nearby in unmarked, waiting for the word.

The bus or, rather, it was more like a coach, pulled to a stop near the huge closed doors of the second hanger space on the lot. Amy, their woman on the inside, said there were at least eleven girls, some due imminently, some a month or so out. The youngest was fifteen, the

211

oldest, other than Amy who looked nothing like her twenty-eight years, was nineteen. Other than one Latina, who Amy did say looked the spit of Jenifer Lopez, so there was that, all the women were Caucasian. Some things never changed. Gia could never figure out, especially coming from a blended, albeit European, family, why the purists wanted white kids. Had they seen Irish pale, freckled, easily burned skin? She was happy with her skin colour, a creamy beige and loved when it darkened in the sun. No accounting for taste. Or history.

The trouble started when one of the women, a young stringy-haired blonde, fell to the ground just as they trooped out in single file to the waiting vehicle. Armed guards had appeared, parading around waving their weapons, and when Amy broke from the line and dashed to help the girl who was rolling in pain holding her belly, one of the guards hit her on the side of the head with his gun, and Amy fell to the ground. Gia saw red.

But she knew her job. She radioed in "officer down", and gave the details as the other women were marched on to the waiting bus.

"We need to get in there," Gia muttered low to Kai, who like her was creeping forward, weapon drawn. "Amy could be in real trouble. We can't let anything happen to her or her baby. Let's go."

The closer they got, the more they heard. Help was on its way, but how soon? It had been decided that the bus should be followed to its destination, so the whole crew, including doctors at the new site, could be taken into custody. Gia and a few other officers would search the then empty hanger and arrest any stragglers. It had seemed a simple plan. No one was to be hurt. Simple was best, right?

The blonde was writhing in obvious pain and Amy, brave officer that she was, crawled over to her, holding her own head where the gun had whacked her. A tall pale-haired man strode from the first building, brandishing another weapon, and shouting orders. He wore a white sleeveless vest and camouflage cargo pants. He was the Alpha, that was for sure. Several heads swung at his command, shoulders were straightened, guns raised. Gia and Kai couldn't hear the orders but two men broke rank and hurried to the two women prone on the ground. Amy was shouting something and the blonde was weeping amidst groans loud enough for them to hear. *Shit*, it seemed like she was in labour.

One of the men kicked her in the side and Amy howled, throwing herself in front of the other woman. That's when Gia snapped.

"I'm going in. Radio the others again. All hands. *Now!*"

"No," Kai said. "You can't! We have to wait!"

"And let Amy and her baby face the consequences? No fucking way."

And she'd hurried off down the short steep path to the open road leading to the compound area. As she began to run, the squad car peeled to a halt on the path behind her and two officers leapt out. She heard Kai yell at them to go with Gia and waiting for them to catch up was the hardest thing ever, but she did it. Together the three ran to the scene below, staying as quiet as possible till arriving at the yard area. Then they ran, pointing their guns and shouting, *"Police! Drop your weapons and hit the ground. Now!"*

It was a blur, in the end. As Gia sat in the cool architect-designed house in Donegal, remembering, forcing herself to remember, she began to shiver, despite the mild night. Hoyt Jansen, the alpha male in charge had turned and laughed, seeing one lone woman hurtle towards him, as the two other officers turned on his crew to protect the others being loaded into the bus.

Gia barrelled towards her fallen colleague, her own gun aimed at Jansen, where she saw with blinding clarity, the arm, lion tattoo to the fore, point directly at her co-worker.

"No!" she howled. *"You'll kill them both, you bastard!"*

And hearing her roar, he turned on her and fired. Once. She yelled at him as he took aim again, *'No, no, no, not*

213

the baby, please not my baby!' and he, laughing, fired again.

It was the second shot that did it.

He wasn't sure afterwards what alerted him to a mood-change in the house, but Flynn woke from his restless sleep with a suddenness that was shocking. He reared up from the bed, knowing only something was off. With enough sense to pull on sleep pants, he stepped quietly from his room. Experience taught him that charging in was a way to ensure things went to shit. He crept noiselessly down the short hall to the open-space living room. His gaze went immediately to the couch. Empty. Concern on the rise, he edged around the perimeter of the room, eyes darting about, checking for any security breaks. All seemed in order. Where was she?

He knew in his gut she wasn't in the bathroom. He wouldn't have awoken with such alacrity for that, and he trusted his instincts enough at this stage in his career to listen to a shift in the norm. It took a second for him to realise there was also a sound that was different. Pausing, he closed his eyes and paid attention. There. He focused and moved forward, saw the curled-up shaking figure hugging the glass.

Fuck. She was in a bad way and unaware of his presence. He needed to tread slowly. Speak softly. Advance with care. He did all three. Crouching before her, he placed one hand gently on the top of her head which was buried in hands resting on drawn up-knees. The sound was not keening exactly, just a low wail. Not loud enough to be instantly recognizable as pain but definitely not an okay noise to be emanating from anyone in the dead of the night. Shit, he didn't know what had brought this on, didn't know what to do about it, just knew he needed to hold her, needed to offer comfort and solace. Needed to do that more than he needed his next breath. He sat, wrapped his arms about her trembling shoulders and hauled her onto his lap.

"It's okay, sweet girl, I've got you. It's okay now, Gia, you're safe and I'll have you warm in no time. Take a deep breath, sweetheart, and let it out slow and easy. I have you. I have you." He spoke more words, gentle soft words of nothing and nonsense. He rubbed his hands slowly up and down her chilled arms and, as she burrowed into his chest, he felt her begin to relax, inch by steady inch.

He kept it up, his low chatter, knowing that whatever it was, a nightmare or a memory, would fade. They always faded. Some took longer than others, some stuck, like glue that had to be peeled back, eased off. She shifted on his thighs, settling more comfortably and wrapped her arms about his body, just above his waist. Her hands lay flat to his back and in minutes they were moving, sliding, stoking his skin, learning his muscles. It was bloody disconcerting but he knew it was a form of self-care, nothing more overt than that. She needed to feel another human, a body and warmth she could trust. And she could trust him with her life. He knew, in that moment, that he would take a bullet for her, in a nanosecond, no thought needed. And not because they both wore the uniform, so to speak. It was a scary thought, as he held her, realising how important she'd become to him. How she'd slipped in under his normally alert radar to nuzzle into his heart. To find his centre and belong there. While the feeling, in and of itself was strangely beautiful, the reality was terrifying. What was he to do with this? As her mouth found his bare chest and tasted, he jerked back from his almost dreamlike state of inertia.

"No, darling, you can't do that. You're just tired and emotional. You don't mean it. Here, turn around." He tried to twist her so she could slide to the floor. He didn't need her getting turned on, mixing up her fear with lust. He was turned on enough for both of them. If she made serious moves on him right now, he'd be fucking toast.

She didn't budge. "I do need you. I need you to show me you forgive me. That it's okay. I was doing my job. I

215

need you to love me, just a little, so I feel okay again. Please, Flynn, kiss me. Make love to me. I need you."

Fuck. *Fuck.* He wasn't made of iron. His body was responding rather heatedly to her wriggles on his thighs, as she rubbed her bottom against his length, pressing her soft yet firm flesh all along his now very hard cock.

"Gia, no. You have to stop." But he knew he sounded like the liar he was.

And then she looked up at him, eyes of amber like drenched pools, her stunning upper lip quivering slightly.

"Don't you want me back? You said we were hot together. I thought you meant it. Show me. I need to believe it. Please, Flynn."

Well, then.

He'd find a way to justify it later. He was good at that. He could write a report that recorded everything the brass wanted to read while skimming on the chances taken, the corners cut. The lives in the balance. He could rewrite history with the best of them. He would definitely be rewriting this tomorrow morning. He bent his head. The first taste of that lip was a gentle press, a featherlight touch. Her soft groan of need pierced through him and all gentleness was lost. That quickly, that desperately. He devoured. His tongue delved in, searching, giving, receiving and he was lost. Abandoning restraint, he kissed her the way she should always be kissed: passionately, honestly, like it would be her last. Like it would be his. Like it was her first, like it was his. A kiss to cherish, a kiss to remember. A kiss like no other.

They lost themselves. Changing angles, shifting positions, leaning into each other, caressing and stroking, using all of their bodies. In some part of Flynn's poorly functioning brain, he knew this kiss was momentous. A new road. A new way forward. No one could kiss like this and go back. His body was straining, urging him to take things further but he ignored it. This moment was as close to perfect as he had ever felt. Even their night of amazing sex hadn't been this otherworldly. This special. He felt like they were in a world of their own. And even as that thought filtered in, he remembered she was in a state of high anxiety.

He eased back. He slid his hand up into her hair and anchored her head. Lifting his mouth a fraction from hers, a mere breath so they could continue to breathe each other in, he said, "*Gia*," because he needed her name on his lips as much as he'd ever needed anything.

"*Flynn*," she gasped back. "God, I want you so much. I need you. Hold me. *Have me.*"

Have her? He was starting to believe he couldn't *not* have her. "You have to be sure. I know you're upset. I won't take advantage. We can stop right now, or just kiss. We don't have to do anything else." And he meant it. He also really hoped she'd override him.

She did. "No, Flynn, kisses are no longer enough. I want all of you. Every scrap of your skin, every inch of your bones, every ounce of your heart. I want it all."

Christ. She tilted his face to hers, looking straight into his eyes, hers burning with honest intent. Okay, then. She was sure. Groaning he lowered his mouth to her neck, her collar bone. Her nipples were hard against the skimpy fabric of her T-shirt and he tugged the strap off her shoulder even as he kissed her through the cotton. Rolling it down he feasted on her breasts and with a low moan she threw her head back and offered them more fully. She tasted like nectar. Like iced lemonade on a hot day. Like all things summer. And she was his. For tonight, anyway, and if he could persuade her, for a lot longer than that.

Turning she straddled him, her sleep shorts leaving very little to the imagination as the sides rolled up to where her thighs met her torso. A quick study, he slid one hand down along her body, briefly pausing on that quirky ribcage and on down, down and under the elastic waistband.

"I can take them off," she gasped, instinctively undulating her body against his erection.

"No need. Not now. No time. I have to touch you, to feel you." And when his fingers encountered her small nest of hair, he groaned. She was everything that was a woman, her scent, her touch, her skin, her sex. It was all beautiful, and so damn inviting. He slid his fingers down further, thanking the clothing god for making such stretchy fabric and muttered a sting of filthy words as he found her so wet and, fuck, so tight. Adjusting her so his hand fit better he slid two fingers inside to the sound of her harsh but needy gasps of encouragement. She began moving, using the friction and rhythm of his hand to relieve all her tension. He pressed the heel of his palm to her clit and used a circular motion to send her higher.

"Shit, Flynn, that feels so good, I'm so close, *please* don't stop." Her words were frantic, and sexy and wild and he wallowed in it. He was doing this to her. He was making her come apart. And no one but him would help put her back together.

"You're safe, darling. I have you, remember. All the way, have you." And when she shuddered and tightened about him and called out his name, he thought he'd never had a greater gift in his life.

Gia collapsed on him, panting, replete, exhausted. *Satisfied.* Her head was pressed against his chest so the thundering of his heart was like a drumbeat to her senses. That gave her pause. She needed to get him inside her. That gorgeous cock of his needed to find a home. She knew the perfect place.

"Hey," she said, dropping small kisses across his torso. She circled one of his nipples and tugged gently with her teeth. His hiss was most gratifying. "Hey, grab a condom, we need to finish this."

There was a sudden stillness to him that immediately unnerved her. Had she overstepped? "Flynn? What is it? Don't you want to? I'm pretty sure I can feel evidence to the contrary."

She tried to pull away, but his arms banded about her,

holding her in place. She felt a thistledown kiss land on her head and then his cheek rested there. What the hell? Had she read everything wrong? Got mixed signals? The signal currently pressing suggestively beneath her open legs was not lying, he was very definitely turned on, so what was the problem?

One of his hands began a soothing seductive journey up and down her back, the other held her head against his chest. She breathed him in, immeasurably comforted by him while still finding his scent incredibly intoxicating.

"I don't have condoms with me," he admitted quietly. "I never thought to bring one."

Gia was stunned. "But . . . but you're a man. You have sex, right? I mean I know you do. You had sex with me before. Every man I know carries condoms in his wallet. I usually do too. In fact, there may be one in my wash bag, I'll go get it." She tried to stir but he held her closer.

"No. I left mine behind deliberately. I was determined, I *am* determined not to have sex with you."

Miffed, she said smartly, "What do you call what we just did? Chit-chat? I call it sex."

He sighed. "I mean penetration. Intercourse. Fucking. Whatever the cool word of the day is. I know I would never not use a condom, so felt I was safe."

"From me?"

"From myself."

She was baffled. And yet, intrigued. "You said we shared hotness, though, and I can feel that wasn't a lie. So, explain. We are consenting adults, Flynn, it *is* allowed."

Flynn shifted a bit, easing his legs out straight, and settling her more comfortably. She could still feel his erection, that had not abated. So maybe there was still a chance she'd get lucky a second time. And he would too.

"After you lost the baby, I was . . . floundering. I didn't know what to do. How to help you. You refused my calls, didn't open my emails. You changed your phone. But I needed answers. I did some research." His voice was steady now, his heartbeat evening out.

Gia, on the other hand, felt a chill sneak up her body and her muscles tense. Research? On what? Her? Oh hell, this wasn't good.

Flynn continued, appearing to be unaware of her plight, his hand still stroking her back. "I discovered that one in five pregnancies ends in miscarriage, and that it is usually within the first trimester. I studied the reasons, or causes, I studied the figures of a likely repeat, I studied all the statistics. I know you are healthy, young, fit. So, I figured it was nothing from your side. And also, that sometimes, as my own doctor told me, there is no reason. It just happens. But I don't like *it just happens*. Then I began doing more research and discovered that studies from 2019 show that the man's sperm can sometimes be the cause, some DNA fragmentation. Or, basically, faulty sperm. You could have lost the baby because of me, Gia. I will never put you at risk like that again. Never!"

Oh fuck. Shit, shit and fuck it again, and all the curse words in the entire universe. What was she supposed to do with that? Sitting up quickly, she lied through her teeth.

"It *did* just happen, Flynn. The doctor said there was nothing wrong with me. You *cannot* blame yourself. I won't allow it. I'm sure your swimmers are strong little buggers. Are you never going to have sex again? You could always double up on the condoms and I'm on protection, if you still fancy me." She tried to make light of it, to brush it off. To take that stark hollowed look of his face. Had he been thinking that all this time? God, she was going to hell.

"There are lots of ways to have sex, as you so rightly said earlier. But am I ever going to take the chance of getting a woman pregnant again? No. I'm not. Not unless I'm in a committed relationship. So that I can be there for her if it happens again. If it is my fault. I've seen a doctor and he concluded my sperm is in full working order, but that could be a misdiagnose. So no, I'd prefer to be married, with my wife knowing my concerns, beforehand obviously, and we'd try for a baby on purpose. By choice."

The sudden silence and the equally sudden realisation seemed to hit them both at the same time. Gia stared at him in the dark, her eyes opening wide as she stated the very obvious fact that they had both inconveniently forgotten.

"But we *are* married."

Chapter twenty

He stayed quiet for the first half hour of the loop walk. Or at least didn't bring up the massive elephant that had not only been in the room this morning, but was lumbering along behind them even as they climbed steadily. Gia had resisted at first but on reflection, realised that going for a hike, in designer gear of course, could well be something their pretend married couple might do. He'd made French toast and bacon and she had stumbled into the kitchen when the smells of sizzling meat and coffee had alerted her to breakfast. Last night had been both beautiful and awful and they would talk about it, but away from the house, away from where she'd been dragged back into some kind of waking nightmare and he'd admitted to both desiring her and fearing sex. What a fool he was. He hadn't explained it well at all. The truth of his fear just spilled over. It wasn't supposed to have been like that, but here they were, hiking the Stroove loop on Inishowen pretending to be madly in love, waiting for their dream baby to fall into their laps.

Last night, after her dramatic reminder that of course wasn't remotely news to either of them, they'd been stunned into silence and to say any mood of lingering passion was well stamped out was being overly generous.

He'd sat her aside, stood, hauled her to her feet and with a curt, "We'll discuss this further tomorrow," he'd fled. He was not only a fool but a coward along with it. He doubted she slept any better than he, but here they were. Hiking. Swigging water like they knew hydration was a requirement, backpacks with snacks including nuts and chocolate. Fresh socks, in case. What pools of water they were expecting to be submerged in after the long dry spell was neither here nor there. They had the technology, as the saying went.

"Are we going to talk or are we going to *talk*?" Gia broke the last stretch of silence, having, good cop that she was, checked no one was within earshot. They'd passed, and been overtaken, by other walkers.

It was a glorious day, the sky a blue so pure it should be in paintings. A few high puffy clouds making it picture perfect. The sea, a precise reflection of the sky was broken only by the odd errant wave and gulls swooped and dipped, sea birds squawking as they dove and dipped before their eyes. A magical day, if, that was, you weren't dreading and avoiding a particular conversation. The 'we are still married and could indeed be having hot sex' conversation.

When Flynn had parked at the small car park heralding the beginning and end of the eight-and-a-half-kilometre walk, they had donned their backpacks and picked up their water bottles. Before Gia could stop him, he took her hand in his and began walking to the trail, saying, "Married, remember?" though whether he was referring to the real or the pretend version was not clear, even to himself.

He played tour guide. They stopped at various places along the route, and he pointed out specific sights and the obligatory flora and fauna. Flynn loved rural Ireland, in all its components. He'd been to every county at some stage and some held his heart more than others. Connemara, naturally, was his soul place as he and his family had been going there since he was a child. But Donegal and its variety of stunning coastline, glorious mountains, boglands and hills, its parks and small towns, its white sandy coves and hideaways, was a close second. There was a particular spot, about a half hour into the walk where on a clear day, like this day, Scotland was visible. Gia was so impressed he wished he could take the credit, but geography and weather, on this occasion, got the prize.

They rounded a bend and yet another jaw-dropping sight was before them. A steep cliff to the right, a vast expanse of sea on three sides, and a rocky, heather-filled climb to the south-west. They paused to breathe it in and Flynn couldn't stop his arm going about Gia as she leaned her back against his chest. It felt so right. So natural. So easy. She sighed and he knew in his bones she felt the same way. He let his eyes close, for the briefest of moments, to capture the feeling. To preserve it so he could uncover it, in the future, when he needed the essence of Gia to remind him that some things were almost painful, they were so perfect.

"Seeing Scotland has got me thinking," Gia said, as if they were continuing a conversation from before. "Can a decent-sized fishing vessel from Greencastle sail or motor to a Scottish port from here? Undetected? Would that be possible?"

Would it? Flynn did some quick calculations in his head, visualised the map of Scotland, focusing on the westerly side and allowed his brain to do some work. Smart though he was, he needed some help.

Stepping back from Gia and removing his arm, he pulled out his phone and began googling. When the results he needed loaded he showed them to her. She stepped close to him, their arms touching, heads bent over his phone. He pointed out a couple of possibilities and could feel his gut respond. She might be on to something. There was no trail of any of the local boats taking women across the Foyle to Derry, but what if they were taking them farther afield?

Shoving the phone back in his pocket he urged her forward. "We're about halfway, we can turn back or keep going, the length is equidistant. But we should get back and do some research, and I need to make calls to some secure sights and speak to my colleagues in Edinburgh. Thoughts?"

"Let's keep going. Why not? It's actually pretty spectacular and I'd hate to miss the other side. We'll get back either way. If you start on the phone with your contacts, I'll make some lunch and we can plot a realistic route with some maps. I saw a bunch at the house, not sure if they're local, but worth a look. And a big map spread out, rather than a smaller screen, might give us a better feel." She took his hand and dragged him forwards, for all the world like he was a reluctant hiking partner. He followed, allowing the pretence and followed it with a kiss. It was part of the act, he knew she'd understand that, but even so, the lightest of touches, mouth to mouth, was like a mini-buzz, a hiss of promise, a tease.

They walked on, hands held, focus to the front.

Gia took the wheel on their return, dropped Flynn at the top of the lane and drove on to Moville to pick up a few supplies. When she returned, he had a map spread out on the counter and a notebook open with several notations already made. His laptop was also fired up and the screen showed aerial views of what looked like a headland. She bustled about the kitchen putting together a couple of sandwiches and making coffee.

"Thank you, Joe," Flynn said into his phone and turned to take a plate of food from Gia as he hit the end-call button. "Thank you for this," he said, setting it on the counter and then lifting the grainy bread stuffed with ham, avocado, brie and tomatoes. "Looks very tasty."

"My pop is a champion sandwich-maker – he uses a specific mustard his dad used to use, one with green peppers and we always had homemade mayo, so while this is tasty, it's not, alas, a Sullivan special. Here," she poured him a coffee and propped herself against the counter. "What have you got so far?"

Flynn chewed, swallowed and nodded towards the map. "Your idea of a Scottish route is taking form. I spoke to some people who put me in touch with others and, well, you know how it works. Joe, my latest contact out of Campbeltown on the Firth of Clyde, has noted a medium-sized vessel pull in and out of their port, intermittently over the last several months but less in the last six weeks. The *Lady Dolores* is not a fishing boat currently, though it may have been in the past, based in its shape and style, and there is a lot of secrecy about the loading and unloading of cargo. Joe says no one cares, as while the fishing territories or rights are not being interfered with, everything else flies under the radar."

He stopped speaking to take another bite and his moan of pleasure was a dart of joy to Gia. She had never been one to 'feed her man' or anything close to it, so her irrational happiness at his obvious enjoyment baffled her even while it left her equally irritated with herself for feeling almost giddy. It was a fucking sandwich, not a boeuf en croute. She needed a dose of reality.

"Good. That's a start. But where would one go from there? It's not exactly a superhighway kind of place by the look of the terrain." She bent over the map, peering closely at the topography, her finger following the A83. "It would be a long ride – whether there were new mothers or pregnant women, it would be uncomfortable." She straightened to find Flynn looking quickly away from her. *Hah!* Yes, indeedy! These stretch leggings were an exorbitant price but the second she'd put them on and they'd fit like a soft warm glove, she'd thought they were worth it. They hugged in all the right places without being indecent. And best of all they made her ass look pretty damn phenomenal, even to her biased mind. By the slight flush of Flynn's face, he thought so too. Excellent. Money well spent, even if it was police-issue.

He cleared his throat. "*Um. Hmm.* This sandwich is delicious." He put it down. Picked it up. Took a bite. Put it back. Flynn Fitzgerald was flustered. He'd been caught peeping and he didn't like it.

Credit where due, Gia thought, he would never ogle. There wasn't a hint or a whisper of anything untoward, anything of a remotely sexual nature. Of all the women and men who worked alongside him in his station, she saw only respect. Some liking too. And definitely some fancying on the part of his colleagues, But nothing from him. His lady friends must be from outside the job. Maybe she'd quiz him. Embarrass him a little. That could be fun.

But for now, there was work. She poured more coffee and if she made sure to bend a little more than was needed, stretch across the counter more than absolutely necessary? She was only human.

Waiting for their dinner orders to arrive that evening in Kealys, they went over the possibilities. Added in the flight information from a small airfield local to the Scottish port and its schedules and connections to Schiphol in Amsterdam via Glasgow. Menchen had said his intel from there was that Irish babies were sold to international buyers right there in the centre of that Dutch city. They used to deal in diamonds and drugs, but babies, though a longer lead in time and a costly support system, fetched a great financial return. With the birth mothers being offered as little as five thousand US dollars and the prospective parents coughing up close to two hundred thousand and more, it was a lucrative business, though now, hopefully on the wane, at least in Ireland. Gia couldn't be sure about the Bronx; all she knew was the ring her team had been investigating was shut down and Hoyt Jansen had escaped. She was as sure as she could be, especially with the tattoo evidence, that one of his out-sourced gangs continued on through Ireland. Was he here too?

She hoped she was about to find out.

Selecting fish and chips and forgoing a starter, Gia and Flynn ate sparingly. If Miller didn't come back with a positive to meet the mother of 'their' baby, they might have to forge another plan. When Gia felt a hand press gently on her knee, she realised her leg had been jumping. Twitching. Not a good look for a smart lady from Connecticut. A lady of fashion and style would *never* twitch. "Thanks," she mouthed to Flynn and felt an enormous flood of peace invade her body. It wasn't a moment of weakness that he pointed out, he hadn't said anything, just helped her stay in character. Much like she had smoothed his hair back into cool Fitzgerald mode, not straightshooter Flynn, before they left the house. In the past, if her shortcomings, no matter how minor had been mentioned, by deed or word, she'd have been both mortified and furious. This? Nah. She was grateful they were a team, had each other's backs. Could she be maturing? Her brother Nick would get a kick out of that after all the teasing he'd given her over the years for her multitude of career changes.

Miller sidled in when they were sipping a digestive, loitering with intent, hoping for contact. "Wasn't sure yous would wait, but I wanted to let yous know yous can meet the mam tomorrow evening. I'll be waiting here after yeer supper to take yous. No funny business, no trying to make a different deal. The one we have stands. Right?" Without waiting for an answer, he scurried off and Gia and Flynn released matching breaths of relief. They had sauntered casually around the port before eating and there was no sign of the *Lady Dolores*. It had unnerved them, but now they were back on track.

Tossing a handful of bills on the table, Flynn stood and taking Gia's hand led her from the restaurant.

They did some more planning. Not that he'd ever admit it, but the old adage, fail to plan and you plan to fail, were words he tried to keep at the forefront of most of his dealings. Not that he was so rigid that he couldn't go off script.

228

Flynn knew, as much as anyone that sometimes you just had to go with the flow, take a leap of faith, improvise. Christ, he was a walking cliché this evening.

He was wound up inside and it was damn uncomfortable. He, who never let emotions get in the way, who kept a steady hand for all who needed him, was a wreck. From her smiles to her laughs, her quirks to her groans, everything about Gia charmed him. *Everything*. He enjoyed her brain as much as he enjoyed her body. He relished her challenges and her cheek as much as he wanted to hold her and keep her. Mush really. His brain had turned to mush. There had been a moment over dinner when she had turned that wide smile on him and he thought his chest would simply crack right open. It had been direct and honest, no hidden anything and he'd felt it to his marrow.

She'd headed to the bathroom moments before and hadn't returned. For the best. It was late, and though they'd shared another nightcap, they had only discussed work. Wearily, he switched off all but the side light next to the couch. She had point-blank refused to give it up and considering how determined she could be, he let it slide. They'd probably be out of here within a day or so, but he swore to himself she'd get the bed tomorrow.

He tapped on the closed bathroom door as he went by, called a low good night and headed to the main bedroom. There was a lone, dimmed light on, next to the dressing table, so he didn't bother with the overhead, and was unbuttoning his shirt when he felt her. He turned slowly to face the bed and there she was. Sitting, back to the headboard, knees pulled up, reading. He stepped back, bewildered. Had he got it wrong, the whole couch thing? And then he saw, though the sheet was covering her, for the most part she was naked. Or certainly topless.

Christ. This would not do. Bracing his arms on the wooden bed-end, he had to close his eyes as he said, "I'll take the couch. I must have misunderstood you. I apologise for invading your space." Straightening, he began to

rebutton his shirt, out of some ridiculous sense of decency –
he thought *what nonsense*, even as his fingers began to work.

"Stop," she said huskily. "Stop right now and take that
damn shirt off. All the way off. In fact, take everything off.
I want to see you."

Every muscle in his body tensed even as every emotion
soared. Every need he had for her released. "Christ, Gia.
No. I can't. *We* can't." Hands clenched to fists he stared
helplessly at her as she tossed aside her book, tossed aside
her coverings and tossed aside all her own misgivings.

"Yes, we can." And then she spoiled her daring with a
giggle – "I sound like a politician, right?"

Flynn groaned. That mixture of sexy, sinful and silly?
Fucking torture.

"We decided, Gia," he started but his throat dried up
and his heart came to a halt as she crawled towards him on
all fours. Naked. Completely naked.

He was done.

"Gia. Please. Think this through. I can't hurt you, I won't."

But she was having none of it. She crawled all the way
to the end of the bed, reached up as he stood immobile,
helpless before her.

"I want this off." She undid his buttons rapidly and had
his shirt peeling from his shoulders before his head caught
up with his galloping libido. Not to mention the erection
straining against his jeans. He caught her hands in his,
holding them away from his body. Trying to use the little
of his sense he had left. She took everything from him with
only one look, one word.

"Don't make this any harder than it already is." He
squeezed his eyes shut. Opened them, and was drowning
in hers, gazing right back at him. "Yes, you can smirk at
my turn of phrase and yes, I'm so fucking hard for you
right now I ache in places I didn't know existed. But we
can't do this. I won't take the chance of getting you with
child. Of putting you through possibly more tragedy and
grief. Don't ask this of me." His voice was raw, holding

back on so much more he wanted to say. To do. But he had to keep it together. He owed her this. He could still be the issue for the miscarriage and he wouldn't rely on her protection alone. He couldn't. What the hell was wrong with him? Why hadn't he swung by a chemist and bought some bloody condoms. "I'm sorry, Gia. You can't know how much."

A slow, secretive and seductive smile crept across her face, that divine upper lip curving upwards and oozing sex appeal.

"I bought condoms."

The phrase 'the world tilted on its axis' might seem simplistic, trite even, but right at that moment, Flynn Fitzgerald felt his world topple. And fall.

Releasing her hands, his eyes never leaving hers, he stripped his shirt from his body, kicked off his shoes and yanked down his jeans and boxers. Gia giggled at his unmanly display of haste and still watching, a huge grin now replacing the smile, she scooted back up the mattress and shoving her hand beneath the pillow, grabbed a string of foil packets and waggled them at him.

"Thank Christ and you for your forethought," was about as much as Flynn could manage before rounding the bed and throwing himself down beside her. Laughing she threw her arms about his shoulders and angled up for a kiss. Flynn wasted no time taking over and devouring her. He'd spent most of the day in a state of semi-arousal and the urge to kiss her and taste her was almost overwhelming. He forced himself to slow down, gentling a kiss that was already on fire. But even that didn't help. Gentle soft kisses with Angelica Sullivan were beyond mind-blowing. He could feel his skin tingle, his heart speed up, his cock harden even more.

And still he had to know. He had to hear the words.

"Are you sure? Absolutely sure?" It was a croak, a desperate plea, but it had to be asked.

In answer Gia twisted, flattened him on the bed and,

grabbing one of the condoms, began tearing it open with her teeth even as she scrambled up onto his thighs. "Yes," she said as she tossed the foil packet to one side. "Yes," she said as she unfurled the latex down over his length to the sound of some guttural utterings from Flynn. "Yes," she said as she edged her way forwards, lifted her body and slid him home. They gasped, moaned and sighed. The bloody relief was Flynn's first thought. *Finally*. Thank Christ, finally.

She leaned forwards, bracing herself on his chest, her hands pressed to his hard body, and she whispered, *"Yes."*

There was only one response to that. One order of business. Get Gia to fly and at long last, feel again what his body had been yearning for since the wedding. They both began to move, she using him to please herself, which not surprisingly made him ache in ecstasy, and he lifted his hips, pushing deeper and deeper inside her heat. She was panting, the tip of her tongue edging out, tempting and desirable and he couldn't wait. He reared up, took her mouth and banded his arms about her, possessing every inch of her. *"Yes,"* she hissed, this time not just assent but encouragement and he needed nothing else. She wrapped her legs about him like a koala clinging to its mother and the feel of her, plastered to his chest, riding him as if it was life and death, he could feel his own orgasm sneaking down his spine, curling, driving, begging for release. Using every ounce of control, he pulled his mouth from hers and dipped his head to her breasts. He took a hard nub into his mouth and sucked. Hard. *"Jesus!"* That's what he wanted to hear. Gia unravelling. For him. For herself. "I need this, Flynn, so fucking bad." Her voice was almost terse, and he knew she was on the edge, she needed more. So close. He angled his hand down between their bodies, found her swollen tip and pressed and circled at exactly the same time. His other hand reached up and taking a fistful of hair, tugged her head back, positioning her so her half-closed eyes latched to his.

232

"Take it, Gia, take everything you need." And pumping his hips faster, changing the angle slightly, he heard her startled "Oh!" as she flew apart. Her instinct was to collapse straight into his chest but he tugged her hair, just a little and her eyes widened.

"*No*," he ordered. "Ride this out, every last pulse, every last ripple. *Take it*, Gia."

Her head fell back then and her glorious throat moved as she moaned the sounds of release loud and clear.

Feeling her begin to fade, he gave two last hard thrusts, and joined her.

Chapter twenty-one

Gia stirred, shifted, turned to pull a sheet over her chilling body but found it being done for her. Flynn settled the sheet and blanket over her shoulders and rested back. He was lying on his side, one arm propping him up with his elbow bent and his head resting in his hand. He appeared to be wide awake.

"Are you creeping on me, weirdo?" She tried to sound cross, but he had a look of such utter tenderness on his face, she failed badly. She smiled, a small hesitant smile, because she *had* just woken to him staring down at her. And that was a little creepy, in anyone's book.

"Just admiring the view," he said and trailed a finger along her brows and down her cheek.

It barely touched her, yet every nerve-ending noticed. She blinked, unable to believe they were here, in the bed, together and it had been a huge success. Should she kick him out now? Now that she'd been satisfied? His finger kept moving, lightly, smoothly, along the slight tilt of her nose, across her upper lip, then her lower, and back to the upper. It tickled and she smacked her lips together to dislodge his touch. Not that it wasn't ultra-sexy to have this man's eyes track every move his finger made, but it was also a little unnerving. She wasn't used to such blatant scrutiny, such obvious devotion to her face. It was just a face.

She went with words, "You're quite the contrast, Mr Flynn Fitzgerald. I'm not sure anyone would believe me if I were to tell them you can look both dreamy *and* focused. It's a skill for your resumé, that's for sure." She was trying to keep things light, easy. She was leaving when this case was closed and she was already way too fond of the hours they spent together, the sparky mix of companionship and sheer lust.

"I find I don't give a single fuck what anyone thinks. *I* think you are beautiful."

It was said with such intensity, such truth, that she felt her eyes sting. That would never do. That would show way too much investment on her part.

"*Pish*," she said instead. If she could slap her own head, she would. No one said *Pish* when they received a compliment that perfect.

Flynn didn't seem to mind. He rolled and in one swift movement he had her trapped beneath his body, his arms propped on either side of her head, elbows flexed. He leaned down, his mouth pressing to hers, soft and sweet. Over and over. And each kiss was accompanied with the word "*Beautiful*".

Oh, holy God, she was finished. This was too much. Blinking rapidly lest the increasing liquid escape her eyes, she tried to enjoy this moment. Allow it in. Sink in it. It was hers, and dammit, it felt like *he* was hers. She reached up and stroked his chest, her hands skimming his nipples, smoothing down his ribcage, around his back, up over rippling muscles as he held himself above her, only their lower bodies in full contact. She could feel her breath start to hitch, her heart rate kick up. And she could definitely feel some serious heat between her thighs. Could she go again? Could he?

Why, yes, it seemed he could. He began to move, taking

his kisses lower, along her jaw, down her throat, edging along her collar bone to her shoulder and back. Then he began employing his tongue as he kissed and licked his way down her chest, slowly and steadfastly kissing and tasting first one breast then the other. She moaned as pleasure seeped through her, her hips starting to move in response to the ever-hardening presence of his. God, but he was good at this. And still he whispered, "*Beautiful*", over and over like a litany, a prayer.

Dangerous territory now, as he kissed across her ribs, down her stomach. She had scars. Many scars, a few way too recent to be ignored. Dangerous indeed. He was too smart not to notice, not to remember later, when they were collapsed and sated.

Abort, abort, her brain called – *more, more,* her body hissed in reply.

Fortunately, he had one goal in mind, a goal she could totally get behind. He kissed his way down, all the way down and kept going. *Yes,* oh thank God, *yes.*

As if he heard her silent plea, she could feel his smile against her swollen nub as he took it in his mouth, sucked, soothed. Adjusting his position, he brought one hand down and proceeded to slip and slide those magic fingers in and out as if they knew this path intimately. As if they'd drawn the map. It wasn't long, she was so eager, he was so determined to bring her to orgasm, that with only the merest hint of a shift on her part, and the mumbled sound of his continued, *beautiful* as his mouth did the sweetest, hottest, things between her thighs and she was crying out in a mingled version of disbelief and joy that it really did feel that good.

She'd barely time to catch her heaving breath when he reached behind her head, grabbed a condom, made short work of opening it and sheathing himself, and crawled back up her body to kiss her senseless. She could taste herself on his lips and it was strangely arousing. Strangely provocative. He nudged her knees apart and used his erection to slide along her creases and tantalise her sensitive skin all over again. And still he asked, "Yes?"

She gurgle-snorted. It might have been considered a laugh, but she was too hyped up on natural dopamine to care. "*Hell, yes,*" she avowed and wrapped her legs around his hips with as much enthusiasm her tired body would allow.

He slid in, held still. He was over her, weight on his elbows, hands framing her face. His mouth hovered over hers and, as he eased all the way in, he closed his eyes. "*Gia,*" he uttered, the sound almost reverent and when he opened his eyes, he captured her stare, held it, daring her to blink him away. She was mesmerised, enthralled, as she watched him feeling what his body was doing to her. No, scratch that, what *her* body was doing to him, and it was the most powerful feeling in the world. *She* was making him crazy with need, *she* was making him grunt as he moved, faster and faster, until she went with him, angling her hips to meet his, glorying in the sight of his clenched jaw, the slight sheen of sweat on his brow. As if unable to bear it, his eyes squeezed shut at exactly the same time as his mouth took hers with such possession she felt it in every part of her body. And then her tears did fall, slipping from the corners of her eyes in single lines. Tears of beauty and magic. Tears of want and loss. Tears of pure gorgeous satisfaction and release. How could it happen? How could she have another orgasm?

Flynn Fitzgerald, that was how. Flynn Fitzgerald and all his smarts and all his focus and all his mixed-in tenderness and surprises. And let's not forget, duelling magic fingers and tongue, tools of the trade, sure, but not every labourer was also an artisan *and* a genius.

She would have to send a thank-you note to Nick for being clever enough to hook up with Caro in the first place. She didn't have to say why, she could just say thanks.

Flynn dropped his head to her shoulder, inhaling her, kissing her sweetly and as she shifted beneath him, trying to get more comfortable, he rolled from her, hauled her into his arms and cradled her to his chest. "Get some sleep, darling." He kissed the top of her head, dragged up the tangled bed clothes covering them both, and closed his eyes.

She wondered, for a second about the used condom and then figured, that was his department. He'd dispose of it shortly, she supposed. Not her problem.

She yawned, closed her eyes and thought – *darling*.

He shouldn't have said it. It was too much, too soon. Flynn watched her as she slept, the early autumn sun peeping in through the fancy blinds. He wanted to touch her all over again. To have her again. He felt like a man possessed, like a demon who needs his next fix. This was crazy.

Before he did something utterly stupid, he slid from the bed, pulled on his jeans which had remained tossed on the floor. He shook his head. How far he'd fallen. He *never* left his clothes lying about. Anyone who knew him would not recognise the person he was fast becoming. A person who, if at all possible, would climb back into bed and make lazy love to the gorgeous woman still tucked up under the covers. He needed coffee and a stern talking to. He'd have to do that to himself, but he'd often given others a pep talk, a bit of encouragement and when needed, a reprimand. He was pretty sure he was in need of all three.

He switched on the kettle and found the cafetière and the ground coffee. He opened the fridge and discovered bacon still available so set about frying some. It was early, not yet seven, but they had a lot to do and a lot to plan. He busied himself in the kitchen and popped some bread in to toast while he whipped some eggs to make an omelette. There were mushrooms, peppers and cheese and as he prepared them, he realised he was humming. *Humming*. This was not a thing he did. He stopped and thought about it and came to the shattering conclusion that he was *happy*. Happy was for others. Flynn didn't do happy. It wasn't that he was miserable, far from it. He was, instead, content. He enjoyed his challenging job, he cared for his family, he spent the odd evening with some old friends, occasionally, it had to be said. But happy wasn't something he ever allowed himself to feel. It was too tenuous, too unstable. Happy was not to be trusted. Content let you live your life, do your job, be the one people could rely on. He'd seen so much unhappiness in his life on the job that he knew happiness to be a falsehood. He saw his siblings find their respective happy places, but all it proved was that it was obviously *not* for him.

He turned to the sink to wash his hands and with his back to the door, said, "Good morning."

"How did you know I was here? I have super ninja skills!" Warm arms circled his torso, coming to grasp each other around his middle. She snuggled there for a moment, his Gia, and he let the moment in. It wasn't enough. Turning, he took her face in his hands and leaned in for a kiss. Before their lips met, he saw her smile and thought, *yeah*, happy.

"My ninja skills outsmart yours. Perhaps I have ninja ears?" Flynn grinned down at her as he pulled back from the sweet kiss.

"Nah, I've checked your ears. They are regular ears. Which is just as well. Man-ears can be nasty." She reached up and swirled her finger around the rim of his, tugging on his earlobe. "You have lots of nice man parts," she said musingly. "Some are very nice indeed. And what's more, you know how to use them."

"A compliment from Ms Smart Mouth? I'm humbled."

"No, you're not. You know very well you had me in a complete puddle of orgasms a few hours ago. No need to be humble about that. But just to be sure, we should try again. What if you've used up all your skills or it was a fluke?"

Flynn laughed, liking her plan a lot. "Gia," he said, "why did you agree to have sex with me last night?"

"Why?" She blinked theatrically at him, all flashing lashes. "You swept me off my feet, Sir Knight."

He pulled all the way back and folded his arms, quirking his eyebrow at her. And he waited.

She skipped backwards and hoisted herself up on to the island, swinging her legs like a child. "Oh, all right, you master interrogator, you. I wanted to see if what happened at the wedding was a fluke." A slight tinge of pink bloomed on her cheeks. "It was pretty amazing, at least for me. And I've been practically celibate since, well, since, you know." He did know. She paused. Swallowed. "I wondered if I'd imagined how good it was between us, if my memory was making it out to be better than it was. If it would be as good with you again."

He pinned her with his gaze, not allowing her to drop her eyes from his. "And was it? As good?" What a stupid-ass question to ask! You should never ask a question you might not want to hear the answer to.

"No," she said. But she shifted slightly, a tiny squirm as if she wasn't finished. As if she was waiting for something else.

Was she embarrassed? Nevertheless, his heart sank. He'd heard that expression before, had never experienced it. Shit. He had not been expecting that. Last night had changed him. Altered his view on fundamentals he'd assumed were not for him.

"It was *so* much better," she whispered, her blush deepening. It took a second for her words to register. But only a second.

He moved, his mouth on hers before she could continue. His heart was racing, like he'd done a sprint at the end of his five-mile run. He pulled her forwards, her legs automatically wrapping about him, her skimpy top doing nothing to hide her peaked nipples as her breasts crushed to his chest. "*Gia,*" he moaned into her mouth, breathing her in. He lifted her, one hand going beneath her bottom, the other pressed to her back. Edging around the counter he stopped by the stove. "Switch it off," he grunted, his mouth on her neck. She dropped one arm from about his shoulders and stifling a laugh, did as she was asked.

"Breakfast can wait," he said, "I have a change of plan."

He carried her to the bedroom, dropped her to the bed and proceeded to demonstrate how much better again it could be.

"Skills, Fitzgerald, you have 'em in spades." Gia flopped back onto the bed, happy and satisfied. She threw her arms over her head and stretched deliciously. Every muscle had been put through a workout and she was more than okay with that.

"You're pretty talented in the skills department yourself, Angelica. I need a breather after that bout."

"Bout? Is that what you call awesome reciprocal oral sex? Huh. I guess that works too." She turned on her side, tucking the sheet about her chest. So far, so good. He hadn't mentioned her scar. How could she have been so cavalier about it? Stupid, stupid. And when he did refer to it, because he'd surely seen it, detective and all, she'd better have a damn good story at the ready. But then, as it turned out, she'd done her best to distract him in other ways. Turned out she was pretty fricking awesome at it too. She loved when he was distracted by her. He got this look in his eyes that was both fearsome and gentle, however the hell he managed it. Like he'd slay dragons for her but eat her up just as quickly. Either or, she was fine with.

"Come on, slugabed, time to get that delayed breakfast and some work done before we ditch the entire plan and try some more versions of our recent activities." Gia rolled, tangled in the soft fabric of the sheet but was caught around her waist and yanked back to a hard wall of chest.

"One more kiss," he begged and turned her so he could capture her lips.

Trouble was, though no trouble really, it was hard to just return a quick peck because Flynn didn't do quick. He took his earnest thoroughness to a whole new level. Each time they kissed she wondered would it feel the same, this time. It didn't. Maybe one day. They'd run together, become interchangeable, their kisses. But not yet. Not so far.

Sighing in mushy wonder, she broke the kiss and rested her forehead to his.

"You have to stop being so charming. I might become addicted."

"So, my evil plan is working?" Using one finger, he tipped her face up to his, his eyes going serious. "We *will* have a discussion on what happens next, you know that, right? When this case is over, when you return to Brooklyn, this doesn't have to end. We can figure something out."

Oh, you poor deluded man, she thought, her heart shrivelling a little, cracking in the most tender of areas. "We sure will," she said, "but now I need sustenance." She scrambled back. "Last to the kitchen makes the rest of the food. First there, makes the coffee." And she was off, shrieking as he chased after her down the hall, in mock anger. He was being playful. Fun. Not at all what she ever expected from the often taciturn or even plain stern, role he played. The difference was, she now knew which was the role and which was the real him. And damn if that wasn't the most tantalising of all.

He played dirty and passed her out as they rounded the corner into the kitchen so she let him brew the coffee and she relighted the stove. Rewhipping eggs was easy as he'd already prepped everything and soon a breakfast of champions was laid before them.

They ate and discussed the day and the evening ahead. Miller had texted and changed the plan to meet about five that afternoon, and he would take them to meet the expectant mother. They ran scenarios, looked over notes. At one stage they took a shower. It took considerably longer than expected. She'd gone to the bathroom to switch on the hot water and had just stepped under it when two large hands had taken hold of her hips and hot needy kisses began trailing down her back. Oh well, what was a girl to do? She'd never had shower sex before. It was something done in books or on films. Involved athletics and balance, not her best attributes. But here she was, propped up against the tiles, gasping and moaning like a woman on the edge of an orgasm, because within moments that was, indeed, who she was. Gia had a vague thought that she really should tell Flynn's sisters just how fit and strong and *fuck it*, sexy, he was. Maybe they wouldn't want to know but, shit, she felt like shouting it from the rooftops.

They made a late lunch, dressed in shockingly expensive casual clothes, and headed to the car. Gia wore jeans, the price of which could feed a family for a week, and a cotton red-and-white striped sweater. Flynn looked hot as hell in jeans, a grey Henley hanging loose and a navy cable sweater draped European style about his shoulders. She almost called for a recess, for more play time, he looked so fuckable, but shit in a snowstorm, they had work to do.

They drove to the beach at Kinnagoe Bay, down a tiny narrow winding road, and strolled hand in hand along its sandy length. There were cool rock formations and shallow pools that kids would love for netting. There was no one to see them in their married life role, yet they held hands anyway. The skin on his palm was slightly rough considering his mostly desk job and she wondered at that. Another conundrum that made up this unusual man. They sat on the rocks for a while, enjoying the breeze, the saltiness of it and the increasing freshness. Flynn checked his phone periodically as they were hoping Menchen would get in touch when there was a sighting of the *Lady Dolores*.

Gia found she liked the feel of Flynn's arm about her shoulders, the way his fingers caressed her arm in an absentminded fashion, as if he wasn't even aware he needed to touch her. She leaned her head against his shoulder and closed her eyes. Was this what was known as a moment of joy? A slice of heaven? It felt like something pretty special to her. Something to cherish. It was hard to swallow suddenly and she had to blink away threatened tears, which was stupid. Hadn't she just this minute been contemplating how happy she felt? There was no need for fucking tears, for an overabundance of unnecessary emotions.

This wouldn't last. She knew that as clearly as she knew her own name. She was privy to information Flynn didn't know. Information that would change his view of her forever. He'd find out and even if he didn't, she'd probably feel obliged to confess. Regardless, when that happened, however it happened, this little pretend marriage would end. And the divorce papers from their real marriage would finally get filed.

Because of the connection the Fitzgeralds had to Nick, there would be family events in the future, events and gatherings to which she would be invited. Looks like she'd have to be a very busy detective with zero time off when that occurred. She wanted to be a part of her new nephew or niece's life so she would have to make sure that happened in Rome, not Dublin. She sighed. Tried to shake herself from those unhelpful thoughts before she blurted out all manner of inconvenient truths.

"Are you okay? That was a deep sigh from one so slight." Flynn looked down at her, those aqua eyes full of concern. "Are you worried about the case? The mother? If she has the baby while we're there?"

"Yes," she lied, "all of that."

He tightened his arm, turning her so she angled into his chest. "I'll be right beside you. I admit I hope that doesn't happen. But if she does go into labour, there are bound to be professionals to assist. They have done this gig many times; they are equipped to handle it. I may have to absent myself for that part should it happen, not sure *I'm* equipped to handle that."

Gia laughed. The thought of Flynn watching a birthing mother and squirming in discomfort would be a sight to see. "Would you have wanted to attend our son's birth?" Oh, shit. Where had that unruly thought come from? She was so done visualising all things to do with her baby. It was a path she'd already trodden way too many times to be good for her mental health.

She became aware that Flynn wasn't answering. She pulled back, startled to see him blink rapidly and brush a hand over his eyes. "Apologies," he said, his voice raw. He cleared his throat. "That was unexpected. In all the times I scoured online for the best baby crib, the bedding, the clothes, I never once thought about him being actually born. I didn't let myself. But now, imagining you, with your belly full and rounded with our child, imagining being with you as the baby was born, it's . . . it's a lot. So yes, in answer to your question, nothing would keep me from watching our child being born. Nothing in the world."

He stood then, hauled her to him and hugged her so tight she thought she might not breathe ever again.

And it was the most beautiful heart-breaking feeling in the world.

The text came in as they were walking back along the beach, the atmosphere between them a bit awkward. Gia got that. Flynn wasn't a man to show emotion. He wouldn't let people in, wouldn't share much. Wouldn't encourage intimacy. But theirs was not just any relationship. It was built on sex, first and foremost, then on a sham marriage, then workplace colleagues and now? Now they were temporarily a couple, temporarily in a real/fake marriage and she didn't really know what to call it. They were lovers. They were kind of friends. Neither were the forever kind so it was hard to label what they were. It didn't matter anyway. Short term was the only part that was definite.

"*The Lady Dolores just docked*," Flynn read out. "We should head down there and be available for when Miller shows up. Don't want to keep him waiting. He could get spooked."

"Gotcha." Gia was all business. "I'll alert the Buncrana station and our contact in Moville as well as our own crew from Dublin. They drove up last night and are staying in an Airb&b in Cooley. I think that's a few minutes from Moville. They all need to be on alert. Just in case."

They got back into the car and Gia began her calls.

The pier at Greencastle was busy as the evening strollers took in the hustle and bustle of a working port. Some were there for the evening's catch, some just to experience the ambience. The accents, the calling back and forth, the jargon, and the craic were all part of the experience. Several older fishermen were mending nets in the time-honoured tradition and it all looked picturesque and peaceful. What lay beneath would tell a different story. After the solitude of Kinnagoe Bay, it felt busy, bustling almost.

They sat on a bench, legs crossed, grazing their phones like true bored socialites. Menchen strolled by, asked for a light for his cigarette and a hushed conversation ensued. The trawler had docked earlier, as he'd said via text, and very little had been seen since. A couple of crew, one male, one female, had disembarked, got into a vehicle parked down the street, were gone for about an hour and reboarded the vessel with several paper bags, printed with the name of a pharmacy in Moville.

"So, things may be moving for the mama," Gia said reflectively. "I wonder will Miller still let us see her?" Menchen shrugged, obviously as ignorant of a birthing mother as the rest of them.

"He's coming your way now," Menchen mumbled, barely moving his lips around a cigarette. Flynn had produced a lighter, which shouldn't have surprised Gia, but had. He was quite the regular Boy Scout. Always prepared.

Menchen moved on, Miller approached. "Do youse still want to do this? Meet the girl?"

"We do," Gia said imperiously. "I won't be accepting any child unless I can attest to the welfare of the mother beforehand. She could be a drug-addicted imbecile for all we know."

Flynn sighed, theatrically for him. "What my wife is trying to say is, no proof of parenthood, no payment. It's a business deal, therefore we need to see the goods. I don't much care what the baby looks like, they change all the time, I'm told. But the host, so to speak, should have good genes."

Miller looked askance at him. "Jesus, youse are quare folk, but sure follow me, and we'll see."

"I want to meet the person in charge," Flynn stated. "I won't be handing over any money unless I know there is a person at the top who is responsible and has a decent business acumen. I'm used to dealing with professional high-flyers, you understand, so this underhand behaviour is an anathema to me."

Gia had to stifle a snort. God, he could be such an asshole, this husband of hers. But damn if he wasn't playing it just right. They followed Miller across to a side pier and there she was, the *Lady Dolores*, moored alongside the quay. She was a traditional trawler, though on the large size, so could have been company owned rather than a one-man venture. Fresh paint had been applied recently and the decks were clear of any debris or other clutter. Miller indicated for them to precede him up the plank and Gia had the eeriest feeling she was in a pirate movie that would not end well. There might not be parrots and wooden legs, but the feeling as they walked along the deck was akin to a bad remake of *Peter Pan*. This was a boat that had been completely overhauled. A door to the wheelhouse was closed but the one next to it was opened by Miller as he stepped in front of them.

"No funny business, mind," he said. "Don't be asking personal questions of the lass – in any case she won't answer so it will be a waste of time. Watch your heads as you go down."

Gia peered down the narrow flight of stairs. Maybe they were called something different on a boat but she was clueless. At the bottom, a corridor opened up with several doors on either side. Much more spacious than it appeared from the outside.

"Stateroom one on the right, two on the left. That one is where you need to go. The galley is further ahead on the right and the head on the left. The next two doors on either side are bunk rooms and the room at the end is the main room, or eating and relaxing space."

"Where does the mother birth her child?" Gia asked, genuinely puzzled.

"In the cabin, where else?"

Where else indeed. A veritable water birth, it would seem, was the order of the day.

Flynn opened the door of the left-side room and ushered Gia inside to a scene straight out of their worst nightmare.

A young woman was bending over a bunk, one hand gripping the rail along the side, the other knuckling her lower back. The sound emanating from her was more terrifying that the dried streak of blood on her nightdress and the waxy ashen face that turned towards them as her pain eased.

What the ever-fucking hell?

Gia's eyes swept the room. An older woman, not unlike Jackie Carroll, sat in a chair, knitting. A younger man, in scrubs, was adjusting a face mask and peered at them, over the strip of paper.

"Not a convenient time," he said in broken English. "Please vacate."

Gia and Flynn stood, stunned, as the pregnant woman wailed and wailed while another contraction appeared to crawl through her body.

"How many minutes apart?" Flynn asked, all business.

"About a minute," the young man said, not sounding too sure.

"Right," Flynn said. "That's close." Setting aside his sweater, he rolled up the sleeves of his Henley. Walking to the wash basin, he began to scrub his hands.

Gia was mesmerised. "Eh, what the fuck are you doing?"

Flynn looked at her, his face a tad paler than before. "Looks like they might need some help here. And despite what we said earlier, we're going to help." And he tossed her gloves and a mask.

Chapter twenty-two

Like a lot of unusual situations, it is only in retrospect that you think of what should or could have been done differently. At the time Flynn did what came instinctively to him. He took charge and acted. It was obvious, very quickly, that the young male nurse was out of his depth. The older woman was a 'minder' she said, and knew nothing about giving birth.

"Where is the midwife or doctor?" Gia asked as she pulled on gloves and donned the mask.

"Midwife was in the process of helping another birther," the woman said, "so she sent Peter to lend a hand. He's in training."

"Where? Where is she helping the other woman? Here? On this boat?" Gia was ready to go in search, as another contraction caused the young mother-to-be to wail in agony.

The woman shook her head. "Nah, she's up at the house. Young Nell went into labour early like, and when we brought Shona down, she was grand. Not due for a few days and then this happened. She started squalling like a banshee."

Up at the house? That was interesting. From the way it was said Flynn suspected it was relatively close by but it was the first they'd heard of it. He'd get intel on that once they got this child delivered. "Can't you get the midwife here within the next few minutes? This lady appears to be in considerable distress." An understatement of the century. Flynn continued in his mid-Atlantic persona, doing his best to look appalled at the mess around him. He was a numbers man, he needed to remind himself, not a cop called to serve.

"She could be here in ten," the minder agreed, "but why would she? Peter's going to do the job, right, Pete? Or he loses the funding to finish his degree."

The Peter in question shrugged his shoulders. "Minder is not wrong. I must pay debt. But help would be good, for sure."

Flynn assessed the situation as best he knew how. Hands scrubbed, he put on gloves and walked around to crouch next to Shona. He took her hand in his to check her pulse.

"How many centimetres dilated?" he asked Peter without taking his eyes off the screwed-up face in front of him.

"She almost fully dilated last time I checked."

"Shona, look at me, that's right open your eyes. Good girl. You're doing splendidly. My name is Fitz and I'm going to help you meet your baby. Gia here is going to help too but the main work is up to you. Now, you're almost ready to push, so I need you to breathe as normally as you can for the next couple of minutes to reserve your strength. Okay?"

Shona managed a brisk nod, her pained blue eyes, huge in her pale face, latched onto his like a lifeline. The poor kid, he thought, she can't be more than eighteen and terrified.

"Gia, can you get some ice chips for Shona, she must be so thirsty." One look at Gia's face told him she needed a job or she might not manage to stay the course. "Don't worry, everyone, I've done this before." Flynn was aiming for confidence and reliability – his staples. He had, but years ago as a rookie when he'd come across a broken-down car and the woman in the last stages of labour. Fortunately, that mum had been a veteran, five youngsters hale and hearty at home. Her husband worked on an oil rig and this labour had started early. It had worked out, a baby girl, their third, came bellowing into the world with apparent ease.

This situation seemed a little more fraught.

It was about then that Flynn also realised Miller was missing in action. That did not bode well. He may have seen Flynn step into action, not the behaviour of spoiled rich boy Fitzgerald. Couldn't be helped. Shona could. Be helped, that was.

"Gia, change of plan – check on Miller. Find him and ask him to fetch a doctor in Greencastle village – there's bound to be one."

She frowned. "What about, you know, *our* baby?"

"We need to roll with this scenario, whatever the outcome, don't you think? Shona needs to get this baby out and it appears neither madam here or Peter are competently equipped."

Gia faltered, and it was his turn to frown.

"Problem?"

"I don't want us to lose the tag to the main guy," she hissed. "We have to get him, Flynn, you know that."

Flynn paused, seeing her frustration. "Try to get Miller first, hopefully he won't have seen too much here. If you can't find him, come right back. Shona may need you."

"I won't be much use to her," she muttered but, whipping off her mask and gloves, she headed out the door.

Flynn assessed Shona as best he could. She seemed to be losing concentration and focus. Not a good sign. He needed her as clearheaded as she could be for someone in this situation.

"*I need to push,*" Shona suddenly shouted, "*now!*"

Christ, Flynn hoped he was doing the right thing, but the one memory that was clearest in his mind was a word

251

of advice from the midwife partner of a garda colleague. "No one delivers the baby except the mother. Everyone else in the room is there as an assist only. *She* does the delivering, *her* body knows what to do, we just aid the process." Those words had actually made sense and Flynn was grateful for them now.

Bending, he eased Shona around to face him. "Listen to your body and listen carefully. You are the boss here. You're in charge. Your body expects what is about to happen, is ready for it. Let it bring your baby to you. Now, I'm going to help you hunker down so your baby is facing the best angle for its safe passage into the world."

He settled his hands under Shona's arms and helped her into the position so many millions of women used in natural childbirth. He'd seen it on TV. Not the most reputable of references, but hey, one works with what one has.

"Peter, grab those towels and the syringe thing, and be ready to help when I say."

He looked over his shoulder to the grey-faced individual panting with anxiety. Fucking great.

"Hey, you, grab me the towels!" he snapped at the older woman who had finally taken an interest in the proceedings. He turned back to Shona. "Look at me, but imagine your baby coming closer each time you push, okay? You can do this and your baby wants to meet you so badly. Now, the next time you feel it, push with all your might. Push!"

And over the next fifteen minutes, Shona did just that. She slammed it. She listened to her body and she listened to Flynn. Gia snuck back into the room as the baby's head emerged, as Flynn asked Shona to take a moment, while he slipped his hand under the tiny head, and eased his fingers about it to help it slide more easily.

"You are fantastic, Shona," he praised. "Almost there, your baby wants to meet you. One more big push, atta girl, go now, *push!*" and then it happened.

Within seconds a slippery slidey little infant landed in

Flynn's large hands and he flopped back on his heels in shock. *Christ*, they'd done it.

No, *Shona* had done it.

Gia materialised beside the new mother and wrapped a blanket about her shoulders. Peter finally grew a pair and he and Gia helped Shona up onto the bed. The baby was still attached to the cord and Flynn knew the placenta had to be delivered too. That had been a surprise when he'd assisted that mother of five back in the day. He'd been so ignorant of the proceedings. So unaware. He stood next to Shona as she was assisted against some pillows and laid the tiny baby on Shona's chest. Peter took over and helped the young mother finish the birthing process.

Tears streaming down her face, Shona looked adoringly at her new-born, then up at Flynn. "Thank you," she whispered, "thank you so much." More tears and hiccupping and kissing on her infant baby's head.

"Not at all, Shona. You and your baby did all the work."

Gia moved to stand beside Flynn, her arms wrapped around her body like a straitjacket.

"What is it?" she asked.

For a second he didn't understand. Then reality hit and he could feel a rush of cold air flood his body.

"A boy."

That feeling when you want to be sick? The cold shiver down your spine, the flush of heat on your face, the sensitive skin and that awful acid in your jaws? Gia had it all. She was going to throw up and there was little she could do. It was stupid of her not to expect this, but she'd not thought as far as being present at a birth. Of a tiny, perfect, little boy. She could feel her stomach heave and tried breathing through her nose, holding for a few seconds, then releasing. Looking about blindly for an exit strategy, she became aware that Flynn had moved aside, was standing by the sink and peeling off his gloves. She edged closer, to tell him about Miller and hopefully take her mind off what she was feeling inside.

He stood, his back to her, hands braced against the white porcelain. He raised them, must have realised they were trembling, because he clamped them back down, knuckles showing white. He was breathing long and slow, just like she'd been. She wasn't the only one feeling the aftermath so strongly. With a muttered oath he yanked off his paper apron and balling it flung it into a wastepaper basket.

"We should go," he said, gruffly. "Find Miller."

Gia swallowed, embarrassed by her own behaviour. considering he'd been the one right in the coalface.

"He's on deck. Waiting. Hates births, he says. Let's go up." She took his arm and steered him to the door. With a nod to Shona and her infant and Peter and a glare at the minder, they left the maternity ward, such as it was, and escaped for some much-needed air.

Miller was lounging at the side of the boat, smoking lazily. He didn't budge when they neared him, holding them in an intense stare.

"What was that all about?" he demanded. "Yous shouldn't have been there to see the wain being born. It's not right or proper."

Gia swore, covered it quickly with a cough. Right and proper? This from a man who took new-borns from their mothers' arms and sold them to the highest bidder. It would be laughable if it wasn't so tragic.

Thinking on her feet Gia fake-grinned from ear to ear. "Oh Mr Miller, it was splendid! We saw our son being born. My Fitzgerald was amazing," she turned giddily to Flynn, "Darling, you were *sooo* beyond amazing," then back to Miller, "You really should have seen him. So brave, so courageous. I couldn't look, not really, it was too icky, but also *incredible*." She began bouncing on her toes, "When can we take him, our son, home?" If Miller noticed the hitch in her words, the near hysteria, he mostly likely believed she was over-excited, like getting a new puppy.

Flynn reached for her hand, held it firm. Brought it to his chest. Kept it there.

"My wife exaggerates, as usual. It was nothing. A mere lucky chance that we arrived when we did. I took some medical classes as a student so knew what to expect." He waved his free arm in a gesture of dismissal and nonchalance. "Just happy my sweetheart gets what she wants."

Miller switched his gaze from one to the other, pondering, she imagined, on just how weird the couple before him were. He was not wrong. If Gary Miller had been in any way astute, he would have sensed the simmering angst rising from both of them. Fortunately, he was neither astute nor observant.

"Tomorrow," he said. "We usually give them a night with the mam, if it's wanted, and then gone the next day. We'll deliver the babby to your house by noon."

Gia pretended disappointment. "Oh, no. Fitz, darling, I want him now. Why can't I have him now?"

He patted her hand, still held firm on his chest. She could feel the steady, safe, *thump thump* of his heart beneath her palm. If he could do this, so could she. Flynn cleared his throat. "Well, that's not the kind of service I, we, expect. Hell, I just delivered that baby, we should be able to take him now. Why don't you go run it by your boss? I'll throw in a bonus, if we can take him home tonight."

Shit. She hoped they weren't taking any baby home tonight. What the hell would they do with it? *Him.* Flynn hadn't thought this through, surely.

Miller tossed his cigarette overboard and crossed his arms. "I'll ask, but don't be expecting anything. I'll go see him later and text the answer. I still have the number from before. Better leave now, hadn't yiz?"

Gia stamped her foot. Spoiled little madam that she was supposed to be. "This is not at all what we expected. Our friends told us you were professionals. In a professional operation, the customer always gets what they want." She turned to her husband. "Darling, you keep trying to persuade Mr Miller, here. I'll go down and check on our son."

She pulled back from Flynn, her hand feeling bereft at the loss of his touch, but she scampered off so as not to be stopped in her progress. She needed to get to talk to Shona alone, to find out what the young girl wanted.

Hurrying down the stairs and into the stateroom, Gia swallowed and swallowed again. She would not break down. Would. Not. *She* was a professional and knew how to get the job done.

Her luck was in. The minder and Peter had vacated the room, for whatever reason. She hoped tea and toast was on the way to Shona. She'd heard it was the food of nirvana when you'd just given birth. She stopped and stared at the Madonna and child visual before her, half lying in the bed. It was picture perfect and tears sprang all too readily to the surface. She blinked hard. Work to do. She walked quietly to the bed and reached out to place a hand gently on Shona's arm.

"Hey, I didn't want to disturb you but we need to talk," she began.

Instantly, Shona tightened her hold on her son. An unbearable moan slipped from her lips. "No," she whispered. "*Not yet.*"

It was all Gia needed to hear. The mothering instinct was strong in this one, young though she was herself. Gia decided to take a chance.

"Shona, listen to me. This is not what it seems and I need you to be totally honest with me, hard though that may be." She took Shona's hand in hers and rested both back on the baby blanket holding the infant. "Look at me, not him." Her words were quiet but strong.

Shona complied. "What? What do you want? I'm not ready. I'm not . . ." Tears formed, fell.

"*Shhh.* It's fine. It's okay. We're not here to take your baby. Or at least not the way you think. Answer me honestly now, put everything regarding money and your circumstances aside for just a minute. If you could, would

256

you want to keep this little boy?"

Shona bent her head, eyes falling to the head nestled at her breast. She blinked rapidly, trying to clear her eyes. "He's lovely, isn't he? A real little pet." She raised tormented eyes to Gia. "I want to be a mum to him more than anything, but I don't know how. I'm still in school. Me dad wanted to keep him but me mam says no. She says I won't be able to manage but I would, I swear I would. If I could just get her to see him, she'd love him. She's not a bad person, she's just worried for me. For me future."

Gia sighed. It was a tough one. "Do they know you're here? That you are giving him up?"

"No. Or not this way. I told them I'd have him adopted out, but they think it's via an agency. But me friend had hers took like this so I said, why not? Get a few bob to give to me mam, and to pay for college if I go." She sniffed. "But now, now I can't. I just can't."

The tears fell in earnest now and Gia could feel her own heart slice open a little farther.

"We'll figure it out. You do know, Shona, that what Miller and his crew are doing is illegal, don't you? It's against the law."

"But sure, how could it be? I'm signing the papers and all. There's a lawyer. They said it was all legal and everything. They *said*."

Her voice had risen with agitation and Gia felt like a heel for upsetting her. The baby began to fuss and Shona adjusted her hold on the wee one and offered a nipple.

"No. It isn't. They lied. Now, why don't you let me take a picture of you and this little guy and send it to your parents? I bet they'll be thrilled to see everything went well. And who knows, your mother may change her mind when she sees her fine grandson."

Shona frowned. "They have me phone at the house. It's in a locker for safe keeping. But I could give you Mam's number and you could send it, couldn't you?"

There it was again. Mention of the house. Obviously, a

place to keep the girls before they delivered. But where, and why now, on a trawler? Lots of questions. Very little time to get them answered. She whipped out her phone, angled it so she could get the new mother and baby in a classic pose and tapped. "Give me your mother's phone number," she said, quickly opening her text box and writing a message to the grandparents, asking them to phone Gia's number in about half an hour if they wanted an update on their daughter and grandson. Shona rattled it off and Gia hit send. One job done.

"Shona, Fitz and I are not here to buy your baby, or anyone's baby. We're from the police and want to shut down this illegal practice. But we need your help. Can you help us?"

As she spoke, as she told Shona a few more details, the young woman's face lost the little bit of colour it had. That wasn't good. Gia didn't want Shona to faint, and selfishly she couldn't afford the time it would take to revive her. She looked about, saw a bottle of water and handed it over. "Drink, you're most likely dehydrated. Now, where is the house where you were kept before being brought to the boat? And where is this boat supposed to be going? If we didn't take your baby. Where would he end up? Do you know?"

Shona drank some water and closing her eyes in exhaustion she told Gia a few snippets of information. With enough experience under her belt, Gia pressed play on her phone's record button and encouraged the girl to open up. Only a few moments went by before they heard voices getting louder, approaching along the short corridor.

"Remember, they don't know we're pretending about the baby so please don't give us away. I promise you we'll do everything we can to ensure you and your son stay together, okay? *Shh* now." The last words were cut off as the door burst open and Peter, the minder and another man came in.

Gia hadn't seen the man before, but there was something familiar about his size and stance. Had she seen him before? *Think, dammit!*

"*Out!*" snapped the minder. "Baby doesn't get handed over till the paper transaction is complete. Go. You'll hear from Miller when it's time. Out!" She flung her arm towards the door and brooking no arguments, hustled Gia out.

Relieved to be gone from the room, relieved to be leaving that poignant scene, Gia hurried up on deck to find Flynn waxing lyrical to a bored Miller.

"Oh darling, you're not droning on about your newest multi-million-dollar tech deal, are you? You know not everyone is as enthralled by this as you. Forgive him, Mr Miller, he does go on. Now," she turned lovingly to her husband, "I've chosen the name and need to get on to the boutique for the monogramming." She turned back to a stunned Miller. He may or may not have heard of monogramming but she wasn't waiting around to explain. "He *is* such a darling baby, isn't he? Oh, wait, you haven't seen him yet. Well, when you do, you'll see that Bradley Cooper Fitzgerald is exactly the right name for him. Come!" She took Flynn's arm and walked him down the gangplank chattering about letter styles for the baby's bed linen and towels. She glanced back over her shoulder and saw Miller scratch his head even as he lit another cigarette.

"Please tell me people don't actually monogram their baby's things or even their own anymore? That can't still be a society norm, surely?" Flynn opened the car door for her in case they were being watched, dropped a kiss on her lips, which she wished didn't give her butterflies, and eased her in.

"Don't know, don't care. Let's get out of here, I've loads to tell you."

Despite everything, despite the exhaustion and the emotion still simmering below the surface, Flynn couldn't help grinning. "Bradley Cooper? As in the actor? How could you?? Why not James Joyce or William Butler Yeats? Something with a little more finesse, perhaps?"

She jabbed him in the arm as he drove. "Hey, Bradly Cooper has finesse! Have you seen him in that movie with Lady Gaga? *A Star is Born?* He's finessing big time."

He glanced over at her. Still pale, still unsettled. He reached over, took the hand resting on her lap in his and linked their fingers. Keeping the tone light, he said "If you must go American, why not James Dean or even Gary Cooper if it's the Cooper part you like. The poor kid would be shortened to Brad and that's just abysmal."

"Brad Pitt's not too abysmal, I'll have you know. Many a fantasy has been woven around Mr Pitt."

Interesting piece of information. "Does he appear in yours?" He had to ask; it would have been rude not to.

"Wouldn't you like to know?" Her spirit was returning. So that was something. *Would* he like to know?

"We can discuss fantasies later if you like. But as we're home, I suggest we shower, have a drink, eat and work. Are you okay with that?"

"All of that, or at least the first three. But, yeah, we have to work. Dibs on the shower, you can pour drinks."

Flynn pulled the car to a stop, they got out and headed to the front door. It was a balmy evening and a drink on the outside terrace would be like a tonic. She'd probably forgotten there was more than one shower, but he was fine with waiting. With putting together a snack for her and getting some protein into a still fairly shocked body. He could do with some too, he supposed, as he pulled together crackers, cheese and salami. He poured two stiff whiskeys, added a couple of clinks of ice and wandered with the small repast out to the stone terrace surrounding the house. The sun was setting but on the far side of Inishowen, so not visible from their spot but the colours shimmered on the water nonetheless. He placed the food on the picnic table and took his drink across the gravel.

He leaned a hip against the low parapet edging the

lough and breathed in the still air. What a day. What a . . . his thoughts were interrupted and turned to a *what the fuck* when a skimpily clad Gia, hair wrapped in a towel, sleep shorts and tank top leaving nothing to the imagination, sauntered out. She grabbed her glass from the table and joined him by the water. It was the most natural thing in the world to enfold her in his arms. To hold her against his chest and close his eyes. To feel her warmth, her support, her acceptance. No one else would have understood how today's experience affected him.

She knew because she felt it too.

She stirred, shifting slightly in his arms and sipping on the drink carefully balanced in one hand. "You did good today, Flynn Fitzgerald. Real good."

He grunted. Speaking wasn't really an option when your throat felt too big for your neck.

He waited a beat, got it together and kissed the top of her head. "You did great too, Ms Sullivan."

"I bailed," she insisted quietly. "I couldn't watch. I'm sorry I let you down when you needed me." She looked up, her troubled eyes meeting his, a sad smile barely curving her lips.

"It was fine. I knew what to do. And you had to go back and figure things out with Shona, so I'd say we're square."

"Yeah, cos talking to a new momma and actually catching her baby as it slithers out of her body are totally the same thing!" She did a dramatic eyeroll and they both smiled.

Real smiles. Healing smiles.

Flynn pulled back and raised his glass to tip towards hers. "Here's to Bradly Cooper Fitzgerald. May he be as bad-ass as the Bradley part and as suave as the Cooper part."

They drank and Gia added with a chuckle "And as sexy as the Fitzgerald part. At least when he grows up."

They went and sat at the table, spread cheese and cold meat on crackers and tried to relax. Gia was about to inhale her fourth tasty ensemble when her phone beeped. She pulled it from her pocket and threw a worried glance Flynn's way. "It's Shona's mom."

She read the text. Frowned, read it again. "*Huh*, she wants to know who the hell *I* am, taking pictures of her daughter and grandson. What have I done with her Shona, she wants to know? That's a good sign, right? She wouldn't wonder if she didn't care, I'm assuming. I'll phone her. I think it's better I tell what's going on in person rather than in text. Don't worry," she said as Flynn was about to interrupt. "I'll keep it general. But she should get her ass up here to Donegal by morning if she wants to take mother *and* baby home."

"Tell the mother there is no guarantee we can hold on to her baby if she comes any later. We will, of course, find a way, but Shona needs her mum, now."

"On it." Gia got up from the table, strolled to the water's edge again and began dialling.

Flynn gathered their plates and glasses and headed inside. He put some water on to boil, thinking a bowl of pasta with the homemade pesto would be fine for their supper, and then he phoned Gabe to update him with the latest developments.

Chapter twenty-three

They tidied the kitchen after dinner, continuing the discussion from earlier. They were at an impasse. Gia had related to Flynn the information Shona had passed on. And he was irritated with himself for not having staked out Moville more thoroughly. Turned out that five young women (including Shona), all in the late stages of pregnancy, were hiding in plain sight in a Bed and Breakfast in Moville. They were brought there from all around the country. There were several Jackie Carroll type women recruiting vulnerable needy girls, mostly under twenty, mostly in dire financial straits, more often than not without family or boyfriend. They would lie low in the B&B, staying in during the day, going for walks along the seafront at night. They went for walks in twos, always dressed the same, like a uniform, so a casual onlooker wouldn't be aware there were ever more than two. Just two pregnant teens out for a stroll, their nightly constitutional. Nothing to see here.

The woman who ran the establishment was a sister to the minder and they were both childless and very strict, according to Shona. The minder used to be a nun and very definitely hated young women. Shona had confided that she and one of the other girls thought the nun sister was jealous because she'd never had any 'funny business' herself. She'd told them having their babies taken away was punishment for their evil behaviour.

One of the girls had experienced pains earlier that day so the doctor who stayed in the B&B remained with her. There was a possibility of complications but Shona didn't know what. Of course, Shona herself wasn't due for several more days so taking her to meet the prospective parents, Gia and Flynn, seemed like a non-event. But unfortunately for all concerned nature got in the way.

"Shona said, other than Peter, the minder, the sister and Miller there are several other men that come and go. Large men, she said. I met one this afternoon who seemed so familiar, but I can't place him. And get this, one of the men is almost definitely Hoyt Jansen, the Dutchman. Shona said he is large, blond and speaks in a foreign accent." Gia had been excited to pass on all Shona's information but it had been put on the back burner as they both had needed some downtime after the events of earlier. It's not every day one delivers a baby while the other pretends to want to buy it.

Now though, things were getting tough. Gia wanted to get the girls out tonight, sneak in with the car, bundle all four into the back and hide them in this house.

Flynn was against it. "No proper planning involved," he said.

"There doesn't need to be a plan! We go to the house, get the girls, leave. Simple."

"Gia, be reasonable. We can't saunter up to the front door of a B&B and demand the girls come with us. They are, as far as we know, there under their own volition."

"But it's still illegal," she countered.

"What they are about to do, yes."

Flynn sounded weary. He had every reason to be. Physically and emotionally. Maybe he was right. Maybe they should wait till the morning, round up the girls in daylight and then go get Shona from the boat. But what if

Miller had suspected something? What if they all scarpered tonight? What if Shona, understandably, gave the game away? So many fucking known unknowns. Enough to do her head in.

And then there was the other issue. Their future. Or lack of it. Flynn seemed to be under the impression that they could be together after the case was closed. That they could do long distance. It just about broke Gia's heart.

Could she get one more night? Her last? Would it be so bad if the girls remained at the house for one more night so she could have her last goodbye with Flynn. He didn't have to know what was going down, and the young mothers-in-waiting weren't expecting anyone. Gia knew, categorically, that once she met Jansen again the jig would be up. She doubted she would be able to contain her hatred, her anger. Either she would crack and kill him, going against the code of bring the suspect in for interrogation, and then she'd end up out of Flynn's reach because he'd never hang with a wrong cop. Never. Or Jansen would call her on her shit in front of Flynn and she'd end up out of Flynn's reach because, as just agreed, he'd never hang with a wrong cop, or in this particular scenario, a murderer. There was simply no way this was going to end with Gia Sullivan and Flynn Fitzgerald as an actual real couple. Divorce proceedings would be filed imminently and he'd walk away without ever looking back.

It was a truth universally known that a man in want of a wife wanted one he could trust. So that was her out of the running.

"I could be on board with waiting for tomorrow, if you were able to come up with a way to distract me. You know, take my mind off things." She hadn't known her voice could sound coy and sexy but, damn, just the thought of the things they could do to while away the hours was enough to make her insides tremble in anticipation.

Flynn folded the tea towel, *of course he did*, and leaned back against the counter, arms folded across his chest. Silly man, if he was trying to look stern, he was failing. He looked so fucking hot, with his sleeves turned back to his elbows, the fabric of his shirt stretched across his shoulders, the jeans showing off narrow hips and long, strong thighs.

"Distraction?" his voice was a growl, low and hungry.

Yeah, epic fail.

Decision made, no rescue mission tonight, Gia pushed away from the island where she'd been admiring the view of male in all its glory. She peeled off her top, a thrill running through her as she saw Flynn narrow his eyes and clench his jaw. His stance shifted as if he was suddenly uncomfortable. Good. She hoped he was about to be very uncomfortable – in a good way.

She reached him, leaned up to place a soft kiss right on his lips even as her hands got busy with his belt. He shifted, grunted and took her face in his hands to make it a real kiss. A one to remember kiss. Fortunately, Gia was a master multitasker and was experienced at concentrating on two things at once. To that end, she thoroughly participated in the deliciously sexy kiss while divesting Flynn of his jeans. Or at least sliding them down over his hips to his thighs. She broke the kiss, licked her lips, eased back and looked down.

Well, hello there. She licked her lips again, this time slowly, her eyes peeping up at a suddenly still, but rapidly breathing Flynn. She wasn't the only one who needed a distraction.

She slid to her knees, arms reaching around to hold his lower body close, right where she wanted it. "Gia," he groaned. "You don't have to do this."

"Correct," she smiled up at him, "but *God* do I want to!"

His hand tangled in her hair and she got busy. Now, this was a way to take your mind off the business of babies and selling and murderers.

He tasted divine. Slightly salty, slightly musky. All Flynn. She wasn't the most experienced in this type of sex play but it didn't appear to matter a jot. Her aim was to give pleasure. Based on the sounds, the grunts and the sexy whispers, along with the grip on her hair, she figured she was doing an A+ job. To her surprise she found herself getting wet, her core tightening and tightening with each stroke of her own tongue along his length, with each lick across the tip, each time she took him in completely. It was such a turn on, to have your lover utter curse words as an encouragement as you took him deep. So immensely satisfying. Perhaps she could . . .

"No, Gia," he hauled her up, mouth latched to hers as he kissed her hard and long. Finally, he broke away, his breathing erratic, swung her into his arms and strode, as much as he was able with jeans at almost half-mast, to the bedroom. He laid her on the covers, stepped back and kicked off his jeans. He did the man thing, one arm behind his head, hauling the shirt up and over. Very un-Flynn. Very sexy. Within seconds he was sheathed in a condom and lying over her, propped on his elbows. "Are you ready for this?" he growled. "Because I want you so hard right now, I need you with me every second. Every single second. I want you to feel every single touch, every single slide. I want you melting in desire before I'm even halfway done with you. I want *you*, Gia, melting for me."

Wow. Hard to deny that kind of demand. Gia tried to make light of his words in her own head, tried to pretend they didn't matter, it was just sex speaking. Just the need for release making him say utterly lovely things to her. Making her feel utterly wanted and desired. Needed. Loved. But Lord, it was hard not to *feel*. To believe, just for the moment, that what they had was real and lasting and *theirs*.

She closed her eyes to it. To the beauty of it as he moved within her, urging her on. Helping her find her place, her rhythm. He might try to be all masterful and Viking-like, and *shit* he was, but he couldn't deny his inherent thoughtfulness. He wasn't going to take without giving. She doubted he knew how to be that selfish. She came, fast and furious with a long delicious float back to earth. Her heart still racing she opened her eyes to his locked on hers. Oh. *Oh.* God, he was so fucking wonderful. So *him.*

"Are you with me?" he asked, breath catching.

"Hell, yeah," she managed, doing her best not to collapse in a puddle of love and lust and sorrow and pain. "Bring it." He took her at her word. She liked that, that he didn't second guess her words, her decisions. Her needs. He listened. Always.

When he finally dropped his forehead to hers, gasping, sweaty and, for the moment, replete, she welcomed such a feeling of profound peace that she thought she might possibly never ever experience it again. How was she supposed to live without this? That sizzle he, and only he brought to her skin, her belly, her heart? He was the drug and she needed to go cold turkey.

Tomorrow. Or the next day. Soon.

Flynn turned, reached for her and felt cool sheets. Not what he wanted or expected. He rolled over, sat up and peered at his phone. Close to four. Maybe she had a bad dream or the events of the day had simply caught up with her. He pulled on boxers and wandered to the living room, hoping not to find her in a puddle of pain, but completely there for her if she was. Nothing. She wasn't there. A hint of discomfort touched him and he went to the front door, opened it, peered out into darkness. No jeep. She'd gone and taken their mode of transport.

Seriously worried now, he strode back to the kitchen. She would have left him a note, or a text, but he hadn't seen a notification when he'd looked at the time. She wouldn't have been so irresponsible as to go off on her own, no way. No one on a case with a partner did that. It was protocol, never mind good manners.

Any note that starts with *'Don't be mad, but . . .'* was not going to be one he'd enjoy reading but he snatched it from beneath the fridge magnet and read it through.

Fuck. She'd gone on a reconnoitre of the house. He should have known her acquiescence earlier had been too easy, too quick. It seemed she *was* a renegade in some ways, though she wouldn't see it like that. She totally believed she was a team player, one of the crew. She was far from that. As a problem-solver and innovative thinker, she was definitely leader material. Not officially, but that was only a matter of time. Every day when they discussed work, went over the case, the background, he was astounded at her insight. He probably shouldn't be. She'd made detective so early in her career, it didn't take a rocket scientist to figure out how smart she was but science had never been his strong point.

He phoned Gabe who would have arrived in Moville a few hours ago and got lodgings. Flynn had suggested Mac and a couple of backup agents get to Donegal asap, using the air support unit, as it might be needed for transport within the next twenty-four hours.

Gabe answered on the first ring. He usually did. "Mackenzie." His quiet voice was as calm as ever. Always succinct, always reliable.

"I need you to come pick me up at the rental. I find myself without transport."

"Ah. Sullivan gone rogue?"

Flynn grunted. "Something like that. Get here." He disconnected and tried Gia's. Straight to voicemail. Texting was better anyway. No one on a stakeout needed a phone ringing at an inopportune moment. He hoped to Christ she was hunkered down in the car and not sneaking around the premises. She'd see his call and curse him to the devil, but this was on her.

He threw on jeans, T-shirt and jacket, grabbed his designer sneakers and with his gun strapped to the holster on his belt, he went to wait outside on the main road for Gabe.

The lights of Gabe's rental dipped in greeting and Flynn climbed in. "I know. I should have kept a better eye on her, you don't need to tell me."

Gabe shot him a glance. "You are not her keeper, Flynn. You are her colleague."

"Colleague? Is that meant to be a joke? Because we are so far beyond that, Mackenzie. And you know it."

"I do. I am glad you have finally acknowledged it."

Flynn sighed. "It's complicated."

A very un-Gabe Mackenzie snort was heard. "That's unique."

"Shut up and drive." A very un-Flynn Fitzgerald thing to say.

Flynn filled Mackenzie in on the case during the drive to Moville, adding to the earlier pieces of information, explaining about the women, the minder's sister, the extra men. They talked, and debated, the best, safest route out for the women and their unborn, and infants, as well as ensuring they caught Hoyt Jansen and Miller et al and put a stop to the baby-buying ring once and for all. An easy plan on paper or virtually, not so trouble-free in reality.

Especially when vulnerable people were at risk.

"Has Gia told you what happened in the New York case last year? How she was involved?" Gabe asked quietly as he slowed going through the small town before turning left for the seafront and the terraced house that was the B&B in question.

"Not in detail. Just that she was a part of the team on stakeout and that she was there when shit went down but Jansen and a couple of his men escaped. For that reason, she has an extra stake in this case, and I get that it feels personal."

"Anything else?"

Flynn glared at him as they quietly exited the car. "What are you not telling me?"

"Later. Can you see your car?" Gabe began a slow steady meander along the seafront path, his eyes scanning the row of houses facing the road. It was a Victorian terrace and well-kept with a certain amount of wealth visible in its presentation. And the vehicles parked outside.

"No. I don't see it. She probably parked away from here

270

for covert reasons though that has its own issues if you need a quick get-away. There, I see her, up ahead, across from the house with the B&B sign. Behind the post." He motioned with his head towards the second B&B sign hanging on a gate. This house appeared to have a side alley and thus possibly a side and back entrance. Good thinking on their part. Some criminals were smart. Others just had dumb luck. Until they didn't.

Gia spotted them. In fairness two large men sauntering along the road after four in the morning were kind of hard to camouflage – unless they chose to. In this case, Gia had to know he'd turn up and bring the cavalry. It's what she would have done.

"Nice to see you, Mac," Gia said, her voice low but easy.

"You too," he replied.

"Fitz," she nodded at him.

"Sully," he inclined his head.

"Yes," Gabe said dryly. "So much more than colleagues."

He took the glare Flynn sent him and the eye-roll that accompanied Gia's "What secrets have you been sharing with your buddy, Fitzgerald?"

Flynn managed to look affronted, or at least that was the expression he was going for. "Not a leg to stand on, Sullivan. What game are you playing?"

She straightened, all business. "I saw the man from earlier, the one I thought I remembered seeing before? He went in and out again, but didn't appear to have anything with him. They use a side entrance, along the alleyway, about halfway down. There is a door that appears to be unlocked as the guy didn't use a key or spend time with a code."

"Someone on the inside could have opened it for him," Flynn suggested.

"True, but he didn't speak. And at the time I was hunkered down in the front garden on this side of the alley and could hear the door open. Anyway. He is definitely one of the men who was in on the New York ring. Ironically seeing him in shadow gave him away; he has a distinct silhouette, one shoulder higher than the other and a short neck. I see him so vividly now." She took a breath as if the memory was not one to relish.

Gia pointed to a large window on the second floor. Its curtains were open and a figure was walking slowly back and forth, one hand at her lower back, the other resting on a very pregnant belly.

"In labour," Mackenzie noted. "See how she pauses, bends slightly? I'll time it until she does it again and we will see how far apart her contractions are." He looked at his watch, checking the time.

"Look at you, all baby magic," said Gia. "What with Flynn here catching Shona's baby and you doing papa watch, you're quite the gynae duo. Another career perhaps?"

Flynn couldn't help the low chuckle. Here they were, in a serious situation, with potentially serious repercussions and she made light of things. Teased them both as if it was their norm. Their thing. It was . . . nice.

"Right. Eh, no." He realised he'd lost track. "Not another career, thank you. This one is more than enough. Are you satisfied with your surveillance? Is anything clearer? Do you have a different plan?"

"Jeze, so many questions. I don't know, I haven't thought it through. And stop giving me that raised eyebrow disapproving look, there is nothing wrong with taking some time."

"Speaking of time," Mackenzie interrupted. "Her contractions are barely a minute apart. She is going to want to push pretty soon."

"What is it with you two? How do you know so much more than me about women's business? Never mind. The point is, why haven't they brought her to the trawler for delivery? That's where everything is set up, though why I don't know. Could it be they want the babies born at sea for passport reasons? I know Shona was there by chance but there was a delivery room set up and she said that's where it all happened."

"It might have something to do with international waters as babies born at sea then take their birth mother's nationality. However, these young women are Irish anyway, I assume, so that couldn't be the reason."

Gia kept an eye on the house as she pondered this. "Do we know anything about the doctor?" she asked Gabe, as Flynn had passed that information, from Shona, on earlier. "Could he be the issue?"

"Nail on the head, Sullivan. Dr Paul Cooney was struck off a couple of years ago for negligence. He is not supposed to be practising on the island of Ireland or indeed anywhere."

As they contemplated this from several angles, there was a bustle of activity in the upstairs room. Other bodies came and went from view. Moments later, an SUV pulled around the corner and the three detectives slid seamlessly from view.

Something was definitely changing inside.

Things happened pretty fast after that. The car eased down the side alley, braked, but didn't turn off the engine. Gia saw the back car door open. Two figures emerged from the house and got in. The pregnant woman and, she suspected, the minder's sister. Straight away another man entered the car, one they could only assume was the doctor, and the SUV departed. How many did that leave in the house? If, as Gia surmised, Shona still had the minder and Peter and perhaps Miller remain with her at the trawler, that might only leave three women and perhaps Jansen and maybe one other. Should they move in? Call for local backup? Their own guys, preferably. She turned to mention the possibility to her team only to find Gabe in conversation by phone with the Dublin team, now ensconced in the hotel down the road right here in Moville.

He nodded at her, obviously in tune with her thoughts. He finished the call, "They'll be here shortly, with at least one other vehicle to transport the women."

"The local police station can take them. I don't want them in the hotel, too easy a target in case we can't contain the situation," Flynn said, thinking ahead as usual.

Gia had to agree, uncomfortable though it might be, the women were better off under guard until the morning when they could be brought to their families, or at least, the possibility could be discussed.

"So, we go in? Get the women, arrest the others on site and then head to Greencastle and do the same?"

"We can't raid the trawler if the woman is still labouring." Flynn was adamant. "We watch the trawler when we finish here, when we know mother and infant are safe we go in, get Shona and Bradley, and, if I can get an ambulance here, get them and the other mother and baby to a hospital in Buncrana. I'll feel better that they are being looked after. We can put a guard on the door there if necessary, if the situation is still not resolved." He looked at both Gia and Gabe. "We need to remember, these women, or rather their offspring collectively, are worth upwards of a million dollars. Jansen is not going to want to give that up, especially if this is, as Jackie Carroll said, their last venture."

Gia felt a tremor run through her. They were so close, so close to getting Jansen. She really hoped she could get him alone, that she could call him the murdering bastard he was, that she could take him down. To that end, she turned to Mackenzie.

"I need protection. What have you got?"

She though she heard Flynn choke but somehow he managed to turn it into a cough. Ha, he thought he was so funny. But he knew what she meant, what she, as a member of their team needed. She gave him an elbow in the ribs and held out her hand for the gun Gabe was pulling from his pocket.

"This Walther P99 should suit," he said.

"I don't think this is necessary," Flynn began but Gia was having none of it.

"Give over, boss man, I know how to use these. Probably better than you. I'm a cop. Not a garda. I've been carrying since day one on the force. Stop with the protest."

"She's not wrong," was Mackenzie's helpful contribution

as he took out his own Sig Sauer, ensured the safety was on, and stuck it back in its holster.

Flynn looked steadily at Gia, a frown on his handsome lovely face. She could feel his concern, his care, rolling off him in waves. She was thankful, appreciative even, but it was unnecessary. She revelled for a few more seconds, knowing that soon, very soon now, things would be so over between them. Irrevocably ruined.

She knew it, she accepted it, but shit on a Sunday, she did not have to like it.

They made their plan, went over it, went over it again, waited for back-up, explained the plan one more time, nodded at each other in agreement, crossed the street in silence.

It was on.

Chapter twenty-four

One could call these criminals confident, negligent or plain stupid. Whatever word described them didn't matter to Flynn, he was just glad the side door remained unlocked.

"Idiots," Gia whispered as she slid past him. "I'm going through to open the front door for Lennon and Larkin. Meet you at the bottom of the stairs."

Flynn nodded, his attention on the kitchen area and beyond, scanning for anything out of the ordinary. All seemed fine. He followed Gia but with less speed, moving silently, listening for normal house sounds interspersed with movement. If their intel was correct, there were three women upstairs, hopefully alone or possibly with one guard. It should be a walk in the park, but Flynn was experienced enough to know never to take easy for granted. Never assume easy, never expect it. That way everyone stayed alert to the unexpected. The front door was opened quietly by Gia and the two back-up detectives from Dublin snuck in soundlessly. Mackenzie had headed around the back to check on access and egress there, and to foil any escape attempts should things go awry.

They went upstairs, all four of them, and spread out

across the landing and corridors going in opposite directions to find the women. They were well trained, this team, and Flynn didn't feel he had to in any way give instructions or directions. They'd all done similar 'raids' before, as part of ongoing investigations and this was another day at the office in that regard.

Gia showed her intent using hand signals to the others and slipped down the hallway and around a corner out of sight. Flynn felt a tug, a pang of anxiety as she went, and told himself he was being overly cautious. She was a damn fine cop and knew how to take care of herself. Sure, he'd noticed a few scars on her body, but everyone who worked in the field, including himself, got some war wound along the way. Most didn't want to discuss them so he'd stayed quiet though one in her belly had looked more recent. The only cops who bragged were those who had retired and were reminiscing about their glory days, often through a very blurred lens.

Within minutes three bewildered young women were being hustled down the hall, with only a handbag each, and Brigid Lennon began urging them down the stairs. Badges had been shown but the women were, naturally, unnerved. Flynn tried to look unassuming and non-threatening but was aware that didn't always work. Thank goodness for Larkin's easier manner. Of Gia there was no sign but he figured she must be checking the rest of the rooms.

He followed the posse down the carpeted stairway and out the now open front door. They were whispering amongst themselves but seemed resigned to being shunted about. Perhaps this was nothing new, just a different handful of people doing the shunting.

He was about to head back up the stairs when he heard a very definite sound, one no one wants to hear on a job. He pivoted and ran to the back of the house where Mackenzie had been on lookout. Flattening himself against the wall in the kitchen he peered through the glass in the back door. Nothing.

Not good.

Waiting was hard, but he knew that sometimes barging through a closed door caused more harm than waiting for the sounds; they could tell you something more. Waiting was not a fool's game, not everyone had the patience. Flynn did.

There. He heard it. A groan, followed by a grunt. Then some words in a language somewhat familiar to Flynn. It was Mackenzie, swearing in Scots Gaelic.

He was out the door in seconds, swung left, then right, weapon drawn. Gabe Mackenzie was doubled over, hands braced on his knees, breathing. And swearing. Next to him, on the ground, out cold was another man. One of Jansen's it was to be assumed.

Flynn strode over to Mackenzie, rested a hand on his shoulder. "Take it easy, Mac. You're almost there." Getting your breath back, your equilibrium in order, helped you return to yourself.

Slowly, Mackenzie stood, eased one shoulder, then the other. A low grunt and he turned to face Flynn.

"Ah," Flynn said, seeing the blood on Mac's sleeve. "How bad?"

"A scratch. You should see the other guy," he quipped.

Despite the seriousness of the situation, Flynn almost laughed. Ever since the big Scot had hooked up with Flynn's middle sister Ali, he was slowly lightening up. Allowing his humour to come through. He was more relaxed, more approachable. He was almost smiling as he approached, stepping over the fallen body. "He's wounded, not dead. He came around the side of the house, weapon already drawn so must have seen the activity in the house. He had his phone in his hand, looked like it was still lit up so I'm thinking someone heard what went down."

"Did you shoot him?"

"I did. I understand the report will be due asap, but it was necessary. He hit me before I hit him. Ballistics will prove it."

278

Even as Mackenzie was speaking, Flynn's brain was circling back to what he'd just heard. "*Gia*," he breathed and turned to race back into the kitchen just as a car roared to life at the front of the house. "*No!*" He spun and raced through the backyard onto the alley to see the lights of an SUV disappear around the corner towards the main street.

He skidded to a halt, frozen with fear. She was in the car, he knew it. He'd felt it earlier, the creeping anxiety and he'd ignored it. Whatever happened now, was his fault.

"Update?" Gabe's voice brought him back to the present.

"Jansen has Gia. The car just took off at speed. There's no way she's not with him. He'll need her as a hostage."

"You don't know that. Not for sure."

"I do," Flynn insisted.

He pulled out his phone, called for an ambulance for the downed man, and he and Gabe dashed around to the front of the house where the others were standing next to their vehicle.

"What the hell happened?" Brigid demanded. "We were settling the women in the back of the car when we heard two doors slam and an SUV peeled away from the alley. Where's Sully?" She looked about worriedly, caught Flynn's look and swore. "Shit, boss. I should have stayed with her."

"Your job was to get these women safely to the car. You did that. Sullivan is my responsibility. I'm going to do a quick scan of the upstairs where she must have encountered Jansen, then, depending on what we discover, I'm going after her."

He paused. Took a moment.

He looked at his three team members and gave orders. "Mac, get to a doctor, and get that seen to. No arguments. Lennon, you and Larkin get these women to the police station, put them under local guard and meet me in Greencastle as soon as. My guess is he'll try to head out to sea. If my calculations are correct, we have a small window of time due to low tide. Go. See you at the trawler. Mac, come when you're bandaged. I'm going to check the upstairs for clues. Then I'm off. I'll take my rental. Can you drive?" he asked his wounded colleague and friend.

Mackenzie gave him an incredulous stare. "Not worth an answer. Change of plan, my friend. You go after Gia, now. I'll take the upstairs before seeing to my arm. I'll video what, if anything, I find, and forward it to you. The others can get the local garda to house the women and follow you immediately. Go."

For once Flynn didn't mind being told what to do. Gabe Mackenzie was a super sleuth; he'd find a needle in the proverbial haystack so was exactly the right man for that job. Plus, he always carried a medical kit of his own salves and ointments in his car or bag so would most likely dodge the doc and come to the port directly.

Sometime rules had to be bent. Sometimes others saw more clearly. Flynn was more than fine with that.

He ran to his car, gunned the engine and drove to Greencastle as if his life depended on it. Because, he realised as he drove at record speed, it did.

When the shit hits the fan, when all plans go upside down, when you see your life flash before you, well, when all the fucking sayings keep tumbling through your head, you know you're in deep.

Gia knew. Deep as a bottomless pit.

She twisted and turned, trying to get, if not comfortable, at least less scrunched and cramped. The bastard had zip-tied her hands and feet when he caught her, stuffed a rag in her mouth so she couldn't call for assistance, and, adding insult to injury, threw her over his shoulder like a ragdoll before thundering down the stairs and out to his SUV. She wasn't sure if she was more furious with him or herself.

Strangely, she was unafraid. She was curious as to what would happen within the next short space of time but she had let a cold well of certainty sit in her belly. She was going to be hurt, physically, and in a weird way, she welcomed it.

She deserved it. After the reckless, careless way she had behaved with her unborn son, she deserved all the hurt. All the pain. All the extra heartbreak coming her way when she also lost the one man she could actually love. The man she *did* love, *all the way* love. God, she wished she didn't love him, she wished it was just sex, just animal lust and endorphins, just his talented fingers and tongue and supremely agile cock. But no. She had to bloody *like* him as well, care about him, find him so fucking interesting and smart and kind and thoughtful. *All the things.*

Thank God it was a short drive to the trawler. She heard Jansen speak on his phone to, she assumed, Miller, telling him things had changed, to dump the women, and get the boat ready to sail. Miller obviously disagreed because Jansen began to swear, almost lost control of the car and abruptly hung up. He continued to swear, in several languages, and he kept driving.

When the car skidded to a halt, the tang of sea air hit when he yanked open the door. She felt a moment's actual fear when he whipped out a knife and leaned towards her. All her thoughtful bravery and devil-may-care attitude vanished as she saw the blade flash in the moonlight. He slashed through the hard plastic tie at her ankles and hauled her to her feet, unceremoniously, through the rear door of the car.

"*Get on your feet!*" he barked but didn't wait for her to accomplish it. He grabbed her by the upper arm, pulling her along beside him, veered towards the trawler.

Miller appeared over the side, a worried expression on his craggy face.

"What's going on? I'm not dumping any women overboard," he announced. "That's not wot I signed up for."

"You fool, I didn't ask you to drown them. Just leave them here on the quayside, anywhere, I don't care, we have to go now. I have the airfield at Campbeltown on alert – we can be there in a few hours. Get moving."

281

"Well, that ain't going to work for you," Miller said. "For two reasons. The tide ain't ready and there's a fierce fog coming in. So, you're scuppered for now." He folded his brawny arms, a smug satisfied look on his face.

Interesting, thought Gia. Dissent in the ranks. Maybe Miller wasn't so bad.

"I don't care what you do with the women, get them off my boat!" Jansen was clearly losing his shit and it was hard not to be happy about that.

"I'm not dumping a woman in the throes of labour out on the quayside, sure that's barbaric," Miller announced even as he caught sight of Gia's face. "Wait, aren't you the Yank who wants the babby?" His puzzlement was real so it seemed like Jansen hadn't rung ahead with that news.

"She's police," Jansen snapped, fury evident in every fibre of his being. "And I've seen her before, so this time she comes with me." He practically threw Gia over the side of the boat onto the deck, while he climbed up the gangplank.

In the still of the dawn morning came the screams of a woman in the last stages of labour and Miller visibly whitened. "I'll be glad to get out of this business," he muttered. "I hate them screams."

Below deck things were no quieter. Gia was tossed into one of the side cabins, one with bunk beds and very little else. The door was slammed behind her and locked and she fell back onto the bed to catch the breath she hadn't realised she was holding. The noises from next door were harrowing. Somebody obviously hadn't attended to her Lamaze teacher, Gia mused grimly. But then, the young woman was probably scared, alone and in pain. She could scream the boat down for all Gia cared, in the grand scheme.

Time passed. Screams continued, interspersed with moans. Gia ignored it all, busy at work with her trusty penknife that had been hidden in her belt, a reliable method of subterfuge learnt from an old colleague. "*If you can't sock it, belt it,*" he'd said. Glad she'd taken those tips on board, she sawed through the stiff plastic. She wished for Jansen's bigger knife, but wishes were for sissies. She was a pro, she'd practised this, over and over, for fun, dammit. Reality, she was discovering was a little different. A tad more strained. Her hands a tad more sweaty. But the mechanics were the same and in no time she was free. She pulled the rag from her mouth, spat, swallowed, repeated. *Yuck*.

Scanning the small cabin, she looked for ways to escape. It seemed fairly hopeless but there was always a way. Always something to work with, you just had to trust your gut, and trust your knowledge. Working with her penknife and its array of additions, she quickly unscrewed the top bunk bedside rail. A hefty piece of metal was now hers to wield. It wasn't ideal but it *was* a weapon. She slipped the penknife in her pocket for easier access – she was taking no chance now. Her phone had been tossed when she'd first been jumped by Jansen and she presumed it was now found and help would, eventually, be on its way. She wasn't sure who had seen or heard their mad dash from the house, but she would be missed. Did she want Flynn riding to the rescue? That was a tough call. Could she admit to yes *and* no? Would that make her appear weak? So be it. As she waited, knowing things would get worse before they ended, she replayed the lead-up to being caught. She could kick herself, blame herself or just analyse it and learn from it. She chose the latter.

She'd gone down the right-hand side corridor, listening for anything different, off. At first there was nothing, then a small cough. She tapped on the door to the left, tried to open it, realised the key was in the keyhole, turned it and opening the door found a young woman lying on a single bed. She was heavily pregnant but managed to sit up, swinging her legs over the side.

Gia put a finger to her lips, showed her badge and, as the girl's eyes widened and her mouth opened, she darted forward to place a hand over the young woman's mouth.

"No," she whisper-hissed, "no sound. Grab your bag

and phone and go downstairs now. You're not in trouble but the man who has you here, is."

The bewildered and now thoroughly scared girl went to do as she was told.

At the door, Gia took her arm for a second, looked straight at her and asked, "Anyone else on this side of the house?" At the slight nod and a finger indicating further along the hall, Gia mouthed a thank-you and urged the girl towards the stairs, her finger pressed to her lips encouraging silence.

Should she have gone for one of the others? Waited for Flynn? Well, she hadn't.

The carpet was a good mask for her footfall, but for a second she wished she'd worn sneakers rather than her sturdy work boots. Moving as silently as possible, she thought she heard a phone ring, just once, a curt voice and then nothing. Or at least nothing major. A light from under a doorway at the end of the hall went out and then there was silence. She crept along, keeping to the wall, weapon drawn. She was alert to the dangers awaiting her, felt in her gut she was about to meet the bastard Hoyt Jansen for the second time in her life, and felt no fear. Only inevitability.

But what if one of the girls was in there with him, if he was, in fact, inside? Would Gia's entering put her at risk? Should she go for it anyway? She was reaching for the door handle when it flew open, so fast she was completely startled. A hand grabbed the gun from her hand, spun her around and whacked her on the side of her head with it, shoving her to the ground.

"Stupid bitch," growled Hoyt Jansen.

Pain, sharp and bright seared her as she tried to get to her feet. Lying on the floor would get her nowhere, she needed to be up and ready for fight or flight. The sound of that man's voice was almost more painful than the head wound.

He jerked her to her feet, yanked her hands behind her back and tied them. Within seconds he had her mouth stuffed with what she could only assume was an old T-shirt. He frisked her, pulling out her phone, tossing it with her badge on the ground and stamping on it. He pulled her around so she faced him and she could see the realisation dawn.

"If it isn't our brave little heroine from New York City! *Ha!* I'm so happy to see you, little mama. Oh wait, I heard that didn't work out for you."

He laughed then, more a sneer really, and Gia couldn't resist kicking out and walloping him in the shin. It wasn't much but she had to do something. How dare he laugh? *How fucking dare he*?

The result of course was that he toppled her to the bed, slapped her hard across the face, punched her right in the belly where her scar reminded her daily of her failure and reached for a tie for her feet. He took a look out the window and, although Gia had no idea what was now going on outside, if their plan was in full swing the girls would be heading to Brigid's car.

Jansen reached for her, tossed her over his shoulder and, since she was bound and gagged there really was little, at this time, she could do. A part of Gia wished either Flynn or Gabe would come charging out from the kitchen, crash into them, take Jansen out and it would all be over. But only a part. She had a reckoning coming with this man and she wanted to see it through. Before these last few days, she would have said, categorically, she'd nothing to lose. She didn't have a death wish, it wasn't that, but her main aim in life since the previous October was to end this man, one way or another. Now, though? Now she had feelings. Happy, sexy vibes, funny, thoughtful gestures, meaningful chats and heartfelt discussions. *Not* part of the plan.

Gia stretched and lunged, squatted and did side-bends. She needed to be ready, not stiff when her opportunity came. The screaming from the room next door had abated and suddenly into the silence came a different scream. A cry. A baby's cry. Oh, thank goodness, the baby was okay. Gia released a shaky breath. Now that the focus was off the birthing, she imagined Jansen would want everyone off, everyone but her. She imagined he would motor out to sea and dump her overboard. She really hoped he wouldn't knock her out first. Or worse. Probably not. Just a good old-fashioned accidental drowning would suit. He wouldn't know she was a champion swimmer. It might not save her life but it would give her a fighting chance. She'd take it.

Gia pressed her ear to the door, heard a series of noises that usually accompanied a group exiting. Doors, banging of cases, grunts – probably due to the narrow space. Was that Shona's voice? With little Bradley Cooper? God, she hoped they got off the boat to safety, hoped desperately that Shona's parents would come through. More noises and voices, that one definitely Miller hurrying them along.

Silence.

How soon would they toss out the new mother and baby? Not yet surely. How much time had passed? She cursed her choice to not wear a wristwatch like Flynn. She'd become so used to using her phone as a timepiece. Not her smartest decision. Would the others be on the way now? She prayed that she and Jansen would be on tide before Flynn arrived. He was likely to interfere. Or, as he would call it, take charge. Command his team.

Whatever. When the time came, Gia wanted dibs on Jansen.

Braking, easing the car to a stop, engine off, Flynn slid out and shut his car door quietly. He needed the silent approach. The one that came with surveillance, even if it was of the instant variety. He crouched and crept hurriedly along behind some parked cars, keeping the quay where the *Lady Dolores* was moored, in view. As he watched, several things happened at once. Miller threw open the door next to the wheelhouse and ushered a woman and baby out. From this distance he couldn't be sure, but assumed it was Shona and her son. The new mother, if she'd given birth, would not be moving so easily. He prodded them along the deck, up the steps and onto the gangplank.

When they reached the quayside, Shona turned to Miller and her voice carried on the still night air. "You can't leave us here, it's the middle of the night! What am I to do?"

Miller looked as lost in the situation as she. Obviously, this was a new direction and not the normal plan. Scratching his head, Miller mumbled something, but took out his phone and dialled. He gestured for Shona to park herself and her baggage, alive and otherwise, on a nearby bench. Could he be calling a taxi? Were they not going to find buyers for the babies? Flynn looked at his watch. Back-up should be here soon. They couldn't let Jansen get away with Gia. That was not an option.

Angling his head, he saw the SUV, confirming Gia's presence. He texted Menchen, ordering him to the site, asap. The more manpower they had, the better Gia's chances of getting out of this unhurt. Being excellent at compartmentalising, Flynn had refused to entertain the notion that this would not end well for Gia. He had thought only of the possibilities to get her to safety, not what might happen if that didn't occur.

It was too huge. Too *unthinkable*.

Maybe fifteen minutes later, the cabin door opened again, this time with several people bundling out. Another woman, leaning heavily on the young man, Peter. The minder carried a small bundle and Miller and another man, perhaps the doctor, brought up the rear. Jansen was getting rid of all his connections. He was leaving. Was he able to pilot the trawler or would he need Miller? The small party of individuals gathered on the quayside and Miller made some more calls. Flynn crept forwards, sneaking along so he could get to the aft of the trawler before anyone noticed him. He needed to board the vessel. He had to get to Gia. If the rest of the team came, they could mop up the motley crew standing about waiting. They all needed to be questioned. Some would definitely be detained and transported to Dublin. Larkin would see to a bus, he was good at strategic planning and thinking ahead with logistics. The women should be taken to a hospital, they and their infants, to get checked out.

All the while Flynn was planning for eventualities, he was creeping ever closer to the side of the trawler. Heaving himself up and over he landed with a soft thud on a coil of ropes. He sat, listened, readjusted his eyes. It was a different light from low down. Dawn was still over an hour away so he'd use this darkness to his advantage. With any luck there would only be three on board, which unless Gia was incapacitated, meant two to one.

Easy. The unknown was what kind of weaponry Jansen would use. And how desperate he was. Many a criminal allowed themselves to be taken, sure in the knowledge their lawyers would spring them within days, if not hours. People like Hoyt Jansen always had a string of legals at their beck and call, on a retainer, and ready to make the deals. Flynn checked his phone for messages and saw the team were two minutes out, switched his phone to vibrate, and taking out his weapon, moved.

He eased forwards, his tread light, unheard. He was practised at this – maybe not as *invisible* as Mackenzie, but he could hold his own in a contest. The activity on the quay gave him plenty of cover and he slipped unnoticed down the stairs to the narrow hallway. Peeping around he was in time to see Hoyt Jansen come out of the most forward cabin and walk determinedly towards Flynn, who immediately whipped back out of sight. Gia must be in one of the cabins closer to Flynn. Decision time. Jansen had his gun drawn but what his exact intentions were was anyone's guess. Going with years of experience rather than heart's desire, Flynn pulled back, letting the next scenario play out, knowing that Jansen would most likely want Gia up on deck where he could watch her while he

288

manoeuvred the trawler out of the port. If he bypassed Gia, left her locked in below deck, then Flynn could move in and get her, but this way he could watch and learn.

He backed away, up the stairs and lay in wait.

Chapter twenty-five

Can one's heart thunder along? Gia's was doing a fair imitation as she waited, metal bar raised, for Jansen, or whoever, to open the door. She'd felt her heart race before, several times recently as she lay wrapped around a certain detective, but this thundering? Surely it could be heard outside the cabin? She knew that was nonsense, but shit, her fear antennae were alive and kicking.

The door handle turned slowly. She readied herself, settled into her stance. Thanked the gods and her parents for making her play softball as a kid, as she wiggled her hips, the bar angled behind her right shoulder, hands gripped on the long part. The second the first male leg appeared in view, she left fly. The thwack was satisfying, as was the howl of pain. He tumbled into the room, tipping forward to the ground, when she promptly swung and whacked again, this time along his lower back. His gun went skidding across the cabin and Gia didn't waste time collecting it. She wanted out. With the second howl in her ears, she scarpered, metal bar in hand. She charged down the short passageway and up the stairs. She had almost made it to the top when she heard him bellow and charge up the stairs behind her. Fuck, she should have hit him again, on the head. *Stupid, stupid.*

She gained the deck and swung the door behind her but it slammed right back as he hurled the top half of his body through. She felt him reach for her ankle and kicked back, hitting him in the face. Another roar and she grinned, wide and delighted. Whatever happened now, she'd handle. She turned, couldn't help it, she had to see. To know it was him, the man who murdered her baby.

Hoyt Jansen reached up to feel his nose, found blood pumping freely and he swore. Loudly.

"You bitch cop, I should have killed you when I had the chance. *You are going down!*" He waved his gun with one hand, while holding his nose with the other and stumbled forwards. The hand over his nose hindered his sight and he banged against one of the sides of the boat. If it wasn't for the blood oozing through his fingers, she would have said he looked the same. Tall, blond, Nordic-looking. Handsome, in someone else's universe, not in hers.

"No, Jansen. *You're* going down. Maybe not by my hand in this moment, but the police will be here in minutes. You can't escape. You can't even move this fucker of a boat cos the tide is against you. It's over. You might as well give it up and face the music. Your lawyers will try to buy you a sweet deal but not after I give evidence to what you did. Amy barely made it, and that poor woman who you had the guys kick repeatedly? Her baby is happy and healthy, no thanks to you, but because of your kicks she can never have another."

"They won't get me on those grounds – it's your word against mine and you'll be dead so I'll get a slap on the wrist for my business dealings. Nothing more."

"You'll get murder, you bastard! I've written everything down. My lawyer has all the paperwork, my sworn testimony and my medical records." She stood in front of him now. Unafraid. She lightly swung the metal bar, pleased to feel its weight, its heft. Tired of all the guilt, all the trauma, all the secrets. She heard several cars squeal to a halt, doors opening, voices shouting. Back-up.

"The cops. They're here. You're done. Take your shot. I don't care. You killed my baby and you'll be done for murder under the Unborn Victims of Violence Act, whether you kill me or not." Somewhere behind her she heard a noise, a gasp, or a startle of some kind. Was there someone else here? There was no way she'd make it off this boat alive, then.

"I didn't kill your baby, cop. You did. What were you doing racing in front of a crew of armed mercenaries if not putting your life and your baby's at risk? That bullet may have been from my gun, but it was all your own stupid fault!"

How many times had those very words slithered through and through and through her brain, her heart? How many nights had she begged forgiveness from her tiny beautiful baby boy? How many times had she cried herself to sleep, knowing she was a charlatan? A person who pretended to protect and serve when she couldn't even protect her own?

"*I had to, you fuckwit!* I was doing my job, and you were about to kill two women and *their* babies! What the fuck was I supposed to do? Run? Like you? You fucking coward!" And she'd told herself those words many times too. *Doing her duty, protecting her colleague, serving the greater good.* They were cold, empty phrases and meant nothing. Absolutely nothing.

"*Hoyt Jansen, put down your weapon. This is the police. You are under arrest. Put. Down. Your. Weapon.*"

Gia wasn't sure whose voice was calling through the pre-dawn, and she didn't much care. She wanted this to be over. She turned her head at a slight sound close to her. She'd forgotten the other person.

It was a mistake to turn. A mistake to take her eyes off Jansen. A mistake, she thought, as she found herself grabbed, her trusty piece of metal knocked uselessly to the ground, held by the very man she wanted to see behind bars for the rest of his life. He hauled her back against his body, one arm banded her chest, the other up, his hand holding the gun to her temple. She could feel drops of his blood dripping, from his nose, onto her forehead. Gross. She hoped, in that otherworld kind of way, that he didn't have any infectious diseases. Would he go for death by cop? It was a thing, she knew, that got some crims out of all the trouble of a trial and certain prison life. But he wouldn't be that brainless surely? He was a pretty successful businessman, in his own warped way. She knew she was in shock, that her feeling of eerie calm was one way her body and mind were dealing with the heightened danger, the expected finale. She'd take it. It was better than shaking which she felt was the other very *very* close option.

And then she heard him.

"Let her go, Jansen. You're surrounded. You can walk away from this mess with the simple act of lowering your weapon."

Flynn spoke quietly, in a measured tone. It was Oscar-worthy. His best ever acting job. What he wanted to do? What he ached to do? Blow the man's brains out, grab Gia in his arms and hold her till forever ran out.

"Walk away? I don't think so. If I go, she goes with me. If you shoot me, she dies. She's a cop, so even if I don't die by your hand, I'll get life because I can't let her testify. She'll do me for murder. She has to go."

"She doesn't. I can persuade her not to testify." He shifted his gaze and looked at Gia directly for the first time. She was pale, so pale, but oddly still. Her eyes looked blank, not scared or anxious as they should be. As anyone's would. "Sullivan, are you okay?" He couldn't let concern leak into his voice. That would be handing Jansen her life on a plate.

"Peachy," she deadpanned.

Reeling inside from the new information, he nevertheless knew he had to give Jansen a way out, which meant playing the fool, however briefly. "Tell Mr Jansen the truth. He doesn't have to go down for murder. Explain about your miscarriage, Gia – that's what took the baby. Not a gunshot. Then everyone can still walk away from here tonight with a few charges that can be discussed."

Gia's eyes closed, briefly, but not before he saw the bleakness. The lack of concern. It was a terrifying glimpse and did more to make him deathly afraid than anything else that had happened so far.

"I can't," she whispered, opening her eyes and staring straight at him. "It was my fault. I shouldn't have done it. I shouldn't have tried to put another person's life above the baby's. But I did. *I did*."

Tears fell then and Flynn felt like his heart had been ripped in two. Twin streaks carved unearthly paths down her beautiful face. She didn't blink, just let them fall.

"No," he insisted. "We'll state it was a miscarriage." But even as her head tried to shake back and forth in spite of the gun bruising her temple, he now knew the cold hard truth. She'd never said it was a miscarriage. Not once. She *lost* the baby, she'd told him. Lost it. Not as it turned out, if the previous conversation he'd just witnessed was true, and why would she lie with a gun to her head, had it torn from her body by the bastard holding the weapon. Once again, Flynn Fitzgerald, Ace Detective, had made a grievous, erroneous assumption.

A chill, an icy breeze like one felt on a winter's day in the Arctic, slid through him. He felt his pulse slow and everything in his body experience a lull. A pause. It was what he'd trained it to do in moments of sheer blinding fury. So that he wouldn't lose control. Behave in a way unfitting.

Well, fuck that.

"Gia, when I say drop, you let your body fall and I'm taking this guy out. Got it?" If he could distract Jansen by talking to Gia, even if he was asking the impossible, he might get the chance to hit him.

Jansen sneered. "You can't discuss this with me standing here! I'm holding her, idiot! I can hear you, you stupid –"

Then, as if prearranged, Gia acted. She whipped a penknife from the front pocket of her hoodie, flipped it open within a nanosecond and drove it forcefully backwards into Jansen's thigh. With a howl Jansen loosened his hold just enough for Gia to yank herself away and *then* she dropped. She heard the shot as she scrambled away, scooting on her bum. Jansen was down, howling, clutching his shoulder with one hand, and his thigh with the other, his gun skidding along the wooden deck,

"*Why didn't you kill him?*" she screamed. "*Or at least let me do it!*"

"Too easy," Flynn said and holstered his weapon.

Mackenzie and Lennon rushed onto the deck. Mac went straight to Flynn while Lennon went to Gia, checked her briefly, and then bent and gathered up Jansen's weapon, securing it.

Jansen, meanwhile, continued to howl.

Mackenzie took one look at Flynn and obviously feeling now was not the time for a chat, turned towards the others. Brigid was helping an exhausted Gia to her feet and Flynn could only stare.

His life had turned on a dime. Instantly. Everything he'd believed about Gia Sullivan was untrue. She'd lied, by omission, but in a massive way. A huge probably insurmountable way. Why couldn't she have trusted him? Told him what had happened? What did she think he'd do? What *would* he have done? That would take some processing, but all he knew was he needed distance. He had to relook at everything that had resulted from that lie and see where it left him. Left them. He checked the quay, saw several vehicles lined up, several gardaí standing awaiting orders, and knew he needed to snap out of it and get to work. He saw her take a step in his direction, one hand outstretched, but he ignored it. He couldn't look at that pale tear-streaked face right now. She looked so broken.

And so alone.

He really was a selfish bastard. It was as he was

turning, to go to her and take her in his arms, protocol be damned, that the shot rang out. Just the one. It was followed instantly by a scream and a crash. He pivoted fully and saw Jansen go down under the considerable weight of Mackenzie. Good. That baby murderer wasn't going anywhere soon. It was a huge oversight to assume the shoulder wound and knife to his thigh had immobilised him, as he'd lain moaning and writhing on the ground, but not to have checked him for a concealed weapon? That was a fucking disaster. The bastard must have had a back-up within easy reach, probably in his waistband. It's what Flynn himself would have done. Be prepared. If you lose one weapon, you must have another. This was his fault. He should have had Lennon pat Jansen down. Double-check. Immobilise him. Flynn would take that responsibility. The fact that he'd been in shock from what had been disclosed was an unacceptable reason. He was police, first and foremost.

Afterwards, he'd remember it had happened in slow motion. Like as if he was watching a film on half speed. Through a smeared lens. He took his eyes from Jansen being hauled up and handcuffed by Mac, to see a look of horror spread across Brigid Lennon's face. Startled at the image he took in the bigger picture. Blood, a considerable amount, spreading down Gia's face as she took her hand from her head in obvious puzzlement. She stood, for an instant, staring at that red, red hand and before anyone could react, before any of them, even Brigid who was mere feet from her, could move or catch her, Gia crumpled to the ground. She had a look of astonishment, and something even more unsettling, on her face and as Flynn leapt to her side he realised he recognised that look. It was acceptance. And that scared him blind.

Mackenzie, despite his own wound, took over. He ordered several ambulances. One for the women and their babies, one for Hoyt Jansen and one for Gia. It became apparent, rather quickly, that the helicopter was going to be put to use. Menchen rounded up Miller and collected the other thug from the house in Moville and sent them to Buncrana with their crew. The minder, the sister, the doctor and Peter were all driven to the local station in Moville awaiting events later that day.

Dawn came and heralded a new morning.

The paramedics arrived and took one look at a still unconscious Gia, measured her vitals, shook their heads and talked quietly amongst themselves. It was bloody unnerving and Flynn hated being kept in the dark. But he was holding her, refusing to let her out of his arms even as they bandaged her head, trying to stop the flow of blood.

"Head wounds bleed something dreadful, you know," they told him, trying to be helpful. It wasn't working.

"Shouldn't she be awake by now?" he wondered aloud, not for the first time.

"Aye, she should surely," the younger man said, unaware that he was heaping coals on an already hot situation.

"Mac, get over here. Gia needs you." Flynn wasn't above using his friend's particular talents at a time like this, not when the medics couldn't wake her.

Mackenzie came over and crouched by Flynn's side. "Let go of her, Fitzgerald. Let these men examine her properly on the stretcher and then I'll take a look. Ease off now, like a good man." He unclasped Flynn's stiff hands and motioned the two men to carry her inside the ambulance. That done, he waited with Flynn as they checked her over for other possible injuries.

The older man beckoned Mackenzie in. "Are you a trained medic?"

"In a manner of speaking," Mackenzie replied, not untruthfully, and stepped inside.

Flynn watched as he laid hands on her head, the sides of her face and then on her upper chest. He closed his eyes, spoke words in some language Flynn didn't recognise and began what sounded like chanting.

The younger medic frowned at Flynn. "Is he a witch doctor? He's saying some foreign stuff over her. What's that all about?"

If he hadn't been so paralysed with fear, Flynn might have found it amusing. As it was, he didn't rightly care what anyone thought of Gabe Mackenzie and his odd and unusual ways. He trusted Mac with his own life and he certainly trusted him with Gia's.

Time passed. Mac continued to speak to her in a low tone and in an unknowable tongue. The medics were getting restless. They wanted to transport her but Flynn vetoed them. The other ambulances and cars drove off, their work done, their cargo secure.

Mac finally came out, his face drawn, circles deep under his eyes and his expression grim.

"Order the helicopter. We need to get her to a hospital. She has need of a specialist." He rubbed his hand along the back of his neck, as weary as Flynn had ever seen him.

"What? Why? What the fuck is wrong with her, Mac? Why won't she wake up?"

Gabe Mackenzie rested his other hand on Flynn's arm, a gesture of comfort. Of resignation. It was scarier than almost anything so far. Mackenzie never gave up.

When he spoke, the words knifed through Flynn as sharp as any blade.

"She doesn't want to."

His family came. Of course, they did. He'd had a battle with the helicopter pilot, also a trained medic. They wanted Belfast, it was closer, but Flynn got the name of a neurosurgeon from his doctor friend in St Vincent's hospital in Dublin, a man who specialised in troublesome head wounds who worked out of Beaumont hospital and that's where they went. He phoned his parents en route because he knew, as a default member of their extended family, Gia was important to them. Then he phoned Nick. That did not go well. He was taking the next flight from

Nantes. He'd been in Vannes, finalising the boutique hotel he'd set up there, using the charms and talents of a fantastic Kurdistani chef who created meals to die for – that was according to Caro who he phoned straight afterwards to alert her to the state Nick was in and where he was headed.

Gabe must have phoned Ali because by the time they had landed on the roof of Beaumont, had Gia brought in for surgery, and he stumbled into the waiting area, Ali, Molly and Kit were there. Their parents arrived a few moments later, his mother shocked when she saw him, her face visibly paling.

"Jesus, Mary and Joseph, Flynn, are you alright?" She slapped a hand to her mouth, her arm going to Patrick for support. "Have you seen a doctor?"

Flynn was puzzled. He hadn't been shot. He wasn't the one who was presently under a surgeon's knife.

Ali rose and walked towards him. "Have you seen yourself, bro? You're covered in blood." She gestured towards his attire.

He looked down. Ah. Right. Probably looked a little scary alright.

"I'm fine, Mum. It's . . . it's Gia's."

"Well, there's nothing fine about that amount of blood. Please tell us what happened. And sit before you collapse. Actually, hold your tale. Molly, please go get us all some coffee from the canteen. We could all do with it. I'll phone Devlin to bring you some clothes, Flynn. I should reach him before they leave."

"There's no need . . ." Flynn began, but his mother gave him 'the look'. No one challenged the look. He wasn't sure he wanted to change out of his bloody shirt and jeans. They held her blood and that was all he had of her at this moment. And that was just ridiculous.

Molly and Kit went for the coffees, but only after Molly had given him a puzzled look. Perhaps she guessed how he felt. Perhaps she finally put it together. Last autumn when he'd been distracted by the 'miscarriage' of his baby, he'd been off. More aloof. Molly had noticed and tried to get him to talk. He hadn't. Then, at Easter, when Dev and Frankie had announced their happy news of a pregnancy, he'd reeled. Shocked at how the insidious arm of jealousy had crept in and threatened to destroy the genuine joy he felt for his brother and Frankie.

The timing had sucked of course. He'd been prepping himself for the expected birth date of his baby to come and go without too much trauma and then his brother announced his news at the family dinner. Molly had sensed something was wrong, as had Gabe. But he said nothing. Not then. His feelings of being torn apart by envy of his brother, a man he loved, and Frankie, like another sister, had driven him to therapy. A good decision it had turned out.

He was always recommending therapy for others but never saw himself as a candidate. Now that he knew its value, its worth, he could actually mean it when he suggested it in future. By summer, Molly had been going through some of her own issues with Kit and he had sensed she needed to know woes were not the exclusivity of the sisterhood. He had confided. Up to a point. No names were mentioned and he made sure she thought it was a work colleague, someone Molly would never meet, who'd become pregnant by him. Sharing that part of his life with his youngest sister had felt in part a huge relief, and in part a betrayal. Now, seeing her curious and concerned expression, he thought she might have guessed it wasn't a work colleague after all.

He hadn't told anyone how he felt about Gia. That he felt carved in two. That he would not sleep or rest or leave her side till he knew she'd make it. *Not* making it was not an option. His brain had shut down that door and it was vaulted.

"When will Gabe be here?" Ali asked. "He must be driving as he hasn't answered my texts, and you know him. By the book, Mr Straitlaced wouldn't dream of taking a tiny squint to see if his girlfriend was checking in on him."

Gabe. Right. He hadn't told Ali he was hurt. He had better prepare her.

"Now don't freak out," he began and knew the mistake the second he saw her face. He reached out his arm and disregarding his bloody attire, it was probably dry now anyway, he hauled her in for a hug. "He's fine. I promise. A mere scratch and as we know he's an excellent healer. Not just for others, but for himself. And he had the weird salve with him, the one he carries in the car or whatever bag or satchel he carries. Why does he carry a man bag? What police official does that?" He kept talking as she burrowed into his chest, her breathing returning to normal.

His mother came over then and pulled her from him.

"Leave the poor man alone, he has enough on his plate. Gabe will be grand. Sure, isn't he a kind of medicine man?"

"Mum!" Ali was startled back to reality. "I'm pretty sure you're not supposed to say things like that. It's disrespectful."

"Can't think why, I only mean it with the very utmost of respect. Come and sit. Try texting him again. Let him know you're aware he's hurt and you'll wait here for him. Or better yet, send one of those voice message things on your phone. He can play that while he's driving and know your mind is at rest so he can drive safely."

Ali was appeased and, after returning the hug, pulled out her phone and stepped out to make her call. Their mum had that lovely balance of parent and friend, supporter and encourager.

Then the pacing renewed. Or his did. Back and forth he went, unable to sit. Unable to stand still. Molly and Kit arrived back with a tray of cups and goodies and, not long after that, Dev and Frankie arrived with a change of clothes. Flynn thanked them, took the bag and left it aside.

He wasn't ready. Not yet. His mother and father began to do the *Times* crossword, Molly and Kit typed on their work devices and Ali sat with earplugs in, eyes closed, probably listening to whatever baking podcast was the latest in her genre. They all stayed. They all waited.

Hours passed. They moved about. Changed positions, got more sustenance. Went for walks, texted work or friends. Chatted.

Waited some more.

When Gabe walked in the door some four hours after Flynn and Gia first arrived, Ali flew from her seat, a sob in her throat, and threw herself into his arms. For the sister that was the least demonstrative of them all, this was huge. It was sweet, and Flynn wished he could spare a thought to enjoy it. To be happy for her. It was so far down his list of things to care about that he felt like a heel.

Mackenzie held her face in his hands, kissed her, in front of everyone, and then looked at Flynn.

"Nothing?"

"Not a word. They've been operating for hours, Mac. Hours. The doc said she had fragments of the bullet lodged in her head and that it might be a slow process. But this? She shouldn't be under anaesthetic this long. That can't be good." He folded his arms about his chest, and tilted his head back, eyes closed. This was taking too long. He knew it.

Gabe winced as Ali hugged his side and she immediately barraged him with questions. The where, how, when, how much does it hurt questions than no cop wants to answer. He did a neat job sidestepping and explained to the room in general a version of what had happened. It was only then Flynn realised no one had asked him those questions. No one had checked how Gia had been hurt. They'd just been glad he was okay and that she was being seen to. His family were odd. They were also the best.

The chatter had escalated when the door to the waiting

302

area opened and all eyes swivelled in that direction. No one was expected. They were all there except Nick who was on a plane. And Caro who couldn't get here till the next day.

A young man in scrubs pulled a protective surgical cap from his head, rubbed a hand over his eyes and looked about.

"Next of kin for Angelica Sullivan?"

Flynn froze.

Jo stepped forward. "I consider myself in loco parentis. She's a member of our extended family. You can tell me or us indeed, how she is."

The surgeon glanced down at his notes. Puzzled.

"No, Mum," Flynn said. "I've got this. I'm the next of kin."

He pushed away from the wall where he'd propped himself, the weariness having finally set in. Unfolding his arms, he stood straight, braced, looked the doctor in the eye and spoke.

"Gia is my wife."

Chapter twenty-six

The silence was deafening. Until it wasn't.

"No need to take your own playacting to this level, Flynn – the doc just needs someone to sign stuff, I'm sure. Mum can do it," Ali said, still wrapped in Mackenzie's good arm.

Flynn ignored her and looked the doc in the face. "How bad? I need to know everything."

The doctor sighed and rubbed his hands wearily over his face. "I won't lie. It was touch and go there for a while but she's stable now. I got the fragments out, she's stitched up and once the general anaesthetic wears off, she should wake up. I gather, though, she hasn't woken up at all, even at the site?"

"No," Flynn acknowledged curtly. "She went down instantly and hasn't opened her eyes or made a sound since. The paramedics were concerned. They said all her vitals were low. Too low." He stopped, unable to put into words his biggest fear.

"It's early. She needs to come around on her own. She's in post-op now. As her next of kin, you can go in. But only you for now and then only one at a time if she has other family. I'll check back in a few hours. I have your details if you're not here."

"I'll be here." Flynn looked back at the collection of Fitzgeralds all gaping at him. He took a breath. "I'm going in to see her. I know I need to explain but I *am* her husband. We got married over a year ago in Brooklyn." The comical sight of one mouth after another dropping open almost brought a smile but he couldn't quite manage it. Not yet.

He left them, following the doctor to the recovery room and paused for a moment before pulling back the curtain. Fearing the worst, he took the light fabric and swirled it about himself as he moved forwards.

Ah *Christ.*

Paler than pale, tiny in the large bed, wires everywhere. The bandage around her head made her look like an alien and the huge shadows under eyes were the darkest he'd ever seen. Her lips, those beautiful lips were of faded rose and even the natural curl of her upper lip was not cooperating. Her arms lay flat beside her, over the covers, lifeless except for the tubes coming to and from drips and machines. She looked so unbearably unwell he had to grip the end of the bed to stop himself from staggering.

"*Gia,*" her name slid out, soft, gentle, broken. He pulled the plastic chair to her bedside and sat, leaning forward to take one small hand in his. He bent, turned it over and kissed it, on the pulse at her wrist. "I'm so sorry, my sweet darling. So sorry. This is on me. I should never have left Jansen unsecured. I should have had Lennon check for concealed weapons. There is no excuse. None. It's not her fault, she secured his gun, as she should, and then saw to you. You can be sure I'll be owning it, in the report. No one to blame but myself as team leader."

He settled himself into the chair, stretched out his legs and, with her hand tucked in his, told her everything that had happened since she was shot. As he spoke, he realised he also had to contact her station in Brooklyn. They should know there was an officer down. It was only right. Nick

305

had said he'd contact their parents, it would be less terrifying coming from him and they'd be relieved that her brother would be there within a couple of hours. He looked down at his blood-stained clothing and figured he'd need a shower and change before he began to frighten the nurses. And he had to talk to his family. That would be no walk in the park. He was usually the fixer in the family. Now he was the screw-up. The one who needed fixing. He had never in his life experienced this awful feeling of being in pieces. Tiny fragments of himself all scattered to the winds with nothing to hold him together. He hadn't known that a woman, that Gia, could be that bind for him. The one thing that could keep him whole. It was both mind-blowing and spellbinding at the same time.

He sat a while longer. Talking, telling her incidental snippets of information. He mentioned Ali and her concern for Gabe, he spoke of his parents and how they welcomed her as part of their family. He said Dev had brought clothes and that he would, eventually, shower and change. But he couldn't leave.

A nurse came by, took BP and temperatures, checked lines and drips. And frowned at him.

"That can't be hygienic," she said.

It was that, the thought that he might cause Gia more trouble with an infection, that drove him to his feet. He released her hand, positioned it securely next to her side and leaned down to press his lips to hers. A light touch, a slight pressure. Just to affirm to himself that he could. God, he needed the feel of those lips under his. Like a touchstone.

He backed away, walked slowly from the recovery area, on back to the waiting room. They were all still there. Every one of them. They were there for him. And he knew, for Gia. Because she was also one of them. His chest eased, just a tiny, tiny shift, but it warmed him.

"I know you want details but it isn't all my story to tell. I need a shower and to change, thanks Dev, and then I'll be back here." He looked around at all the faces he knew and loved. They were tired now too.

Gabe looked pale but well, considering. He probably had stitches and would need rest, but he and Mac both knew it was his magic ointment that most likely saved him from infection.

Flynn rubbed a hand across the back of his neck, weary to the bone. He looked about at his dear, dear family and decided, what the heck, they should know. They should be aware of why he was so distraught. So involved. Gia could tell her own version when or if she wanted. Later.

"Gia and I married last August, following a brief affair during Caro's wedding celebration. The reason is our own business and we did intend to get a divorce since but, well, it hasn't happened. She may still want one when she wakes up." He didn't say, out loud, the big *IF* word, but he knew they all heard it. "However, for the record, I don't want a divorce. I think we can work something out. Just so you know." He paused. Unsure what else to say. What other information they should know. That he was smitten? That he felt his heart slam to a halt when she collapsed? That he'd give his life for hers this second? What was the point? They could surely see it all on his face.

"I need to talk to the boss and explain my situation. I'll be taking time off, to be here. I won't put this case in jeopardy by not being clearheaded enough to see it through. Mac?" He caught Gabe's eye. "You can take the lead if you're well enough, otherwise hand it over to one of the other crew."

"What can *we* do?" his mother asked. "How can we help?"

Flynn looked down at the small but mighty person and felt a wave of tenderness sweep through him. She didn't ask a bazillion questions, she didn't berate him for not sharing his news before now. That would all come later, of that he was certain, but she knew that right now he needed support, not reprimands.

"Mum, could you make a rota amongst the family so Gia is never alone. I'll be here as much as I can, but, the case aside, I also need to see Jansen himself and deal with some bureaucracy. I don't want her waking to an empty room. Anyone who can't do it, no problem, I'll rope in some extras from work."

"Of course we can do it," Molly interjected. "Mum will coordinate with us, on the family WhatsApp and we'll make sure she's cared for. Promise. I'll take the next five hours as I have work to do on my laptop anyway. The rest of you go home."

Kit spoke then, reaching out a hand to shake Flynn's. "Molly will have a spreadsheet emailed to everyone within the hour. We're here for you. I hope you know that."

"I do." Flynn had to clear his throat and then he nodded and with a gentle hand to his mother's shoulder, he collected the bag of clothes to take with him to the station to report, and opened the door to the main corridor.

Well, shit, he thought, as he rounded the corner to the front entrance. Nick Sullivan came striding through the automatic doors, his brows knitted together in deep concern. Sullivan stopped at the main desk and spoke briefly with the receptionist. Flynn let him, Nick would see him soon enough and without doubt have some words to say.

Nick spotted him and was in front of Flynn within seconds. "Where is she? Hasn't she done enough for your family already? Why did you have to get her involved in this case? For fuck's sake, Fitzgerald, I thought I could trust you?"

Flynn knew it was anger and fear talking, but Gia's brother, his own brother-in-law wasn't wrong. Not really. No, he hadn't asked for her expertise, hadn't asked for her to come to Dublin, but he *was* her boss since she'd arrived. Once again, he needed to take responsibility, whether justified or not.

Man up, he thought. It's your fault after all. "Nick. Come on back and I'll explain everything. The family are all there. Gia is in recovery. She's going to be fine."

He wondered, as he led the tense and exhausted Nick

back to the waiting area, if he'd just told one of the biggest untruths of his life.

She heard him before she saw him and felt him before she heard him. It was muzzy and unclear in so many of her senses. She liked being in the dark. The quiet. She felt safe and secure. She had only a blurry memory of what had happened and she figured if she needed to remember at some stage, she could do that work, when it was time. For now, she concentrated on the soft stroking of her wrist. The soft kisses to her palm. Every so often a soft touch to her lips. They were Flynn's touches, she knew that.

The voices she let in, in a drifting kind of way, were more varied. She heard female sounds, older male sounds, she could have sworn she heard her brother Nick – both quiet and angry. Angry Nick made her heart hurt so she dug deeper into her darkness when that happened. She was pretty sure she heard Jo Fitzgerald, speaking in a regular low tone, over and over. The last time she'd heard it, she began reciting, in her head, the same tones, the same sounds. It was the Rosary. Heard for years in her own home growing up in Brooklyn with staunch Catholics as parents. It wasn't expected of her and her brothers, but she'd often, late at night, when she was very small, heard the rhythmic chant from the living room before her parents turned in for the night. As a teenager she'd rolled her eyes in exasperation at their rituals, as an adult she'd been proud of them for keeping their faith alive in the way that suited them. Now? Now it was the most comforting of sounds, like a warm blanket on a chilly day.

When a new voice was added, a voice she knew so well, she felt tears slip down her cheeks, felt a warm hand brush them away. Felt kisses on her forehead. Momma, she thought. Momma is here. Wondering why that might be true was too much, so she didn't. A part of her knew she wasn't ready yet. She wasn't well enough to join them. To find out what her prognosis was. To find out if Hoyt

309

Jansen was alive or dead. That could wait. It could all wait.

She slept on.

The next time she let her senses open to the world she felt him again. He was rubbing her belly and speaking in a low voice. To her? She tried to focus. Forced her brain to pay attention. It wasn't her belly. It was her scar. He was rubbing some kind of oil or cream into her scar. Who did that? And then she heard some words. Soft gentle words.

"I'm so sorry, little one. So sorry we didn't get to meet you. To know you. To have you. But you were wanted and loved. You are still. You always will be."

A shaky breath, a catching in the throat. And there, the softest kiss on her scar. More tears slipped through her shield, and she wished he would wipe them away. But then she felt his head, laying on her belly, more words, more quiet words. *"Wake up, Gia. Please wake up."*

No, she wasn't ready for any of this kind of pain. The darkness was so much more preferable. She sank back down, down. Safe. Secure.

Alone.

"It's been too long. Why the fuck won't she wake up?" She knew that one. That was Nick. In his cross and frustrated voice. He rarely used it. He was normally a calm man, in control and in charge. Not now.

"What did you do to her? Say to her? That Mackenzie said she doesn't want to come back to us. That's on you, Fitzgerald. She loves her family. Her job. Whatever has gone on between you two? That's what this is about. I know it."

"You're not wrong, Nick. A lot of this is my fault. But I can't right it, till she wakes, and I won't talk about our personal business unless she's okay with it. So, you'll have to wait, along with the rest of us. Go back to Rome with Caro. There's nothing you can do in this hospital room that a selection of others aren't already doing. I'll call the second there's any change." Flynn's voice sounded so sad. So, flat. So without hope.

That wasn't right either.

"Our boss isn't too happy either, Flynn," another person spoke.

How many were there? It sounded like Larkin. Why was he here?

"Jansen is still in custody, according to Mackenzie, and we're not sure how long he can be held without a proper charge. We need Gia for that, if murder is still on the table."

That voice Gia also knew. Brigid Lennon.

Bloody Cop Central, right here in her hospital room. She definitely needed to hear this. It was important. Hoyt Jansen needed to have the murder of her child on his rap sheet. She needed that charge there. She owed it to her son. It wouldn't negate her own responsibility, but it would be something.

"Who is he supposed to have murdered anyway?" Nick asked, his voice coming from the left side of the room.

Gia could feel Flynn on her right side, his hand at her wrist, his thumb doing the calm, even, stroking of her pulse point she often felt as she meandered in and out of consciousness.

Opening her eyes was a step too far, so she tried to clear her throat.

"He . . ." she began and the stroking stopped instantly, her hand carried to a broad chest, the thumping against her palm feeling like a drumbeat.

"*Gia!*" several people spoke at once, in excited tones, and someone called for a nurse.

A glass of water was held to her lips and she sipped. Coughed, and sipped again. Keeping her eyes firmly closed, she just wasn't that brave, she spoke, the sound a raspy grating in the suddenly quiet room.

"Hoyt Jansen killed my baby."

There was a lot of activity after she spoke. Nurses, doctors, specialists, they all came and examined her. Questioned her. It had been six days. Six long days when she'd lain in her bed unmoving, not responding, at least outwardly to all that went on around her. She was exhausted. How that was

311

humanly possible, since all she'd done was lie still, was one of those known conundrums.

Nick finally left with Caro, under oath to say nothing of what he'd heard till she was ready to share, promising to be back as soon as she was discharged and ensconced in the Dalkey house with Jo for more rest. Going back to the flat alone was not an option, surgeon's orders. Not with a recovering head wound.

She closed her eyes and slept some more, happy that she'd faced the real world. But of course, she hadn't. She had refused to look Flynn in the eyes, she couldn't. She knew what she'd see. Relief, sure, but it would be coloured by all the other baggage. The absolute truth that she'd driven headlong into danger, dived right into fray of certain harm, knowing she carried an innocent within her. Throwing herself in front of Amy and the other felled woman had been pure instinct. Cop reflex. Would a woman ready to be a mom have done that?

She couldn't look at him.

Escape into oblivion only lasts for so long and she knew the next time, he wouldn't give her an out. Well, she had a plan. She'd get her choices and decisions out there first. Save him the embarrassment of saying the hurtful things she knew he was feeling. Let him go. Set him free from a perceived obligation. Get those fucking divorce papers signed and filed so they could draw a line under the whole damn thing.

Again, she felt him before she heard him.

"Go away." She thought she'd try it simple and easy. If it didn't work, she'd bring out the big guns. "I want to be alone. And I specifically don't want to be alone with you."

She cracked an eye open then, hoping he'd take the hint.

Yeah, that wasn't happening.

"No, Gia. I won't be leaving. Not until you at least look at me."

She watched as he paced the room. Hands shoved into pockets of his trousers. Gone were the casual clothes of their Donegal caper, back were his suits and shirts and formal ties. But, God, he looked like shit. Thinner, drawn and pale. A resident frown. Tight-lipped. Bone-weary.

"We need to talk about what happened," he said. "We need to –"

"The only thing we need to verify," she said, "is that Hoyt Jansen's second shot from his weapon on the night in question, killed the baby. The doctor's report will support that claim."

"Why wasn't this known before? Why is that not in the official report. I've read it. It's not there. There's no mention of your baby."

"I made that decision. I wanted to deal with this in my own way. I wanted another chance to find Jansen and have him admit it. To my face. He's done that now so I can release my medical records." She sighed and looked away from his intense gaze. It was unnerving how he could see right through her. Or so it felt.

"I didn't want my colleagues to know I was pregnant, let alone that I lost the baby. Grief is hard enough without pity. Without blame."

"No one blames you, Gia. No one."

She wasn't buying that. Not for a New York minute.

"Whatever. I'm ready to say my piece, if that gets a harder sentence on that bastard." She closed her eyes, coward that she was, before that aqua gaze was the undoing of her. Before she fell apart and begged. "Please leave, Flynn. We're done. We're done with the case unless I'm needed as a witness to things in Donegal. And we're done. In general, we're done. Please send in my momma and ask Mackenzie to come by later."

She turned in the bed, giving him her back. There was silence. Frosty and long. Then she heard the door click closed as tears dripped slowly onto her pillow.

The women were great. Her momma and Jo became fast friends. They'd visited every day, stayed for hours, brought

313

food that Gia, in her semi-conscious state could smell but had no desire to wake up for. It got eaten by all the visitors.

He hadn't come back, not since she'd told him to stay away. Predictably that really pissed her off. Had he given up on her so easily?

Mackenzie came. He told her all the things she'd wanted to hear from Flynn. Hoyt Jansen was formally charged with human trafficking. Shona and baby Bradley Cooper were well and home with Shona's parents. The other new mother was kept in hospital for a few extra days, but seemingly the Baby Daddy had stepped up and they were going to try to parent together. The other women were delivered into the relatively safe keeping of social welfare, to be assigned case workers and given help as needed. Miller was out on bail, not considered a flight risk, but was charged and would be sentenced. Menchen had rounded up a few other crew members and Gia had finally remembered that the guy she'd recognised with the odd shoulders, had been one of the 'heavies' ushering the women onto the bus back in Flushing a year earlier.

The doctor, Peter, the minder and the sister were all in the process of being charged and Gia found she really didn't care about that. She was on official sick leave and the report-writing was left to the others. Mackenzie should also have been on sick leave but his wound had healed so quickly that even the doctor had seen no reason to keep him home. Magic salve, apparently.

It had been such a small set-up, the Irish-run baby-selling racket. Compared to the one last year this was small potatoes. Miller had been singing like a canary and tossed Hoyt Jansen and his few drones to the slaughter. He had been, as Jackie Carroll had suggested, closing down the operation. Tying up the last few loose ends. It was going to be back to diamonds, Miller said, keeping the Dutch connection going. And still using Greencastle, but this time in the opposite direction. Bringing diamonds *into* the country via Inishowen and then divvied out in whatever route they chose. It hadn't been decided, but it was all moot now anyway.

"But why sell the *babies* out of Amsterdam?" Gia had wanted to know. "Why not from Dublin or Glasgow? What do they have?"

It was the very simplest, and ironic, of answers, in the end. Family. Jansen had several family members working on security at Schiphol airport and several more actually involved with KLM as stewards and even one pilot. It all made the red tape smoother. The Boston route was new and served their needs well. Several of Jansen's gang, those who'd escaped the Flushing raid, had found Boston to be lucrative.

Jansen had hired Miller through an old pal, and he had recruited Jackie Carroll and the Dublin squad for better pickings, as he'd said. There were still knots in the case to be snagged at, to be unravelled, but Mackenzie was hopeful. As to the charging of Jansen? It got complicated. He needed to be extradited to the US where he could be charged under the Unborn Victims of Violence Act, or Laci and Connor's law, as it was known. Gia's unborn baby lost his life because of Jansen's bullet. No other reason. But that was not the crime for which he was arrested in Greencastle. So, work needed to be done but Gia's records and the testimony of her attending surgeon dealing with those bullets, would stand.

They were hopeful.

"When are you returning to the States?" Mackenzie asked as he helped her pack her bag on the last day in hospital.

The younger women were busy with various work things, and Rosa and Jo were making her room ready in Dalkey, where she'd rest a while before any decisions were made.

"As soon as I'm allowed," Gia said. "I think my mother should go back now, but she insists on waiting for me. I don't want to be a burden on the Fitzgeralds, so would rather vacate as soon as possible."

Gabe settled her into the wheelchair provided and, with her bag slung over his shoulder, began to push her down the corridor.

"Jo Fitzgerald took care of me," he said, "when I had some debris stuck in my shoulder a while back. She was everything that was good. Fed me, entertained me with board games and basically poured more tea than I'd ever drunk down my throat. She loved it and, take if from one who detests asking for, or receiving, help, I was never made to feel too much."

"Good to know, detective. But my real concern is, how many Fitzgeralds am I likely to encounter at any one time? There *is* a whole lot of them."

"He won't come near you if you have asked him not to. Rest easy."

And before Gia could come up with a suitable cutting and dismissive remark, they were at the car and the business of getting settled took over.

Damn Gabe Mackenzie and his astuteness. His ability to cut right through. Gia hated the women who said one thing, insisted on it, but secretly wanted another. She wasn't that woman.

Except she was very afraid she was.

Chapter twenty-seven

"Actually married? You and our brother actually tied the knot? That's some kind of crazy shit, right there." Ali flopped back in one of the chairs next to Gia's bed.

Gia was pretty sure she spoke for all the women in the room. Frankie was strolling about, hand to her lower back, while Molly sat cross-legged at the foot of the bed. Caro was in the other chair, back again from Rome with Nick and Toby, just to check on her, she said. Gia knew Nick would not be happy till she was back in the US, away from a specific male aqua-eyed gaze.

They all knew about the marriage, but Gia had an inkling this conversation was about to get way more personal. She supposed they had a right, in a way. They loved Flynn, that was never in doubt. But now they felt a bit like he'd pulled a fast one, as Molly had put it. That he'd deceived them. He had. But so had she, to her own family. They really needed to come clean, to explain, so when the divorce came through it wouldn't be a shock. It would be an expected relief. The whole Fitzgerald family wanted their golden boy to be happy. Hell, she wanted him to be happy. Just not maybe quite yet. A girl had her standards. Moving on *too* fast was a definite no-no.

"Truthfully, I barely remember the day." *Lie*. "It was over in minutes. Your brother bossed me into it." *True*. "He thought he was being gallant." *True*. "I wish it had never happened." *A little lie*.

"But why? I mean, no one cares if you were at it like rabbits. Were you? At it like rabbits? And if so, when?" Ali, of course, straight to the core of the matter.

Molly hugged a pillow to her stomach. "It was at Caro and Nick's wedding, wasn't it? You looked amazing in that red dress and he was acting all cool and slick."

"Cool and slick? Flynn?" Caro said with incredulity. And there was a moment when they all pondered and remembered.

Frankie was the first to agree. "God, you're right, Molly. Flynn was looking fine over those few days and, wait, didn't you *literally* fall into his arms two nights before it, at the flat? We were all dancing and he came with food from Jo."

"Yes," agreed Caro. "I do remember. And you did look super-hot in that red, Gia. So, like Ali said, so very crassly, were you, you know, at it?"

If Caro's cheeks were tinged with pink, Gia's were suddenly on fire. Oh shit.

"He kissed me outside the flat, that first night. And it was, let's say, memorable. So, by the time he asked me to dance at the wedding, we'd basically had hour upon hour of virtual foreplay already." She grinned then at the open mouths of his siblings. "He's hot, your big brother. Very hot."

Ali theatrically clapped her hands to her ears. "*Lalalala! I can't hear you!*"

Frankie chuckled. "You're the one who mentioned rabbits, idiot!"

"How long did it go on? Did you fall in love?" Molly, the quieter one, reined in the merriment.

Gia cleared her throat. It was time to get real. To tell the truth. All of it.

"Wait, I want more details," Caro interrupted. "It was

my wedding after all."

The truth would have to wait a bit, it seemed.

So, details ensued. Not all of them, not in graphic 'at it like rabbits' form, but some. How they'd had a connection, instant and sizzling. New for her, and she thought, for him. They just clicked. Had one really hot sexy night and then she was gone.

"Did he pine for you all that summer?" Frankie wanted to know.

Gia scoffed. "We didn't communicate again till the middle of August. We both knew it was a one-off, a fling rather than an affair. I was returning to the US and he had his work here."

Molly had stilled, her face paled. "So, it *was* you," she whispered. She scrambled up the bed to throw her arms about Gia. "I thought maybe, but wasn't sure. He never gave a name. You poor thing! I'm *so so* sorry!"

Off balance, and unsure of what exactly Molly was on about, because how could she know, Gia patted her back, her brows raised in question at the others.

"What's going on, Moll?" Caro asked, leaning forward to also rub a hand on her youngest sister's back.

Molly pulled away, sat back with her pillow and turned sad aqua eyes, the mirror of her brother's, to the group waiting on tenterhooks.

"Not my story to tell," Molly said, her voice low, "Flynn shared some stuff with me during the summer that explained his odd and very non-Flynn like behaviour last Halloween, Christmas and then again at Easter. Gia, I think you should explain. If you want to. Otherwise, girls, forget I said anything."

"Like that's going to happen." Ali tore off a piece of scone from the discarded tea tray and bit in. "Spill."

Gia reached for the water bottle, took a long drink, screwed the cap back on as if it was a science experiment and finally looked at each of the kind, generous and sympatico women before her.

"You may not like what you hear. And you certainly won't think much of me afterwards, but here goes."

She told them. About the email she sent to Flynn, genuinely not wanting anything more than to let him know. About him turning up in Brooklyn and practically dragging her to the registry office.

"Was that not kinda romantic?" Frankie interjected, her tone hopeful.

"*Shhhhh!*" From the three other listeners.

"Go on," Caro said.

On she went. Flynn returned to Dublin. She went back to work. She told them simply that she lost the baby in mid-October and that she intended to send divorce papers but kinda forgot.

"And then I was asked over here to help with this baby-selling case because I'd worked a case similar – turned out to be the same guy – and you know the rest. I got shot. I'm going back to the US in a few days. Divorce papers will be mailed. The end."

She flopped back against the soft stack of pillows, unbearably weary. Unbearably sad.

They took a few minutes to digest the info. To remember their brother had gone through this, albeit vicariously, as well.

"Fuck," announced Ali succinctly. "That sucks."

They took another few moments to agree, nod, add sounds of concern.

Then Molly said, "If you didn't want Flynn involved, why have the baby in the first place? You knew in time to do something about it. And secondly, why marry him? I know you said he insisted, but he didn't actually shackle you and drag you, did he?"

She hit hard, this one. Low blow after low blow. As she had every right.

Gia smiled though, because Molly adored her brother. They all did. And she, Gia, was the interloper, the one who had brought such distress to his life.

320

"I didn't know I wanted a baby till I found out I was pregnant. I hadn't even thought of getting married – that was years off, if at all. But then it happened. Yes, we took precautions, your brother is not irresponsible and neither am I, but it happened anyway. I didn't choose abortion because it's not for me. I figured I could bring this child up, care for it, as would my family when they got their heads around it, and Flynn could, you know, dip in and out."

"*Ha!*" Ali snorted. "That was your first mistake. Flynn isn't a dip-in-and-out guy. He's an all-or-nothing guy. Usually all. Look how he's always been with Toby."

Gia smiled. "I know that now. But that's it, in a nutshell. Drama over. You can tell your partners, Nick already knows, but was sworn to secrecy. Sorry, Caro, I begged him to let me say it first. He agreed on condition I told you before I left. After that, he'd tell you. And Ali, Gabe knows too. Same deal. Frankie and Molly, you're welcome to tell Dev and Kit, if you wish."

Frankie wiped at her eyes, then blew her nose. "Dev is going to go batshit crazy when he hears. He'll feel so betrayed."

"I'm so sorry he'll be hurt. That's on me," Gia said. "I made Flynn promise not to tell anyone we were married or pregnant. My own parents still don't know about the baby. I'll tell Momma later today."

"Miscarriages are not uncommon," Caro said softly. "I hope you got help to see you through your loss."

Oh Jesus, this was worse and worse. Now they pitied her, felt sorry for her, the one thing she had never deserved.

She took a deep breath. "I didn't miscarry. I recklessly went into a dodgy situation, threw myself into the fray without thinking, without putting our baby first, and got shot. The second shot killed our son."

And to no one's surprise but her own, she burst into tears.

"You bastard! You selfish fucking bastard!" Dev stormed into Flynn's apartment, shoving his older brother hard in the chest as he went. Once. Twice. "What the fuck, Flynn? Seriously. *What. The. Fuck?*" If the shoving and the language hadn't given it away, never mind the decibel level, the spitfire arrows firing from his blue eyes would have heralded Dev's mood.

Flynn closed his own eyes, blocking the sight of his furious younger brother. Frankie. Gabe had texted him that the women had shared things at an afternoon tea in Dalkey. Ali had been hurt Mackenzie had kept things from her, and now he was going to have to deal with more. He'd already had calls from Caro and Molly, checking in with him. Checking up on him, more likely. He sighed now, made a pass by the fridge and pulled out two beers. He handed one to Dev.

"Sit," he said.

"You think a beer is going to get me to forgive you?" Dev took it all the same, popped the cap and took a drink.

Flynn was puzzled. Forgive him? For what? "You have me at a loss," he said, dropping into the armchair by the window.

Dev took the couch, leaning forward, beer bottle hanging from his hands between his knees.

"I bet I do. You are so far up your own ass you forget you have a family. A family who you've kept at arm's length. A family you hid things from. You. The one everyone goes to with their secrets and you can't fucking return the compliment?" He shook his head, genuine puzzlement on his face. And, Flynn realised, genuine hurt.

Shit. He *had* screwed up. "It's complicated," he began.

"Don't. Just don't give me the 'it's complicated' shite. We all have complicated, man, but we *share* it. You know, with one another. Like a *family*. You really are the most selfish fucking individual I've ever had the misfortune to be related to." Dev surged to his feet, paced, returned to the couch. Sat. "Sorry, I didn't mean to let fly." He swallowed some more very nice craft ale.

"No, I'm sorry," Flynn said quietly. But selfish? How

could protecting them from his pain be selfish? He'd kept his sorrow from them to prevent them feeling pain, his loss. His burden to carry, not theirs. "You all had enough going on – you didn't need mine too."

"Can you hear yourself? Holier than thou shite. How did you feel when you found out about Ali? When you knew what she'd been through and never said? How did it feel when Caro went off to Rome without telling anyone the reason why? Jesus, man, that explanation is drivel. Think it through. Put yourself in my position. How would you feel if what happened to you, had happened to me and Frankie and we'd said nothing? I'll tell you how. You'd feel excluded and unwanted. Like we all feel, now we know. I thought we meant more to you than that. Sure, you're the calm, steady one and I'm the hothead, but you were there for me when I needed you, you helped me. All any of us wants is to help you. But, oh no. Mr Staid and Serious has to deal all by himself. Fucking selfish."

Dev took a breath. A much-needed one considering his rant.

Flynn sipped his beer, turned the bottle around in his hands as he contemplated Dev's harsh words. Had it been selfish? He was so used to being in charge. To being the fixer. The finisher. How *would* he have felt if Dev and Frankie had gone through such a loss, and never said? Left out and unwanted was how. Unnecessary. Redundant. Damn. And when Ali revealed her terrible past, he'd been as devastated as the rest of them, if not more so. As the eldest, *he* should have seen something. He'd felt hurt. Double damn.

Looked like he had some explaining to do.

"I *am* sorry, Devlin. It was out of concern for you all that I didn't say anything. But what you're saying makes me realise I was shutting you out, not protecting you. But I didn't know how to talk about it, and that was frankly terrifying for me. I always know how." He leaned forwards now, beer discarded on the coffee table. Hands hanging

323

loose on his knees. "It was all so fast. From the wedding to the news of the baby, from the marriage to the loss. And then Gia arriving here for a case. It threw me, I don't mind admitting now. And I don't deal well with being thrown."

"I hear you," Dev agreed. "You always have a handle on things. But maybe it's time you trusted *us* to know things for a change. Not how to handle the shit, but to listen to you tell us about it. That's all any of us can do. Could do. And we would have, if you'd let us in."

He believed him, then. His younger brother was as adult as he was, didn't need kid gloves, and would have sat and drank beer or whiskey or endless tea, or run with him in the pre-dawn mornings when things were at their darkest. Or even held the punching bag while Flynn pummelled the hell out of it.

He dropped his head, an alarming sting at the back of his eyes. "Shit, Dev, I really am sorry. Of course, you'd have been here. It wasn't that I doubted you. It was more I was unsure of my own way of handling things. I hate being unsure."

"Well, maybe it's time you allowed yourself the odd human emotion, big brother. You may be surprised to find it won't, in fact, kill you stone dead. It might even help."

Flynn swallowed, his throat not really cooperating. He picked up the beer again, giving himself a second or two to regroup.

Dev, apparently relieved he'd said his piece, stretched back on the couch, crossing his feet, cushion tucked behind his head.

"Shoes," Flynn said automatically and a huge grin split Dev's face as he toed off his sneakers.

"Just testing you!" He smirked, clearly enjoying his own joke.

Flynn stood, needing an activity, the air felt so clouded with emotion, and walked to his kitchen where he made a plate of cheese and crackers, olives and paté. He set aside his beer bottle and took down two red wineglasses and a decent Zinfandel. He set everything on a tray, added some side plates and knives and brought it back to the living area and placed it on the coffee table.

"Oh good, I'm starved," Dev said and swung his legs to sit upright and dig in.

They ate in companionable silence for a short while.

Then Dev said, negligently, "What happens now?"

Flynn's instinct was to brush the question aside, but he paused. This was exactly what Dev had meant by letting the family in, and he could start right now.

"I wish I knew, Dev. I don't want us to end. She means more to me than I could've imagined. When we met last year, at the wedding, I won't deny I was blown over. We'd an instant connection. It was, well, it was what it was. A fling, we both agreed, but when she returned to Brooklyn, I couldn't stop thinking about her. I began imagining ways I could get Mum to have a big extended family get-together with Nick and Caro and Nick's family, just so she'd come too. Yeah, I know, ridiculous. But I was smitten. She was smart, challenging, took no shit from me and made me laugh."

"And let's not forget, hot as hell," Dev supplied.

"That too," Flynn agreed. "So bloody sexy without even trying. And that upper lip? Shit, it gets me every time."

Dev tipped his glass to clink against his. "You had it bad, even then. Huh, I'd no idea."

"That was the plan. Then she sent me the email about being pregnant and while I was shocked, there was an odd sense of inevitability to it – and not remotely in a bad way. It felt like it was meant to be. You know the rest. I pretended to only marry her so the child would have my name, be legal, but I'm not that neanderthal. I seized the opportunity to make her mine, neanderthal though I realise saying that is. Aw, hell. Truth? I wanted her in my life any way I could, and used deception and subterfuge to get it. What does that make me?"

"Horny?"

Flynn snorted. "Be serious."

"Hey, nothing wrong with horny. But now, do you still want her in your life now? After everything?"

"More than ever."

Dev smiled. "That's good. She fits you. She fits with us. With all of us. What's your plan?"

They tossed about ideas but Flynn was exhausted and it began to show. Dev rose and they walked to the door.

"Give Frankie a hug and tell her to stay off her feet." Flynn said.

"Sure, Doc. Whatever you say."

"One more thing. I . . . I'm . . . about the baby, yours and Frankie's. Don't ever think I'm not happy for you. I'm sorry I wasn't as enthusiastic as I should've been. *That* was selfish and I wish I could change my reaction. Show how happy I am for you. Truly." Damn he could feel that bloody sting behind his eyes again. He was a fucking wreck. But his brother needed to hear this, needed to know. He was going to be an uncle again and that was a *real* occasion for joy. And totally separate to his own situation.

Dev blinked. Blinked again. There better not be a crying fest here – that wasn't how they rolled. Flynn tensed. Took a breath. But his baby brother stepped up, wrapped his arms tight around him and hugged, hard. Fuck.

"Thank you," Dev rasped. Cleared his throat. "Thank you. It means the world to hear you say it." And pulling back, slapped him playfully on the cheek, though his eyes were serious as Flynn had ever seen. "Keep talking to me. I need you to know you can."

He turned, opened the door and was gone before Flynn could answer.

It was Gabe's turn next. But not before a few days passed. It stuck in Flynn's craw that Gia still refused to see him. What was that about? But he knew he couldn't barge in and demand an audience – where would the respect be? But in truth he felt fairly disrespected by *her*. Like she couldn't be

SECOND SHOT

bothered to hear him out. Didn't care enough, and his own
pride wouldn't let him push. He'd grovel, if he had to, but
only if he knew there was some chance of it working – he
wasn't completely stupid.

And yet, what did he have to lose? This state of flux
within him could not continue. He flexed his hand, easing
the welcome pain. Jansen had been remanded in custody in
Dublin, for now, and the lawyers were working things out.
The murder charge would stick if they could get him back to
the States, and it seemed likely. But earlier that day, he had
requested some time alone with Mr Hoyt Jansen. Up until
now he'd kept his cool. Kept his distance. Held himself in
check. Then the report from the Flushing raid landed on his
desk. He had access only because of the connected cases and
the fact that the NYPD knew him. Knew of him, if not in
person. He'd helped them on a number of cases in the past,
would do so again, presumably. But Gia's sergeant hadn't
wanted them released. Flynn knew the reason now.
Mistakes had been made. Gia's back-up had barely arrived
on time, despite clear directions, her partner had been hurt
in the midst of the shooting and Amy, their undercover
agent, had almost lost her life and that of her baby.

Gia had saved them all. By throwing herself in front of
Jansen's weapon. But he didn't hesitate. He fired anyway.
Twice. On purpose. He hadn't known she was pregnant
with the first shot, but seemingly, and this part had been
redacted in an earlier report on Gia's insistence, she'd cried
out, begging him not to hurt her baby. He'd laughed. And
shot her again.

Then Flynn had read the hospital report, the one that
would sway the jury or judge. He'd reeled. Literally had to
take a step back as he'd read the words explaining the
surgery, the stitching of her womb afterwards, the enormous
loss of blood and the coma Gia had fallen into for two days.

They'd almost lost her then.

They'd almost lost her again.

He did what he'd done only once before. He broke the

327

rules. Deliberately and with intent. And he'd asked Mackenzie to assist. They'd been given a 'dark' visit, as it was called amongst themselves at the station, and that privilege was very rarely used. Like before, when he'd taken on a dirty ex-priest, Flynn had entered the cell where Jansen was kept. He was alone. No duty officers stood guard outside. No cameras were rolling, all sound was cancelled. Gabe followed him inside, not to participate but to keep watch. On Flynn.

When Flynn saw Jansen sitting casually on his bunk, like he gave no shits about anything, all Flynn could see was Gia's scar. The one he had so lovingly massaged and oiled while she lay in a coma, due to the piece of filth in front of him.

He was a trained fighter, Flynn Fitzgerald. Knew how to hit to cause maximum pain without breaking bones or too much skin. Without leaving too many external marks. He took three shots at Hoyt Jansen and his voice, like steel, stayed steady despite the exertion.

He hauled the criminal to his feet and went on the attack. "This is not going to be a fair fight. This is me, showing you I can get you anytime. And this is me seeking some minor reparation on what you did to Detective Gia Sullivan."

One kick landed with a fancy twist and turn, forcing a yelping Jansen to his knees clutching his belly.

"Get up. If you are man enough to shoot women and infants, you ought to be man enough to take a relatively minor amount of pain. That one was for her first coma."

He lashed out again, this time aiming for the vulnerable lower back. "This one is for the second coma."

Jansen went down, a bellow now, more than a yelp, as his kidneys felt the shock.

"And this, you absolute piece of shit, is for my son."

In the end Mackenzie had to pull Flynn back. He used his fists. Had to. Had to feel something crack, some bone under bone snap. Because when he thought of his never-to-be-born son, he saw a red mist and the only way through it was via Hoyt Jansen.

Now his right hand hurt like a bitch. He'd iced it, swallowed a few pills he'd downed with a finger of Scotch, but still. He paced. Back and forth, the energy simmering just below the surface. If his hand wasn't still aching from his 'meeting' with Jansen, he'd beat the punch bag in his home gym till he could feel nothing. That's all he wanted. An absence of feeling. Wasn't much to ask.

A single knock at the door heralded the arrival of his wing man.

"I brought ointment. It will help." Gabe Mackenzie handed over the small tin and followed Flynn down the hall to the living room.

"Thanks." Flynn opened the tin half expecting a foul odour but it was only mildly odd, a mixture of medicinal and herbal. "News?"

Flynn got his updates on Gia via Gabe from Ali. Yes, it was roundabout and rather infantile, but it sufficed. Gabe took off his jacket and, as fastidious as Flynn himself, folded it over the back of a chair before taking a seat on the couch. Flynn took the chair opposite. It was strangely reminiscent of Dev's visit and he hoped he wasn't in for another tongue-lashing.

"She's gone," Gabe said quietly. "Left this morning with her mother. Ali, Frankie and Molly have spent quite a bit of time with her since the shooting, and they really like her."

"She's easy to like."

"No, she isn't. Not really. She can be prickly, sharp and quick-witted. But so are the women in your family so they get each other. You two get each other. You work. She *does* have a sunny nature, when not in mourning, and one catches glimpses of it when she forgets to remember."

Flynn watched his friend and colleague as he rubbed the slightly sticky salve into his knuckles. *Forgets to remember.* About summed it up for him too. Probably for anyone who has had significant loss. And then the guilt when you have fun, or a laugh, or enjoy a moment. When would that end? Did it?

329

"Well, she's gone. So, there's that." Flynn replaced the lid, handed it back to the other man.

"Are you unwell? When have you ever let something you want slip away without a fight? What are you going to do about it?"

"Do? She doesn't want me, Mac. She said so. In this day and age, I can't go badgering her to be with me. It's not how it works anymore, if it ever did."

"I agree, no badgering. But have you told her you love her?"

Flynn rubbed his good hand over his scratchy jaw. "No. No, I haven't." His hand went around to the back of his neck, easing the strain that seemed to have embedded itself. "I should be honest with her about that, at least. So she'll know what happened between us wasn't about just sex, or the baby, or the job. It was, it *is*, about her."

"Yes, you should. And also, that losing the baby wasn't on her."

Flynn threw Gabe an angry look. "Of *course* it wasn't on her. She didn't *lose* the baby. She didn't misplace him or leave him unintended in a railway station, or put him somewhere and forget him. She wasn't neglectful. He was fucking *stolen* from her! She was saving lives while Jansen was stealing them. It was never her fault!" His voice had taken on a rough edge, a distinct lack of control which he abhorred, and he breathed in deeply to regain his senses.

"But does Gia know you feel that way? Have you actually told her you know it was not her fault?"

Had he? Had he said the words? If he had, had she not believed them?

Fuck. Did Gia actually believe he blamed *her*?

Flynn stood, walked to the chair and handed Mackenzie his jacket. "Thanks, Mac. I appreciate the first aid and the support earlier today. See yourself out."

Before his friend had even shut the door, Flynn opened his laptop.

"I've some planning to do," he announced to the empty room.

Chapter twenty-eight

A month. A whole fucking month. How was she supposed to stay sane with a month off work? She didn't paint or do macramé, she didn't knit or felt. She was reduced to jigsaws and adult colouring books. If they'd been *adult* colouring books, they might have been more fun but she was under orders to let her brain recover. Not get all heated.

Heated? That was a joke. The next time she got heated, in a sexual sense, a new millenium would have dawned. Fucking Flynn Fitzgerald and his clever hands, mouth and other body parts; she was kinda ruined for all other men. Fuck, but she missed him. Every single day. Her language had gone to hell, she swore at the drop of a hat, which would be fine in her job amongst her co-workers but her parents did not approve. At least she was back in her own apartment, two weeks into the four, most of which she'd spent tucked up in her own childhood bedroom, her momma fussing over her as only an Italian – and Irish it seemed, could do.

She glanced around her apartment, a third-storey walk-up in Greenpoint, an up-and-coming Brooklyn neighbourhood, according to the realtor. She liked her space, her view – a quiet leafy street – the hardwood floors, the quirky moulding, and if she leaned a little to the left out her front window, she could see the East River. Who didn't like a waterside view? Back in the 1800s it had been a traditionally Polish and Irish area, now it was mostly Polish, but very arty and a lot of funky cafés and bars. She loved it. The village feel that had an edge. She could walk the river boardwalks on her days off and stretch out in some leafy green areas when she wanted. It was a half hour to the city by train, so she never felt cut off. And best of all, she hadn't left Brooklyn so her parents were somewhat mollified.

But God, she loved being independent. Her mother had been devastated about the baby. Her pop just as cut up, but she was glad their smothering was over. She needed head space and, dammit, she had jigsaws to compile. But instead, getting up from her floor position by the coffee table, she went over to her window, opened it wide, climbed out onto the ubiquitous metal fire escape and sat watching the world go by below.

Early October was simply lovely in New York. The summer heat was a memory, the frost of winter a mere mirage in the distance. This was her time. Or it used to be before last October. The slight evening chill, the beginnings of crisp and fresh, the call of cocoa and mulled wine, it all spoke to her and she really hoped it would again. And fuck it, she'd forgotten her book and her phone to play her music. Standing again she climbed back in and came to a shocked halt as her doorbell rang.

What the . . .? She wasn't expecting anyone. The only place a New Yorker arrived unannounced or uninvited was their family home. Glad of wool socks on her feet, deadening any sound, she moved to her cabinet drawer, opened it and reached for her gun. Greenpoint might be oozing charm but that didn't mean she had to behave like a ninny and not protect herself. She eased her way to the door and put her eye to the peephole. Nothing. The person was either blocking her view on purpose which was not good, or clueless, also not good.

She had a gun and was not afraid to use it.

"Who is it?" she asked. Bold strong tone. One that said, 'I have your number, buddy'.

Silence for a moment, then the person turned and spoke, still not visible as too close to the door, but definitely heard.

"*Gia*."

She'd know that voice anywhere. Everywhere. Forever.

Flynn Fitzgerald was outside her door. Now.

Of all the doors, in all the apartment buildings etcetera, but this was no Humphry Bogart movie. This was her life. Time to face the music. Time to say a proper grown-up goodbye. Time to be the adult.

She slid the bolt and turned the latch. And there he was, all tall and intelligent-looking, his hair mussed, a winter coat hanging open over his habitual shirt and tie. Gorgeous. Tired. Drawn. And uh-oh, furious. That was when she noticed the manilla envelope slapping irritably against his leg. The divorce papers she'd sent him to sign. The nail in the coffin of their brief marriage. He threw her a glare, one she felt to her toes, and strode into her apartment.

"How did you get in?" she asked, her voice not as steady as she'd like. "You're supposed to buzz up to the intercom. You didn't buzz." She was babbling. She couldn't help it. He was here. In her space. Close enough to touch. But so distant, so far from her heart she felt she was in a desert. "Why are you here?"

He'd have to answer her sometime, and not keep glaring at her like he wanted to eviscerate her. She squared her shoulders, took a breath and faced him. A 'bring it on' attitude was what was needed here or they'd never be done. Never move on. *God* but she'd missed this man.

Beautiful. Pale and drawn. So tired. She looked all those things. Things he felt, except the beautiful part – that was all her. But he was here on a mission and nothing, not her fine bones, not her amber eyes, not the delectable upper lip, *none* of it would deter him. Attack was the best form of defence, it was said, so he attacked.

"Why did you lie to me, Gia? Why didn't you tell me the truth?" He barked it out because now he was saying the words, he realised he *had* to say them. He had to know. He'd strode across her living room and paced to a window. Now he turned and he tried not to care that she looked stricken.

"What? What do you mean? I don't know what you're talking about." She did sound confused but how could she not know?

"Seriously? That's what you have? Christ, Gia, why didn't you tell me you'd been shot. That our son died because of a bullet wound? Don't you think I had a right to know?"

He could feel his anger surge again and when she took a step back, he realised he'd raised his voice. Yes, he wanted to be on the attack, but that didn't mean he should scare her. He wasn't a bloody bully. He dragged his hand over his mouth, truly exhausted.

"I want to know why you let me believe, for almost a year, you'd had a miscarriage and all that entailed. I had a right to know."

"Did you though? Why? Yeah, we were married but, you know not *really*. And what good would it have done you? There was nothing for you to do. It was a waste of emotion, you knowing." Her shoulders slumped and she sank to the couch, curling her feet up under her.

"That was for me to deal with. It wasn't your decision!"

She glared up at him. "Jesus, Flynn, before you blow a gasket, take off your coat and sit the fuck down. I can't keep tilting my head backwards."

He found himself doing that. Taking the moment to settle his ire, his stomach and the heart that was slamming into his chest. He was as angry as he'd ever been, but he was also a second away from dragging his mouth across hers in the deepest of kisses. A desperate kiss. A pleading, *begging* kiss.

"I can almost understand why you didn't tell me straight away, actually, screw that, no I can't, but let's pretend I can. There were so many times since then. Christ, Gia, I told you I blamed myself, about the research showing sometimes it's the man that causes the baby to miscarry. Why didn't you say something then? What was the worst that could have happened if you'd told the truth?"

Gia reached for a throw cushion and hauled it to her chest, her fingers tightening about the fabric. If anything, she looked paler. God, he was a bastard to put her through this, but it was necessary, for both of them, he felt it in his bones.

"It doesn't matter anymore, Flynn. Why can't you just leave it?"

"Because it bloody matters to me," he said, his voice raw. "*Why* didn't you tell me?"

Gia's lower lip trembled and her eyes filled. She closed them, refusing to look at him, and his heart stuttered as large tears slipped silently down her cheeks. "Because it was *my* fault. I killed our baby." She gulped and a hand flew to her mouth to stifle a cry.

Gabe had been right. She believed it was her fault. *Oh dear God*, that must rip her to shreds every single second, of every single day.

Flynn could feel his chest tighten but knew he couldn't touch her, not yet. She needed to hear what he had to say.

"Hoyt Jansen is the only person responsible for the death of our son, Gia. The *only* person. This was not your fault. It was his, and his alone."

More twin tears slid down her cheeks and she finally opened her eyes. The pain in them hit him in the gut like a hammer. "I put him in danger," she whispered. "I didn't put him first."

"Answer me this, Detective Sullivan, did you do your job on that day? Did you, or did you not, put your life on the line for others? I read the damned report, Gia. And the doctor's. I know what went down."

Gia swiped at a tear, sniffed and looked him dead in the eye. "But I didn't serve our son. I didn't protect *him*."

Flynn moved. He had to touch her. Hold her. He swung himself off the chair and sat next to her. He pulled the cushion from her grasp and despite her futile attempts to bat him away, he hauled her onto his lap. He cradled her then as the tears fell in earnest. It was the same heart-wrenching agony he'd felt from her in their baby's room in his apartment. And again in their Donegal B&B. And here they were again. It was almost getting to be a habit. But now he knew why the pain was so visceral. So open, still.

He let her cry. He held her as close to his heart as he could. He wanted her to feel his beating with hers, *for* hers, as long as she needed. Maybe it was stupid, childish even, but it was all he had.

She quietened after a while, wiping her eyes with her sleeve. He handed her his handkerchief and she blew. Her face was blotchy and bleak. Her eyes swollen pools of sorrow. He had never thought her more beautiful because she was *real*. In his arms. With him.

"Listen to me, Gia, and know I am telling you what is true. You saved at least four lives that night. Four. You put yourself at risk because you took an oath. You *swore* an oath. We know we can go down on the job, the risk of it, but we hope to never be put to the test. You were tested and you paid dearly for it. But you *saved* four humans. At least four. Amy and her child would be dead, but for you. That other woman and her baby would be dead, but for you. Your partner testified that your actions, and yours alone, stopped further deaths. I know it doesn't bring back our baby, but you are a hero. No, listen to me –" She was shaking her head in instant denial. "A hero. I'm so, so, deeply sorry our baby didn't make it. I'll never not be. But I don't want you defining your future on something you had no control over. You don't have to forgive yourself for your erroneously perceived transgressions."

Finally, a smile, just a little one curled at the edge of her lip. "You can't help yourself, can you? Always with a thesaurus in your mouth. I shouldn't have thrown myself in front of Amy. I should've shot Jansen first."

Flynn took her chin in his hand, angled it so he could look straight at her. "No. Gia. No. If you'd shot him first, without provocation, you'd have lost your job. They all had weapons, they all have rap sheets. They *would* have shot Amy and the others. If it wasn't you in that scenario, you'd see it. Amy trusted that her back-up would protect her. She wouldn't have made it but for you. Neither would her child. And neither would the other woman, the young blonde Amy was protecting, and *her* baby. How would you feel right now if all four, two mothers and their unborn babies, had died because you hesitated, because you didn't do what you'd sworn to do? Would you be able to forgive yourself for that? Because that *would* have been on you. Hoyt Jansen shooting you was his decision. Not yours. *Never* yours."

"You make it sound so easy, so simple," she said, wriggling off his lap to stand and walk to the window. She still clutched his hankie and she used it again, then tucked it into her pocket.

"I don't mean to make it sound easy. None of this, of what you endured, is easy. Not then, not now. But you're a strong, independent woman, full of fire and drive and ambition. I want you to know I'm proud of you. Our son would be proud of you. If Jansen's shot had been two inches to the left, he'd be a gurgling six-month-old, proud as punch of his mama. I will always remember and honour the day he died just as I will always celebrate, in a small way, what would have been his birthday. Please allow yourself to do the same."

He stood wondering if she knew now, really knew, he had not, and never would blame her. If that's what she needed to help her move on, at least he'd given her that.

The trouble was, he wanted to give her so much more. He wanted to give a promise of a life together, a partnership that had nothing to do with being a cop. Would she want it? Or would *he* always be a reminder of her loss?

He was an idiot. Of course she'd see him as an obstacle.

Her happiness depended on him *not* being there every day. She most likely needed the exact opposite of what he needed.

He rose from the couch, grabbed his coat and before he could do something really stupid, walked to the door.

"Are you leaving?" Gia asked, her voice rusty from her tears. "Going? You came all this way to yell at me and you're *leaving*?"

He stopped, his back to her, his jaw so clenched, it hurt. "I can't stay here and not . . . I just can't." He pulled open the door and strode through, shutting it behind him.

What just happened? He was leaving? No. *No way.* Gia was rooted to the spot for a moment, then another and finally she flew across the room to pull open the door. Flynn stood there, arms bracing the door frame, his head bent. She gasped because she thought she'd be racing down the hall after him, like a lovesick lunatic.

He lifted his head, eyes locking to hers. "Fuck it, Gia. I need you." He moved so quickly she'd no time to step back. He straightened and swept her up in his arms. He was nimble for a large man – he had them both inside and the door slammed shut before she could say, *I need you, too.*

He tossed his coat aside and, shifting her in his arms, he gritted out, "Bedroom?"

"Down the hall, left." She had barely the words uttered before his mouth descended devouring hers. Oh God, he kissed like she felt. Desperate, needy, eager. Gia wrapped her arms about his neck, hanging on as she returned his kiss, thankful, so fucking thankful she'd have him for one more time. Just once more. Just to say goodbye. He'd brought the divorce papers, she knew they were done, but, *God*, she needed this.

He kicked open her bedroom door, strode through and dropped her to the bed. "Off," he commanded, his voice a growl, nodding to her clothing. He opened the first few buttons of his shirt and hauled it over his head. So damn hot. He tossed it aside and undid his belt. He reached into his back pocket, yanked out his wallet, opened it and tossed a strip of foil packets on the bed next to Gia. *Oh*. Right. Maybe more than one last time? She could feel heat travel along her limbs as her suddenly nervous fingers grappled with her own clothing. He was staring at her, hadn't taken his eyes from her since he'd dropped her on the bed. It was both slightly unnerving and unbelievably sexy. She scrambled out of her clothes because she was as ready as he was. He kicked his trousers away and stood there, naked before her. He was very, *very* ready. She licked her suddenly dry lips, and at last his eyes shifted. To her mouth.

"Your lips," he growled, low and hungry, "are the sexiest things I've ever seen." He knelt over her on the bed, pushing her back with one hand, the other stoking himself, and then tore open one of the packets and rolled it over his very hard cock. Placing a hand on either side of her head, he loomed over her. "You have one chance, Gia, one chance to say no." He bent, took the hardened bud of her nipple into his mouth and sucked deeply. Jesus, she almost leapt from the bed. She felt it to her core, hot, twisty and divine. "One chance," he said as he swirled his tongue over her other nipple. Every nerve ending under her skin yelled *yes, yes, yes,* as he moved his mouth lower, kissing, sucking, nipping at her exposed flesh. He paused at her scar, blew on it gently, kissed it so tenderly despite the heat scorching between them, and moved south. "Your silence is being taken as acquiescence," he said, low and gravelly as he kissed her hip, her inner thigh, her belly just above her small patch of curls.

See? Even when he was being sexy as fuck, he used the big fancy words. She loved that about him. She loved *him*, God help her. And she really loved what he was doing with his clever tongue. "You can absolutely take it as a yes, oh *Jesus*, yes!" That moaned out as she tilted her hips in exactly the way she needed as he slid his tongue along her seam, dipping in and out, swirling and pressing and listening to what her body told him. It only took moments more. She was so ready, so needy, so hungry for his touch that she flew apart, a cry wrestling itself from her as she broke.

"Yes," he groaned, "Yes, my darling Gia, give me yours. All of yours." He hauled himself up her body, repeating the kisses he given on the way down, and then he simply gazed into her eyes, his so dark now, that aqua-blue a memory. He looked fierce, and brave and warriorlike.

She wanted him inside her so badly she thought she'd come apart again just imagining it.

"I want you so much, Gia Sullivan, I find I am unable to sleep properly without you." He kissed her forehead. "I can't eat properly without you." He kissed her cheeks, one then the other. "I am failing in all things that require concentration, without you." He kissed her chin. "I find life without you is unbearably lonely." He swept his tongue along her upper lip. Darts of desire shot through her. "You make everything better and I *miss* you." This time he took her lower lip in his mouth and sucked at the same time he used his hand to position himself at her entrance.

"Now, now, now!" she chanted. "I need you now." He needed no further bidding. Sliding into her, she felt every inch of him, every nuance of him, every part of him. He lowered his forehead to hers, his breathing ratcheting up to match hers. They were in this together. It always felt like that. She never felt he was making love *to* her, it was always, always, *with* her and that thought brought a well of feeling so deep she thought she might disappear into its darkness. He was everything to her. Not just this, now, the intensity of feeling as he moved, more quickly within her, but the care he showed her. The time he gave her. The way he listened to her. Damn it to hell and back, why did he have to be the fucking *one*?

But now was definitely not the time to ask and answer the big questions. Now was a time for strong shoulders, a hard back, a tight ass. Now was the time to move with him, to raise her hips to meet his urgent thrusts and bask in all the tingles and sparks and shivers and exquisite sensations his body gave to hers. Only his body. Only him.

With a grunt that was more a groan, Flynn collapsed on Gia, his heart hammering, his pulse thundering. Christ, she was magical and like a sprite, she had him completely under her spell. He was hers. Only hers. How would he function if she refused the return of the divorce papers? But she couldn't deny this, what they shared. It wasn't just amazing sex, it was a visceral, tangible connection unlike anything he'd felt before and he was damn well going to fight for it. He gathered her in his arms and turning brought her close to his side.

"We need to talk, Gia, properly and with bare bones honesty. I'm pretty sure this bed is not the place to do it, so why don't you take a shower and I'll go make us something to eat. How does that sound?"

"Why can't we talk here?" She bit his shoulder, stroking her hand over his flat nipple. Sensations crept down his spine and he could feel himself stirring again.

He laughed ruefully, took her hand from his torso and placed it on his hardening cock. "That's why, darling. You're simply too much of a distraction to this yearning body. I feel like I've been parched for years and your touch is the drop of water I need for survival." He twisted, kissed her lingeringly on that gorgeous mouth and got up from the bed. He picked his trousers off the floor and chuckled. "Look what I've become around you? A sloven."

Gia pulled herself up to plop her back against the headboard, the sheet pooled about her waist. "I've no clue what that is but I gather it's not something you were aiming for?"

He looked up from zipping his fly and stopped. Stared. How could he not? The most perfect breasts he'd ever seen, tasted or touched were there, right in front of him. Dusky pink nipples hardened under his gaze and he knew he was in serious trouble. She responded, reacted to him, as readily as he did to her. His mind fogged over just drinking her in.

341

"This is not helping," he ground out, waving a hand in the direction of her upper body and all that beautiful silky, satiny smooth skin. Not to mention nipples that begged for more attention.

"We can talk later," she said, and slid a hand down under the sheet.

Christ, she didn't play fair. He slammed his eyes shut, willing his cock to stay put, willing his eyes to unsee the way her hand moved under the sheet, trying desperately to ignore his rioting pulse and heartbeat.

"You're killing me," he growled and relinquishing all control, he reached for another condom.

She did take a shower and Flynn did make food. Her cupboards were not as well stocked as his own but she had great spices and herbs and the basics for a marinara sauce. Her Italian momma would be proud. He made pasta, added the sauce and grated a ton of parmesan. It was so similar to the meal he'd made her before, in his apartment, she'd probably think he was a one-trick pony. She strolled back into the kitchen, her hair damp and slightly curling, a thick fluffy bathrobe enveloping her slender form. He almost went to his knees with desire when she smiled at him. A full, genuine, I *like* you smile.

Maybe, just maybe they had a shot.

"Sit," he said, his voice gruffer than he'd like, but how the hell could he be expected to act like a normal human when her scent drifted to his nostrils and made him want, all over again.

Gia sat, opened her napkin and picked up her utensils. Put them back down. "I'm not sure I can eat when I know there is a looming conversation around the corner. When I know we are going to have to face reality, and deal with the fallout."

"No. No fallout. Just reality. Eat, Sullivan. You might even be impressed enough to tell your mother I'm worth keeping." He smiled at her, trying to put her at ease. His own nerves were a complete knotted mess, but he was good at hiding. At wearing a façade. He donned it now. "Eat," he said.

And with a sigh she twirled spaghetti like a boss.

"Okay," she murmured over a mouthful. "This is delicious. Maybe you should hang around, you know, just to feed me. Till I'm well again. I've two more weeks mandated sick leave."

He could see the moment she realised what she'd said. A flush stained her cheeks and she lowered her eyes. "Kidding," she muttered.

"As it happens, I also have two weeks. Not mandated, and not sick leave. I took time off."

Her expression was almost comical. "What? Wait. Why? Shit. I never even asked. What the hell are you really doing here? You could have yelled at me over the phone. You could have sent the papers by mail. And now you say you are on vacation? What's that about?"

He put his own cutlery down. Laid them aside. The dinner could be reheated, he supposed. This, he now knew couldn't wait. Shouldn't wait.

He stood and taking her fork from her, put it down and pulled her to her feet. "You're right. We need to do this. Come." He tugged her behind him into the living room. She was a reluctant captive, slowing them down as he reached for the large brown envelope.

"Open it," Flynn said, handing it to her.

With hands that held the merest hint of a tremble, she did and reached into take out the sheaf of papers he knew rather intimately at this stage. She turned the pages, looked at the last, where his signature should be.

"You didn't sign," she said slowly, raising her eyes to his. "Why?"

He took the papers and dropped them to the table where they scattered loosely.

"Why?" He stopped, cleared his throat. "I didn't sign because I don't want our marriage to end. I never want our marriage to end. I want . . . I want us to *be* married." He stopped again, aware that he might start hyperventilating if she didn't react soon.

"I don't understand. Why would you want to stay married? You have to move on. Forget me. This. Us." She blinked at him, in confusion, he hoped, not dismissal.

Man up, Dev would tell him now. Share your feelings. Be honest. Sometimes younger brothers could be a pain. Sometimes they were right on the money.

"I love you. I want to be your husband and I really want you to be my wife."

She started to deny, to pull back but he grasped her hands in his, drew her in.

Tilting her chin up so he could meet her eyes he said, "I fell in love with you when I saw you dancing on the table in Caro's flat. I fell again when I kissed you that night against the door. I fell some more when I saw you in that red dress. And again, when I took you in my arms, in the garden, and in my bed. I fell further when you told me you were pregnant and I couldn't believe how lucky I was, that a failure in protection gave me a chance with you. I married you because I wanted, more than anything, to have you in my life. And even when our hearts were breaking, I loved you. When we bumped into each other on the stairs at the station, I felt as if my heart could beat again. You were back. I would have another chance. Ironically, as it turned out, I thought even then, we might have a second shot."

He paused, uncertain about the glaze that had appeared over Gia's eyes. Was she listening? Had he made a complete fool of himself. Nothing ventured, nothing gained, he could practically hear Dev in his ear. Try again.

"You can't," Gia whispered, her mouth wobbling a little. Her eyes huge. "You can't love me. How could you? Not after . . . everything. You can't. It wouldn't be right."

"Gia, loving you is exactly right. Everything about you, your strength, your bravery, your smarts, your smile, your kindness, they all fill me up. You make me feel whole. As if there was always a place vacant inside me, with a Gia Sullivan sized space just waiting. Waiting for you." He kissed her, a gentle touch to those trembling lips and caught the salty taste of her tears. "Ah darling, please don't cry. Not for this. I'm asking for a chance. If you don't feel the same way, we can take it slow. I can wait."

A surprised gurgle of laughter erupted from a sniffling Gia. "In the background, like a stalker? Not your style, Fitzgerald. I know you're a patient man, but are you seriously telling me, you love me so much you'll wait until I love you back? Are you that arrogant? Or that confident?"

"Yes. No. And yes."

She snorted, her tears making her sound all gurgley. How could he find that delightful? Easy. So easy to find all her foibles and her funny ways a delight. Because *she* was a delight. And she was what he wanted. What he needed.

"I love you," he said again, the saying of it coming easier now. The truth of it, out loud, like a fresh wave of happiness each time. He released her hands and took her face in his, his thumbs stroking the soft skin of her flushed cheeks. "I love you. I want to be married to you. For always. Is there any chance for me? Any hope you can throw my way. Anything?" He tried to lighten his tone because he was losing his mind not knowing if she returned even the minutest of his feelings. He knew the desire was there. That wasn't fake. They both felt it. She couldn't pretend that wasn't true. But could she love *him*?

"Oh. *Oh*." She went on her tiptoes and grasping his wrists with her hands, she placed a featherlight kiss on his lips. He felt it zing through him like an arrow on perfect target. "I didn't dare hope," she said against his mouth. "I didn't dare believe. I didn't dare want." She closed her eyes, their breaths mingling, they were so close. "I didn't dare love you."

She kissed him fiercely then, as if her life depended on his. As if she could never be parted from him. Groaning, he took his hands from her face and lifted her up, her legs wrapping about his hips. Her arms entwined about his neck and they held each other as lovers do. Kissed as lovers do, and he dared to hope. He spread one hand against her back, the other holding her head as he deepened the kiss.

Eventually, he pulled back. Breathing heavily, he asked the question that had bothered him for weeks. "Why didn't *you* sign the papers? Your signature line was as blank as mine."

She placed a hand on his cheek, the gesture so tender he felt his throat tighten. "Oh Flynn, how could I? It would be such a lie. I want to be married to you too, so badly. So much. So much I was a coward and figured if you signed first, it was meant to be. It was over. But if I signed, I was telling a lie. So, I sent them to you. I knew I had to take responsibility, that you were too much of a gentleman to ask for them. A part of me was hoping you'd take one look at the documents and toss them in a drawer and forget about them."

"Why?" he asked, his chest aching for her truth. "That wouldn't solve anything."

She smiled sweetly at him. "But we'd still be married. I could pretend. I could tell myself I would find a way to make you love me. As much as I love you. That there was time."

His heart soared. Sky-dived and soared again. She thought he needed time. The only time he wanted was time with her, loving her. Caring for her. Making a life with her.

"We have a lot of logistical things to figure out," he said, walking to the couch and sitting down, Gia still wrapped around him. "Two weeks holiday time probably won't be enough, but it's a start. Be sure though, Gia. Be really sure. We can get that divorce and start again. Begin dating. Do it the old-fashioned way. Have a new marriage, one based on love, not necessity."

She shook her head. "No. Absolutely not. This is our marriage, as crazy and unorthodox as it's been, it's ours. And it *is* based on love. It was always based on love. Just a different kind of love."

Flynn's chest felt like a band was squeezing tighter and tighter. "We can thank our little boy for that. He brought us together. He gave us joy, however fleeting." He cleared his throat, uncomfortable but so full of love for his lost boy, and for this woman. "He will always be a part of our family, whatever shape and size it becomes. He will always be ours."

Gia sniffed. Smiled and sniffed again. "How did I get to be this lucky? But what if I can't have any more?" She pulled back, her face serious. "The doctors couldn't say. I love you, Flynn, enough to let you go if you want more children and I can't give them to you."

"Don't talk nonsense, Gia. Our son will either be our only, or he'll be our first. We are staying married because we love each other. Regardless of what else happens. Whether we grow in size by whatever means, or we stay as we are, you, my beautiful wonderful wife, you are the love of my life and I promise to let you know that, every day for the rest of our lives."

Gia grinned at that. "Oh," she said, "a Flynn Fitzgerald promise? Those are gold dust I've heard. You better mean it, buddy, or I'll use my considerable skills to remind you!"

Flynn laughed as he tossed her back on the couch, leaning down to capture her mouth with his. Yes, the dinner could be reheated, this moment was as perfect as moments got. Food could wait. And as for his promise to love her every day? The easiest promise he'd ever made. And the easiest to keep.

Epilogue

It took longer than two weeks. It was longer than two months to put things in motion for their life together. Flynn stayed in Brooklyn for his prescribed holiday time and they explored the city, the Burroughs, the sites and most importantly, each other. They had fun. They laughed, they argued, they had more fun making up. If his time away from Dublin coincided with the birth of Dev and Frankie's baby, he was not completely sorry. Of course, little Dylan arrived on the tenth, as expected. With Frankie at the helm, no one doubted it. Flynn and Gia looked at the video of the squalling baby over and over, at the sheer joy in the parents' faces, and they were glad. Glad it went so well, glad everyone was safe and glad they weren't there. Not yet. Not quite ready.

But within a week, something happened, something pretty amazing. The ping on Flynn's phone signalled another video of the infant prodigy and he found he couldn't wait to see it, to enjoy the adorable cuteness of this little boy. To see the love this new family of three, shared. He was putting it back in his pocket, a smile still lingering on his face, when Gia came out of the kitchen and noticed.

"Oh, is it another Dylan fest? Show me, show me!"

And just like that he knew, as his Gia grabbed eagerly for the phone, he knew they were starting to *really* heal. She *ooh*ed and *aw*ed, no tears, just her gorgeous smile as she saw the tiny fingers and toes, the yawns, the scrunches his face made and the bleary-eyed Frankie managing like a champion.

It was December by the time Gia moved from Brooklyn to Dublin. So many strings to be untied, so much red tape, so much political wrangling. Flynn had told his bosses in Dublin that he was moving Stateside and a minor earthquake could be felt around the Police and special Branches buildings. It was not a runner. Not an option.

"Then make Angelica Sullivan's transfer to Dublin a reality, without loss of rank or privilege," he'd said all calm and secure in the knowledge that it would happen. It did.

The beauty of it was she was excited to go overseas as she put it, to work with a team she'd already begun to know. "My parents are five hours away, give or take," she'd said, "granted that can be seven hours flight time but it's a hell of a lot easier to get to Brooklyn than it is to Donegal!" She wasn't wrong.

She dragged him shopping as soon as she arrived in Dublin. She chose the fancy baby shop in Dundrum that he had frequented and purchased gifts for Dylan and also for Siobhán Barry's little baby girl, Imelda. Gia added an extra soft toy, an elephant, and the first free afternoon Flynn had, after Gia arrived, they drove to a small village in Westmeath and knocked on the door of Number 26. Shona opened it, surprise and concern on her face. They quickly told her they just wanted to see how she was faring and if there was anything they could do. The young mum brought them into the family kitchen and there, in a bouncy seat on the table, amidst a selection of cups and plates, textbooks and notebooks, little Bradley Cooper gurgled contentedly. Shona's parents were out, and though she pleaded with them to stay and greet the grateful and seemingly hugely proud grandparents, Flynn and Gia declined.

While Flynn picked up the baby for a cuddle and to

show him the soft plush toy, Gia gave Shona a quick update on the state of the individuals involved and although she omitted that Hoyt Jansen was in jail, for murder, in the US, she made sure Shona knew justice had been done all around. Miller and his crew were serving time and as she went through what had happened to each of the others, Flynn zoned out and concentrated on making the little chap smile. It was so much easier than he'd expected. As he played peek-a-boo, using the elephant as a shield, he thought briefly of the similar stuffed animal on top of his wardrobe and felt a surge of gladness that he hadn't tossed it.

As they were walking down the path a short while later, the baby in its mother's arms in the doorway, Shona took one of her son's chubby hands in hers and waved it in their direction. "Say bye-bye, Bradley Fitzgerald," she called, "Ta-ta so much for me toy!"

"I can't believe she dropped the Cooper," Flynn bemoaned as they drove away. "The best part of the child's name." He glanced at her as they came to a stop sign. He'd never get tired of seeing her next to him. Right there, her hand clasped loosely in his.

His *wife*.

Her smiles were happy ones these days. The past was just that, passed. Over. The future, however, was theirs for the taking.

Gia leaned over, kissed him tenderly on the cheek. "No," she said. "Shona added the best of names, the one with *all* the hero parts. Yours."

Second Epilogue

Five years later, Clifden, County Galway

From the diary of Jo Fitzgerald, August Bank Holiday Monday

It was lovely! Yesterday was even better than Saturday, which was great in its own way. So many locals came this year and the sun shone and in the words of Genesis, the Bible not the pop group, it was good. But, yes, yesterday was as close to perfect as a day can get. Molly and Kit arrived! They're so busy with their venture, FitzElliot, Forensic Accountants, and just flew in from Berlin where their latest case wrapped up. Our Molly, undercover accountant – who would have thought! But they love it and it seems their skills really balance each other's. I worry for her, them, of course I do, but they're happy and that's all a mum wants to know. Kit has spoken to us privately, if unnecessarily, but hasn't said a thing to Molly, I think she'll be delighted when he asks …

The rest of them are here too, so many little ones now, it's louder than when our kids were small! But Patrick and I love it. So much joy, so much love. And then they leave, and that's lovely too. What was especially nice this year was having Caro's Italian family come – and with Rosa and Mikey over for baby Gus's christening, it was a family reunion for them too. Viola loves her new cousins but nobody replaces her big brother. How can our boy be 20! Such a fine young man, so handsome, Mia says he has all the girls swooning. I'd well believe it. Those two, Toby and Mia are joined at the hip. We used to think, Patrick and I, that they might be a match one day, but they really are more like brother and sister. And now that Mia also has a new sibling, little Antonio, they have something else in common. That Bernadine is such a delight. The best thing to ever happen to Marianna. What a blossoming to see in one young woman, once so sad, so unwell and now married to her beloved lady farmer and a mama all over again. We've all taken Bernadine to our hearts, and even Caro has long since got over her frustration with Marianna. Love really does cure a lot of ills.

Dylan and Cian, Dev's two, are rascals, racing about like demons and although Frankie swears they're done, and I don't blame her, Irish twins are a handful, I did see her earlier, holding wee Gus, or Fergus Cooper to give him his full title, with rather a dreamy look on her face, then Dev came scuttling over to take the baby from her and hand him back to his papa.

Pretty soon though, that same little chap ended up in Gabe's arms and that brought such a tug to my heart until I saw him look over at Ali, with such profound devotion on his face, and when she glowed back at him, it hit me. She'd not been drinking alcohol all weekend! I do hope they have some happy news for us – it has taken our Alison so long to trust. She'd never have come so far without The Mackenzie, as I believe he's known in Scotland. I'll say nothing. They'll share in their own good time.

The whole Italian contingent, and the Brooklyn Sullivans, stayed up at the hotel this year, what with Marianna, Bernadine, Antonio, Mia, Toby's other grandparents Valentina and Antonio Senior, along with Naomi and Vito, the lodge was just too small. Even our own gang and their families cram every room now. In another few years I bet it will be just the children, and their parents will repair to the hotel too. But not just yet.

Which reminds me, another lovely thing happened on Saturday, Naomi and Vito got married! Right here in our garden, at our party. It was so touching, so long awaited. That special lady had held out on him for so long. Caro says it was because she was worried if her ex got out on parole he might go after Vito. That ex-husband of Naomi's was a truly bad egg. And then he caught pneumonia in prison and died and not one person shed a tear. Though there were many tears, my own included, as Vito spoke such tender words to his bride under the flowered arch. I think Nick, as his best man, even had a hard time keeping a dry eye.

Patrick and I went for a walk along the shoreline early this morning, thinking we were on our own but came across Flynn at the edge of the property where the engraved stone marker lies. We stopped, not wanting to intrude, and then realised he was talking to Matilda, telling her about the older brother she never got to know. The one none of us got to know. Matilda held a posy of flowers and laid them at the stone and then put her arms so trustingly around Flynn's neck. "I know he would have loved you, Papa, you're the very bestest of papas. Mama says that, so it must be true."

Flynn kissed his almost three-year old on her head and taking her up into his arms began to walk slowly back to the house to darling Gia and their new addition, six-week-old Gus. I don't know why, because I don't think it's an eldest child thing, but Flynn's journey to finding happiness just about broke me. It wasn't until he found Gia that I realised how worried I was that he wouldn't. Patrick always says they'll find their own way, and he's right. Up to a point. But I've never seen the harm of a rosary or two. Sometimes several.

We also walked on by the marker this morning and smiled to see Matilda's offering placed on the ground. Patrick knelt to clear away a few stones and I read the inscription out loud, for the world to hear, just like I always do.

In memory of Patrick Michael Sullivan Fitzgerald.
Never in our arms but forever in our hearts.

THE END